Whispers
of Love

Rosie
HARRIS

Whispers of Love

arrow books

Published by Arrow Books 2010

2 4 6 8 10 9 7 5 3 1

First published in Great Britain in 2010 by
Arrow Books
Random House, 20 Vauxhall Bridge Road,
London, SW1V 2SA

www.rbooks.co.uk

Addresses for companies within The Random House Group Limited can
be found at: www.randomhouse.co.uk/offices.htm

The Random House Group Limited Reg. No. 954009

A CIP catalogue record for this book
is available from the British Library

ISBN 9780099527398

The Random House Group Limited supports The Forest Stewardship
Council (FSC), the leading international forest certification organisation. All
our titles that are printed on Greenpeace approved FSC certified paper
carry the FSC logo. Our paper procurement policy can be found at
www.rbooks.co.uk/environment

Mixed Sources
Product group from well-managed
forests and other controlled sources
www.fsc.org Cert no. TT-COC-2139
© 1996 Forest Stewardship Council

Typeset in Palatino by Palimpsest Book Production Limited
Grangemouth, Stirlingshire
Printed and bound in Great Britain by
CPI Mackays, Chatham, ME5 8TD

To Stefano and Giulia Zappia

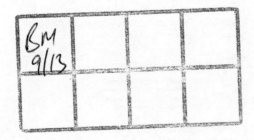

Acknowledgements

Once again my sincere thanks to all at Random House, especially my wonderful editor Georgina Hawtrey-Woore for all her help and patience, and to my agent Caroline Sheldon.

Chapter One

June 1914

A tall, slim figure in a light-blue summer coat and matching blue straw cloche hat pulled down over her dark hair, Christabel Montgomery, her vivid blue eyes clouded with tears, stared unseeingly into the grey, turbulent waters of the Mersey.

It was only a few weeks earlier that she had stood at the very same spot on the Liverpool quayside waving goodbye to her fiancé, Philip Henderson, and now the cold, murky waters had claimed him for their own.

It was all so unreal that it was unbelievable. She had been so excited planning their wedding. Her sister Lilian was to be her bridesmaid, her brother Lewis, best man, and all her family, and Philip's, as well as their friends, were to be there to celebrate the occasion.

They'd waited so long to get married because her father had consistently refused to give his permission and no matter how hard she'd pleaded with him, he'd refused to change his mind. He'd insisted that she must wait until she came of age in September.

Even though she was the eldest daughter, her parents seemed to be reluctant for her to grow up. Much as she loved them both she was tired of having to stay home to help her mother and of being treated the same as Lilian, who was almost six years younger than she was.

'Getting married is not the answer,' Mabel Montgomery had told her dryly when she said she was aching for independence and the chance to lead her own life.

'All you will be doing is changing one authority for another. You may be free from us, but once you are married, you will be expected to conform to your husband's wishes.'

That would be very different, though, Christabel had replied. Philip was only a couple of years older than she was and they had so much in common. They were kindred spirits and not only shared the same views on most things but also enjoyed the same activities.

After a long discussion with Philip's parents, James and Hilda Henderson, who were old family friends and very much in favour of the marriage, Basil Montgomery had finally, if somewhat reluctantly, given his consent.

Preparations had gone ahead for the wedding to take place on Philip's next shore leave which was due in September a few days after her twenty-first birthday, the same month.

She gave a deep shuddering sigh as she thought of all the plans they had made. Still she couldn't believe that none of it would happen and that she would never see Philip again or feel his arms round her, his lips on hers, tender yet demanding.

His parents were beside themselves with grief because there wouldn't even be a funeral. All on board had gone down with the ship and not a single body had been recovered.

The raucous scream of the gulls circling overhead echoed in her head and they seemed to be mocking her. As she left the quayside she shivered and turned up the collar of her coat. The greyness of the Mersey had depressed her and, even though it was June, the keen breeze coming off it had chilled her to the bone.

As she walked away a lump came to her throat as she reflected on the last day she and Philip had spent together. Because of her father's strict code of behaviour she had never before permitted Philip to consummate their love and, eager though he was to do so, he had always respected her wishes. With their wedding date set for only a very short time away, however, they had both given way to temptation.

Although Philip had always been very romantic and demonstrative, as well as tender and affectionate, their lovemaking that day had been a revelation to her. It had brought her such a wonderful feeling of unity and joy that she could hardly bear to be parted from him afterwards. It was only the thought that very soon they would be together for ever that had consoled her.

Now the future without Philip there to share it with her stretched ahead like a blank canvas. There would be no wedding, no more love-making, nothing to plan for or look forward to. She hadn't thought that there might be any adverse consequences but now she felt apprehensive about what they'd done. Was it her imagination, or did the queasiness she felt each morning have something to do with their love-making?

Once away from the Pier Head she felt more in control of her feelings. Although it was overcast and the sun was hidden behind hazy clouds, it was reasonably warm and she straightened the collar of her coat as she walked up Water Street.

On impulse, she made her way to Church Street in the heart of the city, looking around her with interest. She'd never been allowed to have a job but now she thought it might be time to do something positive. It was the only way that she could still make an independent life for herself now that she had lost Philip. Furthermore, it would be better than brooding over the cruel blow fate had dealt her, she thought wryly.

She wandered in and out of the many stores, wondering what it would be like to work in one of them. Her father would probably be horrified; her mother possibly might approve but only if it was one of the high-class establishments in Bold Street.

Christabel felt rather self-conscious as she went into the Kardomah Café. She had never done anything like that before but she was feeling famished. She ordered a pot of tea and a buttered scone and felt very adventurous to be doing so on her own.

As she watched the waitress busily taking orders and serving customers, she wondered if she could do something of this sort, but quickly rejected the idea. Her father would most certainly not approve. He'd be quick to point out that he had spent a lot of money making sure she had a good education and that a job of this kind was not much better than working as a maidservant.

She wondered what sort of work he would consider suitable. When they'd first taken on a lady clerk in his office at the shipping company where he was a partner, he had been incensed but his partner had been adamant that it was far cheaper than employing a man, so eventually he had accepted her.

She toyed with the idea of asking him if she could go and work for him then quickly rejected the idea, realising that if she did that she wouldn't be independent. He would still be able to exert his authority over her and that was exactly what she wanted to free herself from.

By the time she reached home again her feelings of inadequacy and despondency had returned and she went straight to her room. She knew her mother would be expecting her to take afternoon tea in the drawing room, but the thought of having to sit and listen to her mother's friends and their platitudes about her loss made her decide to stay where she was.

When their maid, Mary, came knocking on her door to tell her that her mother was waiting for her, she sent a message back to say she wished to be excused because she had a headache and was lying down.

In her darkened room, Christabel lay on her bed and concentrated on thinking about her future. She had felt queasy again that morning and it worried her. She wished Lewis was at home; he was three years older than her and had always been willing to discuss anything that was troubling her and to offer good advice. It was useless talking to Lilian because she was far too young to understand.

By the time the gong went for dinner she was dressed and ready to face her parents with her ultimatum.

They both listened in silence, exchanging concerned glances with each other as she outlined what she planned to do.

'I think you should give this idea a great deal more thought,' her father stated pompously. 'Your idea of becoming a nurse is a hysterical reaction because you have lost Philip. We do understand.'

'It is nothing of the sort,' she told him hotly.

'Christabel, you have no experience of being out in the world. Nursing may appear to be a very worthwhile occupation, but I can assure you it is not something you will enjoy doing. It's not simply a matter of dressing up in a cap and apron, you know. You would soon discover that you have to do some very distasteful jobs, and that's presuming you could find a hospital that would employ you.'

'And the kind of people you might have to look after are not at all the sort of people you are used to coming into contact with, darling,' Mabel Montgomery shuddered.

'Think of all the blood,' Lilian exclaimed dramatically, screwing up her round, pretty face in horror.

'I know all that,' Christabel conceded, 'but there is probably going to be a war very soon and a great many more nurses will be needed so I imagine they will be crying out for people to join them to care for the soldiers when they are brought home injured.'

'That may be true,' her father admitted, 'there very well might be a war. If there is, then they will want experienced nurses in the military hospitals; women who are strong enough to deal not only with men who may have lost an arm or a leg but also with those who have suffered disfigurement or other gruesome injuries.'

'All the more reason for me to do something about it right away and get some proper training before the war really gets started,' Christabel said, her mouth tightening stubbornly.

'I am sure your intentions are very worthy,' her mother said worriedly, 'but I don't really think that Philip would have approved of you becoming a nurse, do you?'

'I think he would have been very proud of me; it is because of him that I have decided that it's the right thing to do. He would think it was far better for me to be doing something so very worthwhile than to be sitting around moping over what has happened to him,' Christabel defended.

'Oh, my poor girl; I'm afraid you are only talking like this because of the shock and grief you've suffered.' Mabel sighed. 'Leave things as they are for a few months and I am sure we can find some other little job you can do; something far more suitable. Now ring the bell for Mary to come and clear the dishes away, darling.'

'Your mother is right,' Basil boomed. He took a sip of his wine. 'What about the three of you – Lilian, your mother and you – all going on a pleasant cruise for a couple of weeks?'

'A cruise after Philip has been drowned at sea? Do you think I could bring myself to travel on a boat after that?' Christabel asked aghast, her blue eyes flashing angrily.

Mabel laid a cautionary finger on her lips as her husband was about to reply and signalled with her head towards Mary, who had entered the room and was clearing the table.

They talked about inconsequential matters

8

until she'd cleared away their main course and served desert and coffee, then once again Basil Montgomery picked up the threads of their discussion.

This time he went into considerable detail about the strict routine that going out to work would entail. 'It's not only a matter of punctuality, or the length of time you would be expected to work, but also about conforming to the instructions you would receive and the duties that would be expected of you,' he emphasised.

'I am well aware of all that,' Christabel assured him. 'I know it would be a very different way of life from the one I am used to, but I feel it would be far more worthwhile.'

'Well, I am of the opinion that in no time at all you would find it most distasteful,' he told her as he stirred a spoonful of brown sugar into his coffee.

'Not if I am convinced that what I am doing is necessary and of some importance,' Christabel insisted.

'Becoming a nurse and being at the beck and call of doctors and patients can hardly be considered to be of very much importance,' he told her disparagingly.

Their argument continued for the rest of the evening, becoming more and more heated until Mabel declared she could stand it no longer and they must desist, and talk about something else, or she would be forced to go to bed.

'There's no need for you to do that, Mother,' Christabel told her. 'I'm going up to my room so that I can do something positive about my decision. I intend to write a letter to the matron of our nearby hospital – the Wallasey Cottage Hospital in Liscard Road – and ask if she will employ me.'

'She'll probably tell you that with your lack of experience you are only suitable to be a ward maid or a cleaner of some sort,' her father told her scathingly.

Christabel hesitated, wondering if it would be better to tell them the truth, which was that she thought she might be expecting Philip's baby, rather than take such a dramatic step as leaving home. Then the thought of how shocked they both would be deterred her.

After all, she told herself, I might not be pregnant. Feeling unwell might be a reaction to the news of Philip's death.

A week later, when war was much more of a possibility and most people realised that it seemed to be inevitable, her father seemed to relent somewhat.

'If you are still insisting on this headstrong idea of becoming a nurse, perhaps you would like me to make some enquiries for you?' he offered.

'There's no need, as I have already applied,' Christabel told him, 'and I received a letter this morning to say that my name was forwarded to the matron of a new hospital which is being opened at Hilbury.'

'Hilbury?' He frowned, 'Where on earth is that?'

'Somewhere between Liverpool and South-port,' Christabel said as she scanned the letter she was holding. 'It is being made ready to receive casualties should there be a war. It also says that they would like me to report there for an interview and they have sent a map to show me how to get there.'

'So you are determined to go ahead with this idea?' her father said worriedly.

'Of course I am!'

She felt elated but nervous because she knew it was a very decisive step she was taking, but she was convinced that it was the best thing to do. She was still feeling unwell and if she was pregnant, then it was best that she moved away from home before it was discovered.

When, once again, her parents tried to talk her out of committing herself, pointing out the many pitfalls and drawbacks she would be bound to experience, she refused to listen.

'You've told me all these things several times before,' she reminded them. 'It is something I am determined to do, so please don't keep putting obstacles in my way.'

The interview was purely perfunctory. They were anxious to find staff for the hospital as soon as possible and even when she explained that she had no previous nursing experience this did not seem to matter.

'You will live in at the hospital and during your first six weeks you will receive intensive training,' the matron said. 'Providing you pass the examination at the end of that period, you will be accepted as an auxiliary nurse.'

When she told her parents her news over dinner that night they were both aghast at the idea of her actually leaving home.

'We've been talking of nothing else for the past weeks,' she said exasperatedly. 'Surely you both realised I would be going ahead with the idea?'

'We went along with the idea only because we felt it kept your mind occupied and stopped you grieving about Philip,' her mother said quickly.

Christabel felt bewildered. 'War is imminent, you know that and what I am going to do could be very important,' she pointed out.

'If there is a war, then surely you can see that your duty is to stay at home and help look after your sister and provide comfort to your mother,' her father reminded her.

She looked from one to the other in dismay. Her parents both sounded so old and yet her father wasn't even sixty. As far as she was aware he'd never had a day's illness in his life and even though his hair had a touch of grey at the temples, his blue eyes were as clear and bright as her own. As for her mother, she was a few years younger than him and there was no trace of grey in her thick dark hair, and her rounded face was unwrinkled.

It would be at least another ten years before they needed her to be there to look after them and until that day came she wanted to have a life of her own.

Chapter Two

The wards at Hilbury Military Hospital radiated from a central core like the legs of a spider. The entire structure was of prefabricated, corrugated asbestos and tin and when it rained the noise inside was deafening.

The hospital was custom-built and was situated on the outskirts of Liverpool. Apart from the doctors, nurses, clerks, orderlies and those who drove the ambulances, it was staffed by men from the Pioneer Corps. Until it became fully operational, local people were hired to undertake the cleaning and cooking.

At first Christabel found the starkness, the noise as trolleys were wheeled around, and the constant bustle almost unbearable. The strong smell of antiseptic made her feel queasy, especially first thing in the morning.

After the first few bewildering days of settling in, however, she gradually accepted it, even though it was vastly different from what she was used to.

The rules were strict from the moment the new trainees arrived. All thirty of them assembled in the large lecture hall and were told that the next six weeks of intensive training were

14

going to be very hard work indeed. They would be expected to attend lectures every day and there would be severe penalties if they were absent for any reason at all.

At the end of the welcome speech the matron handed them over to the care of Sister Speakley, a grey-haired martinet whose steel-rimmed glasses gave her a sharp, owl-like appearance.

'Sister Speakley will be responsible for your physical welfare as well as your training so if you have any problems at all, then go to her and she will help you resolve them,' Matron told them before she left the room.

Sister Speakley took her place in front of the class and informed them in a no-nonsense tone that she expected high standards from all of them and that they must be neatly dressed at all times. She ended her talk by informing them that they would be sharing accommodation and there would be two girls to each room.

Girls who already knew each other immediately paired up and the rest tried to select the person they thought would be most compatible. Christabel had never before had to share a bedroom with anyone, not even for a night, and when she found herself with a plump, bubbly, red-headed girl called Peggy Wilson she felt extremely apprehensive.

In next to no time, however, they had settled in. She found that there was a surprisingly easy-going comradeship between the two of them and that she quite enjoyed Peggy's company.

Even so, she refrained from sharing too many confidences with her.

War on Germany was officially declared within a month of Christabel's arrival at Hilbury. This factor made those in authority extremely anxious to ensure that the new recruits worked hard to complete their training and qualify as auxiliary nurses, and also that they were prepared to sign an official form to say that they would stay on as permanent staff.

Much as she wanted to do so, Christabel hesitated. She wasn't sure that she could stay there – at least, not permanently – and she didn't know what to do or say to Sister Speakley to explain the situation.

Ever since she had arrived at Hilbury she'd felt nauseous each morning and although it wore off during the day she knew now for certain that she was pregnant and that the situation was serious.

She tried to put it to the back of her mind and to concentrate on the training, which, because of the fact that war had been declared, had been extended to ensure that they were thoroughly competent to work on the wards.

They received a lecture from Dr Murray who was in overall charge of one of the sections of the hospital. He was in his early thirties, good-looking, with thick fair hair and brown eyes and, in many ways, reminded her so much of Philip that she found it hard to concentrate on what he was saying.

At the end of the lecture he waited until she was about to leave the room, then called her over.

'Did you find my lecture boring?' he asked in clipped tones.

'Good heavens, no.' Christabel stared at him, wide-eyed. She wanted to tell him that she had been captivated by every word he'd uttered, but she felt too tongue-tied to do so.

'You didn't appear to be taking very much notice of what I was saying.' He frowned. 'In fact, you seemed to be in a dream most of the time.'

Christabel felt the colour rushing to her face. 'I'm sorry, Dr Murray. You are right, but I was concentrating on what you were saying; I didn't let my thoughts wander.'

Before she could hold them back, tears were streaming down her face and he stared at her in bewilderment.

'I know my lectures are good, but they have never had this effect on anyone before,' he joked.

When she told him that his resemblance to Philip, her fiancé who had been drowned at sea just a few months before they had planned to be married, had awakened feelings and memories that she'd tried to put behind her, he looked discomfited.

'Mop your eyes and then you can tell me about him . . . that's if you want to,' he told her brusquely as he handed her a large white handkerchief.

He listened attentively as she told him all about Philip and the plans they'd had for their future together, as well as the battle she'd had with her parents when she'd said she wanted to become a nurse. The only thing she omitted was the fact that she was pregnant; she let him assume that her hesitancy to sign the agreement to stay on at Hilbury was because of the duty she felt towards taking care of her mother.

'Why let that deter you?'

'Well, you might not be agreeable to my going home to look after her, especially if I had to do so in a hurry,' she said lamely.

'Nonsense! If she was taken ill, then of course we'd make arrangements to release you temporarily. If that's your only concern, then you should go ahead and sign on the dotted line,' he told her emphatically.

Christabel nodded thoughtfully and, for one fleeting moment, wondered if she should also confide in him about her predicament; explain that the real reason for her hesitancy was that she was pregnant and didn't know what to do about it.

Instead, she remained silent and as Dr Murray started to move away, asked, 'I wonder how long it will be before Hilbury receives its first consignment of wounded soldiers?'

'If you stay with us, you will be one of the first to find out,' he said, smiling warmly at her.

Christabel's infatuation with Mark Murray

grew ever stronger over the next few weeks. No matter where she was working, whether it was on the wards, in the sluice room or in the kitchen, she found herself looking out for him and felt quite disappointed if a day passed and she didn't see him.

Peggy pointed out that she ought to be careful. 'People will soon be talking about the way you're flirting with Dr Murray,' she warned.

'Rubbish. I'm not flirting with him,' Christabel defended. 'I admire him, that's all.'

'You know what Sister Speakley said about fraternising,' Peggy reminded her.

'That was with the patients who will all be young soldiers. She said that because they had been injured they'd be very vulnerable and looking for someone to hold their hand. I hardly think Dr Murray comes into that category.'

'No, but he is a doctor and you are only a trainee auxiliary nurse,' Peggy rejoined.

Christabel ignored her advice. She continued to make sure that her and Dr Murray's paths crossed as often as possible. Again she considered whether to tell him that she was pregnant and to ask his advice then she jibbed because she was sure he would be shocked by her behaviour and she hoped that one day they would become real friends.

Her hopes of that happening were dashed when Peggy told her that he was a married man and had two small children.

It was like a slap across the face. For a moment, she didn't want to believe what her friend was telling her.

She stood there completely stunned then felt herself flush hotly. How could she have ever been so silly? she thought ruefully. Her crush on Dr Murray was suddenly shattered and she wondered how she could have been so deluded as to compare him with Philip. True, they both had a shock of fair hair and deep brown eyes, but there the resemblance ended.

As she made her way to her room, she felt an overwhelming sense of gloom. What was she going to do now? Carried away by her foolish dreams she had lost count of time and she realised with a sinking heart that by now she must be three months' pregnant. That meant that even if she had contemplated having an abortion as a possible way out of her dilemma it was out of the question now because she had left it far too late.

She would have to act and fast, she thought in dismay. Another month and it would become so obvious what was wrong that she wouldn't be able to hide her condition.

She felt choked by panic and an inability to think clearly. She daren't go home; her parents would not only be horrified but would also consider it a terrible social disgrace.

For one moment Christabel thought of taking Peggy Wilson into her confidence, but then decided that was probably very unwise. There was nothing that Peggy would be able to do to help her and there was always the chance that she might gossip and tell some of the others at Hilbury.

Once anyone in authority knew about her condition then Christabel was pretty sure that she would be asked to leave immediately.

She tried to tell herself that she still had plenty of time to make a sensible decision about her future and, even though she had no idea what that would be at the moment, she was sure that she would be able to think of someone who would help her or something that she could do.

Long after she and Peggy had gone to bed, turned out the lights and stopped talking, Christabel found that sleep eluded her. Her mind was a confused jumble of what had happened in the past and how she had come to be in such an alarming predicament.

The next morning she felt heavy-eyed and weary and found it increasingly difficult to concentrate on the lecture she was attending. Twice Sister Speakley rebuked her and when the class ended she asked her to stay behind.

'You seem to be very distracted and inattentive this morning,' she commented, her voice sharp with annoyance.

She listened to Christabel's mumbled apology in silence, studying her so closely that Christabel was certain that Sister Speakley would discern the reason.

As she walked away after she had been dismissed with some severe words of caution she felt a fluttering beneath her ribcage and she thought she was going to faint.

For a moment she thought it was stress because she felt so humiliated at being spoken to in such a way by Sister Speakley. Then she forgot all about that as realisation dawned on her that it wasn't stress that had caused the flutter but the baby quickening. The child she was carrying was already capable of movement strong enough that she could feel it.

As she undressed for bed that night she surreptitiously studied her silhouette. The belt of her skirt had been getting tighter for days and as she was wearing only a long white lawn nightdress, she could see that her stomach bulged noticeably; her breasts seemed bigger and were quite tender.

As she crept under the covers her fears mounted. She recalled the exact date when she and Philip had made love and worked out exactly how pregnant she must be.

The results alarmed her. She realised that somehow she must have miscalculated. She wasn't three months' pregnant but was well over four.

In the small hours of the morning the answer finally came to her about what she must do; she must take her brother Lewis into her confidence just as soon as she possibly could.

She and Lewis had always been very close.

When they had been much younger he had always made a great fuss of her and had been very protective. Whenever she had been told off by one or other of their parents and sent up to her room, he'd always managed to find a way to come up and comfort her. They'd become even closer after their sister Lilian had been born.

At eighteen he'd started work as a junior clerk in their father's firm and from then on, when he received his pay packet each week, he'd bought her little treats like a bar of chocolate or a comic. When Lilian found out, she protested so much about it, claiming that it was not fair because Lewis wasn't buying her anything, that in the end he'd been told to stop doing so.

They had still remained close even after he had started going out with Violet, who was now his wife, and she knew that she could rely on him to help her. He was twenty-four, a man of the world, so he wouldn't condemn her or be shocked by what had happened. He would not only be understanding but he would also be able to advise her about what he considered was the best thing to do.

There were only another few days left of the six-week training course to run. Once it ended and the students had passed their final examination, they would all be given a week off before starting work on the wards.

Even though Christabel's parents had been against her becoming a nurse, they would surely be proud of her achievement when they heard that she was now a fully fledged auxiliary nurse.

They were bound to make it an occasion for a family dinner to celebrate. Lewis and Violet would be there as well as Lilian so she would have to find a way of getting Lewis on his own so that she could confide in him and ask him for his help.

At all costs she must be careful that Lilian didn't overhear their conversation. Her sister would be sure to tell their parents and she could imagine the consternation that would cause.

Violet would also probably be taken aback but she could be relied on to be discreet. She would not say a word to anyone if Lewis told her not to. She certainly wouldn't say anything to either Basil or Mabel, because Christabel knew that she was far too timid and too much in awe of her in-laws to face them with such news.

Chapter Three

Christabel's announcement that she was now a fully qualified auxiliary nurse met with a lukewarm reception from her mother because there appeared to be some other exciting family developments that were far more important.

'Take your things up to your room and then hurry back down because we are waiting to start dinner, and it's a special celebration,' her mother told her.

'Of course.' Christabel smiled. She thought the family had forgotten all about her birthday, even though it was such a milestone being her twenty-first, but obviously they hadn't. This was to be a family meal to celebrate the occasion.

'Lewis and Violet have been here for ages and have some special news but I'll leave Lewis to tell you all about that,' her mother added.

'Heavens,' Christabel paused at the foot of the stairs, 'he isn't going to join the army, is he?' she asked in alarm.

'No dear, not as far as I know.' Her mother frowned.

As she took off her outdoor clothes and put them away, Christabel gazed round the familiar setting with a feeling of nostalgia. It was only six weeks since she'd left home yet in that time her entire life had altered so much and there were even more dramatic events to come, she thought morbidly as she selected one of the many dresses hanging in her wardrobe, changed into it, brushed her hair, and prepared to meet the rest of the family.

They were already seated in the dining room; all of them, except Lilian who was considered too young, enjoying a glass of sherry. She went over to where her father was sitting in his usual chair at the head of the table and kissed him perfunctorily before taking her place facing her sister at the other end of the table. She waited to be offered a sherry and felt disappointed when she wasn't.

'Have you heard the latest?' Lilian babbled excitedly, looking from under her lashes across at Lewis who was sitting on the left of his father. 'It's far more exciting than all this gloomy talk of war.'

'It's not merely talk, Lilian,' Basil intervened reprovingly. 'War has been declared and some of our troops have already landed in France. What is more, I gather that, any day now, we can expect to hear reports of actual fighting.'

'I think Lewis has some news for us all,' Mabel said quickly, smiling across at her son.

'Well, yes.' He hesitated, looking at his wife as if for approval, and when Violet gave him a brief nod and a timid smile, he cleared his throat and continued. 'Yes, we do have some news

26

for you.' He coughed nervously. 'Violet is pregnant; we are expecting a baby soon after Christmas, probably at the end of February.'

Christabel felt the colour rush to her cheeks. She quickly took a sip from her glass of water to try and calm her racing heart. 'In February!' The words were out before she could stop them. No one seemed to notice, they were all too intent on congratulating Violet and Lewis, asking if they'd chosen a name yet, and so many other questions that Violet looked overcome with embarrassment.

'So does that mean you are four months' pregnant, Violet?' Lilian asked, her clear, piping voice cutting across the chatter. 'If so, have you quickened yet?'

'Quickened?' Violet's sallow cheeks turned red. 'I'm not sure what you mean, Lilian.'

'Have you felt the baby moving? Are you quite sure it is alive, because a great many first-time pregnancies end in miscarriage; did you know that?'

'Lilian!' Lewis gave her a furious look.

'In our biology lessons we've been told all about what happens when you become pregnant,' Lilian explained looking all wide-eyed and innocent.

'I hardly think that gynaecological subjects are suitable at the dinner table,' Basil said firmly. 'I am sure, Lewis, we all wish to congratulate you and Violet, but now we should change the subject and talk about something else.'

Christabel let her thoughts drift as congratulations were showered on Lewis and Violet. She waited for her mother to remind them that she had just had her twenty-first birthday, and to tell them the news that she had now qualified as an auxiliary nurse, but her mother seemed to have forgotten about her.

Christabel felt rather hurt but, not wanting to steal the limelight from Lewis and Violet, she decided to say nothing. As soon as she could politely do so she said goodnight and escaped up to her room.

'I was late arriving and so I haven't unpacked my suitcase yet,' she explained. 'When I've finished doing that I'm looking forward to having an early night. It will be so wonderful to be able to sleep in my own comfortable bed again.'

Once upstairs she undressed and put on her dressing gown but she had no intention of going to bed. Her mind was far too active to even consider sleeping. She wouldn't be able to rest until she'd found a way to talk to Lewis on his own. She wondered how long it would be before he and Violet came up to bed.

Several times she went out on to the landing and listened with growing impatience to the sound of voices from below. It seemed they were all still in the dining room because she could hear the chink of cups and smell the tantalising aroma of coffee; she would still have a considerable wait.

It was almost an hour later before she heard her mother call out to let Mary know that she could come and clear away and to ask her to make sure that there was a jug of water and glasses in each of the bedrooms. Ten minutes later they all started to say goodnight to each other and make their way upstairs.

Christabel drew back into her room, peeping out through a crevice in the door to see if there was any possibility of waylaying Lewis.

She felt a surge of relief when she saw that Violet was coming upstairs at the same time as Lilian and guessed that her father had detained Lewis so that he could have a private word with him.

After that the waiting seemed to be interminable. Her mother came up to bed but still her father and Lewis remained downstairs. She was so tired that she'd almost given up in despair when she heard the drawing-room door open and heard the two men come out. She breathed a sigh of relief when she heard her father say, 'I'm going to lock up for the night so perhaps we can talk about it again tomorrow.'

As Lewis was about to walk past her door, Christabel called out to him in a whisper.

'Heavens, you startled me,' he exclaimed. 'I thought you'd be in bed and asleep by now, since you came up over an hour ago.'

'Lewis,' she said as she laid a hand on his arm. 'I desperately need your advice. Can we go for a walk first thing tomorrow morning before any of the others come down to break-fast?'

He frowned. 'Of course, but can you tell me what it is about? You sound as though there is something dreadfully wrong,' he said, his voice full of concern.

'There is, that's why I don't want to talk about it here in case someone overhears us and you know what a little chatterbox Lilian can be.'

He nodded understandingly. 'Eight o'clock? I'll be waiting at the end of the drive for you? Are you sure you don't want to give me some idea of what it is about?'

She shook her head. 'Thank you, Lewis, I knew I could depend on you. I'll tell you every-thing in the morning.' She closed her bedroom door quickly, not giving him time to say anything else or question her further.

It was a cool, hazy September morning as Christabel made her way down the drive to meet Lewis. He was already waiting and, without a word, he tucked her hand through his arm as they set off at a brisk pace down the road together.

'Now come on, what's all this cloak and dagger stuff about?' he asked, squeezing her arm as they turned into the next street, 'Are you in some kind of trouble?'

It took Christabel several minutes to formu-late what she intended to say to him because each time she started to speak the words seem to stick in her throat. In the end, she blurted out, 'I'm pregnant, Lewis, and I don't know what to do. I need your help.'

'Pregnant!' He looked down at her, a shocked look on his handsome face. 'You surely don't mean you've become involved with someone since you've been at Hilbury?'

'Heavens, no.' She shook her head. 'It happened before then, on Philip's last leave. As soon as I suspected, I knew I had to get away from home before Mother guessed. That's why I decided to train as a nurse. It was the only way I could think of to get away from home without them stopping me.'

Lewis let out a long, soft whistle. 'Why on earth didn't you tell me earlier instead of packing your bags and leaving home. That's only made matters worse.'

'I wasn't completely sure . . . I . . . I half hoped I was wrong and that everything would come right again and that my feeling sick was some-thing to do with the shock of losing Philip,' she mumbled, her face red with embarrassment at having to talk about such matters with her brother. 'Even when I arrived at Hilbury and found that I was still being sick most mornings I tried to convince myself that it was the change of environment and the smell of antiseptic or else the different kind of food I was eating because the symptoms always wore off by lunchtime.'

'You could be wrong,' he said hopefully. 'It might be shock and so on.'

'No, I know for certain that it isn't any of those things,' she said despairingly.

'So you are absolutely sure?'

Her colour deepened. 'After last night I am quite positive. You know what Lilian said, when she asked Violet about whether she had quickened.'

'Yes.' He frowned, and waited for her to continue.

'Well, I have, too. Several times I've felt the baby moving and I know it is there and growing bigger all the time because my clothes are all too tight for me. That's why I need your help, Lewis; don't you see, soon it will be obvious to everyone. I won't be able to stay at Hilbury and I can't come home.'

'Are you quite sure that you don't want either Mother or Father to know?'

'Of course I don't! You know perfectly well that they'd be terribly shocked.'

'Would they?' He frowned thoughtfully. 'They might be quite understanding. After all, you were planning to get married the next time Philip came on leave.'

'No!' Her chin jutted. 'I don't want them to know anything at all about it.'

'So what are you planning to do, then? You won't be able to go on working as a nurse.'

'I know that; I've left it too late to have an abortion, and I want to have this baby and then have it adopted. I'm hoping that that will be the end of the matter and I'll be able to get on with my life again.'

Lewis stood stock still and grabbed her by the shoulders and stared down at her in disbelief. 'Do you know what you are saying, Christabel? This is me you are talking to.'

'Don't try and talk me out of it,' she said, pulling away from him and starting to walk again. 'I've thought it all through and that is why I want you to help me.'

'So what are you hoping that I can do about it?' he asked in a bewildered voice.

'I can't ask Father to increase my allowance and no matter how frugal I am I know it won't be enough to live on once I am no longer at Hilbury, so I want you to help me find a cheap room somewhere and pay the rent for me until after I've had the baby.'

'That's a rather tall order, Christabel. I have increased responsibilities of my own now that Violet is pregnant. I'm not sure that I can afford it.'

'Please, Lewis; I'm depending on you. You earn a good salary and I'll pay back every penny it costs you as soon as I am back at work again. I'm not asking you to install me in a house of my own, I only want one small room in a cheap lodging house or somewhere like that and, of course, it must be in some other part of Liverpool.'

'Where on earth do you think you are going to find a place like that?'

'I don't know but I thought you would. There must be cheap rooms around the dock area, some of those small streets off Scotland Road, somewhere like that.'

'Most of those are overcrowded slums. Two or three families all living together under one roof, sharing everything from kitchens to lavatories,' he told her flatly.

'I know, and I don't mind. I've become used to sharing a room with someone since I've been at Hilbury.'

'It's not quite the same though, is it? I imagine everything is scrupulously clean at Hilbury and—'

'But I have to find somewhere, Lewis. Look, we have to get back before anyone misses us and wants to know why we went out so early.' Her voice rose and she smothered back a sob. 'I'm counting on you to help me to find somewhere to live and then, after I've had the baby, please would you help me to arrange for it to be adopted?'

Lewis looked taken aback. 'All right, all right. I understand the fix you are in, but I do need time to think this through. When did you say you thought this baby was due?'

'About the same time as yours; sometime in February. So you see the predicament I am in and how much I need your help.'

'I'm still of the opinion that you should tell Mother, or even the Hendersons – after all, it *is* their grandchild.'

'That is right out of the question,' Christabel told him. 'If you won't help me, then I'll find someone else who will or I'll get rid of it myself somehow.'

'Christabel! You are overwrought; you don't know what you are saying.'

'So you will help me?' She looked at him pleadingly. 'I'm counting on you, Lewis.'

'I'll have to think about it,' he said evasively. 'I think we'd better be getting back now or they'll be wondering where we are.'

'I can rely on you to help me, though?' Christabel persisted as they began to retrace their steps.

'There's an awful lot involved,' he parried. 'It's not just a question of finding you somewhere to live, but also arranging where you can have the baby. If you want to keep it quiet, then it will have to be a private nursing home and they are very expensive.'

'I've told you I will pay you back every penny. I'll go back to Hilbury the minute I've had it,' she promised.

'What if they don't agree to take you back? When they hear you are going to have a baby, they'll probably dismiss you.'

'They're not going to know, though, are they? I'll tell them I will be taking some time off to look after Mother. You could write them a letter saying she has been taken ill and asking if I can have a few months off to look after her.'

'Christabel!' Lewis stopped and stared at her

in disbelief. 'I can hardly believe that you can be so devious.'

'Would you write the letter? Not yet, of course,' she added hurriedly. 'I want to go on working for as long as possible. With any luck, I won't need to leave Hilbury until November.'

Chapter Four

Christabel was extremely conscious that her body was rapidly changing and there was no disguising the fact that it was thickening.

Each day when she put on her nurse's uniform it seemed to be that little bit tighter and she became increasingly worried about how long she was going to be able to manage to keep the fact hidden from Peggy, who shared her room, never mind Sister Speakley and everyone else at Hilbury.

It wasn't until she went home one weekend in late October and her mother commented that she seemed to be putting on weight, that she decided the time had come to leave Hilbury.

That weekend she went to see Lewis on the pretext that she wanted to find out how Violet was.

'You are only home for a couple of days and you are going to spend time visiting them? I didn't think you liked Violet all that much,' her mother said tetchily.

'I thought you would be pleased because it seems to be the polite thing to do,' Christabel said smiling tightly.

'Yes, perhaps you are right. Maybe I should come along with you.'

'No, you rest, Mother. You can see Violet at any time,' Christabel said quickly. She guided her mother towards an armchair. 'Why don't you sit down, put your feet up and have a little nap. I'll only be gone for an hour or so and when I come back we'll have a nice cup of tea and I'll tell you all my news.'

To Christabel's relief Violet was in her bedroom resting when she arrived so she wasted no time in telling Lewis that she now felt she had to leave Hilbury as soon as possible and asking him to do whatever was necessary to make it possible.

'I've given it considerable thought and I don't think writing to the hospital is the answer,' he told her.

'Why ever not?'

'Well, for a start, they'll think it strange that I write to them and not Father and, furthermore, what will we do if they reply and he gets hold of the letter?'

'Then why not come to Hilbury and collect me? They won't think that strange; they'll think it's very urgent and that you're doing your best to help. They'll understand that you've come because Father is staying at Mother's side. In fact, it will make it look all the more serious.'

'Very well, but where will you go?'

'I was hoping you would be able to find me a room first,' Christabel told him impatiently.

'Somewhere that is very cheap and far enough away from home so that there is no chance of me ever bumping into anyone I know.'

'I have made one or two enquiries. I thought it might be a good idea if you went over to Wallasey, but everything over there is quite pricey, far more expensive than here in Liverpool.'

'Then can you find something around the docks? I'm not likely to meet anyone I know there, and it will be cheap,' she asked him.

'It's not a very desirable area, Christabel; you won't like it there.'

'It will do; I'll only have to be there for a few months, until I've had the baby. After that I will be going back to work at Hilbury.'

'If you are quite sure, then I'll see what I can arrange,' he promised. 'As soon as I've found somewhere for you I'll let you know and then, providing you like it, we can decide when I will put the other part of our plan into action and I will come and collect you.'

'I'll need to be out of Hilbury as soon as possible, though. Could you rent the room and then come for me at Hilbury? You don't have to let me know when it will be; taking me by surprise will be all the better because I won't have to pretend that I'm shocked by your news.'

Christabel was on tenterhooks when she returned to Hilbury. Every time someone called out her name she hoped that she was being summoned to Matron's office and that she'd find Lewis waiting there.

The week dragged by and she began to wonder if he'd let her down, then, on the Thursday, when she'd almost given up hope, the call came.

She was helping Peggy to put clean sheets on a bed when Sister Speakley came bustling over. 'Nurse Montgomery, Matron wants to see you at once in her office,' she told her sharply.

'What have you done wrong this time?' Peggy grinned as Christabel straightened up and headed for the door.

'Nurse Montgomery!' Sister Speakley's voice cut like a whip. 'Smarten yourself up before you report to Matron. Your cap is lopsided and your apron strings are not tied correctly.'

'Yes, Sister.' Christabel obediently straightened her cap as she hurried to the door. Once outside the ward, she almost broke into a run in her eagerness. Lewis and Matron were in such a serious conversation when she arrived that her affected surprise at seeing him there went unnoticed.

'Nurse Montgomery, I'm afraid I have bad news for you. Your brother tells me that your mother has been taken ill and has asked if you can return home and take care of her. Normally I would not permit a nurse just to leave without notice, but, under the circumstances, I am prepared to make an exception. You may collect whatever you need from your room and meet your brother in the main hall. I hope you will be able to return to your duties here soon.

'Kindly let me know how matters progress and when we can expect your sister back,' she added, looking at Lewis. 'It is most unfortunate that you need her at home as we are getting very busy and, of course, we have trained your sister to nurse sick and wounded soldiers, not one of her relatives.'

'We do understand that, Matron, and we greatly appreciate your understanding and cooperation,' Lewis told her gravely.

The moment they were outside Hilbury, Christabel let out a long sigh of relief. 'You did that so well, Lewis, that I almost believed Mother really was ill,' she congratulated him.

'Be that as it may, I can't say that I am very proud of what I have done. I am not at all sure that I am doing the right thing in aiding and abetting you in this matter. What are we going to do at Christmas? Mother will be expecting you home for at least a visit, so how are you going to deal with that?'

'In the same way as we're dealing with things now.'

Lewis frowned. 'I don't understand?'

'I'm relying on you to explain to Mother that there has been an epidemic or a rush of casualties, and that I am needed at the hospital and am unable to get any time off.'

'That's all very well, Christabel, but with only Lilian still at home, it's going to be a rather quiet Christmas for them. They're bound to miss you.'

'Then you must make sure that they don't. You and Violet will have to visit them a little more often and make sure they aren't lonely.'

'That may not be as easy as it sounds,' he grumbled. 'Remember, Violet will be heavily pregnant by then and she will probably want to rest a great deal.'

'So will I,' she reminded him. 'At least she won't have to hide away and be cut off from all her friends and family,' she added pointedly.

When he didn't answer she slipped her arm through his and squeezed it affectionately as they reached the railway station. 'You *have* found me somewhere to live, haven't you?' she asked anxiously. 'Where is it?'

'It's in Wilcock Court off Scotland Road. It's only one room and it's on the second floor and not very salubrious. I've rented it in your name; well, that is, as Mrs Montgomery, and I've paid four months' rent in advance.'

'Oh Lewis, thank you!' she said, relieved. 'Mrs Montgomery,' she looked up at him and laughed, 'so I'm married, am I?'

'It was impossible to find anyone willing to let a room to a single lady,' he told her as they boarded a train for Liverpool Exchange. 'As far as the landlady is aware, I am your husband and I've told her that I am about to go to sea and will be away for several months. Her name, by the way, is Maggie Nelson. She's a rather rough sort of character, but then so are most of the landladies in that area.'

'Have you told her I'm pregnant?'

'No, I thought perhaps it was better not to do that in case she refused me the room. As a rule they don't want crying babies, if it can be helped.'

'It won't take her long to find out, though. There will be one quite soon, won't there?' Christabel sighed, rubbing her hand over her extended stomach.

'When she does, then you can let her know that it won't be any problem because you have been booked into a private clinic to have the baby. When you come home afterwards without the baby, you can always say it has died or something. I'm sure you are capable of making up a suitable story.'

'Yes, and then I will be packing my bags and telling Mrs Maggie Nelson that I am going home to my mother until you come home from your unknown destination,' Christabel told him.

'Good, that's all settled and clear in both our minds,' Lewis agreed.

'You haven't told me about the clinic yet,' Christabel reminded him as they left the Exchange and started to walk towards Scotland Road.

'I've written down all the details. They want you to go along sometime before you are due to give birth to provide them with various details. Don't forget, you are also booked in there as Mrs Montgomery,' he added.

As they left the busy office area behind, Christabel noticed the streets were becoming shabbier, and when they turned into Wilcock Court, she drew in a sharp breath of dismay because there was such an air of gloom and neglect over the place.

It was mid-afternoon; most men were still at work, but there seemed to be women clustered together on every doorstep. A few were shouting at children who were playing in the gutter, or swinging from ropes tied to a lamp post, but most were simply talking to each other and the majority of them looked unkempt and even dirty to her fastidious eye.

'Surely this isn't where the room is?' she asked in alarm.

'I told you it wasn't very salubrious,' Lewis retorted in a disgruntled tone.

'Which house belongs to Maggie Nelson?'

'It's the end one,' he stated, 'and since there's no one standing outside gossiping, maybe she doesn't fraternise with her neighbours very much.'

To Christabel's relief the heavily built middle-aged woman who answered the door to them looked reasonably clean and wholesome in her dark dress and clean floral apron.

'This way Mr and Mrs Montgomery,' she invited.

She led them up the stairs and along a narrow

landing to a medium-sized room that contained a narrow bed and wardrobe at one end and an armchair and a round wooden table and two straight-backed chairs at the other. Across one corner was a dark red cotton curtain which she pulled to one side to reveal a work shelf with narrower shelves above it containing an assortment of cups, saucers, plates and tins for storage. On the main shelf there was a gas ring, a tin kettle and a washing-up bowl; underneath the shelf were two buckets, one containing fresh water.

'There you are, everything you need,' she said proudly. 'You can refill the bucket with water from the tap in my kitchen whenever you need to do so. The other bucket is for your rubbish and you bring that down and tip it into the bin out in the back yard. By the way, that's where the lavatory is. You'll have to go through my kitchen to get out of the backdoor,' she added as an afterthought.

'I see. I hope that's not too inconvenient,' Christabel murmured.

'It hasn't got to be, has it?' Mrs Nelson answered tartly. 'That's the way it is and I've been letting rooms out for so long now that I'm used to it. Anyway,' she went on, 'I'll leave the pair of you to settle in. You won't be staying as well, will you, Mr Montgomery?' She frowned, looking over at the narrow bed.

'No no,' Lewis said hastily, taking out his watch from his waistcoat pocket and consulting it.

'I have to return to my base, I must leave quite soon.'

'Then in that case, I'll leave the two of you to say goodbye. I hope Mrs Montgomery will be very comfortable here once she's settled in.'

The moment the door closed behind Mrs Nelson, Lewis handed Christabel the details of the private clinic. As he buttoned up his coat and prepared to leave he made her promise to go along there as they'd requested.

'Of course I will, but there's no hurry. It's ages and ages away so stop worrying. When am I going to see you again?'

'I'm not going to call here again. You heard what I said to Mrs Nelson, I have to report to my base. That means I am leaving Liverpool right away.'

'Yes, but we must meet up from time to time, Lewis,' she begged. 'I'm going to be terribly lonely. I'll want to know what is happening at home and surely you will want to know that I am all right.'

'It will be difficult, Christabel. I've done what you asked me to do; I've found you a room and booked you into a clinic. The rest is up to you. If you don't like being cut off from me and the rest of the family, then you should have done as I suggested in the first place and taken Mother or Philip's parents into your confidence. If you'd done that, then you could have gone home and spent the next few months in comfort instead of in this horrible place.'

46

'What happens when I actually go into the clinic, after the baby is born, I mean? Are you going to be there to arrange all the legal details and deal with all the papers that will have to be signed if it is to be adopted?'

'I'll try to be there but, remember, I have Violet to consider too. Our baby is due at the same time and she must be my first priority.'

He held out his arms to Christabel and hugged her close. 'I'm sorry little sister, but you must see that I am being torn in two over this. That's why I wish you had been more open about it and confided in Mother.'

'That was quite out of the question,' Christabel said determinedly, pulling away from him. 'I understand it makes things difficult for you, Lewis, and I do appreciate all that you have done for me,' she told him, smiling wanly. 'You will try and see me, even if it is only occasionally?' she persisted anxiously. 'I'm so scared Lewis,' she added tearfully. 'Couldn't we meet in the park now and again, perhaps in St John's Gardens; that's not very far from here, is it?'

'Very well, I'll try and do that.'

'When?' Her face brightened. 'Can we meet there regularly? Perhaps once a week?'

'No, that is far too risky. I'll meet you there in two weeks' time and we'll see how that goes,' he said firmly. 'I'll try and be there at one o'clock and, with any luck, Father won't notice my

47

absence from the office. If he does, I will have
the excuse that it is my lunch hour and that
I'm doing some shopping or something for
Violet.'

Chapter Five

Christabel felt utterly desolate after Lewis had left. She sat down on the edge of the narrow bed and looked around in dismay. This was to be her home for at least the next three months and already she not only hated its drab appearance but also felt claustrophobic there. She wished she could afford new curtains or a new rug to brighten the place up but since she was no longer earning and in future, once she'd spent her meagre savings, would have to rely on Lewis for every penny she spent she knew she couldn't afford them.

Rousing herself, she went to look in the curtained-off corner that acted as a kitchen to see if there was any tea and milk to make herself a drink. The place was completely bare. Shocked, she went back and sat on the bed and tried to think what she must do. Although it was already dusk outside it meant she would have to venture out to buy some supplies otherwise she would have to go hungry until the next day and she was now starving as she'd missed out on lunch.

She walked across to the window, rubbed a space clear on the glass, and stared out. The fog that had been threatening earlier had closed in and the women who had been standing out in the court gossiping had gone inside. There were only one or two older children still out playing.

Taking a deep breath, she picked up her purse and decided she would have to go and do some shopping. Mrs Nelson came out into the hallway when she was halfway down the stairs.

'Going out, Mrs Montgomery?' she said in surprise.

'I need to buy some food and things,' Christabel explained.

'Oh, well, if it's a pinch of tea and a spot of milk, I can let you have those, enough to last you until morning.'

'No, I need several other things as well,' Christabel told her.

'You mean to make a meal for tonight? Remember, you only have a gas ring to do your cooking on, so you won't be able to do much more than boil up some potatoes or make a drop of soup. If you want anything cooked, then you'd better bring it down to me and I'll put it in my oven for you,' she added.

'How very kind of you, Mrs Nelson, I'll remember that.'

'As a matter of fact, I have some scouse simmering away on the hob right now and I'll be happy to share a bowlful with you,' Maggie Nelson went on. 'It will be far better than for you to go out foraging at this time of night.

I can tell you the best places to shop and it will be a sight easier to find them in the daylight than it is in this fog.'

'Well . . .' Christabel hesitated. She did feel scared of venturing out and wasn't even too sure if she would be able to find the shops or even find her way back to Wilcock Court afterwards.

'You go on back up to your room and have a rest and come down about six o'clock and I'll have it all ready on the table for you. If you'd like a cup of tea now to keep you going until then, there's one already brewed and I don't mind if you drink it down here in my kitchen or take it back upstairs with you.'

'I'll take it upstairs with me, if you don't mind, thank you, Mrs Nelson.' Christabel smiled.

When she came back down a couple of hours later, Christabel was surprised to find how tasty the scouse Mrs Nelson served was and how cosy it was in her landlady's kitchen.

She had never in her life had to cook for herself and she had no idea how to go about preparing a meal like the one she'd just enjoyed so, having thanked Mrs Nelson and praised her cooking, she suggested that she might like to provide her with a cooked meal every evening.

'Oh, I don't know about that,' Mrs Nelson exclaimed. 'I always cook something for myself, so I suppose it wouldn't be too much trouble,' she added thoughtfully.

'I'll pay you of course,' Christabel told her quickly.

'Not used to looking after yourself then, is that it?' Mrs Nelson queried.

'No, not really. Apart from that, as you already said, it won't be easy to cook very much on a gas ring.'

'I also said I would be willing to pop anything you wanted roasting or baking into my oven,' Mrs Nelson reminded her.

'It mightn't always be convenient for you to do that, though,' Christabel pointed out.

'No, that's true enough,' Mrs Nelson agreed as she reached out and took Christabel's empty plate and carried it over to the brownstone sink.

'Would you like a helping of pudding?' she asked as she lifted a dish of Apple Charlotte out of the oven.

As they ate, Mrs Nelson expounded on the theory of providing Christabel with a regular meal. She pointed out that it would mean extra shopping and that she would need to know if there were any foods that Christabel didn't like. By the time Christabel went back up to her room, however, a deal had been made.

With hardly any shopping necessary, no cooking and very little cleaning to do, Christabel found it difficult to occupy her time until her baby was born because she had no money to spend on entertainment, and was now paying Mrs Nelson for her meals.

After she'd attended the clinic as Lewis had told her she must, and made quite sure that they understood that she wanted to have the baby adopted the moment it was born, she didn't see the necessity to buy a layette for the child. Anyway, she told herself, she couldn't afford to buy wool for knitting and she wasn't much good at sewing.

Wilcock Court was only a couple of turnings away from Scotland Road where there were plenty of shops and a large market but they were not the sort that interested her. Most days, she made her way to the city centre and walked around the shops there, making sure that she avoided the really high-class stores like Henderson and George Henry Lee and the fashionable places in Bold Street, in case she bumped into her mother or someone who knew her.

She usually settled for a coffee and a snack in a Lyons Corner House or the Kardomah Café at lunchtime, just enough to keep her going until the evening when Mrs Nelson would have a hot meal waiting for her.

Sometimes in the afternoons, if it was very cold or raining, she went to a matinee, sitting in the cheapest of the seats.

It was warm in the cinema and watching what was happening on the flickering screen took her mind off her own plight. She watched anything and everything. When it was a romantic film it sometimes brought back so many memories of Philip that she had to walk out.

Even though she'd hardened her heart to the past, she knew she was still vulnerable. She was also racked with guilt about what he would think about her giving up their baby. There were days when she worried deeply about this and wondered if perhaps Lewis had been right when he'd wanted her to tell her mother, but she knew she hadn't the strength to face up to her father's wrath. Perhaps, if she had told Hilda Henderson, she would have understood. As Lewis had said, it was their grandchild, after all, and once they were over the shock of what had happened they would have helped her.

As Christmas approached she felt homesick. She was also worried that her mother might not believe Lewis when he told her that because they'd received so many casualties at Hilbury after the terrible British defeat at the battle of Ypres, she wouldn't be able to come home for Christmas.

However, the newspapers were so full of reports concerning what had happened at Ypres, and how the British soldiers were digging themselves into the trenches on the Western Front, that both Mabel and Basil accepted what Lewis said.

'It's going to be a very quiet Christmas for them with only Lilian there,' Lewis told her as they sat in a Lyons Corner House catching up on what was happening in the family.

'Not really, you and Violet will be there for Christmas Dinner,' Christabel pointed out.

'I'm not too sure about that, it will depend very much on how Violet is. She doesn't really feel well enough to go visiting. Unlike you, she has to spend a great deal of her time resting in bed.'

'At least she is in her own home and can fill in her time doing things that interest her. I have to exist in a pokey little room where it's impossible to even cook my own meals,' Christabel grumbled. 'What's more, it's in such a horrible, slummy area that I am almost too scared to go out. In the evenings, all I can do is sit and read and the newspaper is full of dreadful accounts of what is happening to our soldiers who are at the Front.'

'Really?' He looked surprised. 'Violet is always knitting or sewing things for the baby when she feels well enough to do so.'

'There's no point in me doing that, is there, since I am not going to be bringing my baby home. You have made all that clear to the clinic, haven't you, Lewis? I am counting on you being there to deal with all the paperwork immediately the baby is born.'

'Don't worry, the matron at the clinic will let me know as soon as you go into labour and I promise I'll do my utmost to be there,' he told her stiffly. 'I still don't agree with what you are doing because I still feel that you should go home and tell Mother that you are expecting a baby, but if you are sure it is what you want, then I will stand by your decision,' he told her abruptly, pushing back his chair and standing up to leave.

Several times over Christmas her gloomy little room was so cold and dreary that Christabel wondered if perhaps Lewis was right and she should go home. Then the thought of the shock and horror she'd see on her parents' faces, the explanations she would have to make and the admonishment she would receive, especially when they heard that she intended to have the baby adopted, stopped her.

She'd stuck it out until now, and there were only a couple more months to go, she told herself. She made a chart of the days left and began marking them off each morning but, even so, the time still dragged.

By the end of January, her only contact, except the fortnightly meetings with Lewis, was with Maggie Nelson when she went down for her evening meal. She felt so big and cumbersome that she no longer had the energy to go into the city centre any more and she still felt nervous of walking around the Scotland Road area on her own.

Lewis was sympathetic, but he was very worried about Violet, who had been confined to bed by their doctor and was far from well. At the end of January he told Christabel that he couldn't spare the time to meet her any more.

'You will come to the clinic, though, Lewis, when I have to go in there?' she asked in alarm.

'I told you I would, and you know I always keep my promises,' he said stiffly.

'Yes, but what about if Violet needs you to be with her? Her baby is due at almost exactly the same time as mine.'

'Stop worrying! I've said I'll come to the clinic, and I'll be there. It will all work out and everything will fit in smoothly. Now go and pack a bag with the things you will need to take with you to the clinic and as soon as your labour pains start, call a taxicab. Here,' he handed her some pound notes, 'buy any extras you think you might need and keep plenty of change in your purse so that you can pay for the taxi.'

Lewis's optimism was short-lived. There were serious complications with Violet's pregnancy and Dr Ferguson, the Montgomerys' family doctor, warned Lewis that there was every possibility that their baby would be stillborn. Furthermore, he was very concerned about how Violet would react if that did happen, because she was so extremely overwrought.

'I know you have engaged a resident midwife to take care of her, but perhaps you should also warn your mother; she might want to be with your wife to comfort her.'

'No, no! Whatever happens I don't want Mother worrying,' Lewis told him, 'so I beg you not to mention it to her, or to my father.'

'Of course not, Lewis, if that's the way you

want it,' Dr Ferguson agreed, but he looked rather disapproving.

'Thank you.' Lewis held out his hand.

'Try not to worry yourself too much,' Dr Ferguson told him gravely. 'Your wife is in capable hands, remember, and the midwife will send for me if there is any change and she needs my assistance.'

Lewis stayed at his wife's bedside most of that night; towards dawn the midwife said she thought Dr Ferguson should be summoned. Between them they did everything possible for Violet. Shortly before breakfast time a baby girl was born and Dr Ferguson broke the news to Lewis that it was stillborn.

'I have sedated your wife to help her recover from the ordeal she's been through,' he told Lewis.

'Does she know that the baby is dead?' Lewis asked worriedly.

'No.' Dr Ferguson pursed his lips thoughtfully. 'I must warn you, though, Lewis, that I'm worried about what her mental state will be when she's told; someone responsible should be with her.'

'I'll be here; perhaps I should be the one to tell her.'

'No, Lewis.' Dr Ferguson shook his head. 'I think she needs another woman here. As I said earlier, perhaps your mother or even your sister. Christabel could be a great help now that she's had nursing experience.'

'No!' Lewis remained firm. 'I'll deal with it myself.'

'Very well. I'll come back again in a couple of hours and see how your wife is. In the meantime, think about what I have said.'

'Yes, of course,' Lewis assured him as he accompanied him to the door. An audacious plan was already forming in his mind and he wondered if he dare mention it to Dr Ferguson.

Lewis felt that the decision had been taken out of his hands when, an hour later, he received a call from the clinic to let him know that Christabel had been admitted and had given birth in the early hours of the morning. He could hardly believe it when he was told that it was a girl.

Torn between his promise to Christabel and his duty to be with Violet, he told the midwife that he had to go out for a while on urgent business.

'Are they both all right?' he asked anxiously when he arrived at the clinic. 'Can I see them?'

'Mother and baby are both fine, Mr Montgomery,' the matron gushed. 'Of course you can see them. Perhaps you will be able to persuade your wife to cooperate with us. She had a perfectly straightforward delivery but now she is refusing to have anything at all to do with the baby; she won't even attempt to breastfeed it,' she went on.

'Have you made the arrangements for it to be adopted?' Christabel asked him anxiously the

59

moment Matron discreetly withdrew from the room and left them together.

'Don't worry, everything is in hand,' Lewis assured her.

'She's been trying to make me feed it.' Christabel shuddered. 'She put her in my arms, Lewis, and she is so sweet and fragile that I found it unbearable to hold her for a single moment. I knew I must have nothing whatsoever to do with her or I would never be able to part with her.'

'Don't worry, you just lie there and recover; I'll arrange the adoption and deal with everything,' Lewis said awkwardly.

Matron was looking very tight-lipped and rather puzzled as she accompanied Lewis to the door when he left the clinic a short time later. In accordance with her undertaking of absolute discretion, however, she made no comment. She merely nodded when Lewis stepped into the waiting taxicab carrying the newborn baby in his arms, saying he hoped his wife would be well enough to come home within the next few days.

Chapter Six

A week later, Lewis came to the clinic to collect Christabel and pay the bill. Even though she still felt rather shaky, Christabel was determined to put the past behind her and make a fresh start.

Even so, she felt immensely relieved when Lewis said that there was no need for her to go back to Wilcock Court as he had already told Mrs Nelson that she no longer required the room.

'I've booked you into a hotel for the night and then you can return to Hilbury tomorrow,' he told her.

'If they'll have me,' she said in a cautious voice.

'I've already told them that Mother is better and so they are expecting you in the morning.'

'You seem to have thought of everything,' she commented, looking at him in surprise.

'I've done what I thought you wanted me to do,' he said a trifle impatiently. 'Now, I'll put you in a taxicab and then I must get home to Violet and the baby.'

'Oh, she's had her baby, has she?' Christabel said in surprise. 'You could have told me.'

'I didn't want to upset you,' he said, looking uncomfortable.

Christabel blinked back the tears that were threatening at the memory of the appealing little scrap she had held in her arms a few days earlier. Deep down she knew her decision had been for the best because there was no way she could have looked after it. Not unless she'd involved either her parents or Philip's, and she felt it wasn't right for their reputations to be brought into disrepute because of her actions.

'What has she had?'

'A little girl,' he said tersely. 'We're calling her Kay.'

'The same as I had!'

He looked at her quickly, conscious of the wistful note in her voice. 'You're not regretting your decision, are you?' he asked sharply, as he hailed a cab.

She shook her head. 'No, of course not. You did what I asked of you. Thank you for arranging everything so well, I knew I could depend on you,' she added with a grateful smile. 'So, when am I going to see your baby?'

'Whenever you next manage to get time off and you come home for a visit,' he told her as he helped her into the cab. Before he slammed the door, he gave the driver directions and then gave Christabel money for the fare.

Apart from an enthusiastic welcome from Peggy, Christabel found that her arrival back at Hilbury passed almost unnoticed. To her surprise and relief she found she was still sharing a room with Peggy and working on the wards supervised by Sister Speakley.

The only difference was that before she'd left there hadn't been many patients; now the wards were packed to capacity, there were even men lying on makeshift beds in the corridors, and Christabel found being rushed off her feet utterly exhausting.

At the end of the day she felt so drained that all she wanted to do when she came off duty was lie on her bed and close her eyes. A great deal of Peggy's chatter about all that had gone on in her absence went over her head. Peggy mentioned so many new nurses and doctors that most of the time she had no idea what she was talking about and often she let her thoughts drift.

More and more, she found she was wondering what had happened to her baby. She'd had no idea when she'd made plans for it to be adopted that she would feel the parting so much; there were days when she felt as though a part of her was missing.

Being absent for so long also had an effect on her work. There were so many new procedures and rules that for the first couple of weeks she was struggling to keep up and frequently made mistakes or misunderstood instructions, something Sister Speakley was quick to notice.

'Your work is far from satisfactory, Nurse

Montgomery, so if you are still worrying about your mother, then I suggest that you go home for a couple of days and set your mind at rest,' she ordered, halfway though the second week.

Christabel was more than happy to comply. She hadn't been home since October. Although her mother had seemed to accept the explanation of why she couldn't come home at Christmas and had realised that she couldn't keep in touch because of the high security measures, Christabel was worried in case somehow or other she discovered the real reason for her absence.

The two days she spent at home reassured her that she need have no worries at all on that score. Both her parents were pleased to see her and when she told them that she was not allowed to divulge what had been happening at the hospital they said they quite understood.

She'd had an uneasy moment when they went to see Violet and her new daughter Kay. Her mother was such a proud grandmother, exclaiming how perfect the baby was, and pointing out that little Kay had the Montgomery blue eyes.

Christabel couldn't help feeling a twinge of remorse that she'd said nothing about her own baby when her mother had added, 'My only grandchild, and she looks just like you did, Christabel, when you were that age.'

Lewis handled the situation in his usual diplomatic way and the next minute they were talking about more serious matters to do with the War and its effect on everybody at home as well as the soldiers on the Western Front.

Even so, Christabel was relieved when it was time for her to return to Hilbury. She knew that from now on her work there would be far more demanding than when she'd first decided to become a nurse, but she was determined to focus on nursing to the exclusion of everything else.

On her return, she found her whole attitude to the patients was different. At first, each time a new batch of wounded men were brought into the wards she'd been sickened by the sight of some of their appalling wounds, but now she found she could look at gangrenous limbs, horrendous flesh wounds and sup-purating sores with detachment. It was almost as if the soldiers were no longer individuals, merely impersonal bodies that she was handling, and because it no longer worried her she became more dexterous when helping with the dressings.

Sister Speakley was quick to notice this and when casualties started arriving after the second battle of Ypres, she began to give Christabel more responsibility.

Many of the wounded, Christabel discovered, were her own age and those well enough to do so often tried to flirt with her or one of the other young nurses. Peggy claimed that cheering them up was as good as any medicine they could administer. Christabel didn't agree with her theory and remained aloof and she soon found that the patients noticed this and treated her with respect.

The one exception was Karl Blume, a young German. Blond, with pale-blue eyes and chiselled features, he spoke fluent English. His injuries were slight; a broken shoulder and a flesh wound in his chest. He was not confined to bed and, to her annoyance, he followed her constantly and tried to engage her in conversation, even though she usually ignored him.

Whenever she had any time off duty, she usually took a stroll round the perimeter road and, more often than not, Karl would be there. The very thought that he must be watching and waiting for her irritated her.

When he overheard her telling Peggy that she was going home for the weekend, his eyes narrowed. 'Take me with you,' he ordered.

For a moment, Christabel thought he must be joking. 'Patients are not allowed to go outside the hospital grounds,' she reminded him.

'Not officially, so if you tell me the time you will be leaving I will join you along the road.'

'You can't do that. You'd be caught. The MPs would spot you in your hospital blue uniform and take you into custody and you'd be severely punished!'

'I would wear my khaki uniform.'

'A German officer's uniform, are you mad?'

She stared at him in disbelief. His nerve astounded her. Surely he must know what the punishment would be if he was caught.

'Well? Will you let me accompany you?' he challenged.

'Most certainly not,' she told him sternly.

In the two days that followed Christabel went to great lengths to avoid Karl. She toyed with the idea of cancelling her leave, wondering what her own position might be if he followed her and then claimed that she had agreed to his going with her. As she changed out of her uniform into her own clothes, she hoped he'd abandoned his preposterous idea and that he wouldn't be at the station.

He was and, to her astonishment, he was wearing a British uniform. He nodded but she ignored him even when he raised his stick to his cap in a formal salute as she walked past him.

As they waited on the platform she was conscious of him walking up and down with a measured tread, tapping his stick rhythmically against his trouser leg.

He occupied a different carriage to her, but when she alighted at the Exchange he was right there at her side as she made her way out into Tithebarn Street.

Christabel tried desperately to think of what to say to stop him from following her, but then, when she turned to speak to him, she discovered he was no longer there. She looked around but he seemed to have completely vanished. Puzzled, but nevertheless relieved, she wondered if she ought to report him when she returned to Hilbury or whether it was best to say nothing about it.

Determined not to let it spoil her weekend, she put it out of her mind.

Her parents seemed pleased to see her; her mother thought she looked thinner than when she'd last been home, and worried whether this was because she wasn't getting enough to eat or whether she was working too hard.

Lilian wanted to know all about the patients and said she wished she could become a nurse because she was fed up with having to stay at home and help her mother.

'You are too young at the moment,' Christabel told her. 'Anyway, think yourself lucky that you have such a comfortable home and time to go out with your friends.'

At dinner, her parents dominated the conversation. Her father talked endlessly about the war and how he would deal with the situation were he in charge. Whenever her mother managed to speak, she bemoaned all the shortages of food and everything else. Lilian said nothing and although Christabel found their conversation tedious she tried hard not to show it.

Neither her parents nor Lilian had any idea about what it was like to go short of anything, she realised. They lived in the lap of luxury, she thought, as they enjoyed an excellent meal and generous helpings on all their plates. Her mother complaining so bitterly about shortages made her want to tell her about the squalid poverty she'd witnessed in Wilcock Court, but she knew that she couldn't do that without revealing why she had been living there.

As her father settled down to read the *Liverpool Evening Echo*, she could almost hear Maggie Nelson saying, 'I never buy a paper because they're a waste of money. You can read all the latest news from the lurid headlines on the placards for free.'

She remembered how Maggie had shopped, buying a joint of lamb for Sunday roast, having it cold on Monday, minced on Tuesday, in a pie on Wednesday, and with an assortment of vegetables as scouse on Thursday. Then it had been fish and chips on Friday and bread and scrape on Saturdays – or sausages and mashed potatoes, if she had enough money before it started all over again.

Maggie had been forced to be frugal yet she rarely grumbled, Christabel recalled, even though she had no luxuries at all in her life and had to make every penny do the work of two.

She was so kind, and looked after me so well, yet I never even thanked her, she thought guiltily. I left Lewis to tell her that I no longer wanted the room.

When Lilian began talking about the new baby it made her feel uncomfortable. She had not intended to visit Lewis and Violet this time but Lilian was insistent.

'It's months since you last saw her and you'll be amazed by how different she looks,' Lilian enthused. 'I had no idea that babies grew so quickly.'

The next afternoon Christabel agreed to go and visit Violet with her mother and Lilian. As her sister had foretold, she was amazed. Little Kay was now almost four months old and no longer a tiny little thing who spent most of her time asleep but plump and lively and taking notice of what was going on.

Her gummy smile and occasional gurgling laugh brought smiles to all their faces. Lilian sat cradling her until Violet suggested that Christabel might like to hold her.

For a moment, the thought of holding the plump little body in her arms horrified Christabel but she didn't know how to refuse. As the baby looked up into her face, her deep-blue eyes staring straight into her own, Christabel felt her heart thudding.

Kay was the same age as her own baby would have been, and it might just as well have been her own child that she was holding in her arms, who was looking at her so intently. She couldn't help wondering where her own little girl was and whether or not she was as loved and well cared for as little Kay was.

Mabel was so proud of little Kay, making much of the fact that she was her only grandchild, and

Christabel once again wondered what her parents' reaction would have been if she'd confided in them when she was pregnant.

When she went to bed that night she found herself wondering if perhaps Lewis had been right after all and whether, as her parents loved his little Kay so much, they would have accepted her child?

It was now too late to do anything about it, she thought sadly. She had given up her baby and now she had no idea at all where her baby was; she could only hope that her child had found love and that she was well cared for and happy.

There was one thing she could do, she resolved. First thing in the morning before she caught the train back to Hilbury, she would go and see Maggie Nelson and thank her for all she'd done for her.

Maggie was astonished to see her on the doorstep. She greeted her enthusiastically and looked startled when Christabel handed her a big bunch of red roses.

'For me?' she gasped. 'No one has ever bought me flowers before in the whole of my life.'

Over a cup of tea she expressed sympathy for Christabel's loss. 'Your husband told me that you'd lost the baby,' she said, laying one of her work-worn hands on Christabel's. 'Perhaps there will be another one soon,' she added. 'You're such a lovely couple that you deserve to have a family, you'll make lovely parents.'

Her words made Christabel feel so guilty about the way they had deceived her that she almost broke down and told Maggie Nelson the truth. Then, realising that it would not do either of them any good, she held her tongue. It was all in the past, she reminded herself, and she'd resolved to start afresh, so why burden Maggie Nelson by telling her?

The train was on the point of pulling out as Christabel rushed on to the platform. As she settled into a corner seat she suddenly wondered if Karl Blume had also caught it or whether he was still at large and, if so, what she ought to do about it.

Chapter Seven

Peggy Wilson clamped a hand over her mouth, her grey eyes filled with astonishment, when Christabel walked into the room they shared, dumped her bag on the floor, and flopped on to the bed with a groan of weariness.

'What on earth is wrong with you?' she laughed.

'I feel half crippled,' Christabel groaned. 'I've had to walk from the station because there was no transport,' she grumbled, kicking off her shoes and massaging her aching feet. 'Do you know why?'

'All leave has been cancelled. There's a hue and cry going on because that German patient, Karl Blume, is missing,' Peggy told her. 'The Military Police are here investigating.'

Startled, Christabel sat bolt upright. 'Oh heavens! He followed me to the station!'

Peggy looked startled. 'You mean when you went home?'

'That's right. He'd heard me telling you that I was going home and he asked if he could come with me. Of course I told him it was impossible, but he was on the same train as I was and he was wearing a British officer's uniform. Heaven knows how he managed to get hold of that. I didn't speak to him, but he got out at the Exchange, the same as I did, and then he just seemed to vanish.'

Peggy looked worried. 'When the officer in charge of the investigation was checking the staff list, Sister Speakley told him you were on weekend leave. Perhaps you ought to go and let them know you're back . . . and about Karl Blume.'

'What do you mean?' Christabel frowned.

'Well, you do know where he went, even if he didn't go with you,' Peggy pointed out.

Christabel looked uncertain. 'I'll think about it,' she demurred. 'You keep quiet and say nothing . . . right?'

'I'm certainly not going to say anything. I don't want to be in trouble,' Peggy blustered, her face flushing. 'I still think you should let someone know,' she added, leaving the room before Christabel could answer.

As she put her shoes back on, Christabel decided that she would go and tell Sister Speakley what she knew about Karl Blume's disappearance.

'You did the right thing in reporting this to me, Nurse Montgomery,' Sister Speakley told her approvingly.

Privately, she wondered if Nurse Montgomery had led the young German officer on, but there seemed to be no point in making an issue about it since the Military Police had taken the matter over and it was out of her hands. All she need do was send Nurse Montgomery along to speak to Sergeant Williams who was in charge of the inquiries. If he believed her story, then everything would be cleared up quickly and quietly and the nursing staff would be exonerated over any carelessness on their part in allowing Karl Blume to leave the hospital.

Christabel mentally rehearsed her story to make sure that she made it clear that she had not in any way collaborated with the young German. Every detail, however, went out of her mind when she entered the office the military police had taken over, and she recognised the sergeant sitting behind the desk as Dennis Williams, one of her former patients.

'Nurse Montgomery!' He stood up and leaned across the desk to shake her hand.

'You're looking well, Sergeant Williams. Are you fully recovered?' she asked, smiling up into his dark eyes.

'As a result of your nursing I am quite fit again,' he told her with a mock seriousness that had them both laughing.

Convincing Dennis Williams that Karl had followed her was simplicity itself. He was so relieved to have information about the missing German that he didn't question her story.

'And you say that as far as you know he simply disappeared when you reached the Exchange.

Are you quite sure that he didn't follow you? You see, he might be hiding somewhere near your home.'

'I suppose that's possible,' Christabel agreed. 'You don't think he's dangerous, do you?' she asked worriedly.

'I hope not, but, you never know, these Huns can be crafty devils. Are both your parents at home?'

'Yes and my younger sister. Oh dear, if he causes any trouble or hurts any of them, I'll feel so guilty!' Tears misted the intense blue of Christabel's eyes as she gazed up at him.

'Try not to worry. We'll soon have him back in custody now that we know where he might be,' Dennis promised. 'I've got a vehicle and a team of men outside and we'll go straight to your home and make a thorough search of the neighbourhood. You'd better come along with us; I'll need directions on how to get there. Do you have to ask Sister Speakley for permission, or are you ready to leave right away?'

'I had better inform her about what is happening, as I am supposed to be on duty in about an hour.'

It was a bumpy ride in the army truck, but sitting in front next to Dennis, reminiscing about the people they'd known when he'd been a patient, Christabel was barely aware of any discomfort.

Their exchange of gossip didn't keep her from worrying about what might be happening if

Karl had followed her home and was hiding out nearby.

'Now where would he most likely go?' Dennis cut across her thoughts. 'Think carefully. From what you've told me, he's wearing a stolen uniform, impersonating a British officer. He's in a strange place and knows no one. Is there anywhere in your garden where he could hide? If so, he might have taken refuge there and if anyone confronted him, concoct some story about losing his memory and wandering off from the hospital.'

'It is possible he could be hiding in our summer house,' Christabel agreed. 'What if he's not there, though?'

'Aah, then we will have to see what your family can tell us. We'll also check the railway station to see if he has tried to get away by train. After that, we'll search every street in the vicinity and between your home and the hospital. If we have to do that, then I will alert the local police and get more troops drafted in so that we can widen the search area until we do find him.'

'That could take days!'

'Then let's hope he's skulking in the summer house. I'll get my men to look there first,' he said as he parked the truck. 'Can we get into the garden without disturbing your family?

Karl Blume had reacted true to form and had taken refuge in the summer house. When Christabel let Sergeant Williams and his two

77

men in through the side gate and Karl found the doorway barred by two military policemen, he tried to make a run for it.

The shouts and commotion aroused the entire household; Lilian came running out of the back door with their dog, Prince, beside her. Sensing danger, the huge black and brown Alsatian bounded down the garden and within moments had the German's arm clenched between his teeth.

'Will one of you get this animal off me?' Karl shouted, looking from Christabel to Lilian, his voice edged with panic, as he tried to free himself from the grip of the snarling animal.

'Christabel, what are you doing back here? What is going on?' her father exclaimed as he came rushing from the house followed by her mother who looked scared to death. 'We thought you had gone back to Hilbury?'

Without waiting for her to reply, he called Prince to his side and then, squaring his shoulders, stepped forward to where the two military police were now holding Karl while Dennis was fastening handcuffs on to his wrists.

'What the devil is going on here?' he demanded. 'Why are you taking this man prisoner, sergeant? What's he doing here?'

Dennis stood to attention and saluted smartly. 'Your daughter has helped us locate this man,' he explained. 'It seems he followed her when she left Hilbury and has been hiding out here ever since.'

'Good heavens. Is he dangerous?' Basil asked in alarm.

'Well, he's a German prisoner of war, sir. He doesn't appear to be armed in any way but, for all we know, he could be a spy,' Dennis said gravely.

'I see.' Basil stroked his chin thoughtfully. 'Is there anything further we have to do, sergeant, or will you deal with him now? I'd like to take my two daughters inside, away from all this commotion,' he added as he began to shepherd Lilian and Christabel away from the scene.

'You've nothing to worry about, sir, we're taking him away immediately. Nurse Montgomery will have to accompany us. She will be needed to give evidence.'

'Oh dear, surely that isn't really necessary,' Mabel intervened. 'I think poor Christabel has gone through quite enough . . .' her voice trailed away as Sergeant Williams fixed her with a steady stare.

'I understand your feelings, ma'am,' he told her politely, 'but rules are rules in the army. I am sure you appreciate that, sir,' he added, turning to face Christabel's father.

'Yes, yes. Of course. You must do as you think necessary. You have transport?'

'Yes, sir, parked in the road outside the front of your house. We'll take the prisoner and make him secure while you say goodbye to your daughter.'

79

'Can we offer you some refreshments before you start on your journey, sergeant? Tea and a plate of sandwiches, perhaps?' Mabel offered.

'That would be most acceptable, ma'am, but I am afraid duty calls. Some other time perhaps.'

'Fine action on your part, my girl,' her father applauded, his hand resting heavily on Christabel's shoulder for a brief moment as they stood on the doorstep.

'I was only doing my duty,' she murmured.

The righteousness in her father's voice lingered in her thoughts as they drove away. Aware that Karl Blume and the two military policemen were only separated from her and Dennis by a coarse canvas sheet, she remained silent as they drove back to headquarters.

'Wait here, this shouldn't take long,' Dennis ordered as he pulled up at the barracks, killed the engine, and jumped down.

'You mean you don't really need me to give evidence?'

'I'll let you know after we've booked the prisoner in,' he told her as he walked round to the back of the truck.

Christabel looked at Dennis questioningly when he rejoined her ten minutes later.

'Now that's all finished with, I think we should celebrate,' he said as he let in the clutch and roared out of the camp.

'Where are we going?'

'I know a restaurant where you can still get

steaks,' he told her. 'It's a bit of a dive, noisy and smoky, but the grub is out of this world. I don't know about you, but I'm starving,' He reached out and squeezed her hand. 'We'll start the evening there, OK?'

The food was everything Dennis had promised it would be. He drank beer and she sipped at a glass of well-chilled white wine. The noise was overpowering and made conversation almost impossible.

They danced once. Dennis held her in a bear-hug to try and protect her from being elbowed and jostled, but it was much too claustrophobic for enjoyment.

Eventually, they left the restaurant. It was a pleasant early spring night and as they strolled back to where they had parked his army vehicle, Christabel felt as if she was suspended in time. The street was thronged with soldiers and civilians, men and women, all intent on finding enjoyment, but she felt as if she was not part of it, merely an onlooker.

'You don't have to report back to Hilbury Hospital until tomorrow, do you?' Dennis asked softly as their vehicle came in sight.

'No . . . not really.' She looked at him, startled.

'Shall we find somewhere to stay the night?'

Her breath caught in her throat and she wondered if she had heard aright.

'Together?'

'Why not? Come on, there's a war on. Snatch a little happiness while you can. You're not going to tell me you're one of those shrinking violets, who leads a man on and then dumps him,' he challenged. 'It's not as though we've only just met,' he added persuasively when she made no answer.

'And I suppose you know of a quiet little hotel where they ask no questions?' she said with a trace of cynicism.

'Of course I do!' he whispered confidently as he pulled her into his arms.

As his mouth was about to take possession of hers, Christabel placed her fingers over his lips and pulled away, shivering slightly. She liked Dennis Williams but she only wanted him as a friend. Memories of being in Philip's arms and their passionate lovemaking the night before he'd sailed still dominated her thoughts and she shook her head.

'Perhaps I'd better take you back to Hilbury,' he said in a hard voice as he released her and, squaring his shoulders, stepped back. He fished around in his pockets for his cigarettes and held out the packet to her. When she shook her head he selected one and lighted it. 'So do you want to tell me what it is I've done wrong?' he asked as he exhaled a cloud of smoke.

He listened in silence as, hesitantly, she told him about how her fiancé had been drowned at sea only a short time before they were due to be married.

She gave only the briefest of details and said nothing at all about the baby she had given up for adoption; that was still something that filled her with such remorse that it was too raw to talk about to anyone other than Lewis.

When she'd finished, he dropped the remains of his cigarette on the pavement and ground it out with his heel, then he put his arm round her waist and drew her close.

'There's a war on, Christabel,' he said softly, pushing her hair back from her face with his free hand and kissing her on the brow. 'It must have been a dreadful ordeal, but you can't go on living in the past for ever. You can't plan for the future, either, because there may not be one, so why not live for the moment? Why not let us enjoy the pleasure of each other's company while we can?'

Chapter Eight

Christabel smiled to herself as she read the note that had been handed to her by the army orderly. It was from Dennis to say that he was starting a week's leave on New Year's Eve and asking if he could he meet her.

The nurses at Hilbury had drawn lots to decide which of them should have time off over Christmas and who would wait until New Year. Christabel had been disappointed when she'd found that, once again, she would not be sitting down with her own family for the ritual meal of turkey and plum pudding. Christmas had always been so much more festive in their home than the New Year celebrations.

She'd consoled herself with the thought that Christmas 1915 wouldn't be the same at home this year because although Lilian would be there Lewis would be absent.

It had come as a shock to all of them that he'd been called up for service and had opted for the Navy. After he'd finished his training at Portsmouth he'd been posted to the *SS Kilbraid* and was now somewhere at sea.

Christmas at Hilbury Hospital had been more enjoyable than she had envisaged it would be.

They had made decorations to hang in the wards by cutting up wrapping paper and discarded document slips into narrow strips to make paper chains.

They had put up sprigs of holly and mistletoe and decked out a fir tree with baubles made from cardboard and cotton wool. At the very top, they had pinned a huge star cut from a piece of metal which they'd polished until it shone like silver.

Now that she had the added bonus of knowing she would be celebrating New Year with Dennis, she tried to decide whether she should take him home and perhaps even invite him to spend some of his leave with her family.

She'd only been home twice since the debacle with Karl Blume and she wondered if her father still regarded her as 'brave' and Dennis as something of a hero. Or, more important still, whether her mother's invitation to Dennis to come and see them again still held good.

She had seen Dennis several times since then, but only very briefly, and always in the company of other people. Remembering the night he had wanted them to spend together brought her out in a cold sweat. Whenever she thought about it, recalling how disappointed he'd been by her refusal, she wondered if it would be better if she had nothing more to do with him or, for that matter, with any man.

Peggy was the only one she could confide in and she'd been surprised that Christabel had turned him down. 'Others have affairs,' she pointed out defiantly.

'Think of the risks, though. Supposing I became pregnant,' Christabel muttered.

'You wouldn't if you took precautions,' Peggy mused thoughtfully as she brushed her hair.

'What sort of precautions can you take?'

'You've got me there,' Peggy admitted. 'We never talked about those sorts of things at home. Our home was a bit like a nunnery; no one admits that anything like that goes on. Now you know why they believe in the Immaculate Conception,' she giggled.

When Christabel asked Peggy what she thought about her taking Dennis home for the New Year, Peggy shrugged.

'If you are really serious about him, and you think your father liked him, then why not?'

Was she serious about him? It was a question Christabel asked herself over and over again. Looking back on that incident she always felt uncomfortable about it and had been more than a little surprised that he had wanted to see her again.

Now, she tried to analyse her feelings for Dennis and to decide whether or not she would miss him if he suddenly went out of her life for ever.

Perhaps, if she took him home and he met her family and even stayed for a couple of days, it might give her the chance to find out what their true feelings for each other were, she told herself.

When they met early on New Year's Eve, and she told him her plan, he seemed to grow taller and puffed out his chest as if determined to impress her.

'You don't mind, then? It may not be very exciting. My parents lead a quiet life and my younger sister is only sixteen and very childish for her age.'

'I can't think of a better way to start 1916,' he told her solemnly.

'I'm not too sure what sort of reception we will get because they don't know we're coming,' she warned.

'Surprise is the best form of attack,' he told her confidently.

Although Dennis was in a jubilant mood, Christabel felt dubious about what her parents would say. As it was, when they arrived mid-afternoon, everyone was affable. Christmas at The Laurels, although Violet and little Kay had been there on Christmas Day, had been rather quiet and now the family welcomed the diversion of not only Christabel being home but also a visitor as well.

Lilian brightened like a drooping flower which had been taken from a cold greenhouse and placed in a sunny window. Her round face dimpled and her eyes glowed with excitement when Christabel asked if they would mind if Dennis stayed with them for a few days.

'I am so pleased,' she enthused. 'Mother has invited some of her friends to dinner tonight so this will make it a real celebration. Dennis is perfect to let the New Year in,' she went on. 'He's so dark and handsome that he is bound to bring us all luck,' she added, smiling across at him coquettishly.

As she relaxed in a hot bath before dressing for dinner, Christabel congratulated herself on how well her plans had gone. She was quite amused by Lilian's reaction; her little sister was growing up, she thought fondly.

When she was ready to go downstairs, she studied her reflection with satisfaction. She had chosen her favourite dress and the vivid blue velvet not only matched her eyes but also clung to her like a second skin. I have a much better figure now than when I first took up nursing, Christabel thought, as she twisted and turned in front of the cheval mirror.

She had taken a great deal of trouble with her hair, piling it high on her head, and using hot tongs to curl it into fronds and ringlets around her face. She pinched colour into her cheeks and smoothed a trace of Vaseline on to her eyebrows and eyelashes to make them shine.

Confident that she was looking her best, she went downstairs. The rest of the family was already gathered in the drawing room. She felt disappointed when her entrance went unnoticed. Lilian was playing the piano and Dennis, who was standing at her side turning over the sheet music, never even glanced up.

Her mother's friends arrived before Christabel had a chance to interrupt Dennis and Lilian. They were all pleased to see her and eager to hear about her life as a nurse that she had to leave it to Lilian to entertain Dennis. By the time midnight was imminent, and Dennis was sent outside to act as harbinger of the New Year, she realised that she had barely spoken to him all evening.

Dennis brought in the traditional lump of coal and piece of bread and was rewarded with a hot toddy before he did the rounds, wishing each and every one of them a happy and prosperous New Year.

It was shortly after midnight when the last of the guests left and Mary was finally able to start clearing away the remains of the evening's festivities. Within an hour, the entire house was wrapped in silent darkness and Christabel wondered if she dared to nip along and see Dennis for a few minutes to make sure he was settled in and explain why she'd neglected him all evening.

Cautiously she opened her door and tiptoed along the landing. She paused outside Dennis's room, ear pressed against the closed door, but there was no sound at all. Biting her lower lip, she turned the handle, letting out a sigh of relief as it opened smoothly.

She made sure she closed the door behind her, before whispering his name aloud. When there was no answer, she edged towards the bed, stretching a hand out to touch him, feeling for his face, his hand, his shoulder, to let him know she was there.

When she failed to make contact with any of these she ran the flat of her hand over the bed. There were no contours at all. The bed was empty.

Christabel stood perfectly still for several minutes, trying to collect her thoughts, wondering where he was; surely he hadn't left? He'd seemed to be enjoying every minute of the evening, even though it was in Lilian's company. He had appeared to get on well with her father, and her mother had remarked more than once what a nice young man he was.

Perplexed, she started to go back to her own room but, halfway along the corridor, she heard a sound that stopped her in her tracks. From downstairs she could hear the rise and fall of voices followed by a smothered, giggly laugh.

A feeling of jealousy churned inside her. In one second it was as if all her dreams of possible happiness with Dennis were ruined – because of Lilian, of all people.

She wanted to burst in on them, let her parents know what was happening, but humiliation because he found her own sister so attractive stopped her from doing so.

Her anger collapsed. Shivering and utterly deflated she crept back to her own bed and lay there, trying to close her mind to what was happening until, eventually, she sank into an exhausted sleep.

She woke next morning wondering if it had all been some terrible nightmare. As she watched Dennis and Lilian exchange sly glances across the breakfast table and saw the lovesick dreamy smile that played on her sister's lips, she knew it was not a figment of her imagination; Lilian was infatuated by him.

As she struggled to hide her annoyance, Christabel became aware that Lilian was staring at her, a questioning look on her face. As their gaze locked, Lilian's big grey-blue eyes had a feline watchfulness, as if she was waiting to see what Christabel's next move would be.

Some primitive instinct of self-preservation welled up inside Christabel. She knew it was useless to draw her parents into the argument. They would take Lilian's side and say she was overreacting; they always had, ever since Lilian was a tiny toddler.

When, as they were growing up, Lilian had taken her treasured dolls or scribbled in her books or hidden them, her mother had always said it was probably her own fault for leaving them lying around. It would be the same now. She would be blamed for bringing Dennis to stay and then neglecting him all evening.

Refusing to play Lilian's game, Christabel smiled at her sister and suggested, 'Why don't you and Dennis go for a walk this morning while I stay and help Mother?'

For a moment Lilian looked taken aback and the challenge went from her eyes, leaving them as soft and grey as the sky outside the window.

Christabel sensed Lilian was about to refuse. It had been a calculated risk but one she was confident of winning. She knew Lilian was covetous but she also knew from the past that she had always lost interest in the things she had hidden when she found it didn't worry Christabel that she had taken them.

She had not considered Dennis. He looked from one to the other of them with a puzzled frown then came round the table, taking Lilian's hand, affirming his readiness to go with her.

Christabel turned away, hiding her chagrin.

Lilian and Dennis returned late for lunch, laughing and apologetic, their cheeks flushed from the cold, their eyes bright with excitement. They teased and wisecracked, sending secret messages across the table until Christabel felt she could stand the atmosphere no longer. When the meal was over and the rest of the family gathered in front of a roaring log fire in the drawing room, she slipped quietly away and made a telephone call to Hilbury.

'What on earth has happened?' Peggy gasped when she was finally brought to the phone.

'I'll explain later,' Christabel told her. 'Could you ring back, to my home, and tell whoever answers that I'm needed back at the hospital immediately?'

'But you've still got two days of your leave left . . .'

'Never mind that, please, just do as I've asked.'

Christabel hung up before Peggy could ply her with any more questions. A few minutes later, as she was kneeling in front of the fire, pretending to warm her hands, she heard the phone ring. Her father rose from his chair and went out into the hall to answer it.

'That was a Nurse Wilson from Hilbury Hospital, Christabel,' he said as he came back into the room. 'She said you were needed back at the hospital. I asked her to speak to you herself, but she rang off. She sounded quite perturbed!'

'Oh dear, they did warn us that a new intake was due,' Christabel murmured, standing up. 'It looks as though I will have to go. Sorry about this.' She smiled at her mother apologetically. 'There is a war on,' she added tritely.

'You've only just got here,' her mother sighed.

'I'll come again soon,' Christabel murmured, kissing her mother's cheek. 'Are you ready to leave, Dennis?'

'Me?' He looked taken aback.

'Must Dennis go, Mother? He still has several more days of his leave left,' Lilian said quickly.

'Well . . .' Mabel looked questioningly at her husband.

'Please say he can stay, Father?'

Lilian's breathless entreaty, delivered in her most cajoling voice, seemed to clinch the matter.

'If that's what Dennis wants to do, then of course he can stay,' Basil smiled benignly.

Peggy looked bewildered when Christabel arrived back at the hospital and she learned what had happened.

'Why on earth didn't you have it out with them, not simply give in like that?' she asked.

'It went wrong,' Christabel admitted. 'I counted on Dennis coming with me. I'd decided to stop prevaricating and agree that we could stay together somewhere until I was due back here.'

'I'd say it was as well things didn't go according to your plan,' Peggy told her bluntly. 'In my opinion, it isn't worth risking your reputation for a man like that.'

An hour later, when she was called to the telephone, Christabel's heart soared with excitement, expecting it to be Dennis. Then it plummeted into her shoes when she heard her father's clipped voice.

'Lilian . . . here?' she repeated in a puzzled voice. 'Of course she's not here, why should she be?'

The blood drained from her face as her father told her that Lilian and Dennis had left the house within minutes of Christabel's own departure. 'They hoped to reach the station before your train left because you left a coat or something behind,' he told her. 'I thought that perhaps they'd decided to bring it to the hospital.'

94

As she replaced the receiver, Christabel knew in her heart that they had gone away together. She hadn't left anything behind. Lilian must have devised that story so that she could leave the house with Dennis and she wondered where the two of them had gone.

Christabel phoned home very late that evening, hoping to speak to Dennis and find out what had happened.

'Your train had already gone by the time they reached the Exchange,' her father told her. 'So Lilian showed him around the city and they stayed and had a meal before returning home. Dennis has only just gone upstairs; I can call him, if you want to speak to him.'

For a moment Christabel was tempted to say yes, feeling quite sure that her father would discover that Dennis was not in his room but in Lilian's. Then, knowing it no longer mattered to her, she said there wasn't time as she had to go back on duty.

'Would you like me to let him know you called when I see him at breakfast tomorrow?' her father asked.

'No, thank you,' she said firmly, 'there's no need, it's not important.'

Chapter Nine

Christabel was determined not to let the flir-
tation between Dennis and Lilian upset her.
After all, she reasoned, in some ways it was
her own fault because she had made it clear
that all she wanted from him was friendship.
Also, she had to admit that Lilian had grown
into a very pretty girl and it was only natural
that Dennis would be attracted to her.

Even so, she was sure that his infatuation
would be short-lived. She hardened her heart
and decided to say nothing to Lilian except to
make it clear that she wanted nothing more to
do with Dennis.

When she went home, which was not very
often, she was relieved to find that she felt no
jealousy or remorse as she listened to Lilian
burbling on about Dennis and how wonderful
he was. She was able to listen with smiling
detachment.

When her mother joined in and also began
singing his praises, she escaped by going to
visit Violet who was missing Lewis and was
very worried about his safety.

Kay was now such a lovable baby that
Christabel wanted to spend as much time as

possible with her and Violet seemed to be more than happy to let her take Kay out for a walk. She rarely came with them so Christabel had the child's undivided attention and, even though it stirred up painful memories, she enjoyed every moment of their time together.

Back at Hilbury she immersed herself in hospital life to such an extent that she almost became estranged from the real world and was slightly taken aback when she received a letter from her mother to say that Lilian and Dennis were married and that Lilian was no longer living at home but had gone with him and his unit and now they didn't know where she was because she was not allowed to disclose their whereabouts.

Although Christabel told her mother that she had no idea where they were, she always brought the matter up whenever she went home and seemed to think that she ought to be able to find out where Dennis was stationed. Christabel found it difficult to convince her mother that there was nothing she could do to help.

All through the summer months, Hilbury, like all the other military hospitals, was stretched to its utmost capacity as the war esca-lated, and Christabel found herself working exceptionally hard. At night she often felt so exhausted when she came off duty that she was too tired to eat. All she wanted to do was sleep and put the latest news about the Battle of the

Somme, which had now gone on for several months and had resulted in heavy casualties, out of her mind.

It was late August when she next made a visit home. She'd intended to do so ever since the Battle of Jutland a couple of months earlier; she knew her parents and Violet would be terribly worried about Lewis because the naval forces had been involved.

When she arrived home, she was shocked by her father's appearance. He looked as though he had aged ten years since she'd last seen him. His hair was grey, his face drawn; he'd lost weight and seemed to be a shadow of his former self.

'He's been looking like that for months now,' her mother sighed when Christabel commented on how ill he looked.

'Have you called in the doctor?' she asked worriedly.

'I don't think there is any point in doing so; I put it down to business worries and the fact that we are still not sure where Lilian is living.'

Christabel was not convinced and, when shortly before Christmas, Basil collapsed from a fatal heart attack, although she was deeply saddened by the news, she was not really surprised.

Her mother was distraught and the fact that they were unable to locate Lilian only added to her distress. Violet did what she could but she was so busy looking after Kay that she was not a great deal of help and it was left to Christabel to arrange the funeral and Christabel had no alternative but to ask for leave from Hilbury, promising that she would return the moment she could locate her sister and arrange for her to come home and take care of their mother.

Sister Speakley was most understanding. 'You have plenty of leave due to you, so don't worry if it is a matter of a couple of weeks,' she told Christabel. 'Having said that,' she went on quickly, 'you are one of my most reliable nurses, so I look forward to you being back as soon as possible.'

It was mid-January before Christabel managed to locate Lilian's whereabouts and even longer before Lilian agreed to move back home to take care of their mother.

Christabel delayed her return to Hilbury for a few more days because Violet asked her to stay for Kay's second birthday. Lewis was still at sea and because she had no immediate family of her own, Violet felt desperately lonely.

Back at Hilbury, Christabel wondered if the war was ever going to end. There were times when she treated men who had been so horribly injured in one or other of the ongoing battles that she felt she was in a living nightmare. Occasionally, she wondered how it would feel like to live once again without being surrounded by barbed wire and people in khaki uniform and all the rules and roll-calls that were part of each day.

Days became weeks, then months, and still the massacre went on; the wounded arrived, were operated on, patched up and moved on. The nursing staff automatically knew how to deal with most injuries; they were no longer sickened by the sight of blood, the stench of putrefying flesh or the agonised cries of the wounded.

Christabel managed to get home for two days over Christmas 1917 but her mother and Lilian, who was now pregnant, complained so bitterly about everything, including the shortage of food, that every time she sat down for a meal with them she felt guilty about eating any of what they had.

Dennis had been sent to France and for several weeks there had been no letter from him, which worried Lilian a great deal. She was afraid he might come to some harm and wanted him home before the baby was born.

It was August the following year before the war news took a turn for the better. By October the Allies had recovered France and Belgium and spirits began to soar. When they learned that the allies had pushed the Germans back beyond the Hindenburg Line and that the Kaiser had abdicated everyone was optimistic that the war would end soon. When Armistice was declared in the second week of November, they were overjoyed.

As the weeks passed, rumours about the hospital being closed down were rife. Christmas 1918 was a strange mixture of elation and uncertainty about the future. As the bitter winter reluctantly gave way to spring, Christabel felt restless. Her job was no longer rewarding, or satisfying. The men in their care were, for the most part, well enough to leave hospital. In ordinary circumstances they would have done so in order to free beds for the newly wounded, only now that the fighting had stopped the flow of wounded men had ceased.

The end at Hilbury came quite suddenly. A fleet of army vehicles arrived at dawn one morning in late March. Those well enough to be sent home were dispatched, those who were prisoners of war were marched into waiting vehicles and taken away to secure camps. The army personnel attached to the hospital were driven off in separate trucks.

The nursing staff were left marooned and without any information about their future. Two days later a Ministry official arrived and handed out dismissal notices. Staff were told that they could apply to be transferred to a civilian hospital if they wished.

Christabel decided she needed time to think before taking such action. At the moment, she welcomed the thought of a rest from it all. It was almost spring and she toyed with the idea of spending the summer months free from routine and pressures of all kinds but, because

Lilian was still living at home, she wasn't sure if she wanted to live there too.

When she received a letter from her mother to say that Lewis was on his way back, and his boat was due to dock within the week, she made up her mind to go home. She longed to see him again. It would be like old times, all of them gathered together.

Christabel's unexpected arrival brought exclamations of surprise from her mother. After she had hugged and kissed her, she stared in surprise at the number of cases Christabel had brought with her.

'Does this mean you have come home for good?' she asked.

'That's right, Mother. They've closed Hilbury down, everyone and everything gone.'

'Why didn't you let us know?'

'It all happened so suddenly. You know what the army is like. Orders came from the top and they acted immediately, so there wasn't time to send you a letter.'

'You could have phoned.' There was a hint of displeasure in her mother's voice.

'Yes, I'm sorry. Anyway, it doesn't matter now, does it?'

'Lewis is home. He's here at the moment with Violet and Kay.'

'Tremendous! Where are they?' Without waiting for her mother to answer she burst into the dining room and was immediately enveloped in a bear hug by Lewis, who had recognised her voice and was waiting to greet her.

For a moment she was taken aback because she hadn't seen him in his navy-blue sailor's uniform before.

'Are you so proud of your uniform that you don't want to change into civvies?' she teased, laughing up at him.

'It's not a case of being proud of it; I can't find anything in my wardrobe that still fits me,' he laughed, straightening his shoulders and pulling himself up to his full height.

'Yes, you *have* broadened out a little!' She stepped back, holding him at arm's length and studying him critically, her head tilted to one side. 'A great improvement, I'd say.' She grinned.

He grabbed her to him, kissing her heartily on both cheeks. 'And you look fine yourself,' he told her. 'A lot older, of course. In fact, I would say quite grown-up,' he teased.

'Come along, Christabel, slip your coat off, you're just in time for lunch. I'll tell Mary to lay another place,' her mother told her.

'I'll take my things upstairs, first,' Christabel murmured. 'I won't be a moment. I must freshen up.'

She turned and went out of the room and picked up one of her suitcases. Her foot was already on the bottom stair when her mother came hurrying after her.

'Wait, Christabel. Hold on a minute. We . . . we

didn't know you were coming home . . . your room isn't ready.'

'That's all right. I can put clean sheets on the bed, or whatever needs doing, later on. I'm only going to take these upstairs out of the way.'

'Christabel, you don't understand. Dennis is using your room.'

'Dennis!' Christabel turned sharply, a look of annoyance on her face.

'Well, yes, dear. We didn't know you were coming home; you didn't write and let us know and now that Lilian is back, living here with her new baby, he had to have somewhere to put all their stuff.'

Christabel felt she wanted to hide in a corner and cry. She knew she was being childish but she'd so looked forward to coming home, to her own room and possessions, and now it was like living in a hotel, she thought sadly.

'Leave it until after lunch, dear, and we'll see what arrangements we can make. Perhaps Dennis could move their things into Lewis's old room.'

'Don't bother, I'll use that room,' Christabel said resignedly.

Later, she stayed upstairs for a long time until the light began to fade, staring out of the window, watching the diamante patterns emerging on the darkening sky as, one by one, the stars emerged, trying to work out why she was feeling so resentful about Dennis's invasion of her home.

* * *

Next morning, her mother was the only one up when she went down to breakfast.

'Since it seems to matter to you so much, Christabel, you can move back into your own room any time you wish,' Mabel told her coldly.

She looked up, ready to apologise, to explain why it was so important to her, but her mother had turned away and Christabel was uncomfortably aware that she had upset her and that it was too late to make amends.

Chapter Ten

Christabel found the tension in the Montgomery household was palpable. She wondered if the edginess they were all feeling was because, in different ways, they were all missing her father. The house certainly seemed to be a different place without his authoritative presence.

From the moment she'd come home she'd noticed that everyone seemed to be arguing about something or snapping at each other over trivial matters, when they should have been one of the happiest families in the land.

She had returned from nursing far more worldly-wise but none the worse for all the grim sights and experiences she had encountered. Lewis had been at the Battle of Jutland, and had been torpedoed at the Dardanelles, yet he'd come through both of these harrowing engagements completely unscathed, at least physically. He was now home again and had resumed work in the family shipping business where he'd taken over his father's partnership in the firm, which meant he had a lot of extra responsibility.

Christabel was aware that both her mother and Lilian seemed to be uneasy about her being there. Most of the time there was friction between the three of them and frequently it was almost unbearable.

Partly, Christabel reflected, it was due to all the fuss they both made about Lilian's little girl. Marlene expected to be the centre of everything that was going on. Compared to the way Kay was being brought up, Marlene was thoroughly spoilt by both her mother and grandmother. As a result, she was constantly throwing tantrums and screamed if she couldn't have her own way.

Since Lilian had been at home looking after her mother they'd developed a close bond and Christabel sensed that Lilian resented her being there or offering an opinion about anything. She wasn't sure why, but she suspected that Lilian was afraid that she might want to take over the reins and run things herself. In fact, nothing was further from her mind.

She didn't intend to stay at home a moment longer than she had to because she found it far too claustrophobic. She had plans for her future and spent a great deal of time and energy working on them.

The one thing she did enjoy, and which she knew she would miss very much if she went away again, was visiting Violet and taking little Kay out and about.

Kay was a pretty little girl with dark hair and big expressive blue eyes. Violet was a good mother and, as a result, Kay was bright and well mannered; she asked so many questions that Christabel found it stimulating to be with her. She enjoyed taking her down to the Pier Head to see all the ships or on one of the ferry boats across the Mersey to New Brighton.

When the weather was unsuitable for those sorts of outings, they often spent happy hours looking at family photographs. Kay especially loved the ones of when her father, and her aunts, Lilian and Christabel, were small.

'Grandma always says that I look exactly like you in those pictures,' she told Christabel. 'When I'm grown up I'm going to be a nurse just like you were in the war,' she added with a big beaming smile.

Seeing how enraptured Lewis and Violet both were with Kay frequently revived disturbing memories for Christabel of her own child. Although she knew she'd had no alternative but to have her adopted, the very fact that her baby would now be the same age as Kay sometimes brought a stab of regret over what she'd done. It also made her all the more interested in Kay's progress and sometimes she had to hold back for fear of upsetting Violet or being told that she was spoiling the little girl.

It was yet another reason Christabel decided that the time had come for a change. She decided to organise a family get-together so that she could tell them what her intentions were for the future.

Lilian looked dubious when she mentioned it to her. 'You mean have a proper party?' She frowned. 'We haven't had one of those for ages but have you given any thought to all the work it will entail? I have enough to do looking after Mother and Marlene without taking on anything extra.'

'We'll time it for Kay's birthday. She'll be five in February so we can plan it for then and tell her we're all going to get dressed up and that there will be a birthday cake with candles on it, she'll love that,' Christabel went on, ignoring all Lilian's protests.

At the very last minute, on the day of the party itself, Christabel decided that the occasion demanded a new dress. She wanted one that was the very latest fashion so she went to Liverpool's Bold Street. Having bought the dress she felt it needed one of the new hairstyles to complete the effect which meant going to the hairdresser's and this made her even later arriving home.

They were all gathered in the dining room ready to start the party when she walked in. The straight-cut apple-green silk dress skimmed her knees and had floating panels of darker green chiffon draped from the waist. With it she wore a matching sequined headband positioned straight across her forehead so that it partially concealed her new hairstyle.

Her appearance stunned them all; they stared at her in silence.

'Oh, Chrissy, what have you done to yourself?' Lilian's squeal of horror started everyone talking at once.

'It's the latest fashion,' Christabel retorted,

tilting her head and pirouetting round so that the floating panels flared out seductively.

'It certainly shows off your legs and you've a good pair of pins, old girl,' Dennis chortled.

Lilian gave him a warning look as she saw her mother frowning uneasily.

'What is that thing you have on your head, Christabel?' her mother asked in a puzzled voice.

'It's a headband.'

'It looks like some sort of Indian headdress with those feathery things in it,' Lilian scoffed.

'Don't be silly.' Although she smiled, Christabel removed the offending piece.

The gasps when they saw her new hairstyle were even greater than the furore caused by the shortness of her dress.

'In heaven's name what have you gone and done to yourself, Christabel?' her mother exclaimed. 'What's happened to all your lovely long hair?'

'By the look of things she's had it chopped off for one of the new short cuts,' Dennis laughed admiringly.

'It *is* very short!' Violet murmured.

'It's called a bob,' Christabel told them, running her hand over the back of her head and then trailing her fingers down her face to where the side hair was swept forward dramatically on to her cheeks just below eye level.

'You look naked!' her mother told her, her eyes travelling from Christabel's long, slim, bare neck to the low cut neckline of her new dress.

'It will take time to get used to, but I rather like it,' Christabel defended.

'Then it seems you are the only one who does,' her mother told her scathingly.

'You'd better learn to like it,' Christabel laughed, 'I can hardly put my hair back on again, can I?'

'No, Christabel, I realise that you can't do that, but you'd better make sure you wear a hat when you go out. I don't want people seeing you make such a spectacle of yourself. Either that, or else stay indoors until it grows again,' she added tetchily.

'Mother, we've got to move with the times,' Lewis defended as they took their places at the table and he saw the tears glistening in Christabel's eyes.

'Lewis is right, Mother. I'm sorry you dis-approve but I need to look not only smart but also fashionable in readiness for my new job, so I'm trying to make the most of myself,' Christabel affirmed as she passed the plate of sandwiches to her.

'A new job? What sort of job? You never said you were thinking of going out to work. Does it mean you're going to a new hospital? I thought you'd given up nursing for good.'

'I've been offered a post as nurse-companion to a young girl who is recuperating from tuber-culosis. As part of her treatment, she is being sent to live in Switzerland,' she explained.

'Switzerland!' Her mother's reaction was a

mixture of disbelief and consternation. 'Surely you could find something nearer home,' she grumbled as she stirred the cup of tea Lilian had placed in front of her. 'I shall be so worried about you. All that snow and ice everywhere and all those mountains, you could so easily break a leg, you know.'

'Mother, Fiona Gleeson is recovering from TB. She isn't fit to undertake anything energetic, let alone ski. She has been sent out there by a Harley Street specialist because the alpine air is considered to be very beneficial. I have been hired as a nurse-companion. My job will be to entertain her and make sure that she has plenty of rest. It will also be my responsibility to ensure that she eats the right foods, and takes the medicines prescribed.'

'And what about her family? Where will you live? Will there be servants to look after you?' A torrent of questions poured out from all sides.

'Fiona's parents will come out and visit her about once a month. There's a housekeeper and servants to look after the chalet. All I have to do is keep Fiona company and make sure she sticks to the rules laid down by her specialist.'

'Won't you find it very dull?'

'Dull?' She shrugged. 'I've never been to Switzerland before so it will be quite an exciting experience. I've been told that the scenery there is absolutely magnificent.'

Her vivid blue eyes hardened as she stared at her mother. 'The fact that I am going away will make things better for you all. It will give Lilian more space. Now that she has a child and all the paraphernalia that entails, as well as the fact that Dennis is home, means we are very cramped.'

'There's no need for you to rush off or to go to the other side of the world; this is your home as well, and there's plenty of room here for all of us,' her mother told her quickly. 'I'm not entering into an argument with you, but the thought of you going off to Switzerland worries me, whatever you may think,' she added huffily.

'Dissatisfaction with what you have seems to be one of the aftermaths of the war with you young people,' she went on reflectively. 'Only this morning Mary handed in her notice and told me that she will be leaving at the end of the month because she's getting married and moving to Scotland. I must say, it came as something of a shock to discover that she's been engaged for almost two years. I've never even thought about her having a life outside our home.'

Christabel was about to point out that they'd always taken Mary for granted, rather like they did herself, but she decided it was time for them all to remember that the real reason they were all there was not to have a family argument but to celebrate Kay's birthday.

'Do you want some more jelly and blancmange, or are you ready for someone to light the candles on your cake, Kay?' she asked, smiling across the table at the little girl.

'I'm ready for my birthday cake, Aunty Chrissy. I'm waiting to blow the candles out,' Kay said eagerly.

'Then we'll ask your daddy to light them right this minute,' Christabel told her. 'Would you like me to help you blow them out?'

'Yes please.' Kay held out her hand to Christabel who rose from her seat and went round to the other side of the table to stand behind Kay's chair.

'Now don't forget that you are supposed to make a wish, Kay,' Lewis told her as he applied a light to the five little candles and they all commented on how pretty they were as they flickered and then burned brightly.

Christabel squeezed Kay's hand reassuringly as the five-year-old took a great big breath and then blew it out in the direction of the candles as hard as she could.

'They're all out,' she exclaimed, clapping her hands excitedly. 'Now can I have my wish?'

'Your wish?' They all looked at her uncertainly.

'I think you are supposed to keep what you've wished for a secret or else it won't happen,' Violet explained.

'I can't do that or it will be too late and then it will never happen at all,' Kay whispered, her eyes misting with tears.

'Too late? I don't understand what you mean by that.' Lewis frowned.

114

'Aunt Chrissy will be gone away to Switzerland and then it will never happen.'

'Whatever do you mean, what are you trying to say?' Violet asked, looking puzzled.

Kay took hold of Christabel's hand and then reached up and pulled her face closer so that she could whisper in her aunt's ear. 'I want you to give me your pretty headband, Aunt Chrissy, so that I can wear it to remind me of you all the time you are away,' she said with a tremulous smile.

Chapter Eleven

There were times when Fiona Gleeson behaved as if she was nine rather than nineteen, Christabel thought as, half asleep, she struggled into her dressing gown and padded into the adjoining room to see why, yet again, Fiona was ringing the bell for her.

She even looks like a spoilt child, Christabel reflected, as she regarded the willowy figure propped up in the four-poster bed, clutching an oversized golden-furred teddy bear to her chest. Fiona's straight blond hair fanned out over the mountain of lace-edged pillows like an exotic shawl, framing the girl's delicate features.

'Fiona, did you ring?' Christabel asked, smothering a yawn and running a hand over her own ruffled hair in a vain attempt to smooth it back into its sleek bob.

'You know I did; you weren't still asleep, were you? It has been light for ages and ages!' The silver-blue eyes were accusing, the pale lips petulant. Two bright spots of feverish colour pinpointed her cheekbones.

'Yes, I was asleep,' Christabel admitted. 'After all,' she added, 'I have been up twice during the night to attend to you.'

'Well, that's what you are here for,' Fiona said petulantly.

Christabel smiled patiently but said nothing.

When she had first applied for the job of looking after Fiona, only daughter of Sir Henry and Lady Margaret Gleeson, it had sounded enchanting.

There would be snow, blue skies, sunshine and a crystal-clear, sparkling atmosphere. She'd be living in a luxury chalet-style house overlooking a picturesque village bright with flowers. It was a popular resort for wealthy people who could afford to indulge in their enjoyment of skiing and tobogganing.

Fiona's parents had painted such an idyllic picture that she'd had no hesitation about accepting the post. After the tension-wrought atmosphere at home it had sounded like the perfect solution.

St Moritz was every bit as enchanting as the Gleesons had predicted. It had been chosen as the most suitable place for Fiona's recuperation, not only because it was considered to be the finest of the Alpine resorts, but also because it was one of the main tobogganing centres, a sport in which both Fiona's father, and her brother George, intended to participate whenever they came to visit her.

What the Gleesons had not told Christabel was that their daughter was not only an invalid, but also thoroughly spoilt and excessively demanding. She was given to tantrums when she couldn't have her own way and this made her an extremely difficult patient.

Christabel often found herself thinking that it had been easier to control an entire ward of wounded soldiers than this one delicate-looking girl. She would have found it even more difficult if it had not been for the arrival of George Gleeson.

Fiona's brother had been sent out by his parents to make sure that everything was all right and that Fiona had settled in, and he was to report back on her progress. He was tall and extremely handsome. He had a shock of thick fair hair, hypnotic green eyes, a deep mellifluous voice, and a bold, yet charming manner. From their very first meeting, Christabel liked him.

George was something of a disappointment to his family. Following on from Eton he'd gone to Cambridge, but in his second year there he'd been sent down after a drunken brawl. It was the end of his academic life; instead of following his father into banking, he had trained as an actor. His classical features had won him several small-time parts.

His training, however, had imbued him with a voice of such melting quality that he had only to speak her name for Fiona to listen to his advice and do what he asked of her.

Determined not to let him see how charming she thought he was, Christabel treated him with cool reserve. This, she noticed with interest, seemed to intrigue him and she sensed his visits to St Moritz were not merely to check on his sister's health.

The visit from George had a most beneficial effect on Fiona. He insisted on taking her for a drive each day while he was staying there. Once she was warmly wrapped up in a chinchilla jacket, with a matching fur muff and an ear-hugging cloche hat, they would drive out in one of the jingling two-horse sleighs that were so popular in the resort.

George always invited Christabel to accompany them, and insisted they must stop for afternoon tea at one of the many café-restaurants. George's gallant attentions and witty conversation would bring a sparkle to Fiona's eyes, and even Christabel found herself smiling as he regaled them with anecdotes about his life in the acting profession.

Even so, the first time George asked if he could take her out for the evening, she demurred even though she knew she would have enjoyed the opportunity very much.

'Why ever not? You seem to enjoy my company when we take Fiona out for a drive.'

'Only because it's a pleasant diversion for Fiona,' she told him primly.

'So don't you think it might be an equally pleasant diversion for you if we went on our own?' he teased, his gaze holding hers.

'It is out of the question because Fiona is still far from well and it's my duty to see she is never left alone.'

When he nodded in agreement with her decision, turned on his heel and walked away without another word, Christabel almost cried with vexation.

To spend an entire evening in his company, without Fiona being there with them, would have been wonderful. His dashing good looks, his charm, his manner and his voice combined to make him a most attractive man and one she wanted to get to know better.

When George returned a few minutes later to say he had arranged for the housekeeper, Madame Frederique, to remain on call that evening to attend to Fiona's needs, Christabel stared at him in amazement, too taken aback even to thank him.

'I'll call for you at nine o'clock,' George told her. 'We'll dine at the Carlton Casino Restaurant and then we can dance afterwards. Their orchestra plays this new jazz as well as the more conventional dances,' he said, grinning boyishly at her.

Christabel spent the rest of the day in a state of indecision. She wondered what the Gleesons' reaction would be if it ever reached their ears that she had left their daughter in the care of domestic staff while she went dancing with their son.

Fiona will have retired for the night long before nine o'clock, she reminded herself, *and in all probability she will be asleep before I leave with George. There's even a chance that she won't waken again before I return home, in which case she need never know that I have been out.*

Since George is the one who has made the arrangements I am only obeying orders, she told herself. Anyway, it would be quite a long while before news of the incident could possibly reach the Gleesons' ears, that's if it ever did, and it would be time enough then to worry about their reaction.

Having reached a decision, she then rescheduled their normal evening routine to make sure that Fiona would be ready to retire early and, if luck was really on her side, would be asleep before George called to collect her.

Discreetly, she slipped away to the kitchen to have a word with the housekeeper about her plans. Madame Frederique, although eager to please George Gleeson, knew only too well how petulant and demanding Fiona could be and was quick to point out the hazards of their scheme.

'Let us give her a special treat,' she suggested, anxious to avoid any sort of confrontation. 'What about serving supper in her room after she is in bed? I will prepare her favourite dishes, ones I know she delights in. And perhaps she could have a small glass of wine; one that will make her sleepy, yes?'

'That sounds wonderful!'

'And we will say nothing about you going out, eh? If she should waken, I will be on hand, and I will say you have retired early with a bad head, and that you are not to be disturbed. Yes?'

Having settled that part of the arrangement, Christabel wondered what she should wear. Knowing that her duties were to chaperone and care for a young invalid, the evening dresses she'd brought with her were restricted in colour and style, and more suitable for family dining than accompanying a handsome man to a smart restaurant

The only dress she had packed that remotely looked suitable for a dinner-dance was the pale green one with floating dark green chiffon panels that she had worn at Kay's birthday party, but she wondered if it was rather too risqué for such an occasion.

It was either that or one of her more formal dresses, she decided, since there was no time to indulge in a shopping spree. Moreover, even if she had the opportunity, she couldn't afford to do so.

The first part of the evening seemed endless and everything seemed to go wrong. Fiona was irritable and obstreperous. She rejected the idea of having her supper served on a tray and it took a lot of persuasion to make her change her mind.

'Only if you stay and read to me while I eat it,' she said, pouting.

'Very well.' Christabel struggled to keep her voice calm although inwardly she was feeling increasingly anxious.

Madame Frederique saved the day by producing such an appetising spread, promptly at seven o'clock, that Fiona was suddenly eager to eat. She scowled when Christabel reminded her that she was to have her supper in bed, but reluctantly gave in when Christabel remained resolute and insisted that she had to keep to their agreement.

'You've not rested at all, Fiona, since we returned from our drive,' she pointed out. 'Tomorrow you will be too tired to go out at all.'

Fiona pouted childishly, clutching the huge teddy bear to her chest, burying her face in its soft golden fur and ignoring what Christabel was saying.

Firmly, Christabel took it from her and propped it against the pile of pillows alongside her as Madame Frederique placed the bed tray across Fiona's lap.

The appetising food, wine and warmth of the room soon took their toll. Fiona had barely eaten the last morsel of the delicate ice cream and fruit confection, which had been made specially for her, before her eyelids were drooping and her attention was no longer on the book Christabel was reading aloud to her.

Very cautiously, Christabel removed the tray and placed it on the table by the bed, but she went on reading aloud for another few minutes until Fiona's breathing became deep and regular. Then she closed the book, drew the covers up so that they covered Fiona's arms and shoulders, and, picking up the tray, moved quietly from the room.

Persuading Fiona to have her supper in bed had taken far longer than Christabel had expected it to. It meant that she now had less than half an hour in which to get ready.

Even so, she felt elated by George's reaction when she went into the sitting room where he was enjoying a sherry while he waited for her. Immaculate in evening dress, his green gaze moved appreciatively from her shining cap of hair to her high-heeled sandals and back up again with a smile of complete approval.

Christabel slipped the filmy lace shawl she was carrying round her shoulders. 'Ready?'

He grinned. 'Your carriage awaits!' With an exaggerated bow he crooked his arm, so that she could slip her hand into it.

They made the short drive almost in silence. When they reached the Carlton Casino, he seemed to be both amused and delighted by her reaction, as well as by the attention they received as he escorted her inside.

Once they were seated, he ordered their food and selected the wines without deferring to her at all.

It was the first time she had been anywhere in St Moritz, apart from accompanying Fiona to look at the many exquisite shops, and she was very impressed by her surroundings. The lighting came from massive crystal chandeliers, there were heavy, loganberry-red draped curtains at the enormous windows, and the sumptuous seating was upholstered in a matching fabric. Everything blended so harmoniously that it was the perfect background for the elegant diners.

Christabel was aware that a number of the people present seemed to know George. Men acknowledged his presence with friendly nods and a number of the ladies smiled in his direction.

He responded in kind but made no move to join any of the other parties, or to introduce Christabel to anyone and, although she appreciated that she had his whole attention, it did make her feel rather like Cinderella.

When the dancing started George was on his feet at once, leading her out on to the floor. With one arm firmly round her slim waist, he guided her into the rhythm of waltz, fox-trot and polka with the ease of a skilled dancer.

To Christabel, already light-headed from the wine, it was intoxicating. She had always enjoyed dancing but she had never had such a skilled partner before. It was as if they were floating on a cushion of air, their steps faultlessly matched, and their bodies swaying in perfect unison to the music.

At any other time, she might have found the intricate jazz numbers far too complicated to follow, but, under the golden glow from the glittering chandeliers, it was as if every step she took synchronised perfectly with his.

As they circled the dance floor while the band played the final waltz, she began to wonder if Fiona was all right and to feel just a little guilty about deserting her.

When they arrived back, George ordered the driver to wait as he escorted her to the door and exchanged a few brief words with Madame Frederique, who assured him that Fiona had not awakened all evening.

After George left, when Madame Frederique insisted that she must have a glass of hot milk and some arrowroot biscuits before she retired, Christabel suspected that Madame was hoping for a detailed account of her evening's entertainment.

Although she had never felt more alert, or so wide awake, Christabel had no intention of sharing such secrets with her. The night had been a revelation to her, and not only about George and his lifestyle; it had also made her realise how lonely she was. She desperately wanted to go to her room to analyse every minute detail of what had taken place.

Making the pretence of smothering a yawn, she took the tray from Madam Frederique's hands and went straight to her room, not even pausing to look in on Fiona to check if she was all right.

Chapter Twelve

Christabel knew that even though the relationship between her and George was purely platonic, keeping it hidden from Fiona was not going to be easy even though they both agreed that it seemed to be the sensible thing to do.

Fiona led such a sheltered existence that she was alert to even the slightest change in the daily pattern of what was going on around her. Three weeks later, when they'd returned from one of their afternoon drives, and George had asked her if she would like to go out with him again that evening, Christabel was aware that Fiona was listening to their conversation and she felt uneasy.

A few minutes later, when Fiona challenged them about what she and George had been whispering about, Christabel realised that her hesitation and their surreptitious exchange of glances had alerted Fiona that there really was something between them that she knew nothing about.

Fiona did not pursue the subject, but Christabel knew her well enough to realise that her curiosity had been aroused and that she probably wouldn't let the matter drop until she had ferreted out the whole story.

Before George left, he found the opportunity to tell Christabel that he had made the same arrangements as before and that Madame Frederique was happy to look after Fiona that evening as she had done on the previous occasion.

Christabel felt uncertain about whether or not to go through with it. She enjoyed his company and appreciated that he accepted that she didn't want any involvement other than their being good friends. When she tried to explain her misgivings to George, however, he became annoyed and dismissed her worries about leaving Fiona knowing they were socialising together as ridiculous.

'All we do is eat, talk and dance together, so what harm is there in that, for goodness' sake?'

'None whatsoever, and I very much enjoy your company,' she admitted.

'Good, because I enjoy yours. It's refreshing to find an attractive girl who is a good listener. It must be your guilty conscience,' he teased.

'There's nothing for me to have a guilty conscience about since we've both agreed we are simply good friends and we both want it to remain that way. As I've already said, it's leaving Fiona which is worrying me. Supposing she is taken ill while we are out and I'm not there to look after her?'

He shrugged dismissively. 'If you feel uneasy

about coming out with me tonight, then forget I ever asked you. I'll call for you anyway, in case you change your mind,' he muttered as he moved towards the door.

Cheeks burning, Christabel retreated back into the room feeling annoyed as well as hurt and humiliated at being treated in such a cavalier manner.

She was acutely aware that Fiona had witnessed what had happened. She saw the cunning look on her pale face and a malicious gleam in her blue eyes. She waited for her to say something, but Fiona remained mute, a half-smile playing on her pale lips as if she was enjoying the situation.

For the rest of the evening Fiona was unbelievably obedient, almost docile. So much so that Christabel felt increasingly apprehensive and wondered what she was up to.

Fiona accepted that her supper would be served in her room as soon as she was in bed without demur. She didn't even ask Christabel to read to her. The moment she had finished eating, she reached for her teddy and snuggled down to sleep without any fuss whatsoever.

'I feel so tired, I think it must be all the fresh air this afternoon,' she murmured, as she slid down under the covers and allowed Christabel to tuck them in around her shoulders.

Christabel's heart was stirred by the sight of the outline of the skeletal-thin figure which barely raised a mound under the silken covers.

As she was leaving the room, she paused for a moment and looked back. Fiona's face, framed by its halo of fair hair, looked so ethereal against the lace-trimmed pillows and Christabel felt a stab of guilt about leaving her, even though she knew that Madame Frederique would take every care of her.

It was a fleeting thought and quickly surpassed by the sudden rush of excitement as she recalled that, within the hour, she could be back at the Carlton Casino enjoying her evening with George, if that was what she wanted.

The memories of their previous visits, the delicious food, the glamorous setting, the glittering lights, the sophisticated crowd and the exciting music they had danced to filled her head as she hurried to get ready.

As she slipped into the pale green dress and stood in front of the long mirror to arrange the floating dark-green chiffon panels, a movement from the doorway startled her. She held her breath as she saw that Fiona, a ghostly figure in her floor-length white lawn nightdress, was standing there watching her.

'That's a very pretty dress. I don't think I've seen you wearing it before. Are you going somewhere special?'

Christabel felt hot colour staining her cheeks as their eyes met in the cheval mirror.

She bit her lip. 'I'm going out for a meal and to a dance with your brother,' she said quietly.

'With George?'

When she hesitated, Fiona moved into the room and perched herself on the edge of Christabel's bed. 'I've never been to a dinner-dance, Christabel. I think I would like to go with you tonight.'

'That's out of the question, Fiona. You're not well enough. It'll be very noisy, and it's an extremely smoky atmosphere. It wouldn't be wise, not in your state of health.'

Fiona stared at her in silence for a minute.

'It was because of the state of my health that I was sent out here to St Moritz, wasn't it?' she sighed.

'That's right.'

Fiona gave a supercilious smile. 'And you were hired to nurse me because of the state of my health, weren't you, Christabel?'

Christabel nodded.

'I wonder what my parents would say if they knew you went out and left me on my own in my state of health. Especially if they knew you were going out with George . . .' her voice trailed away, but her eyes were shining with malice.

Christabel frowned uneasily. 'What are you trying to say, Fiona?'

Before Fiona could answer there was a noise from downstairs and they heard Madame Frederique greeting George and showing him into the drawing room.

'I'm sure my brother will think you look very lovely,' Fiona murmured.

'Thank you!' Christabel tried to accept Fiona's compliment calmly, but inwardly she felt perturbed as she wondered what the girl was leading up to.

Stretching out a hand, Fiona touched one of the floating chiffon panels of Christabel's dress and then moved towards the door, still holding on to it so that Christabel had no choice but to go with her or have her dress torn.

Against her will, Christabel found herself being led down the stairs to where George was waiting.

'Christabel's ready and she's wearing such a pretty dress that she looks really lovely,' Fiona pronounced, as they entered the drawing room.

George's eyes met Christabel's over his sister's head and she tried to flash a warning, but she wasn't even sure herself what kind of game Fiona was playing.

'I've never been to a dinner-dance so I've decided I'm coming with you,' Fiona announced.

'Don't be silly, Fiona!' George remonstrated crossly. 'Back to bed this instant.'

'No! I'm coming with you and Christabel,' she repeated firmly, two red flushes of colour staining her cheeks.

'Fiona, stop this nonsense. You know you are in no fit state to go dancing.'

'True but I also know that I'm in no fit state to be left alone,' she told him coolly.

'You're not being left on your own. Madame Frederique will be here looking after you.'

'Either you take me with you, George, or I shall tell our parents that you and Christabel are carrying on with each other. I shall tell them all about what the two of you have been up to,' she added, smiling sweetly.

'Up to? We haven't been up to anything,' George told her. 'We've simply gone to a dinner-dance. It's what grown-ups do,' he added with a forced laugh.

'I only hope Father will believe you and see it your way,' Fiona replied innocently.

'Look, I'm taking Christabel to a dinner-dance, nothing more! After all,' he defended, 'it's not very amusing for her to be shut up here with you twenty-four hours a day, now, is it?'

'It's what's she's paid to do. She's only a servant, you know.'

'Fiona, that's unforgivably rude.'

'Unforgivable? What an apt choice of word, George. That's probably the very expression Father will use when he hears you've been taking Christabel out. You know how outraged he always is when he catches you playing around with any of the servant girls back at home. In fact,' she went on smugly, her eyes fixed on his enraged face, 'it's the reason he turned you out, isn't it?' She smiled vindictively. 'I heard him say that it was cheaper to give you an allowance, so that you could live away from home, than to have to pay young servant girls hush money to go quietly and not make a fuss when they were pregnant.'

George's face blanched beneath its tan. 'You are absolutely despicable, Fiona! I suppose you've been listening at keyholes again?' he jibed.

'Of course, but Father doesn't have to know this time,' she went on unperturbed. 'If you took me with you, then I wouldn't want him to know about you taking Christabel to dinner-dances!' She laughed softly, her delicate features suddenly sharp and waspish. 'If you took me along as well, then I would hardly be likely to give the game away, would I?'

George looked helplessly at Christabel. 'What do you think we should do?'

'The Carlton Casino is far from suitable for Fiona,' she said stiffly. 'The smoky atmosphere and all the noise won't do her any good at all.'

'It won't do me any good, either, if she tells the old man that I've been taking you out,' George interrupted. 'If he cuts off my allowance, I'll probably starve to death. The play I was in has finished and I haven't another part in sight.'

'So you're going to take me with you? Oh, thank you, George.' Fiona's flushed face was wreathed in smiles as she hugged her brother. 'I'll be ready in ten minutes. Come and help me dress, Christabel,' she ordered over her shoulder.

Christabel was astonished by the change in Fiona's behaviour once they reached the Carlton. Her petulant attitude vanished as she absorbed the scene around her. She begged for some champagne and when George ordered it she drank her first glass so quickly that Christabel was alarmed and protested strongly when George poured out some more for her. She was even more concerned when Fiona demanded that George should give her one of the long, dark cigarettes he was smoking.

Ignoring Christabel's warning that smoking was harmful for her, Fiona fitted a cigarette into a long jade holder she'd taken from her evening bag and proceeded to light up with the enjoyment of someone who was already used to smoking.

By the end of the evening, Fiona was utterly exhausted. Her face was flushed, her eyes glazed, and she was too fatigued to even walk and made no protest at all when George picked her up in his arms as if she was a child and carried her out to the taxi. She seemed to be almost asleep when they reached home so he carried her straight up to her bedroom.

'Don't be too long, we must talk about this. I'll fix myself a drink while you settle Fiona for the night,' he whispered conspiratorially to Christabel as he left the bedroom.

Christabel didn't attempt to fully undress Fiona; she simply removed her dress and shoes and pulled the covers up over her before joining George in the drawing room.

A week later, Sir Henry and Lady Margaret Gleeson arrived in St Moritz unannounced. Two hours later, following a heated confrontation,

Christabel had been dismissed and Fiona was on her way home to England with her parents.

As she stood in the snowy road outside the chalet that had been her home at St Moritz for such a brief period, her two suitcases at her side, Christabel tried to focus her thoughts on what she was going to do.

The interview with the Gleesons had been short and bitter after they'd heard Fiona's version of events.

After a stormy confrontation they had given her a month's wages, although they pointed out that she didn't deserve a penny after the way she had flirted with George and neglected Fiona.

They refused to let her travel back to England with them and it was with great reluctance that they met her pleas for the money to pay her fare home.

Going back to England was the last thing Christabel wanted to do. In her letters to her mother she'd written such glowing accounts about how wonderful it was in Switzerland and how happy she was in her new position that it would be impossible to simply arrive home and say the job had ended. Unless, of course, she claimed that Fiona had died.

A shudder went through her at the thought of telling such a monstrous lie. She wasn't superstitious, but she felt that was pushing things a little too far.

If only the Gleesons had not decided to depart in quite such a hurry, she might have had time to make some plans. They had shut up the house and turned her out into the street all in the matter of a few hours.

She wondered who had contacted them and told them what was going on. She suspected it had been Fiona. Madame Frederique would hardly have done something like that since it meant she had lost her job as well.

George hadn't even been given the chance to defend himself since they hadn't taken the time to get in touch with him. Slowly it dawned on her that since they hadn't even spoken to him he wouldn't even know they'd been in Switzerland or anything at all about what had happened.

Christabel pressed her hands to her temples, trying to calm the throbbing that she was afraid was building up into a searing headache. If George was still in St Moritz, she reasoned, and if he didn't know that Fiona had gone home, then perhaps that changed her situation completely.

If George enjoyed her company and found her as good a listener as he professed she was, then perhaps he might let her stay with him, she thought hopefully.

If she could persuade him to do that, then there might be no need for her to return to Liverpool, at least not immediately.

All she had to do was convince him that his

parents had resolved to take Fiona back to England for some reason connected with her treatment, and that she wanted to stay on in Switzerland, even though it meant losing her job.

Feeling more relaxed now that she felt she was in charge of the situation, Christabel picked up her suitcases and made her way to the hotel where she knew George was staying.

Chapter Thirteen

George was surprised to find Christabel waiting for him at his hotel when he returned from a day spent on the ski slopes with some of his friends. This turned to concern, however, when he heard the reason why she was there.

'You're saying that my parents have been here in St Moritz and gone straight home again?' he exclaimed in bewildered tones. 'Are you sure, Christabel? I can't imagine my old man passing up a chance to spend some time here enjoying a spot of tobogganing after travelling such a long distance.'

'They seemed to be in a tremendous hurry,' she explained.

'Even so, I can't understand them returning to England without even seeing me! Didn't Fiona tell them I was still here?'

'I don't think they gave Fiona much opportunity to tell them anything,' Christabel told him evasively. 'They were too busy insisting that they intended to take her back to England immediately.'

'I see!' He ran a hand through his hair, and then his face cleared. 'It's probably something to do with her treatment; another specialist, or something. So when are they bringing her back?'

'I don't think they are. They certainly never mentioned it.'

'And yet they left you behind?' He raised his eyebrows in surprise.

'They told me my services were no longer required,' Christabel told him. 'They gave me the money for my return fare because I said I didn't want to travel with them. That was because I wanted to see you and explain what was happening,' she added quickly.

George gave a long silent whistle. 'So what are you going to do now?'

'I don't really know. I'll have to return to England and try and find work, I suppose, so I'd better go and make some travel arrangements right away.'

'Hold on, there's no rush, is there? Let's go for a meal and we can talk about it and see if that is absolutely necessary.'

'That's very kind of you, George. I must admit I hate the thought of having to go back to Liverpool and tell my family that I've lost my job, but I don't think it is possible to stay here in St Moritz even for one night because everything is so expensive,' Christabel gulped, twisting her handkerchief nervously and avoiding his eyes.

'I have an idea that might appeal to you,' he went on. 'Come on, I'll tell you all about it while we're eating. I'll arrange for you to stay here at my hotel for tonight,' he added briskly taking her arm and guiding her across the road towards a smart little restaurant.

He waited until they had been served before he spoke. 'I really do think I might have the answer,' he assured her.

'Oh, and what is that?'

'Well, it would mean you would have to live in London. Would that matter? Do you really need to return to Liverpool? My agent has told me that it might be to my advantage as an actor to return to London.'

'I don't understand the connection.' Christabel frowned.

'Well, if I am going to live there permanently then I need someone to take care of things at my flat, a sort of live-in housekeeper.'

She frowned questioningly as if still not quite sure what that had to do with her but inwardly she felt exultant.

'I'm offering you the job.' He smiled.

'Of being your housekeeper!' She looked at him in feigned astonishment. 'I'm not sure,' she demurred.

Over dinner George explained about the letter that he'd received from his agent telling him that there was a challenging part for him in a new modern play by Jules Lowry that was soon to open in London. He had already accepted on George's behalf so it was imperative that George return to London immediately.

He could talk of nothing else. Lowry was one

of the leading playwrights and his agent had read the play and described it in glowing terms. The fact that he had a part was exciting enough but George was elated beyond belief because he had been selected without even going for an audition.

'I really am starting to be noticed,' he told Christabel. 'I began to think I would never get beyond bit parts. Now it probably means that my name will be up in lights outside one of the big London theatres.'

Although she was pleased for him, Christabel was also concerned about what the future would hold for her if she accepted his offer as George seemed to take it for granted she would. Although at present they were very good friends, she would be little more than a servant, she reflected, and after the humiliating treatment she'd just suffered from his parents she didn't like the idea of that at all.

Also it meant that if she were living in London, she wouldn't be able to see little Kay very often and she longed to see her niece. She had missed her so much while she'd been living in Switzerland. Kay had just started school now, and Christabel felt she was missing out on all her formative years.

Yet, did she want to go back to Liverpool? she pondered. She certainly didn't want to return to living with her mother, not while Lilian and Dennis were still there.

Probably, if she did go back to Liverpool, the

moment Lilian knew she didn't have a job she'd expect her to take over at home and be the one to look after their mother so that she and Dennis could move to a home of their own.

'Come on, Christabel; make up your mind,' George prompted, raising his glass. 'This is the nineteen twenties and you're an emancipated young woman, so what are you being so coy about?'

She stared back at him for a long moment. 'I was thinking about what people might think about us living together in the same flat and what they might say!' she murmured.

'What utter rubbish; anyway, what does it matter. We both know that we would lead a blameless existence.' He laughed. 'Come on, Christabel, and enjoy the freedom we fought for; people's outlooks have changed since the war ended. Surely you don't want to turn the clock back to Victorian days? It's a new century, a new world; people are no longer inhibited by false modesty and dubious values. Live life to the full and enjoy every minute of it, that's the motto for our generation, so let's make the most of it.'

'What happens if your parents hear about your new play and come to London to see you in it? If they come to your flat they are bound to find out I am living there,' she pointed out.

'They wouldn't be seen dead at my place,' he assured her. 'My flat is a nice enough little place, but far too Bohemian for them to ever visit. They have their own London house in Belgravia, so you can put that worry from your mind right away.'

Christabel found that she enjoyed living in London with George. His flat was comfortable and it was quite easy for them to get from there to the theatre as well as to the shops in the West End and the more exciting Chelsea area.

Christabel found the flat was equipped with everything she needed. She had her own bedroom, which was even larger than his, and they shared the living room space.

George was easy to look after and very considerate and, most of the time, he left her to her own devices. All he asked was that she did the cooking when he ate at home, kept the place in order, and made sure that his clothes were always ready for him to wear.

George left for the theatre around mid-morning, leaving her free to organise her day as she wished until the evening. Then she dressed in one of her many pretty frocks and went to the theatre where she would watch the play from the wings until he came off stage. Then they would join the other actors and their friends and enjoy the night life in London's West End. They rarely arrived back at the flat until two or three the next morning.

There was no performance on Sundays so, if the weather was uninviting, they often stayed in, reading the newspapers, or playing records.

George owned one of the new wind-up gramophones and they both enjoyed listening to jazz. On those Sundays when the sun was shining, if they were feeling energetic, they sometimes strolled along the Chelsea Embankment or walked in St James's Park.

Christabel delighted in their Bohemian existence. Her hair was shorter than ever, she even risked having an Eton crop, but George didn't like it so she let it grow back into a shaped bob with the slightly longer side pieces curved forward on to her cheeks. She followed the latest fashion trends with enthusiasm, making regular visits to the West End shops trying on all the very latest styles. She had good legs, so the Chanel outfits, with their low waists and knee-length skirts, suited her extremely well.

Except on Sundays, when they listened to jazz, she rarely played the gramophone when George was at home since he preferred listening to his new wireless. She thought it looked ugly. She hated the complicated contraption made up of accumulators, batteries and a speaker. A lot of the things he listened to were, to her mind, extremely dull and uninteresting, but he was never happier than when fiddling with the various knobs and locating different stations.

George was so enthralled with his new toy that he even planned to sit at home and listen to the broadcast of the Royal Wedding on 26 April, when Prince George would marry Lady Elizabeth Bowes-Lyon. Christabel insisted that since they were in London and it was such a great opportunity to witness such a historic event, one that was regarded as the highlight of 1923, they should go and watch the procession.

In the end, she won, but only because the Archbishop of Canterbury had forbidden the ceremony to be broadcast, fearing that some of the populace might not show due respect. Men in pubs might even sit and listen to the ceremony with their hats on.

Christabel found it exhilarating to mingle with the cheering crowd outside Westminster Abbey. She thought Lady Elizabeth Bowes-Lyon already looked every inch a princess as she stepped down from the state landau. She was wearing an ivory dress of fine chiffon moiré, embroidered with silver thread and pearls, and it had long sleeves of fine Nottingham lace. As she took her father's arm and walked along the red carpet into the abbey, her eight bridesmaids carrying her train of point de Flandres lace mounted on tulle, Christabel thought it was the most romantic moment she'd ever witnessed.

But George's mind was on other matters. It was time for him to leave for the theatre and he was anxious for them to go otherwise he would be late.

Christabel told him she wanted to stay to see the royal couple emerge from the abbey after the service and to savour the moment.

'Well, if you really want to do so then it's up to you, but you'll have to do it on your own, so do take care because there're bound to be pickpockets about,' George warned. 'I'll see you later at the theatre, and we'll go for a meal.'

Minutes later, when she felt a light touch on her arm, Christabel recalled his words and her heart thudded with fear. As she turned and looked up into a pair of steely black eyes, her heart raced for quite another reason.

'Alex, what are you doing here? George has just left for the theatre, shouldn't you be there?'

'Heavens, no! I'm his agent not his keeper. I don't have to turn up at performances.'

The rest of the day passed in a dream. As soon as they could free themselves from the crowd they walked together in St James's park, quite oblivious of the fact that the weather had deteriorated and was now overcast. Christabel had only met Alex a few times and knew very little about him, except that he was an American and, according to George, one of the top agents in the business.

They dined together at the Café Royal and danced the evening away. On the dance floor their steps matched and their rhythm was in perfect accord, almost as if their two bodies were a single entity. It was a sensation that was entirely new to her, so very different from George's dancing.

That was not surprising, she mused, since he was very different from George who was like a big brother to her, considerate and easy-going. This man with his saturnine features had a look of ruthlessness about him that, the first time she'd met him, had sent a shiver down her spine.

Alex Taylor was tall, broad shouldered and handsome with almost jet-black hair and deeply tanned skin. His features were strong and inscrutable; there was an air of mystery about him that she found intriguing.

When Alex finally put her into a taxi it was after midnight. Christabel had completely forgotten that she was supposed to join George at the theatre. When he arrived home just after one o'clock in very ill humour because he was afraid she had come to some harm, she was already in bed and asleep.

The next day, Friday, they hardly spoke to each other. She knew he was sulking, but decided it would only make matters worse if she told him where she had been.

The following week George announced that on Saturday he wanted to watch the Cup Final. When she protested that neither of them was interested in football, he pointed out that it was a very special football match; for the very first time, it was being held in London at Wembley Stadium.

His enthusiasm for the match, which was between Bolton Wanderers and West Ham, amused her. He had always considered football to be such a common game. It had only been when he was told that King George V was to be amongst the spectators that he had been so eager to attend.

She expected him to ask her to go with him and was surprised when he didn't. It wasn't until he was leaving that she realised that his not taking her to the Cup Final was meant to be a punishment, a way of showing his displeasure over her not showing up at the theatre after the royal wedding.

Christabel spent the entire day with Alex Taylor.

He was still very much a mystery to her. She knew nothing of his background, but when they were together she found that such things didn't seem to matter. Merely being in Alex's company was enough to set her pulse racing. She even forgot how quickly the time was passing and, in a sudden panic, found herself rushing to get back to the flat before George returned home.

Overcome by guilt, she did her best to prepare a special meal, dishes she knew George enjoyed, and uncorked a bottle of his favourite wine ready to pour him a glass the moment he walked in the door.

When the hours ticked by and the meal she had taken such trouble to prepare was ruined, she wondered if George was staying out late deliberately. Perhaps he was doing it as a form of retaliation because he wasn't keen on her seeing Alex Taylor and was annoyed that she'd taken no notice when he'd told her so.

At midnight, when there was still no sign of him coming home, Christabel decided not to wait up any longer but to go to bed. The next morning, when she realised he hadn't come home, she began to feel alarmed. She knew it was no good phoning the theatre because, as it was Sunday, it would be closed.

She began to panic in case he had walked out on her because of their arguments about Alex. She checked his wardrobe and felt much calmer when she found that all his clothes were still there. She tried to think constructively and even toyed with the idea of phoning Alex. In the end, she summoned up the courage to go to the local police station and report him missing.

The desk sergeant consulted a ledger on the desk in front of him and she tried to be patient as he ran his finger down a long list of entries. 'George Gleeson? I'm afraid he has been taken into custody,' he pronounced grimly.

George, and other enthusiasts attending the match, had been caught up in the melee when thousands rushed the turnstiles. Fighting had ensued. The police had eventually restored order, but George, along with a great many others who happened to be carrying hip flasks containing whisky, had been charged with being drunk and disorderly.

Reluctantly, the police allowed Christabel to see him for a few minutes. She was distraught when she saw how dishevelled and unshaven he looked. There was a fanatical gleam of anger in his green eyes as he confronted her.

'Shall I let Alex know what has happened so that he can contact a solicitor and make sure you are properly represented when your case comes to court?' Christabel suggested.

'No, that won't be necessary. I've decided that I am going to conduct my own defence and I've been rehearsing what I shall say.'

Christabel stared at George in disbelief, wondering how he could be so arrogant and so self-assured under such frightening circumstances.

'Supposing they don't believe you?' she said hesitantly.

'Don't worry; I'll be able to convince them that they have made a mistake and I'll be released on the spot.'

She saw him frown with annoyance when she shook her head in disbelief.

'You'll see! And afterwards I intend to sue for damages for wrongful arrest,' he said confidently.

Christabel tried hard to make him change his mind, but he was unwavering in his belief that there was nothing at all to be worried about and that he would be able to convince the judge that there was no case to be answered.

At first he was emphatic that he didn't want her telling Alex what had happened. Then when he heard that his appearance in court wouldn't be for at least a week he accepted that although he'd been given bail it would be better to tell Alex what had happened before he read about it in the newspaper.

'You and Alex are both going to be there I hope,' he stated the morning the case was to be heard and he was getting ready to go to Court. 'Afterwards we'll celebrate with a slap-up meal and I'll buy you both all the champagne you can drink!'

Christabel assured him that she would be there. What she didn't tell him was that they'd talked endlessly between themselves about the case and Alex had agreed with her that it was very unwise of George not to have a lawyer defending him.

Looking demure in a new navy cardigan suit and a matching cloche hat she had bought specially for the occasion because she thought everything in her wardrobe was far too bright and flamboyant, Christabel felt very nervous as they took their seats.

Alex had warned her that the press was bound to be there taking photographs, so she had made sure that George was wearing a new white shirt and a well-pressed, dark grey suit. Standing in the dock he looked as cool as a cucumber as he delivered his carefully prepared speech in a strong, clear voice.

Despite his eloquence, or possibly because he was far too outspoken and because he was an actor, the judge decided he wanted to make an example of his misconduct and George was sentenced to eighteen months' imprisonment.

His punishment was far more severe than the sentences served on any of the others who had been charged with him and Christabel felt numb with disbelief.

She calculated that even with time off for good behaviour it would be the following autumn at the earliest before he was free again. Where on earth did that leave her, she wondered? Even if George agreed to her staying on in his flat while he was in prison, would she be able to afford to remain there all on her own? Living in London was so terribly expensive; she would most certainly have to try and find a job.

Apart from that, she though worriedly, what would happen when George's parents discovered that he'd been sent to prison? They might decide to either sell the flat or rent it out, and she shuddered to think what would happen if they discovered she'd been living there with George.

She decided that there was only one person who would understand the position she was now in and who could advise her about what was the best thing to do, and that was Alex Taylor. But, as she turned to speak to him and saw the hard inscrutable look on his face, she wondered just how much she could count on his help.

Chapter Fourteen

Christabel would never forget the night she had arrived at Alex's Mayfair flat after George had been sent to prison. He'd asked no questions, simply invited her in as if there was nothing at all unusual about her calling on him so late in the evening. He had taken her coat, led her into his massive lounge, sat her down on the comfortable sofa, and then poured her a brandy.

He had occupied an armchair opposite her, silently nursing his own drink, waiting until she'd drained her glass before speaking.

'Are you all right now? Do you want to tell me what's happened?'

He listened in silence, his eyes gave nothing away. When she had finished telling him that George had been sent to prison, he refilled her glass.

'Drink this. Then try and get some sleep.' He patted her hand consolingly. 'We'll talk again in the morning. Things will look different then, I promise you.'

He took her through to the bedroom, handed her a navy silk pyjama jacket, and then left her. The room was enormous, and so too was the bed. She undressed and slipped in between the cool silk sheets and waited. She felt slightly muzzy with all the brandy she'd been drinking and was asleep almost at once. When she woke, daylight was already showing behind the curtains.

She groped her way to the bedroom door and opened it. The lounge was in darkness. As her eyes grew accustomed to the dimness she could make out the shapes of the furniture. Alex was sound asleep lying on the sofa and covered over with a blanket.

She crept back into the warm, comfortable bed feeling guilty that he'd had to spend the night on the sofa.

She lay there dozing and turning over in her mind her feelings for Alex. She found it impossible to understand why he meant so much to her. She sometimes wondered whether it was because, with his dark hair and dark, hypnotic eyes, he reminded her of her brother Lewis. In her heart she knew this wasn't the case. Lewis had vivid blue eyes, like her own, and Alex's hair was not just dark, it was jet black.

If you analysed Alex's appearance, Christabel thought dispassionately, you would see that his features had a certain Latin quality. His skin was so tanned and smooth that his clean-shaven cheeks gleamed. His dark eyes had a cold, watchful brilliance that screened his thoughts. She had never known anyone quite like him.

Even his shoulders seemed to be exceptionally wide. George, with his shock of fair hair, was so different. Just by looking into his eyes, because he was so transparent, she could usually tell exactly what he was thinking.

With Alex there was always uncertainty. Although he seemed to be interested in her, she was never entirely sure what his feelings for her were.

He didn't try to please her, or attract her attention. There were no gifts or bouquets of flowers. Always she was the one who was anxious to please him, to fall in with his plans, whatever they were. In some ways, she knew she was behaving like a lovesick schoolgirl.

She re-examined in minute detail every moment she'd been in his company from the time they'd met. There had been a great many memorable hours spent together while George was in the theatre. There had been walks in London, drives out into the countryside and boat trips on the river. It had been more than mere friendship; it had been like a courtship. A very proper courtship conducted by a man who seemed serious about his intentions.

She was suddenly roused to find Alex standing at the bedside holding a cup of tea for her. She felt a moment's unease because she hadn't heard him come into the room and wondered how long he had been watching her.

'I have to go out,' he told her in clipped tones. 'When you are dressed, why don't you go and collect all your belongings?'

'You mean I can stay here while George is in prison?' she asked in surprise.

'Don't you want to?'

'Yes – that would be wonderful. Only you can't sleep on the sofa.' She looked up quickly and caught a gleam of amusement in his dark eyes before he masked it under lowered lids.

'I don't intend to do so. You fetch your things. We'll sort out the sleeping details later,' he told her, looking at his gold Rolex. 'I must go, or I shall be late for the theatre.'

'The theatre?' She looked dumbfounded.

'I'm not only an agent, representing George and some other actors, but I'm also a producer. I'm in charge of the company putting on the play that George had a part in.'

By the time Alex returned later in the day, Christabel had collected all her clothes and other possessions from George's flat. She had no idea where to put them, so they were piled up in one corner of the otherwise immaculate living room.

She saw him frowning at the sight of them as he crossed to the drinks cabinet and took out a bottle of sherry and poured them both a glassful. He sat down on the sofa and patted the seat beside him.

'We must have a talk,' he said tersely. 'I need to know how you come to know George.'

'We met in Switzerland. I was working as a nurse-companion to his sister Fiona when she was recuperating from tuberculosis,' she said briefly.

'I see.' His lips curled sardonically. 'And what happened to your patient?'

157

She was silent for a moment, staring down at her hands which she held tightly clasped in her lap.

'Her parents came and decided to take her home.'

'And left you behind in St Moritz?'

'They wanted to take her to see a new specialist in London. For personal reasons I didn't want to return to England right away,' she said stiffly.

'You mean you decided to stay behind with George?' The mockery in his voice made colour flare in her cheeks.

'George was my patient's brother. He was very kind to me and always the perfect gentleman,' she defended.

'Aah! His sort usually are,' he commented dryly.

'His sort?' She frowned. 'What exactly do you mean?'

He looked at her, raising his eyebrows mockingly. 'Are you telling me you don't know about George and his sort?'

She shook her head.

'He's never tried to make love to you all the time you've lived with him?'

'Of course not. We're good friends and he's always been the perfect gentleman.'

'That's because he doesn't care for women; not in the way most men do,' Alex told her dryly.

Christabel felt the colour flooding her cheeks.

She had never thought about it before, and what about the servant girls Fiona had mentioned? She'd never quite believed that. In a way she'd been grateful that there was only camaraderie between her and George because she still hadn't put Philip out of her heart.

'You don't think that any red-blooded man could share his flat but not his bed with someone as attractive as you?' Alex questioned.

That night, Alex didn't sleep on the sofa.

Alex was an experienced lover. When, shaking with nerves, Christabel told him she'd only ever made love once and that had been with Philip before he'd left on his fatal voyage, he smiled and told her not to worry.

He taught her so much, showed her that loving could be an art as well as a physical release. He was such an exciting lover that when she was in his arms she felt as if she was being transported to another world and no two journeys were ever the same.

Sometimes he was gentle, his strong, sensitive fingers tuning her body to its ultimate pitch. The quick-breathing eagerness of his mouth, as he explored every inch of her skin with the utmost delicacy, carried her to heady and exhilarating peaks of excitement.

At other times he could be harsh, demanding and almost brutal; intent on his own satisfaction and oblivious of whether he hurt her or not. Even these moments brought a wild ecstasy to her senses until she cried out for release, with a rhythm and ferocity that matched his own.

Her feelings for him were so intense that she couldn't bear the thought of losing him. Yet, for all his momentary fervour and passion, he was cold. As the months passed she was concerned because she felt she had no hold over him at all except their lovemaking. It worried her. She didn't want this to be a casual relationship; she wanted to spend the rest of her life with Alex Taylor. Above all, she wanted marriage.

As the time approached for George to be released from prison she decided to put Alex's feelings for her to the test so she suggested they should visit Liverpool so that he could meet her mother and brother. To her delight, he agreed and said they would drive up there in his new Alvis motor car.

'Does your family know that we've been living together?' he asked as they left London behind them and headed North.

'No, of course not. Mother would be horrified. She thinks I am still in Switzerland nursing.'

They were both silent, lost in their separate thoughts as they covered the miles between London and Liverpool. Even when they stopped to refuel the car and took a break for refreshments, Alex had very little to say.

It was early evening when they finally reached Liverpool and she directed him to her home. Christabel felt a sense of unease as she introduced Alex to her mother who seemed to be looking much frailer than she remembered. Her hair was now quite white, her round face showed a network of fine lines under her eyes.

'Would you and your friend like to freshen up before we sit down to a meal, Christabel?' she enquired after asking Alex if they'd had a good journey.

'I've put your friend in Lewis's old room, so can you show him where it is? Your room is exactly as you left it,' she added with a faint smile. 'This time there has been no one using it while you've been away,' she assured her.

It felt good to be home. Christabel lingered in her bedroom, touching the familiar furniture, looking at the pictures and ornaments that she'd treasured as she was growing up.

She flung wide the window and leaned out, smelling the cold tang of the Mersey. The glow from rows of street lights patterned her view reminding her that the nights were drawing in and that summer was almost over.

Like my life, she thought, as she combed her hair and renewed her lipstick. *I've reached my thirties, my spring days are over. I'm becoming an old maid*. She smiled confidently at her reflection. She would marry soon. She was sure that Alex was on the point of proposing, possibly either tonight or tomorrow.

She found that Alex was already downstairs and in the drawing room with Lilian and

Marlene. She paused in the doorway, struck by the contrast they made; her sister and niece both being so petite and fair seemed to make Alex look even darker.

She stood there unnoticed for several moments watching with amusement as Marlene demanded his full attention. Marlene was no longer the chubby toddler Christabel remembered her as but a plump little six-year-old with a halo of fair curls. Because of all the attention she'd had from her mother and grandmother in the intervening years she was now an extremely precocious little chatterbox.

To her surprise, Alex seemed to enjoy Marlene's company and when Lilian said that she and Marlene would take him for a walk the next morning he readily agreed.

'It will give you the opportunity to have more time with Mother,' Lilian explained to her. 'I'm sure there are lots of things you want to talk about and you won't get much of a chance when Marlene is around.'

It wasn't what Christabel wanted; she wanted to be with Alex, to be the one to show him familiar landmarks. She was also looking forward to taking him to meet Lewis and Violet and, above all, Kay.

Most of the time she only half listened to what her mother was saying because her own thoughts were distracted by wondering about what Lilian was saying to Alex.

She did, however, become interested when

her mother started telling her about the problems Lilian was having with Dennis.

'He ill-treats her, you know. Sometimes she has terrible bruises. Mind, he is always very careful and they are always where they don't show, or where, if they do, Lilian can cover them up. Her arms are often black and blue and she says there are marks on her back and other parts of her body that would shock me if she showed them to me.'

'He never hits Marlene though, does he?' Christabel asked.

'No, that's one good thing. He does treat Lilian very badly, though; he's quite a brute when he doesn't get his own way, especially when he's been drinking.'

'Perhaps you should ask Lewis to have a word with him,' Christabel suggested. 'Would you like me to mention it to him?'

'No.' Her mother shook her head. 'I haven't told him about it because I know how busy he is. I am sure that if I did, he would only say that what goes on between husband and wife is their affair and refuse to interfere.'

When Christabel went to see Lewis she fully intended mentioning the matter, but all her attention was taken up by seeing Kay again. She, too, had changed in the ensuing years and was now a leggy nine-year-old and rather quiet and reserved. She had straight dark hair in a pigtail and a rather severe fringe, and Christabel felt it was like looking at one of the photographs of herself at that age. There was still a special affinity between them and Kay seemed to be delighted to see her. She even said how much she'd missed her and was eager to tell her all about what she did at school.

The weekend passed all too quickly and even though Alex hadn't whispered the magic words she was waiting to hear, she considered it to have been a pleasant interlude.

As she fastened the locks on her suitcase and prepared to leave she wondered if he might propose on the way home.

Humming to herself she went downstairs and was pleased to find Alex deep in conversation with her mother. They stopped talking as she walked into the room and Christabel sensed tension in the air. She wondered what they'd been talking about and looked from one to the other enquiringly, but neither of them made any attempt to enlighten her.

The weekend was far from being the success Christabel had hoped it would be. Alex hadn't proposed; in fact, he had seemed to be on edge and was anxious to get back to London. The only good thing about the trip had been seeing Kay again.

When she asked Alex if he'd enjoyed their visit, he was so curt that she felt mystified. He didn't seem to want to talk; it was as if his mind was fully occupied with some problem. When she asked him what was worrying him he was so evasive that she felt uneasy and wondered if it was what her mother had said to him that had upset him so much.

They were both silent on the return journey. When they reached London she couldn't believe she had heard aright when Alex said he would drop her back at George's flat.

'I have a business meeting to go to in the morning and I need time tonight to prepare what I am going to say, so I won't be very good company,' he explained.

'All my make-up and things are at your flat,' she protested.

'You can come and collect them some time tomorrow,' he told her brusquely as he lifted her suitcase out from the back of the Alvis and handed it to her.

'Collect them? What on earth do you mean, Alex?'

'George will be home in a couple of days' time, so you'll need to get things ready for him. Can you come and collect your stuff in the evening?' he added crisply, ignoring all her questions as he slipped back behind the wheel and put the car into gear ready to drive away.

Christabel didn't answer. She felt too choked by tears to trust her voice. She had no idea what had happened between them that was making him react in such a way and too much pride to question his decision.

Whatever could her mother have said to him that had made him change towards her so suddenly? she wondered, feeling bewildered and utterly distraught. It was as if Alex had no feelings for her or her welfare at all. He was virtually throwing her out on to the street.

As all her expectations of marriage to Alex came crashing down around her she was now positively looking forward to George coming out of prison.

Chapter Fifteen

Christabel soon discovered that prison life had changed George. Gone was his easy-going, happy-go-lucky approach to life. He was moody, bitter and increasingly short-tempered. An added blow to his pride was the fact that the understudy, who had taken over his part in the theatre, had proved to be such a good actor that it had been decided to keep him on in the role. George was offered an understudy part; when he turned it down his contract was terminated.

Christabel suspected the decision had been made by Alex but she said nothing. She'd neither seen nor spoken to him since their weekend in Liverpool. When she had gone round to his flat the following evening she'd found that the locks had been changed and she was unable to get in. Two days later a courier had arrived with all her belongings; she'd looked in vain to see if there was a note inside from Alex, but there wasn't one.

Now that George was home Christabel felt as if she was living under a cloud that was becoming ever darker. Invariably, he was under the influence of alcohol and his mood was morose and argumentative. Often he stayed in bed until midday and then mooched around the flat half-dressed, finding fault with everything she did.

Because he was no longer going to the theatre he sat in a dejected trance, drinking whisky and fiddling with his wireless, searching out new stations, until she felt that she could scream from listening to the weird distorted sounds, high-pitched shrieks and other strange, oscillating noises.

She tried to ignore what was happening by playing records, often the same ones, over and over on her gramophone, and playing them so loudly that the loudspeaker sent the sound of jazz echoing into every corner of the flat.

Their nerves were stretched to breaking point and they quarrelled incessantly. Neither of them, it seemed, could do right in the other's eyes. Often Christabel would put on her coat and walk the streets, wondering what to do for the best.

The answer came in a way she'd never even contemplated. She returned one afternoon to find George frantically packing his belongings into suitcases.

'Collect up what you can of your things, we've got to get out as quickly as possible,' he told her. 'I've not paid the rent for months and the landlord is sending the bailiffs round; they'll grab anything they can lay their hands on.'

'Where are we going?'

George paused and looked up from what he was doing. 'I'm going back home, but I don't know what you are going to do,' he told her bluntly.

Ten minutes later they were both standing on the pavement outside.

'Here', he fished in his pocket and brought out a crumpled five-pound note, 'this will help tide you over. Take care of yourself,' he added as he hailed a taxi.

Christabel felt shocked. George didn't want her, Alex had changed the locks on his flat, so what on earth was she going to do? she wondered. She didn't have a job or even enough money to rent a room, so it was impossible for her stay on in London. There was only one thing she could do, and that was to go back home.

Her mother seemed rather surprised to see her, but Christabel explained her visit by saying that she hadn't been feeling well and thought she needed a holiday.

'Oh, I thought you'd come because your friend is staying here for a few days,' her mother commented, giving her a shrewd look.

'My friend?' Christabel looked puzzled.

'Yes, dear. That rather nice young man you brought down from London.'

The colour drained from Christabel's face. 'Do you mean Alex Taylor?'

'That's right! He's been such a wonderful help and support to Lilian, that I sometimes wonder how she would ever have got through this dreadful divorce business without him,' Mabel commented.

'You're talking in riddles, Mother. What divorce?'

'Lilian and Dennis, of course dear. I thought I told you about it when you were here. Didn't you see it in the newspaper? The *Liverpool Echo* had a lovely picture of Lilian.'

'It wasn't in the London papers,' Christabel told her.

'What a pity, it was such a lovely one. Alex went to court with her. He's been such a tower of strength, and so attentive ever since. He's been taking Lilian out and about to try and take her mind off what she's been through,' Mrs Montgomery went on guilelessly, completely unaware that each word was like a knife turning inside Christabel.

'Where are they now?' Christabel interrupted, cutting short her mother's burbling.

'They've taken little Marlene over to Wallasey. Your Aunt Agnes hasn't been too well and I sent her over a pot of quince jelly because it always was a favourite of hers. Our own mother always used to give it to us when we were children if we weren't feeling well and I thought it might bring back memories for Agnes and cheer her up. I daresay she already has some in her own store cupboard that she's made herself, but it was about the only thing I could think of . . .'

'When will they be back?'

'Oh, they'll be home in time for dinner and it will be quite a surprise for them to find you here!'

'Yes, it will, Mother. You won't say a word to either of them, will you? Would it be OK if I went up to my room and stayed there until dinner time? I'm so tired.'

Mabel looked bewildered. 'Yes, dear, if that's what you want to do.'

Christabel spent a long time deciding what she would put on. She wanted to look glamorous enough to impress Alex, and put Lilian into the shade. Yet, at the same time, Christabel thought, she didn't want to rouse her mother's suspicions that there was a feud developing between her and Lilian. All her memories of what had happened when she'd brought Dennis home had been revived.

It had only been a question of her pride being hurt when Dennis had taken up with Lilian, but this time it was different. At her age, it was high time she was married and settled down, she thought grimly, and Alex was the man she wanted to marry.

She heard Lilian and Alex return, and her sister's simpering laugh and Alex's deep chuckle at something Marlene had said. She pictured them all together in the room downstairs as Marlene had her supper and said goodnight to them all before Lilian took her upstairs and tucked her into bed.

She gave Lilian time to go back down again

and to relay any messages from Aunt Agnes to her mother, and for all of them to sit down at the dinner table, before she put in an appearance.

'Hello, everyone!' Christabel paused dramatically in the doorway and felt elated as she saw the look of shock on both their faces.

She had chosen a knee-skimming slinky red dress and draped a black silk scarf at the neckline and she knew she looked sensational. Her gaze rested on Alex, curious to see his reaction. She was not disappointed. There was open admiration in his dark eyes, and his smile was so warm and intimate that for a moment it was as if they were the only two people in the room.

Reassured, she accepted a glass of sherry and joined in the exchange of family small talk. Throughout the meal, however, she was conscious of the closeness between Lilian and Alex. They were sitting side by side, and it was as if there was an aura around them that separated them from everyone else at the table. Each subtle touch or sideways glance between them revealed their feelings for each other and Christabel's heart sank. It became increasingly obvious to her that she had lost her hold on Alex.

Nevertheless, she was determined to make a stand and, as soon as she managed to get Lilian on her own, she accused her of trying to steal Alex away from her.

'What on earth do you mean?' Lilian gasped her blue-grey eyes wide with surprise.

'It wouldn't be the first time!'

The colour drained from Lilian's face. 'Are you by any chance referring to Dennis?'

'You know damn well that I am,' Christabel retorted.

'You are more than welcome to have Dennis back, Chrissy,' Lilian told her sweetly.

Christabel ignored her jibe. She knew she was on the point of making a fool of herself unless she was careful. It was always the same when she quarrelled with Lilian. Her sister always remained cool and calm and sweetly docile, yet at the same time inflicted spiteful barbs that not only found their mark with unerring accuracy, but also managed to sting her into reckless retaliation and say things she bitterly regretted afterwards.

This time, however, she wasn't going to be drawn into saying anything she might rue later on. Alex meant so much to her that she was determined to keep cool and win.

Christabel laid her plans carefully. During the week, Alex went back to London. The play George had once had a part in was on each night at the King's Theatre and because Alex took his responsibilities as producer very seriously he felt it was imperative that he should be there as often as possible.

In his absence, Christabel regaled them by saying what a good friend he had been to her

173

after George, the actor she had been house-keeper to, had been arrested.

'Arrested?' Lilian looked surprised.

'We knew nothing of this!'

Lilian and her mother both spoke at once, their faces registering concern and dismay.

Christabel sighed, bit her lip, and pretended to look embarrassed. 'George was arrested the day of the Cup Final at Wembley. Quite by accident, he and some others got caught up in some sort of skirmish, and when the police found that George was carrying a hip flask, they arrested him on the grounds of being drunk and disorderly. He wasn't, of course,' she stated emphatically.

Her mother looked shocked. 'They actually sent him to prison?'

'Yes. For eighteen months.'

'Oh, Christabel! Why on earth didn't you write and tell us at the time, my dear? Why didn't you come home?' her mother exclaimed aghast.

'I was too upset to think clearly. Anyway, Alex said I could stay with him until George was free . . .' Her voice trailed off as she dabbed at her eyes.

'How on earth could you do that? Alex told me that he has only a one-bedroom apartment!' Lilian exclaimed.

Christabel didn't answer, but the knowing look she directed at Lilian made her sister colour up.

That had given her something to think about, Christabel thought as she saw the jealous gleam in her sister's eyes. It didn't need any further explanation to let Lilian know that she and Alex had not only been living together but had also been lovers.

It made her feel good. She hoped Lilian was hurting inside as much as she was. One way or another she was determined to win Alex back, and even if it meant causing Lilian distress, she was prepared to do it.

Christabel smiled to herself, remembering how their father had described it as the act of an impulsive child when Lilian had married Dennis Taylor and now, she told herself, Lilian was acting the same way over Alex and it was really only infatuation on her part.

That evening, when Lilian was not present at dinner, she learned that she had gone up to London to be with Alex and that she'd taken Marlene with her. Christabel decided it was time for more direct action. If Lilian wouldn't listen to her, then she would have to try and get her mother on her side and convince her that Alex was not a suitable companion for Lilian.

Her mother sighed. 'I will try talking to her, of course,' she agreed. 'I certainly don't want her marrying him on the rebound from that other terrible man. In fact, after what you've told me, Christabel, I'm not at all sure that I should have Alex Taylor in my house ever again. Perhaps when they come back from London we can think of some diplomatic way of telling him that he is no longer welcome here.'

They were saved from having to carry out what would have been, for both of them, a most unpleasant task by the arrival of a letter from Lilian a couple of days later. Its London postmark set alarm bells ringing in both their minds.

Mabel waited until she had finished eating her bacon and egg and was on her second cup of tea before she opened it. She scanned it quickly before emitting a tiny shriek of dismay and then passed it across the table to Christabel.

Christabel took the sheet of notepaper from her mother's shaking hands and read it with a mixture of shock and disbelief.

Dearest Mother,

By the time you receive this Alex and I will be married and on our way to America. We're taking Marlene with us because we intend to make a home there for a while.

I'm sure now that Christabel is back home she will take every care of you.

Wish us luck!

Your ever loving daughter,
LILIAN

Christabel fought back the sour taste in her mouth as the words seared themselves on her brain. She wanted to scrunch the letter into a ball and throw it down on the table in disgust, but instead she passed it back to her mother without a word.

'This is a terrible shock,' her mother murmured as she took the note and read it through again. 'I don't know what Lewis is going to say when he hears about it.'

'I'm afraid there is nothing he can do,' Christabel said resignedly.

'He will be so worried, though. He has already explained that business is not good and he is finding it hard enough to maintain this house as well as his own. I dread the thought of having to go and live with him, but it may come to that because he's said I can't afford to employ a full-time housekeeper and I'm certainly not able to cope on my own.'

Christabel went over and put her arms round her mother. 'You won't have to do that now, will you? I'll take care of you,' she promised, kissing her on the brow.

She'd not only lost Alex for good, Christabel thought sadly, but Lilian had also made it clear by going to live on the other side of the world that, as the spinster, she was the one who was now expected to stay at home and look after their increasingly frail and dependent mother.

Chapter Sixteen

1925 started badly for Christabel. A few days into the New Year her mother went down with a chill which developed into pneumonia and left her weak and lethargic. For several months she remained confined to the house, making no effort at all to pick up the threads of her life. She lost weight, she looked tired and drawn, and was so listless and disinterested in what was going on around her, that gradually, one by one, her few remaining friends stopped visiting.

Even when the weather improved she claimed that she felt too weary even to go window-shopping in the city centre with Christabel, something which at one time she'd loved to do. Instead, she stayed in her bedroom day-dreaming about the past or reading the letters she received from Lilian.

On arrival in America Alex had met up with an old colleague, Sam Baldwin, who had a financial interest in film-making, and he'd been instrumental in persuading Alex to move to Hollywood to produce a film he was backing.

For quite some time, apparently, Alex had predicted that films were destined to be the foremost entertainment of the future, so he had jumped at the opportunity to become involved in the new medium.

'Lilian's description about all the marvels and intricacies involved in making a film is childlike in its naïveté,' Christabel told her mother. 'All this rigmarole about sets, cameras and cutting-room floors, is so garbled that I'm quite sure she has no idea what she's talking about. Lilian never has understood anything mechanical which is why she was never interested in learning to drive a motor car.'

Once they had moved to Hollywood, Lilian's letters became less enthusiastic about America. She was desperately homesick and lonely and complained that most of the time she only had Marlene for company. Time and time again she complained that Alex was so engrossed in his new life that she felt neglected. It was a state of affairs that brought a degree of satisfaction to Christabel but heart-rending distress to her mother.

The days came and went, and Christabel found she was becoming almost as lethargic as her mother and unable to find the enthusiasm to reconstruct her life. It was as if she was lulled into a state of complacency that left her impervious to everything around her.

She'd always taken it for granted that as a result of the shipping business that had been her father's and was now being run by Lewis, the family were comfortably off, but now Lewis was continually warning both her mother and herself that they would have to start making some changes.

One of the first economies Lewis insisted on was that the dark-blue Austin 12 motorcar that had always been the Montgomerys' pride and joy would have to be sold.

Christabel had enjoyed driving it and it had been one way of getting her mother out and about. Now, as her mother insisted on staying indoors, saying that walking tired her, Christabel spent more and more of her time visiting Violet and Kay and then taking Kay out.

She enjoyed Kay's company and took a special interest in her progress at school. She encouraged her to read and helped her with her hobbies. Anything was better than having to listen to her mother either worrying because she had not heard from Lilian, or worrying because she had, and the news was not to her liking.

Lilian eventually wrote to tell them that the film Alex had helped to produce was finished, and was receiving rave reviews from the critics. Christabel once again felt a flicker of alarm about how aimless her own life was apart from her interest in Kay.

Lilian's letters suddenly were filled with glowing accounts about the film stars she was meeting, and the social life she and Alex were enjoying. As letter after letter arrived full of details of the Beverley Hills parties, the First Night premières, the lavish cocktail parties, the exciting soirées, the glamorous poolside barbecues and the fabulous balls, Christabel felt envy, jealousy and anger churning inside her. She should be the one in Hollywood, being escorted to these events by Alex – not Lilian.

Instead, she was vegetating in Liverpool and achieving nothing. Love and marriage seemed as far away as it had ever been and she felt more frustrated and lonelier than ever. Her chagrin reached a new height when a letter arrived from Lilian telling them that she was pregnant again.

Mabel immediately became dewy-eyed and sentimental. She talked incessantly about her own pregnancies, and about Lilian's babyhood in particular, because Lilian had been the prettiest, the cutest, the smartest and the most loveable of her three children.

Christabel tried to shut out her mother's reminiscing but it was not easy. Mabel would constantly find things that reminded her of when her own children were small, and would dwell on what lovely little girls Kay and Marlene were. She deplored the fact that Christabel was not married with a family of her own.

'Lilian must come back here to England, to her own home, before it is too late for her to travel. I don't want my grandchild to be born

181

in America; I want it to be born here, in Liverpool,' Mabel kept saying.

'Why? This isn't their home now; they have their own place in America,' Christabel pointed out.

'That has nothing to do with it,' her mother protested and insisted on writing to her and ordering her to come home.

She became extremely agitated when Lilian wrote back and said that was impossible because Alex was already involved with his next film and they wanted to be together when the baby was born. Minutes after reading this, she had a massive heart attack and collapsed, still clutching Lilian's letter.

Christabel immediately sent for the doctor although, from her nursing experience, she knew that there was nothing he could do; she also summoned Lewis, who was stunned and shocked at the news.

They telegraphed Lilian although they knew she was hardly likely to return for her mother's funeral. Lewis took control and arranged the service and interment and afterwards, once again, reminded Christabel that there would have to be changes. He had delayed them as long as possible because of the state of their mother's health but now the large family home would have to be sold.

In a state bordering on panic, Christabel began to weigh up her own personal situation and carefully to consider all her options. She wished she had kept up with her friends in Liverpool, people of her own age who would understand her dilemma and be able to offer valid advice about what she should do.

The idea of going back to nursing sent a shiver through her. Since coming back home to live she'd come to appreciate the difference a comfortable home could make. A hospital environment with its stringent rules and rigid routine was certainly not the sort of lifestyle she ever wanted again.

In an attempt to cheer her up, Lewis invited her to a dinner held by one of the shipping companies. There she happened to meet an old school friend, Jessica Thompson. She seemed surprised when Christabel said she was living at home even though her mother had died and asked her if she would be interested in taking a trip to Argentina with her.

Christabel stared at her in astonishment. It seemed as if Fate was holding out a helping hand and helping her to reach a decision about what she ought to do with her life

'How long did you have in mind?' she asked tentatively. 'You do mean as a holiday?'

'More or less.' Jessica smiled. 'If you are not working, it wouldn't matter how long it was, would it?'

'No, not really,' Christabel admitted.

Jessica sighed. 'I recently had an operation and my specialist is against me going back unless I have someone who has medical training with me, but I find the thought of hiring a stranger extremely off-putting. With an old friend like you, it would be quite different. It could be good fun, in fact! And you do have nursing experience, Christabel, so now, what do you think of the idea?'

'Why Argentina?'

'Well, I'm married now, to Freddy Newland, and he is part-owner of a polo club out there. I only came to England for my operation because I thought the treatment here would be better.'

'I see.' Christabel tried to sound non-committal, but her thoughts were spinning like a whirling dervish, she felt so excited. Freddy was about ten years older than her and she remembered him from when they'd all been members of the tennis club years ago.

'How about it, then, Chrissy?' Jessica's voice brought her back to the present. 'Nurse or travelling companion, or whatever you want to call yourself. You'll have a generous salary, a room of your own, your own maid and all expenses paid. As soon as I'm feeling fit again, I can promise you a super social whirl. You'll love it! Now, do say you're going to come with me?'

'Well . . .' She hesitated. She very much wanted to take up the challenge, and to set her life in motion again.

'I'm sailing from Liverpool in ten days' time, so you'll have to make your mind up pretty damn quick. Shall I go ahead and book your passage?'

'If you're quite sure you think it will work out.'

'Of course it will! It'll be absolutely perfect.'

'Then I'll come!'

'Wonderful!' Jessica hugged her enthusiastically. 'Here's my telephone number; get in touch if there is anything you need to know. I'll phone you and arrange final details.'

Lewis was astounded when Christabel broke the news to him. He begged her to think about it carefully before deciding. He even warned her that, if they didn't get on, she might find herself stranded in Argentina.

'I have thought about all that and if it doesn't work out, then I'll think of it as a holiday.'

'That's all very well, but shouldn't you find a place of your own here, first of all, so that you have somewhere to return to if things don't work out in Argentina?' he questioned.

'There simply isn't time for me to do that,' she pointed out. 'Jessica said they sail in a few days' time.'

'Couldn't you follow on afterwards?' he suggested.

'No, I have to travel with Jessica. That's the whole purpose of her inviting me – I'm to be her companion,' she pointed out. 'As a businessman, you must realise how important it is to keep your promises.'

'I do, but there is the question of our family home. There's all the furniture and possessions to be disposed of, as well as the property.'

'Couldn't you do it, Lewis? You are here on the spot and I'm sure Violet will help you. There's nothing at all that I want so you can sort out anything you would like to keep and then sell the rest or do whatever you want with it.'

Before she left Liverpool, Christabel disposed of anything of sentimental value. Dry eyed, she burned all letters and greetings cards she'd received over the years. As she watched them blacken and curl, before collapsing into a pile of grey ash, she felt a sense of freedom; it was as if she had finally released herself from the past.

As owner of one of the leading polo clubs in Buenos Aires, Freddy Newland held a unique place in the hierarchy of the local society. Whenever Jessica felt well enough they wined and dined with all the most important business people, as well as government officials and leading socialites, and on these occasions Christabel found she was being included.

In addition, she and Jessica were fêted by the many 'ladies only' clubs and societies. Jessica, who had met most of the ladies behind these organisations when she had been in Buenos Aires previously, played the field. She accepted invitations only if she considered a visit to be worthwhile. Otherwise she would decline, winning her hostess's commiserations when she explained she was not feeling strong enough to socialise.

If anyone noticed that her health rarely presented any problems for the more important social events of the season, or whenever there was a polo match in which her husband's team were participating, good manners prevented them from mentioning it.

For Christabel, the entire scenario was new and exciting. She had completely shaken off her lethargy and, like a butterfly emerging from a chrysalis, happily played her part as Jessica's attentive companion both at the many social gatherings and as a spectator at the polo field.

Her lack of knowledge of the sport was no handicap whatsoever. In fact, in some ways, she found it was an excellent opening gambit. There were always plenty of knowledgeable men on hand to instruct her on the intricacies of the game.

Within a few months of arriving in Argentina, Christabel had a working knowledge of such terms as 'chukkas' and 'divots', and could comment intelligently on the skill of each of the four players in Freddy's team, or even of those in the opposing team.

Christabel found that although it could be a wonderful existence at the Newlands' palatial home in the exclusive residential area on the outskirts of Buenos Aires, it very much depended on Jessica's mood as to how much she could participate in what was going on. Jessica preferred to reserve her energy for the social gatherings that followed rather than expend it watching polo, and she made it clear that Christabel was there to look after her and not simply to enjoy herself.

'Freddy said the other day that when we left England you looked like a middle-aged frump. More my nurse, than my companion,' Jessica commented a trifle maliciously one day as Christabel helped her dress to attend an evening function. 'Now look at the difference! You are so full of energy that I feel tired out just watching you!'

Christabel smiled. She did sometimes feel as if she'd taken on a new lease of life – at least until she was in the middle of an interesting conversation with Freddy or someone and Jessica demanded attention. This immediately brought her down to earth and made her realise that she was there in the capacity of a companion, which was only a glorified servant and not really as one of their friends.

'How long did you say you'd been back with your mother?' Jessica frowned.

'Too long! I lost track of time. It's hard to believe it now, but after Lilian went off with Alex, I almost felt as if my life were over,' Christabel admitted.

'I can understand that. If I lost Freddy, I'd feel there was nothing left worth living for and I'm sure it would be the same for him even though I must be something of a burden to him in my state of health.'

Christabel recalled their conversation a couple of weeks later when Jessica was rushed to hospital for an emergency operation. Freddy was distraught and sought solace in drink.

Night after night he sat nursing a bottle of whisky, refilling his glass over and over again. For Jessica's sake, Christabel tried to restrain him but he took no notice. Finally, in desperation, she took all the bottles of whisky from the drinks cabinet and hid them in her bedroom in the hope that it would give him time to sober up before Jessica came home.

It was the last place she thought Freddy would think of looking for them but she was wrong. Sometime after she was in bed that night he came bursting into her room accusing her of stealing his whisky. He was already drunk and she assumed he must have been drinking the brandy which she hadn't bothered to hide, knowing that his preference was for whisky.

She lay very still hoping he would think she was asleep and would go away, but he was not to be deterred. Grabbing hold of the bedclothes he pulled them off her and threw them to the ground. Then he grabbed hold of her. He was strong and well muscled and although she fought like a wild cat she was no match for him.

He completely ignored her plea to let her go, and her offer to return his whisky if he would leave her alone.

'I intend to have my whisky and you as well,' he told her contemptuously. 'Who the hell do you think you are, Christabel, trying to dictate what I can and cannot do in my own home?'

Bruised and sore, Christabel stayed in her room the whole of the next day, asking the maid to bring her meals up to her as she felt unwell. She felt horrified by what had happened and didn't want to have to face Freddy again on her own. That night she pulled a chest across the room to barricade her door in case he tried to get in again.

Two days later, Jessica came home from hospital. She insisted on coming down to dinner that night even though Christabel thought she ought to rest and have her meal brought up to her.

She looked very pale and barely ate anything. She waited until the end of their meal before levelling her accusations. Her anger, heightened by her sense of inadequacy because of her illness, was frightening in its intensity.

Her onslaught took Freddy and Christabel by surprise. 'You're imagining things, or else you've been listening to gossip from the domestics, Jessica,' Freddy blustered.

'So Manuel is a liar when he says he saw you coming out of Christabel's room well after midnight?'

'Servants gossip. They put the wrong interpretation on things . . .'

'So you have never been into her bedroom?' Jessica pressed a hand to her chest as if in pain. 'I want the truth, Freddy.' Her face was ashen, her vivid red lipstick made her mouth look like a scarlet gash, and her eyes were darts of sharp light as she turned to look at Christabel.

'Come, darling,' Freddy placed a protective arm round her shoulders, 'you are over-wrought. This illness has taken a lot out of you.'

Jessica pushed him away. 'Don't you dare touch me! I don't want you near me until I get to the bottom of this. What have you to say, Christabel? Was Manuel telling the truth? Did he see Freddy coming out of your room?'

Christabel bit her lip. At first, she had decided to say nothing, but now she felt the need to defend herself. 'Probably,' she admitted. 'I had hidden his whisky because he was drinking far too much and he came in to get it and . . . and he raped me.'

'Raped you!' The scorn in Jessica's voice brought the colour rushing to Christabel's cheeks. 'You mean you enticed him in there! The two of you have been having an affair behind my back.'

'Look, my darling,' Freddy intervened quickly, raising his hands suppliantly, 'you know that is utter nonsense because you are the only woman I have ever truly loved,' he told her glibly, avoiding Christabel's eyes. 'You know I would never dream of doing anything like that, knowing how much it would hurt you.'

'Only because you know that if you did, I would throw you out and you'd be penniless,' Jessica retorted scathingly. 'Have you told Christabel that? Does she know it's my money that provides the lavish lifestyle you enjoy?'

'Why should I tell Christabel about our private affairs? There is nothing between us. She means nothing to me. I've only treated her as one of the family because you regard her as a close personal friend.'

'That was in the past. From now on, she's no friend of mine!' Her anger still blazing and her features distorted, she turned on Christabel. 'You betrayed my trust,' she fumed, 'that is something I can never forgive. You know how I feel about Freddy and yet, behind my back, you became his lover.'

Christabel waited for Freddy to admit what had happened, but he remained mute and avoided her eyes. Christabel felt her insides tighten and she fought back the sour taste in her mouth.

'I'm sure he was quite ready to take what was on offer,' Jessica sneered. 'He always has had a penchant for servants. A bit of rough, if you know what I mean,' she added coarsely.

Christabel bit her lip, her face flaming with anger and embarrassment. Jessica might be justified in her onslaught on Freddy, but she refused to take the blame for his actions.

Stung, she appealed to him to put the record straight. 'Tell her, Freddy! Tell Jessica the truth about what happened.'

'For Christ's sake, Christabel, stop making a mountain out of a molehill. I was worried out of my mind over Jessica, and I turned to you for a word of comfort and reassurance. You took advantage of that and, momentarily, I strayed. It's something I bitterly regret, so let's leave it at that.'

She stared at him in disbelief, unable to credit what she was hearing. 'Not a word of that is true,' she gasped.

'Please!' Jessica pressed a hand to her forehead. 'I've had all I can take. Pack your things and go.'

'Go! What do you mean?'

'I should have thought that was plain enough. You are dismissed. I don't want you under our roof another minute!'

'You can't just turn me out,' Christabel said indignantly, 'I have nowhere I can go.'

'That's your problem, Christabel; it's something you should have thought about before you started carrying on with my husband.'

'Freddy, tell your wife that I am telling the truth; admit that you broke into my room and raped me. I'm being treated no better than a servant caught stealing,' Christabel said desperately.

He shook his head. 'You know quite well that what happened was your entire fault, Christabel,' he said smugly. 'Jessica controls the purse strings, so there is nothing I can do to change things.'

Chapter Seventeen

The moment her trunk was packed, Christabel called a cab, and moved into a hotel in the centre of Buenos Aires. She felt humiliated and angry about what had happened.

She took a long bath, changed her clothes and then ventured down to the hotel restaurant where she ordered a light meal and a glass of wine. As she sipped her wine she tried to sum up the situation and decide what she was going to do next, because she was apprehensive about her future.

Although she'd saved every penny of her wages since she'd been with the Newlands, she knew quite well that it wouldn't last all that long once she had to start living on it. It was important that she reserved enough for her fare back to Liverpool and that would account for a sizeable chunk of it.

Did she want to go back to Liverpool, she mused? While she was on the same side of the Atlantic as Lilian she wondered if she should pay her a visit. Lewis had written to say that Lilian had miscarried the baby she'd been expecting and, remembering how despondent she'd felt after losing her own baby, even though that had been her decision, she thought Lilian might welcome a familiar face, someone from her own family.

It would mean meeting up with Alex again, of course. Still, that was all in the past. It was hard to believe how besotted she'd been about him. After her recent ordeal at the hands of Freddy she had no interest in him – or in any other man, for that matter.

The distance from Buenos Aires to Hollywood was far greater than she'd anticipated, and by the time she'd arrived and found where the Taylors lived, she was almost penniless.

Alex answered the door and for a moment he stared as if seeing a ghost.

'Christabel?' His voice was a mixture of surprise, disbelief and apprehension as his eyes travelled from her face down to the suitcases piled up at her feet.

'You've taken us by surprise, but you'd better come in. I take it you have come to stay,' he added dryly as he helped carry her luggage into the hallway.

Hearing their voices, Lilian called out, 'Who is it, Alex? We're not expecting anyone.'

'It's me, Lilian,' Christabel answered before he could do so. 'I thought it was time I paid you a visit.'

'Christabel! It can't be! Why on earth didn't you let us know you were coming?' Lilian gasped as she came rushing out into the hall.

'It's so wonderful to see you,' she enthused as

they kissed and hugged each other. 'I've been feeling really homesick recently since . . . since . . .' She struggled for words but couldn't go on.

'Lewis wrote and told me about the baby and I am so sorry,' Christabel said softly.

Lilian swallowed hard and then regained her composure. She grabbed hold of Christabel's hands, holding them tightly as she held her at arm's length and stared at her in disbelief. 'My God, Chrissy, I do believe you're even thinner than when I last saw you!' she exclaimed.

Christabel shrugged nonchalantly. She had to agree that, compared to Lilian, she certainly was slim. Both Lilian and Alex looked overfed and dissipated. Since she'd last seen him he'd grown a moustache which bristled above his top lip like a baby hedgehog.

'Marlene, come and greet your Aunt Christabel. I don't suppose you remember each other after all this time,' Lilian added. 'Come along, poppet,' she urged, pulling forward a plump little seven-year-old with light auburn hair curled into the same face-framing style as her own. 'Say hello to your Aunt Christabel.'

'Come, come, a kiss will do,' Alex admonished ebulliently as Marlene held out her skirts and gave a wobbly curtsy. 'She's not auditioning you for a film part, so you don't have to try and make an impression!' he added with a laugh.

Over dinner that night, Alex's meteoric rise as a film mogul was a much-discussed topic and Lilian was so full of news about all the famous people they met that for a moment Christabel felt envious.

'America is such a forward-looking country that there are a great many outstanding opportunities for those who are prepared to take risks or who have initiative,' Alex stated pompously. 'Hollywood in particular has so much to offer the entrepreneur.'

'Perhaps you should stay here with us and find out for yourself,' Lilian suggested.

Christabel bit her lip and didn't answer. America might be a new beginning, but would it bring her fulfillment? Would it ease the deep ache in her heart? she wondered. Seeing Marlene again brought back vivid memories of her own child. Not for the first time she wondered if she had made a terrible mistake in giving up her baby.

'With your figure, Chrissy, you could make a mint in films,' Lilian went on. 'Isn't that right, Alex?'

'Indeed, although it would take quite some time to train you before you would be able to get a part since you have no acting experience whatsoever,' Alex pointed out.

'Well, that's out of the question, then,' Christabel smiled, 'I would need a job that paid me right from the start, if I am to stay on here for any length of time. Do either of you have any suggestions?' The pace of life in Hollywood would be even greater than it had been in

Buenos Aires. There would be so much happening, so many new faces all around her, that her days would be filled. Would that ensure that she would be able to forget all her other worries and frustrations? she wondered. 'I've had enough of nursing and being at everyone's beck and call,' she added.

'That's a pity, because the job I was going to suggest would entail you being a jack of all trades,' Alex told her. 'I was about to suggest you became my PA. I think she'd fill the bill, don't you, Lilian?'

'PA? What on earth is that?'

'Alex means you'd be his personal assistant,' Lilian explained.

'You mean his secretary? Oh, I could never do that. I don't write shorthand and I have no typing ability.'

'He already has a secretary. No, he means someone to do all the fiddly little jobs he hasn't time to do; someone to meet visitors when they call to see him and he can't be bothered to see them; someone to smooth the ruffled feathers of the actors and actresses when he rubs them up the wrong way.'

'I'm sure you would be perfect for the job,' Alex agreed. 'Shall we say you'll give it a try?'

'I'd have to find somewhere to stay first,' Christabel demurred.

'Nonsense, you can stay with us; it will be wonderful having you around and we will be able to catch up on all the family news when you're not working,' Lilian pointed out. 'Lewis's letters are always so brief and Violet never writes at all. I did hope that Kay and Marlene would write to each other now that they are old enough to do so, but Marlene says she can't even remember her cousin. I'm sure Kay must remember Marlene – after all, she is three years older, but then they haven't seen each other for so long,' Lilian sighed.

'That's another reason why I want you to stay, Christabel, even if it is only for a few months. It's so long since we were last together that I feel isolated from the family. Sometimes I feel I want to come back home.'

'You've made plenty of friends here and you have a busy life,' Christabel reminded her. 'Perhaps what you need is a break; a holiday back in Liverpool might do the trick.'

'Yes, that's true, but of course there is always Marlene's career to be considered and it might hold her back if we did that.'

'Marlene's career? Heaven's, she's only a child!' Christabel smiled.

'I know, but she's already on the way to stardom. Do you remember Jackie Coogan who co-starred with Charlie Chaplin in the film *The Kid*? Well, that's what I want for Marlene. She has so much talent that with Alex's connections, it should be possible for her to be a child film star like Jackie Coogan was.'

'Well,' Christabel floundered, 'you know more about these things than I do.'

'A year or so later two young sisters Dorothy and Lilian Gish appeared as Henrietta and Louise in *Orphans of the Storm*,' Lilian went on, warming to her theme. 'I know Marlene has just as much talent and I'm determined that one day she'll play a leading role and have her name up in lights. In fact,' she added proudly, 'I've been grooming her for stardom.'

'I suppose you always dress her in pretty little dresses with matching ribbon bows in her hair like she's wearing now?' Christabel remarked.

'That's only part of it. I've spent hours encouraging her to do a little dance and to hold out her skirts prettily as she makes a curtsy and a bow. I've also instructed her on how to pose and look coy as she smiles for the camera and I've encouraged her to "perform" for the benefit of our friends whenever they come for dinner. I'll get her to recite the little poems and sing the little ditties I've taught her for you.'

With Alex there to introduce her to everybody and to ensure she understood what was expected of her, Christabel's early days at the film studio went quite smoothly.

At first she had difficulty in adjusting to the American idiom, and their different way of thinking. They were all so articulate, so detailed with their descriptions, and so voluble. They regarded her as overly reticent and far too restrained and controlled.

When Alex asked her to check over some publicity copy for the film he wanted to promote, everyone, except Alex, was highly critical of the changes she made. They thought her writing was far too clinical and that it was lacking in fervour. Her words, or so the advertising panel claimed, were devoid of passion.

'Christabel, it may be in perfect English but it has no selling power,' the Director of Promotions told her.

Devastated, she turned to Alex for an explanation, but he only shrugged aside the criticisms that had been levied at her work.

'Take no notice; they would criticise you no matter what you wrote,' he said dismissively. 'We made a great team once, Chrissy,' he added, 'so perhaps we will do so again, you'll see!'

'I think you've got it all wrong, Alex. The people in the Promotions department don't like the way I've handled the copy and I know they want me out. They criticise my words, and my approach – everything I write or do, in fact. They say—'

He waved his hand, silencing her and dismissing her words in one gesture. 'I've already told you it's of no account.'

'How can you say that? If I can't hold down this job, then I have no alternative but to go back to Liverpool.'

'No, no, no! That's what I'm trying to tell you. Think of being my PA as the bottom rung! From now on you are going to move so high up the ladder that people will be writing eulogies about you instead of you struggling to write words of praise about them.'

Christabel looked completely bewildered. 'What on earth are you talking about, Alex?'

'You. You are going to be the biggest discovery of the decade. In fact, you are going to be the *star* in my next film.'

'You really are crazy, Alex. I can't act. I don't even like having my photograph taken.'

'You have the sort of perfect cut-glass English accent that all Americans envy and admire,' he told her. 'You also have the cool, sophisticated manner that the camera loves.' He rubbed his hands together. 'I'm planning for you to play the leading lady in my next picture!'

'Leading lady, at my age? You simply aren't making sense, Alex. It's a preposterous idea!! Why don't you spend your energy on promoting Marlene's career as a film star? Lilian is longing to see her name up in lights.'

'Mmm?' He frowned dismissively. 'Time enough for that.' He placed a hand under Christabel's chin and, turning her face sideways, studied her profile critically. 'Don't worry, I'm sure the make-up department will be able to work wonders,' he assured her. 'They'll be able to transform you so that you can look any age from sweet sixteen upwards,' he teased.

Christabel looked sceptical. 'Why should you want them to do that when there are so many beautiful women already available here in

Hollywood and many of them are already established as accomplished actresses?'

'I repeat, you have the English elegance, the clear voice and faultless accent, as well as the cool bearing. What is more, it is all without any visible effort because it is the way you have been brought up; it all comes quite naturally to you.'

'That is something that anyone can achieve with the right training if they have acting ability.'

Alex shook his head. 'Believe me, no matter how hard they try, the results always look contrived.'

Christabel smiled thinly. What Alex was telling her was music to her ears, balm to her jaded feelings, but she remained dubious. 'Why have you decided to try and make me a star? Why not Lilian? She's as English as I am.'

Alex laughed uproariously. 'She may be, but she's hardly leading-lady material.'

'And I am?'

'You have elegance, presence, bearing, the ability to assimilate instructions and accept constructive criticism. Christabel, if you put yourself in my hands, I'll make sure you reach the top. I'll make a *star* of you. Your name will be up in lights outside every cinema in England as well as here in America.'

Her thoughts were in complete turmoil. Outwardly she appeared to remain perfectly calm, but her nerves were zinging. She studied

Alex speculatively. He was still attractive and still had the ability to make her pulse quicken.

'Don't take too long to make your mind up, the opportunity won't last for ever.'

She'd been down that path once before, she reminded herself, and her nerves had been stripped raw when he had deserted her for her sister. For that reason, she told herself firmly, this must be a business arrangement and nothing more.

In her heart she was doubtful if that was going to be possible, even if he did agree with her on that point. Alex was so charismatic! There was an animal magnetism about him which she automatically responded to no matter how hard she tried to avoid doing so. If they were working together, then would their constant closeness cause problems?

She didn't need to take time to think, she told herself sternly. For Lilian's sake she couldn't risk anything happening between them.

Even so, she found it took a tremendous effort to shake her head, signifying that she was not prepared to go along with his proposition.

Chapter Eighteen

That evening when Christabel broke the news to Lilian and Marlene that she had decided to return to England, they both pleaded with her to stay on in Hollywood.

'I thought you were happy living here and working for Alex,' Lilian said in surprise.

'It's been a wonderful experience and I've most certainly enjoyed staying with you, Lilian.'

'Then why are you leaving?'

'Suddenly, for some reason, I feel homesick,' Christabel explained. 'You know how it is, you said yourself that sometimes you feel you'd like to go back to England.'

'I want you to stay so that you can see me become a film star,' Marlene sobbed, flinging her arms round Christabel's neck and hugging her tightly.

'I will still be able to go and see the film you are in at the cinema in Liverpool,' Christabel pointed out.

'Will you?' Marlene's tears stopped immediately and she gave a beaming smile. 'You promise?'

'I promise, and I'll take Kay to see it as well so that she knows you have become a film star.'

'I didn't know they had cinemas over there, Aunt Chrissy.'

'Yes, they have several, and I will make sure I see your film,' Christabel assured her.

'The reason I didn't know was because I can't remember ever being there.' Marlene pouted.

'You have been there, but of course you were just a baby, so that is why you can't remember. Perhaps one day your mummy and daddy will bring you again on a visit,' Christabel told her.

She looked questioningly at Lilian as she spoke but Lilian shrugged her shoulders non-committally.

Alex made no comment at all about her leaving and, much to her annoyance, Christabel found she had to ask him for the wages that were due to her.

'By rights you should forfeit your wages because you haven't worked out your notice,' he told her.

'I understand, but I would like to leave immediately.'

'The decision is yours, of course,' he said curtly.

'I need my wages, otherwise I haven't enough money to pay my fare back to England.'

'You could always work your passage, I imagine.'

Christabel frowned. 'Are you deliberately trying to make things awkward for me?' she flared.

'I thought it might help you to see sense and

to realise you could do very well for yourself here in Hollywood, if you were prepared to take my advice.'

'I've already made my mind up, Alex, and I've decided that I am returning to Liverpool and I want to do so as soon as possible,' she repeated stubbornly.

'Ah well,' he shrugged his shoulders, 'in that case, I'd better help you, I suppose. Here you are, then.' He opened his wallet and drew out a wad of notes and handed them to her.

'What's all this? It's far more than what is due to me.'

'The wages that are due to you certainly won't pay for your passage back to England,' he told her cryptically.

Christabel felt uneasy. She knew he was right but at the same time she didn't want to accept his money because she felt it placed her under an obligation to him. She had been intending to ask Lilian if she could loan her some money without Alex knowing.

'Go on, take it,' Alex thrust the bundle of notes into her hand, 'call it a loan, if that makes you feel any better,' he added as he turned on his heel and walked away before she could say anything.

Three days later, Christabel was on her way back to Liverpool. Lilian and Marlene came to wave her off, both of them saying tearfully how much they were going to miss her.

'Mind you write and let us know you've arrived safely, and from now on keep in touch,' Lilian told her.

'Don't forget to go and see my film, Aunty Chrissy,' Marlene called after her as she went up the gangway.

It was a bleak, cold crossing and Christabel spent a great deal of time in her small cabin mulling over her situation and wondering what to do when they eventually docked in Liverpool.

Although the money Alex had loaned her had paid for her passage, there was not very much left over to cover any extras, so she tried to be very frugal during the journey.

It also meant that once she reached her destination she would be virtually penniless. She knew her parents' home had been sold after her mother died, so she had nowhere to go unless she went straight to Lewis and Violet's and asked them if she could stay with them for a while.

It was a cold and grey late-November day when they docked in Liverpool and Christabel felt chilled to the bone after the warm sunshine of Hollywood. She had no idea what her next move should be. For several minutes she stood on the quayside trying to make up her mind whether to try and find a room or go straight to Lewis's.

Common sense prevailed; she didn't think it

was fair to descend on them without some prior warning. She was longing to see them, especially Kay, but now that she was back in Liverpool she wasn't at all sure that she wanted to do so right away.

They hadn't been in touch all the time she'd been in Hollywood. In fact, as far as she knew they probably thought she was still in Argentina unless Lilian had written to Lewis and told him that she was staying with them.

Now that she was back in familiar surroundings she was determined to stand on her own feet and make a life for herself and she wanted to do that before she went to see Lewis and Violet.

If she could manage to find herself a job, she'd have enough money to rent a small flat or some comfortable lodgings. That way she would be able to retain her independence and not have to rely on help from anyone.

The plan seemed sound but when she came to put it into practice she immediately met with difficulties. She had so little money she knew she could only stay in a hotel for a night or two at the very most and then she must look for cheap lodgings until she found a job and could afford something better.

Locating the sort of accommodation she wanted in a fairly respectable area proved impossible. The room she eventually rented in Dalrymple Street was not even as good as the one she'd had in Maggie Nelson's house when she'd been waiting for her baby to be born. It was small and squalid, the paper was peeling off the walls and there was an overwhelming smell of damp and decay.

The first night she was there she'd been eaten alive by fleas and the small red blisters that appeared on her arms and neck were visible for days afterwards.

At night when she was in bed, after she'd blown out the candle, the cockroaches came out but if she lighted the candle again they always scuttled away behind the cracks and torn wallpaper before she had a chance to catch them.

Finding a job of any kind proved to be equally daunting. There was so much unemployment in Liverpool and she had no special training or skills to offer aside from her nursing.

As the days became weeks what little money she'd had left over after paying her passage home had almost gone and she still hadn't found any work even though she had exhausted every avenue she could think of – except begging.

She knew she no longer looked smart and because of this she felt miserable. Her hair needed attention and her clothes needed washing but apart from managing to rinse out her underwear and drape it over the back of a chair to dry there was no way she could wash and iron anything else. Money was so short that she couldn't afford to take her clothes into a laundry.

As her living standards dropped so did her

hopes of finding a job. In the beginning she'd applied for office work and then at some of the high-class dress shops as a sales assistant. The story was always the same: they were laying off staff, not hiring them.

In the end she capitulated and applied for work at one of the Liverpool hospitals although she'd been determined never to do nursing again. The woman she spoke to looked at her in disbelief when she said she'd trained and was fully experienced.

'Really?' she said sceptically. 'So where was that and why did you leave?'

When Christabel told her that the hospital where she'd trained had been the military one at Hilbury and that it had closed at the end of the war, the woman lost interest.

'That's so long ago that you would probably need retraining as there have been so many medical advances and new ways of doing things since then,' she stated.

'Surely you must have some vacancies for nursing staff,' Christabel insisted.

'No,' the woman shook her head looking Christabel up and down in a disparaging way, 'we don't even want any ward maids or cleaners,' she said dismissively.

It had been the last straw. Christabel felt utterly depressed as she came away. She wondered what on earth she was going to do. She couldn't bring herself to stand in one of the queues outside the many soup kitchens that had been set up in some of the warehouses in the docks area for the unemployed, even though the smell as she walked by was tantalising.

For almost a week she managed to exist on tea and toast for breakfast, a cup of hot broth made from an Oxo cube at midday, and whatever she could find for the rest of the day. Her hunger was magnified because of the cooking smells that permeated from other rooms in the house. It made the life she'd known in Wilcock Court when Maggie Nelson had provided her with such appetising meals every day seem like heaven by comparison.

Memories of those days and the sad outcome dominated her thoughts and more and more she felt herself longing to see Lewis's little girl again. Kay would be ten now and she wondered if she had changed very much since she'd last seen her.

Once or twice she walked down the road where they lived hoping to catch a glimpse of Kay but she never did. The house looked so different from how she remembered it that she wondered if they were still living there.

One afternoon, shortly before Christmas, she plucked up the courage to knock on the door. The woman who answered was a complete stranger and she was too smartly dressed to be a servant.

Christabel asked if Mrs Violet Montgomery was at home and the woman shook her head.

'I can't help you,' she said and made to shut the door.

When Christabel put out a hand to stop her doing so the woman added firmly, 'I don't know who you are, but they don't live here any more.'

'Mr Montgomery is my brother, can you not tell me where they are living now?'

The stranger stared at her for a moment then said, 'Somewhere over in Wallasey, but I've forgotten the address. Rolleston something, I think it was.'

'Do you mean Rolleston Drive?'

'Yes, it's something like that,' the woman said dismissively and began to close the door again before Christabel could ask for any further information.

Back in her shabby little room, listening to the noise of a heated row that was going on above her, she felt utterly despondent and knew she could stand living there no longer.

She'd had no success in finding a job and when Saturday came and she realised after counting out the few coins in her purse and finding that she didn't even have enough for a loaf of bread, let alone to pay the rent on her room, she resolved that, regrettably, the time had come to swallow her pride and to go and ask Lewis if he would help her.

She counted out the coins again and hoped that there was enough to pay the boat fare across to Wallasey. She would probably have to walk once she got to Seacombe, because she didn't think there would be enough left over for the bus fare from there to Rolleston Drive.

Chapter Nineteen

Christabel stayed in her room all Saturday morning packing up her belongings and hoping that the landlady wouldn't come knocking for her rent until midday. Her plan was to be out before then.

She wanted to leave going across to Wallasey until the afternoon, hoping that that would be the most opportune time to find them all at home, although since it was the last weekend before Christmas there was always the possibility that they would be out shopping.

She had no idea what number in Rolleston Drive they were living at, so, although she was footsore having had to walk all the way from Seacombe Ferry, she walked the full length of the tree-lined street, studying all the houses, and wondering if she would be able to recognise which one now belonged to Lewis.

She was admiring a very attractive detached house on the opposite side of the road when a tall, good-looking man and a young girl approached from the opposite direction and turned into the small driveway leading up to the front door. Christabel recognised Lewis immediately and, before she could stop herself, called out his name.

He paused and looked back over his shoulder. As she crossed over the road towards them he turned and raised his trilby staring at her in disbelief. 'Christabel?'

'Surprised to see me?'

'Yes, I am rather,' he said as he hugged and kissed her. 'We received a Christmas card from Lilian saying you'd been to see them but she made no mention that you were coming back home so I presumed you'd returned to Buenos Aires.'

'I've been here in Liverpool since November. It's taken me a while to find my feet,' she added with a deprecating laugh. 'I expect you've completely forgotten me, haven't you?' she remarked turning and smiling at Kay.

'No, I do remember you, Aunt Chrissy.' Kay beamed. 'You used to play with me and take me out.'

'That's right. You were only a little girl then; now you are almost as tall as me. You'll be eleven next February, won't you?'

'Yes, fancy you remembering,' Kay said hugging Christabel enthusiastically.

'Well, come along, let's all go indoors, Violet will be surprised to see you, Christabel,' Lewis commented as he unlocked the front door and ushered her inside.

The house was warm and welcoming, beautifully furnished and Christabel could tell at a glance that Lewis was making a success of his life. Violet appeared to be as quiet and withdrawn as ever but she did show surprise when she saw who their visitor was.

'I think this calls for a little celebration,' Lewis said, breaking the slightly awkward silence. 'Find some glasses, Violet, and I'll bring out the sherry.'

'Are you coming to stay with us, Aunt Chrissy?' Kay asked as the three grown-ups clinked glasses.

There was an awkward silence, then Lewis and Violet both spoke together.

'I expect your Aunt Chrissy has made other plans,' Violet said quickly.

'Great idea! Of course you must spend some time with us, Christabel,' Lewis invited.

'Thank you, Lewis, I would love to do that,' she replied quickly before her brother could change his mind.

'Aunt Chrissy, will you come and stay for Christmas, please?' Kay begged. Her blue eyes were shining as she slipped her hand into Christabel's, tugging at it eagerly.

'It depends on whether your mummy agrees or not,' Christabel told her. She had seen the swift exchange of looks between Violet and Lewis, and guessed that it was probably the last thing Violet wanted to happen but she was also quite confident that she wouldn't dare go against his wishes.

'Is that what you want to do, Christabel?'

218

Violet asked hesitantly. 'If so, then you'll have to give me a few days to organise a bedroom for you.'

'Don't forget it's Christmas Day next Friday, Mummy,' Kay piped up excitedly.

'Surely the bed in the spare room is always made up ready, isn't it?' Lewis asked in surprise.

'Well, yes, but . . .' Violet stopped, overcome with embarrassment. 'It might be slightly dusty in there. I've had so much to do that I gave it a miss this week when I was cleaning upstairs.'

'I'll dust the room for Aunt Chrissy,' Kay said eagerly. 'Please, Mummy! I want her to stay.'

'Well, if you are all sure then that sounds wonderful; I'd love to stay for a while.' Christabel smiled. She couldn't believe her luck. Their invitation solved all her immediate problems. Free accommodation, in the sort of surroundings she was used to – what could be better? she thought with relief.

'Would you mind coming back to Liverpool to help me collect my belongings either tonight or perhaps tomorrow morning?' she asked Lewis giving him a warm smile.

Violet found that having Christabel staying with them proved to be rather traumatic. They'd only had news of her once or twice since she'd been in Buenos Aires and it had been like seeing a ghost when she appeared on the doorstep with Lewis and Kay.

Lewis inviting her to come and stay with them had been understandable, but she'd thought it would only be for a few days over Christmas; a week, at the most. Now Christabel had been staying with them for well over a month, and she showed no signs of leaving.

Yet how could she explain all this to Lewis without him thinking she was being unreasonable? Christabel was so helpful, sweetness itself, in fact, and always anxious to help in any way she could. She was particularly good with Kay and was always ready to play games with her or listen to her read. She knew Kay was extremely fond of her and would certainly miss her when she did leave.

To some extent this was what worried Violet so much. Christabel monopolised Kay and it was having a bad influence on her. Kay had become quite spoilt and rather precocious. Unless Christabel decided to leave soon it would be the Easter holidays and Kay would be at home for about three weeks. If Christabel was still staying there with them then she was bound to insist on taking Kay out all the time and then she really would be spoilt.

The one thing that irritated her even more than the way she spoiled Kay was the frequent comments Christabel made about how like the Montgomerys Kay was.

'She not only has Lewis's dark hair and blue eyes, but she even has the same slim build,' Christabel pointed out repeatedly.

No one knows better than I do, Violet mused, *that Kay doesn't look the slightest bit like me.* She had even regarded it as something of a bonus since she knew only too well that she was exceptionally plain, but it was different when someone else pointed it out.

'What's so odd about that?' Violet questioned.

'Nothing really, except that she doesn't seem to take after you or your family in any way at all.' Christabel smiled. 'Most children seem to inherit likenesses from both their parents, but not Kay. You can identify everything about her as being inherited from the Montgomery family.'

Violet found these comments very upsetting but when she commented on it to Lewis, intending to ask him to tell Christabel to stop making them, he merely shrugged and told her she was becoming neurotic. After all, he pointed out, Christabel was quite right because Kay did have his colouring and since he was her father he couldn't see anything very surprising about that.

Although Violet tried to dismiss the matter as being of no consequence, it worried her. She found it impossible to ignore what Christabel had said and was constantly studying Kay and scrutinising not only her looks but also her habits.

Christabel was right: Kay wasn't the least bit like her, Violet thought miserably. It wasn't simply looks – that was understandable, as

Lewis had pointed out – but it was even her manner and her way of speaking. Kay had Lewis's turn of speech, his mannerisms and his attitude to things. She even had the same flashes of temper which flared up in seconds and died down just as swiftly.

Violet was so unsettled by these revelations that she found other disturbing thoughts began to invade her mind. What if there was an underlying reason why Christabel was right? she asked herself. Could it be that the reason Kay had inherited all these traits was because, even though Lewis was her father, she wasn't really Kay's mother?

She knew it was a preposterous thought, but she had been so very ill when her baby had been born that she couldn't remember very much about what had happened. She had been in so much pain and so terribly weak that it had all been so confusing. She'd been devastated when, after all the hours of agony she'd endured, she thought she'd heard the doctor say that her baby was stillborn and that she would never be able to have another.

She recalled drifting in and out of consciousness for several days wishing that she could die as well. If her baby was dead and she couldn't have any more children, then there was nothing to live for because having a child of her own meant so much to her.

Days later, when she was well enough to be

propped up in bed, she'd been in tears when she realised that her baby was in the crib alongside her bed and had been there all the time.

Lewis had consoled her, telling her not to worry. They had a beautiful little girl and that was all that mattered. He'd also explained that because she'd been too ill to look after the baby after she was born the nurse had fed her from a bottle. Nevertheless, the baby had thrived and everything was going to be all right from now on.

From then on she'd hardly given it a thought. Now she found that she couldn't sleep at night for worrying about it. She spent hours and hours going over every minute detail relating to Kay's birth.

The more she thought about it, the more convinced she became that Christabel's insinuations might be justified and it was possible that Kay was Lewis's child but not hers.

Supposing, she reasoned, he had replaced her dead baby with his love child, thinking that because she was so anxious to have a child of her own she would never know the difference?

She knew it was an absolutely outrageous idea and highly improbable, but try as hard as she could she found it was impossible to put it out of her mind.

Christabel had been staying in Rolleston Drive for well over six weeks before Lewis suggested that perhaps she'd like to go over to Liverpool to visit their parents' grave, and he would accompany her the following Sunday afternoon.

Violet was very much in favour of it and couldn't wait to have both the house and Kay all to herself.

The moment Kay heard what they were arranging she threw a tantrum because she wanted to go with them.

'No, Kay, it's impossible for you to come because it would mean you would probably be late getting back and you have to be up for school on Monday morning,' Violet explained.

'We could go over on Saturday, then it wouldn't interfere with Kay's schooling at all,' Christabel suggested.

Violet demurred and remained adamant that she didn't want Kay to go with them.

'OK, OK, you win!' Christabel held up her hands in mock surrender. 'I'm sorry, Kay, I got it all wrong. Never mind, we'll have some days out when you are home from school over Easter.'

Lewis cut short the argument. 'We'll all go on Saturday,' he said decisively. 'We'll have lunch at the Adelphi Hotel and afterwards go and visit the graves and then we can be home again in good time for Kay's bedtime.'

Violet was on the point of saying that wasn't what she wanted to do, but a warning look from Lewis silenced her. She knew it was no good arguing with Lewis once his mind was made up so she accepted the inevitable.

Kay was not so easily mollified. Life had been so different – quite wonderful, in fact – since Aunt Chrissy had been staying with them. Aunt Chrissy took her part whenever her mum and dad scolded her, or wanted her to do something she didn't want to do, whether it was tidying her room or going to bed.

Aunt Chrissy was so much more fun to be with than her mum. They had such good times together. She bought her sweets and ice creams, took her to the pictures on Saturday afternoons when it was too wet to do anything else, and, whenever they went shopping, Aunt Chrissy always bought her a present. Sometimes it was a puzzle, or a book; at other times it was something pretty to wear.

Best of all was when she went out with her aunt on her own and she liked the idea of just the two of them visiting Liverpool; it was far more appealing than all of them going as a family.

Later that morning, after Lewis had gone to work and Kay to school, Violet brought up the subject of the forthcoming trip.

'Are you saying that I seem to have undermined your plans, Violet?' Christabel questioned.

Violet's face reddened, but she said nothing.

'Is it because Kay is so fond of me?' Christabel persisted, 'or is it because you are tired of having me living here?'

225

'Well, naturally, I have been wondering what you have decided to do about your future,' Violet prevaricated. 'Surely you need to get a job and earn some money? You can't sponge off Lewis for ever,' she added spiritedly.

'I don't intend to,' Christabel promised. 'It's only a temporary arrangement.'

Ever since she'd been staying in Rolleston Drive she'd been borrowing money from Lewis and she'd kept concocting stories about her money being tied up in America, and that she was waiting for it to come through. Lewis knew the truth and she'd promised to pay back every penny once she found a job, but she was surprised that Violet was shrewd enough to see through her story.

'The trouble is, I'm not able to find the sort of job I want. There's not much call for writing publicity copy for films here in Liverpool, so I'll probably have to go to London.'

Violet looked relieved but she said nothing and Christabel could tell from the way her lips tightened that she was waiting to hear something more definite than that.

'I'll leave right after Easter,' she promised. 'I would like to go before then, but I've promised Kay that I will have some days out with her during her holidays and I don't want to upset her by letting her down. Is that all right?'

'I suppose it will have to be. Have you told Lewis?'

'Not yet, but I will do. Perhaps we could

226

leave it for the moment, until the end of the school holidays, otherwise Kay might get upset and I'm sure you don't want that to happen.'

Chapter Twenty

Christabel made the most of her time with Kay during the Easter holiday. Easter Sunday 1926 fell on 4 April and although there was still a chill in the air, most of the days were bright and sunny.

They went out almost every day and even though she promised both Violet and Lewis that she wouldn't spoil her with too many treats, Christabel spent every penny she had on making sure Kay enjoyed every minute they were together.

Christabel took her somewhere different most days, setting out shortly after breakfast and not coming home again until very late in the afternoon or early evening.

Violet was far from pleased, especially when Christabel said she'd thought that it was the best way of helping her.

'It means we are both out from under your feet all day and since you don't like anyone in the kitchen when you are cooking, I thought you would be pleased.'

'There are plenty of other ways that you could help,' Violet grumbled. 'Kay needs to learn how to keep her room tidy, for a start. There are books and pencils everywhere.'

'I'll make sure Kay makes her bed and leaves her room in order each morning before we go out,' Christabel promised. 'If there is anything else I can do to help, you have only to ask me.'

Violet didn't take Christabel up on her offer; instead, she continuously grumbled about all the extra work having a visitor made until in the end even Lewis grew tired of listening to her complaining and pointed out that Christabel wasn't a visitor, she was family.

It also made both Christabel and Kay all the more eager to get out of the house and stay out as long as possible.

They never planned in advance but waited to see what the weather was like before deciding where to go.

If it was bright and sunny, they were quite adventurous; if it was raining or very overcast, they often went to look round the shops in Liscard and then to a Milk Bar for their lunch before strolling home again around tea-time.

Kay loved the sunny days when they went to New Brighton and Christabel let her mess around on the shore. They would buy fish and chips and sit in one of the shelters on the promenade and eat it out of the newspaper. Afterwards, they would walk around the fairground and even go on one or two of the rides.

'Will you come on the ride with me, Aunt Chrissy?' Kay always asked. Laughing and holding each other tight they'd spin round in one of the chair rides, or sit side by side on the galloping horses on the roundabout, both of them giggling as they soared into the air and then bumped back down again.

'Mum hates anything like this and she certainly wouldn't come on one,' Kay told her.

'Does your dad ever take you on one?' Christabel asked.

'Only when we come here on our own because Mum says it's very common to go on the rides and she won't let me do it.'

One day they went all the way to Southport because Kay had never been there and very much wanted to go.

'You mightn't be able to see the sea, you know,' Christabel warned her. 'It goes out so far that you can't even see it.'

On the way there she told Kay all about when she was nursing at the military hospital that was between Liverpool and Southport.

'Can we go and see it?' Kay asked eagerly.

'It won't be there now,' Christabel told her. 'After the war it was closed down and I expect they've built either factories or a housing estate there by now.'

Once, when it was too cloudy to go to New Brighton, they went over to Liverpool to look at all the shops. They'd had lunch at the Kardomah Café and afterwards Kay wanted to go and see the house where her father had grown up.

'You grew up here as well, didn't you, Aunt Chrissy?' Kay asked as they stared at the old family home. 'You and Aunt Lilian.'

'Yes, we did, but that was a long time ago.'

'Have you ever lived anywhere else in Liverpool?' Kay asked.

'Yes, in Wilcock Court.'

'Where's that? Can we go there?'

For one impulsive moment Christabel thought of taking Kay there; then common sense prevailed and she knew that it would be a silly thing to do.

For a start, she reminded herself, it had been ten years ago when she'd lived there, and there'd been a war on. So much had happened since then. It was quite possible that Maggie Nelson was no longer living there or even that she might be dead. If she was alive, then Maggie was bright enough to work out that Kay was about the same age as the baby Christabel was expecting while she'd lived there.

'One day, perhaps,' Christabel prevaricated, aware that Kay was waiting for an answer.

'Why not now?'

'It would take too long; it's in another part of Liverpool altogether and we have to get back. Your mum would be very cross indeed if we were late after she's cooked a meal for us, now, wouldn't she?'

'I suppose so,' Kay agreed resignedly.

'Come on, then. Are we going to walk down to the Pier Head or catch a tram?'

'If we're late, then it had better be a tram, I suppose,' Kay muttered.

'Well, we have time to walk and it *is* all

231

downhill,' Christabel told her. 'Come on, we'll walk. Shall we count how many steps it takes us to walk from Bold Street to the Pier head?'

Linking arms they began counting but they gave up long before they reached Tithebarn Street, both of them agreeing that it didn't really matter.

On board the *Royal Daffodil* ferry boat they decided to walk round on the top deck.

'Can we see the part of Liverpool where you used to live?' Kay asked as they hung over the rail watching as the boat pulled away from the landing stage and headed across the Mersey towards Seacombe on the other side.

'Probably, since we can see at least half of Liverpool from here,' Christabel laughed. 'Look, I can see the cathedral.'

'I can see the Liver Birds perched on top of the Liver Building. Do you think that one day they might fly away?' Kay giggled.

'Let's hope not, otherwise we wouldn't know when we were in Liverpool and, judging by the time on the clock face up there, we really shouldn't be in Liverpool now but back home in Rolleston Drive; we still have a long bus ride before we're there.'

They were late and although it was only by a few minutes, Violet was very annoyed.

'What's the point of me cooking you a proper meal when you don't bother to come home in time?' she grumbled.

'Why all the fuss? You were only just about to dish up,' Lewis said frowning.

'That's not the point. I am trying to teach Kay punctuality, but how can I do that if no one backs me up?'

'I'm sorry. It's my fault. I rather lost track of time,' Christabel apologised. 'We're here now, though, and I must say your casserole smells delicious, Violet.'

'Aunt Chrissy was showing me places she knew in Liverpool,' Kay piped up. 'You know, Dad, the house where you all grew up and where Granpy and Granny Montgomery lived,' she went on, almost choking on her mouthful of hot food as she tried to eat and talk. 'After that we were going to see where Aunt Chrissy lived after she left school, somewhere called Wilcock Court and—'

'Kay, stop talking with your mouth full,' Violet said sharply. 'I've told you before about doing that; you're old enough to know better. It's high time you learned some manners.'

'Sorry.' Kay looked crestfallen, hunching her shoulders as she stared down at her plate.

'For heaven's sake, sit up straight,' Violet admonished. 'I won't let you go out with your aunt again if you are going to carry on in this fashion when you get home.'

The rest of the meal passed almost in silence. Lewis made one or two comments, saying how worried he was about the impending miners' strike and the effect it would have on Liverpool as well as the rest of the country if it actually took place.

233

'It will probably affect the shipping lines pretty badly.'

'There's no coal exported from Liverpool, so how can it make any difference to us?' Violet asked.

'Exporting coal is the lifeblood of this country in so many ways,' Lewis stated. 'Ships need coal to fuel their boilers and without coal, most of which comes from South Wales, shipping will be at a standstill.'

He expounded on his theory of what should be done to prevent the strike happening while they ate the jam roly-poly and custard that Violet had baked, but no one else said anything.

The moment they were finished Violet ordered Kay up to bed saying that if she had to slouch over the table as she'd done all through the meal, then it must mean she was tired and needed an early night.

Kay went without a word and didn't even say goodnight to any of them.

'I'll help Christabel to clear up here and wash up, so you go and sit down and take it easy,' Lewis told Violet. 'We'll make a pot of tea and bring it in when we've finished the dishes and we can all sit round the fire and drink it.'

'You wash up! You've never offered to do that in your life before,' Violet said scathingly. 'You wouldn't know where to begin.'

'I'm sure that Christabel can tell me what I have to do.' Lewis smiled. 'Go on, put your feet up; you've cooked the meal, it's only fair that we clear up afterwards.'

'Christabel is probably the one who needs to take it easy since she's been trailing around Liverpool with Kay ever since breakfast time this morning. Poor child, she looked quite worn out. She must be exhausted since she didn't even bother to argue when I told her to go off to bed,' she added.

'I'm fine and I enjoyed my meal,' Christabel told her as she began stacking up the dirty plates. 'Lewis is right, we should be the ones to do the dishes, so go and take it easy.'

The moment they had carried everything through to the kitchen, Lewis made sure that the door was shut before he turned to face Christabel. 'What the hell were you thinking about, saying that you would take Kay to Wilcock Court? The very idea of taking her there sends shudders through me. What if old Maggie Nelson had still been living there? I'm sure she would have remembered you. What would you have said if she'd started asking questions about your baby?'

Before Christabel could answer, the door opened and Violet was standing there. It was obvious from her startled, wide-eyed look that she had overheard what he had said.

'I thought I would come and see if you needed any help,' she muttered, looking from one to the other. 'What baby were you talking about, and who was Maggie Nelson?'

'Someone we knew when we were growing up,' Christabel said quickly.

'Wilcock Court? That's near Scotland Road, isn't it? I'm surprised that you knew someone living in such a slummy part of Liverpool.'

'It was a chap I met when I was in the Navy; his mother lived there,' Lewis muttered.

'Christabel said it was someone you knew when you were growing up. So which was it?'

As Lewis opened his mouth to speak Violet clapped her hands over her ears. 'Don't bother to invent any more lies,' she said bitterly. 'I can work it out from what I overheard. All these years you've been lying to me, Lewis,' she said accusingly.

Lewis looked at her in bewilderment. 'What in heaven's name are you talking about, Violet?'

'As if you didn't know!' she gulped.

'I don't know; I haven't the faintest idea what you are on about. What lies? I've never lied to you about anything.'

'I heard what you said . . . about Maggie Nelson . . . about her knowing about the baby. I've had my suspicions, but I didn't know that she was in it as well,' she sobbed, pointing an accusing finger at Christabel.

'Then perhaps you should calm down and listen. It's a simple enough explanation.'

'I bet it is, but then the pair of you are liars. I never want to speak to either of you ever again.'

Lewis caught her by the arm. 'Will you stop and listen to what we want to tell you, Violet?'

'No, I won't!' She pulled her arm free. 'Don't touch me! You'll have to sleep down on the sofa because you're never coming into my bed ever again. You can't use the spare room, because your sister is in there,' she added as she slammed the kitchen door.

'For goodness' sake go after her, Lewis, and tell her the truth,' Christabel told him.

'That will mean implicating you and telling her that it was your baby we were talking about.'

'So be it. It doesn't mater, after all this time, *who* knows.'

'It will mean explaining to her that you had it adopted at birth.'

'So what does that matter now? After all, it's the truth.'

'I don't know,' he shook his head from side to side, 'she's far too overwrought at the moment to take any notice of what we say and, for the life of me, I can't understand what she is thinking right at this moment.'

'Then go and talk to her and find out. It's obvious that she's dreadfully upset about something.'

Lewis began to walk out of the kitchen, then hesitated. 'Perhaps it would be better to leave it until the morning, she might have calmed down by then and will listen to us and understand.'

Christabel didn't answer; it seemed pointless to do so. She finished tidying up in the kitchen then went upstairs herself. She found the bathroom door locked so she went into her bedroom, undressed, and put on her dressing gown.

Violet stood by Kay's bed for several minutes, looking down at the sleeping girl with tears in her eyes. She didn't need an explanation from Lewis, she'd had her suspicions for a long time. Even so, she knew it wasn't fair to keep punishing Kay because of her own unhappiness.

As she heard Christabel coming upstairs she quickly went into the bathroom and locked the door. Shaking, she waited for the house to quieten down so that she could go to her room. She wondered what she was going to do if, despite what she had said earlier, Lewis had already come up and was in bed. If he was in their room, she'd have to go and sleep downstairs because she couldn't bear to have him anywhere near her, not after what she had heard him and Christabel talking about.

She'd been right all along, it seemed, about Kay. She looked round the bathroom which was so full of their personal items. The toothbrush holders, Kay's and Lewis's, both streaked with toothpaste because they both always used too much and didn't rinse the brush properly afterwards.

As Christabel tried the bathroom door again

and called out asking if she was all right, Violet looked round desperately for something to use to defend herself with if Christabel managed to force the door open.

The only thing she could see was Lewis's cut-throat razor so she grabbed hold of it. When she heard Christabel walk away she was astonished to find that she'd been holding it so tightly that she'd drawn blood even though she hadn't felt a thing.

Suddenly it seemed like a sign. She wasn't superstitious but surely this was the answer. She couldn't go on living under such a cloud, not knowing if she really was Kay's mother or not. Worse still, if she wasn't, and Kay looked so much like Lewis, then who was her mother? It was all too much . . . but then she stopped herself. What if it was Kay who found her? She put the razor down, tended the small wound, and quietly left the bathroom.

Chapter Twenty-One

Christabel and Lewis, like everyone who knew her, found it extremely difficult to come to terms with Violet's suicide. Lewis, possibly because he had been the one to find her a few days later, lying unconscious on the sofa with an empty pill box at her side. It was as though his mind was incapable of taking in what had happened. 'I thought she was merely sleeping; taking advantage of the peace and quiet because you had taken Kay to the pictures,' he told Christabel.

He had made a cup of tea for them both and brought it through, intending to sit and have a quiet chat with his wife. When he'd touched her arm to let her know that her tea was on the table beside her, she hadn't responded.

He'd called a doctor but it was much too late to do anything. By the time Christabel and Kay returned from their outing, her body had been taken away. Lewis was told there would have to be an inquest which he found unbearably upsetting knowing what a reserved person Violet had been.

Her presence was everywhere, no matter where he looked or turned. At any moment he expected to hear her voice calling out to him from another room. Or that she would suddenly walk into the room, dressed in her neat dark skirt and white blouse, anxious to see if there was anything they needed.

He kept telling Christabel that if only he had some idea what had led to her taking such a drastic step, he mightn't feel so angry, bewildered and confused.

When she'd said that perhaps her staying with them for so long had been something of an imposition, he'd dismissed such an idea as nonsense.

'Violet always coped so well with domestic matters,' he insisted, 'so I'm quite sure that didn't have anything to do with it.'

In the days that followed Violet's funeral Christabel watched uneasily as Lewis tried desperately to pull himself together, but it was not easy for him. His mind appeared to be a seething turmoil of doubts and unanswered questions which seemed to grow longer each day as he tried get on with life for Kay's sake.

When Christabel told him that she had to go to London for an interview, he became very annoyed.

'I postponed it so that I could attend the funeral but if I don't go this week then I will be out of the running for the job I'm after,' she explained.

'If only Violet had left a note to give me some idea of why she has done such a terrible thing it might help me to understand. It breaks my heart to think that she was so unhappy and in such distress and that I didn't even notice. I loved her so much that I would have done anything in the world to make her happy,' he sighed.

Christabel watched with growing concern as he searched the entire house, hoping to find a message of some kind; looking in every drawer and cupboard, searching page by page through the books in the bookcase, and even those on the shelves in the kitchen. He even rummaged in all the wardrobes, going through Violet's clothes in case there was a note or letter in one of the pockets. He searched through the drawers where she kept her underwear and stockings in the hope he might find some clue. He hunted everywhere, but there was no note or letter or anything else to set his mind at rest.

As far as he was aware, they'd been idyllically happy. They had a nice house in a pleasant district of Wallasey. He had a good job, and he was generous with the housekeeping money. In addition, he'd given Violet a separate allowance so that she always had money of her own to buy clothes, or spend on treats or outings for herself and Kay whenever she wished to do so.

He knew Violet idolised Kay and he had no idea how she could bring herself to abandon the child when she was reaching an age when she needed her mother so much.

He accepted that having Christabel staying with them might have caused Violet a certain amount of stress over the past month. He was well aware that Christabel and Violet were not close.

For some reason they had never taken to each other. After their first meeting Lewis's sister had joked about him marrying such a plain-looking woman. 'You always had such a reputation in your younger days for being something of a rake and you always had such beautiful girls on your arm,' she'd persisted.

They'd laughed about it, and agreed that it had all been part of growing up. He'd retaliated by reminding her of all the boyfriends she'd had in her stormy younger days, and yet she was still not married to any of them.

'I knew from the moment I first met Violet that she was the woman I wanted to marry!' he'd told Christabel.

'And you've never regretted it?' Christabel probed.

'Never for one moment,' he said decisively.

Other people might think Violet was withdrawn and even lacking in personality because she was so shy, but to Lewis she was pale, mysterious and wonderfully serene. She was the perfect loving wife, as well as being a tremendous friend, and an excellent mother.

In short, their marriage was everything he'd ever hoped it would be. The realisation that she'd been so desperately unhappy and had ended up taking her own life was appalling; it both puzzled and disturbed him.

He couldn't understand why she'd not said something to him since they had always been able to talk openly to each other about anything.

It was this reticence over what had been upsetting her that concerned him deeply and led him to think that it must have been something extremely personal. And since whatever it was obviously had only been troubling her quite recently, he suspected that it might have something to do with Christabel's arrival.

Had she overheard the conversation between him and Christabel after Christabel had been about to take Kay to Wilcock Court and misunderstood it? Or was it because Christabel made such a tremendous fuss of Kay?

He knew she'd upset the child's routine, and that she had, in so many subtle ways, undermined both his and Violet's authority.

They'd both agreed it was annoying, but surely that wasn't sufficient reason for Violet to take her own life? In the evenings, though, she'd been quieter than usual, he reflected. He'd attributed that to the fact that she was happy and contented.

Looking back, he realised that there must have been far more to it than that. Several times he'd caught her studying him, an anxious look on her face. Had there been something of tremendous importance she wanted to say, but didn't know how to start?

He wondered if Kay had any idea about what had been worrying her mother. Or if there had been anything unusual happening recently that he knew nothing about. The trouble was she was so distraught over her mother's death he didn't dare increase her anguish by questioning her.

It was difficult enough for an eleven-year-old to understand about such things as suicide and he didn't want to say anything that might make her feel guilty in any way, or possibly think that in some way it was her fault.

Life was going to be difficult enough for both of them now and the last thing he wanted was to lose Kay's trust. He'd have his work cut out bringing her up single-handed through her formative years when a mother was so important, especially to a girl. He'd do it, though! He'd do it for Violet's sake, he vowed.

The funeral was a morbid affair. Kay wept copiously throughout the simple ceremony. Lewis felt such an agonising sense of emptiness that he was too overwhelmed with sadness to find the words to console her. Shaking with grief, he could do no more than hug her close to him.

He took the rest of the week off from work so that he could be with Kay and he tried his best to comfort her, and help her to come to terms with what remained of their life.

Without Violet's presence the house seemed

to be an empty shell, he thought, as he threw away a vase of dead flowers. It lacked the warmth and atmosphere of a home. It seemed ridiculous, but even the shine had gone off the furniture; everything was lifeless and disorganised.

For Kay's sake he struggled to maintain their usual routine. Breakfast, lunch, high tea and a bedtime drink punctuated their day. He did his best in the kitchen, but nothing tempted Kay to eat. She picked at her food, and said she wasn't hungry, but he suspected it was because the meals he prepared nowhere near equalled the ones Violet had served them.

He made a half-hearted attempt at cleaning the house, more to keep himself occupied than anything else. He couldn't stand the silence; it grated on his nerves.

He tried his best to tolerate it and encouraged Kay to play some music on her gramophone, hoping that listening to that might help to distract her mind from the loss of her mother.

The following week he sent Kay back to school. He'd phoned first, and had had a talk with the Headmistress, who'd agreed to keep a special eye on her and to let him know immediately if there were any problems.

He also decided to return to work himself, but knew that first he'd have to find a housekeeper and he wasn't sure how Kay would take to having a stranger there in their home.

She'd simply have to adjust, he told himself

wearily, because he couldn't manage to run the house *and* go to work.

Kay certainly appeared to be a lot better now that she was back at school, and mixing with her friends again. Night times were the worst. Frequently he heard her sobbing in her sleep or calling out for her mother and he found it heartbreaking.

The very next day, as he was boiling eggs for himself and Kay for their tea, Christabel turned up unexpectedly.

Lewis looked bewildered. 'Christabel! What are you doing back here? Didn't you get your job in London after all?'

'Aunt Chrissy!' Kay threw herself into Christabel's arms, hugging her and kissing her. 'You've come back! I thought I was never going to see you again either. Promise you won't go away again, please?' she begged.

'I hope I won't have to do so, darling,' Christabel told her, hugging her close, 'but it all depends on whether your daddy wants me to stay and look after you both.'

'Aunt Chrissy can stay, Daddy, can't she? Say you want her to; that we both want her to stay?' Kay begged, her voice shrill with anxiety.

'Well . . .' Lewis hesitated, looking from one to the other. 'Are you quite sure you know what you'll be taking on if you decide to stay and run our home?'

'I've thought it through. I know what I'm doing,' she told him confidently.

'You'll be giving up so much, Christabel. It will be like being married, but with all the chores and worries and none of the pleasure,' he pointed out grimly.

'As I said, I have thought it through and I'm fully aware of what I'm doing,' she repeated. 'I have the choice of staying here or going to London and taking this job. If I do that then I'll probably end up living in a block of over-priced flats. The alternative, if you'll agree to it, is making my home here with you in Wallasey, and looking after you and Kay.'

'If you take this job, it's not very glamorous and there's no chance of promotion, you know,' he told her dryly. 'It will be a daily round of cleaning, cooking and looking after Kay and me. After the high life you've grown accustomed to in the past you might find it pretty dull.'

'True, but at least I'll be able to organise my day as I like. If the sun's shining I can take a walk in the park without having to ask for permission to do so.'

Lewis still looked dubious. 'You are sure it's not simply a passing whim?' he persisted. 'Kay's had enough upheavals in her life, I don't want you suddenly deciding to walk out on us and upsetting her all over again.'

'No! I've never been more serious about anything in my life,' Christabel assured him. 'I'll remain as long as you need me, Lewis.

I give you my word that I will stay until Kay is grown up and ready to leave home, if that's what you want; or at least until she is old enough to look after herself.'

Chapter Twenty-Two

There were some difficult times in the first few months after Violet died. Kay was very depressed and clingy. She rejected her food and seemed to be unable to stop crying because she was convinced that it was all her fault. Often she was too upset to sleep on her own and on several occasions refused to go to school.

Christabel was extremely patient and understanding, even taking Kay into her own bed at night whenever she was very distressed. Gradually, she helped her to accept what had happened by constantly reassuring her that it wasn't in any way her fault. She promised her that she would stay and look after her until she was grown up,

Kay accepted her as a friend as well as a surrogate mother. Even so, Lewis played a very important part in her life. He had come to mean so much more than the average father did.

No one, not even Lewis, seemed prepared to voice an opinion as to why Violet had taken her own life. Christabel kept recalling the conversation Violet had overheard between her and Lewis about Maggie Nelson and although she said nothing whenever she thought about it, she felt a frisson of guilt.

She suspected that what Violet had heard, together with her frequent comments about Kay looking more like Lewis than herself had upset Violet. Even so, Christabel couldn't really understand why she had taken it so much to heart as Lewis always appeared to be such a devoted husband.

Once or twice, in a roundabout way, she tried to talk to Lewis about it and to sound out his views, but Lewis refused to discuss the matter.

Whenever she raised the subject he became so tight-lipped and angry that she suspected there was something she didn't know about their background. Since it was obvious he had no intention of telling her she finally dismissed it as something that would have to remain a mystery and tried to close her mind to the idea that Violet's suicide was in any way her fault.

She had always got on well with Lewis when they'd been growing up, and she still enjoyed his company so when he asked if she was sure she wanted to stay and look after them, she assured him she was.

'It will mean putting my life on hold for a time because I don't think I could cope with a job as well,' she pointed out.

'I wouldn't expect you to do so; we'll have a proper agreement so you can regard this as work,' he told her and she agreed and accepted it as a way of earning her living.

Lewis left Christabel very much to her own devices when it came to running his home. In return, she cared for him and Kay as efficiently as any wife. Their home was warm, clean, well decorated, and an open house to Kay's friends.

In addition to paying all household expenses, Lewis made Christabel a regular allowance and invariably took the bus and the ferry boat to work so that she could have use of the car during the day. He was always willing to stay home and look after Kay in the evening if she wanted to go out on her own.

She liked sharing meal times and their concerns over Kay, planning outings, reading the same newspaper, and discussing what was going on in the outside world. Jointly they budgeted for family expenses and they often had friendly arguments over what they should do at the weekends or where they should go on holiday, all of which meant that their lives were not all that different from those in any average home.

In many ways it was an ideal arrangement for them all. Occasionally, Christabel wondered what would happen if Lewis ever met anyone he wanted to marry. He kept very fit and although he was now almost forty he looked younger and was still quite a catch. She knew she couldn't share a home with another woman, and she certainly didn't relish the thought of having to move out and be on her own again.

Whenever these thoughts came into her mind

she would study her brother, and hope that he was far too comfortable to make any changes. He enjoyed plain food and simple meals which suited her style of cooking. He liked his home to be run in an orderly way so she made sure that it was. She organised his wardrobe, and took his suits to be dry cleaned regularly. He never had to ask for a clean shirt or look for socks or underwear because they were always ready and waiting. And so, too, were freshly laundered towels, as well as the brands of toothpaste and toiletries he preferred.

She looked after Kay with the same efficiency. Kay adored pretty clothes and loved shopping so Christabel taught her how to choose discerningly so that she got value for money. No matter how much she longed to have a particular dress or pair of shoes, Christabel always persuaded her to look at others first to make sure they were really what she wanted. Liverpool had a wonderful selection of shops so there was plenty of scope for comparison of both quality and price.

Kay reminded her so much of what she'd been like at the same age that sometimes Christabel felt she was reliving her own youthful days. And because Kay's features were almost identical to her own, Christabel found it easy to advise Kay on what suited her best.

As the years passed and Kay was no longer a leggy schoolgirl, Christabel often found herself thinking about her own child. She would be the same age as Kay and also on the verge of womanhood, and Christabel wondered if she was as well cared for and as happy as Kay was.

Everything was going so smoothly that Christabel felt a sense of irritation when, a couple of weeks before Christmas 1929, they returned from one of their shopping sprees in high spirits about the presents they'd bought for Lewis to find that while they'd been out he'd received a telegram from Lilian saying they were in London and that they wanted to come to stay over Christmas.

'What are you going to tell her?'

'I don't know,' he frowned, 'I can't tell her anything at the moment because I don't know where she is. There's no address on the telegram. It rather looks as if they simply intend turning up on the doorstep. If that happens, then I suppose we will have to make them welcome.'

'Does she give any idea of how long they will be staying?' Christabel asked, holding out her hand for the telegram so that she could read it for herself.

'Did you say they're coming to stay with us for Christmas?' Kay asked excitedly.

Lewis shrugged hopelessly. 'It rather looks as though they are,' he commented dryly.

'Typical of Lilian to take it for granted that we will be pleased to see them and willing to put them up,' Christabel said crossly.

* * *

As she cleared the debris from the dining table after their Christmas dinner, Christabel wished she could turn the clock back so that she and Kay and Lewis could have celebrated Christmas on their own as they'd done in the previous few years she had been living with them.

Whether it had been the wine, or the excitement of having so many visitors, Christabel didn't know, but the only thing that had seemed to go right was the cooking. Even Alex couldn't find anything to complain about with the dishes she'd served. The turkey had been succulent and the accompaniments were cooked to perfection. The wine was at the correct temperature, and even the Christmas pudding dished up the right lucky charms to everyone. She had even remembered to buy some Christmas crackers.

Looking back, it might have been better to have missed them out, since they'd caused so much trouble when they'd been pulled. Lilian had insisted on everyone wearing their paper hats, and had acted like a spoilt child when hers had been torn accidentally. She'd refused to accept the one Alex offered her, but had insisted on trying to repair her own.

Conversation was erratic, and futile; trying to talk above Lilian's tirade was impossible. Alex grew more and more argumentative and that only made matters worse.

Kay and eleven-year-old Marlene spent most of the time sending eye signals to each other and long before the meal was over they were both giggling over anything and everything.

The moment she could do so, Christabel had persuaded everyone to move from the dining room to comfortable armchairs in the sitting room. She handed Kay and Marlene a small box of chocolates and suggested they took them up to Kay's room. She then served coffee, mince pies and brandies for those who wanted them, and breathed a sigh of relief when, in next to no time, Alex had fallen asleep, and Lilian had picked up a magazine to read.

Quietly she had slipped away into the kitchen where even the debris from Christmas dinner seemed like a haven of peace. Stacking dishes had a calming effect on her nerves. By the time she tied an apron round her waist, filled the sink with hot, sudsy water, and plunged the first batch of dishes into it, she was feeling quite sanguine. Leastwise, she was until the kitchen door opened and Lilian appeared.

'I thought I'd come and give you a hand,' she whispered in a conspiratorial tone.

'There's no need! I'm quite happy.'

'You wash and I'll wipe, like in the old days when we were growing up,' Lilian said brightly.

'It's all right, Lilian. Go and sit down with Alex and talk to Lewis!'

Lilian pulled a face. 'They're both asleep. Alex drank far too much wine. Still, I suppose he felt he had to, it was the only way to keep sane over dinner, wasn't it?'

Christabel didn't answer. Giving vent to her feelings she picked up a pile of plates and plunged them into the water, splashing soapsuds everywhere.

'Steady on, Christabel!'

'I did warn you. It's no place to be when you're dressed up to the nines. You'll ruin your dress, and I haven't another apron.'

'Don't worry! I'll tie a towel round my waist if you're going to splash like that.'

Christabel didn't answer, but concentrated on what she was doing.

'I thought this would be a good opportunity for us to have a nice little chat,' Lilian said brightly.

Christabel stiffened. 'What about?'

'Marlene has asked Kay to come back with us to London. It will be so nice for her to mix with younger people and go to some parties and have some fun.'

'Really! You'll have talk to Lewis about it.'

'I've already suggested it to him and he doesn't mind,' Lilian said quickly. 'We'll be leaving first thing Saturday morning because we have to get back for a New Year's Eve party in London. Alex has all sorts of things lined up to do with business as well as social commitments. You don't mind Kay coming back with us, do you?'

'I would much prefer her to stay here and study.'

'Oh, Chrissy! You sound as old as you look!

257

Let the girl have some fun; she'll have such a wonderful time with Marlene, they get on so well together,' Lilian said airily.

Christabel decided that it was futile to argue since Lilian had already persuaded Lewis that it was a good idea and she was quite sure Kay wanted to go. Instead, she made Kay promise that she would come home immediately after New Year's Day so that she could do some revision before the new term started.

'Very well,' Kay agreed reluctantly, 'that's if Uncle Alex can spare the time to bring me back.'

'There's no need to trouble him,' Christabel told her quickly, 'you can come home by train on the Friday.'

'All on my own?'

'I don't see why not. Find out which train you'll be coming on, and phone and let me know. Ask Aunt Lilian to take you to the station and I'll meet you at Lime Street, OK?'

'Yes, Aunt Chrissy. Gosh! I can't take it all in.'

'Don't forget to let me know the time of your train as soon as you can,' Christabel reminded her as she waved them off.

Kay phoned on New Year's Day, babbling on excitedly about what a wonderful time they'd had the night before.

'So what time is your train on Friday?' Christabel asked.

'I haven't had a chance to find out. I'll phone you again tomorrow,' Kay promised.

When she phoned the next day it was to say

258

she'd been invited to a party on the Friday and also one on the Saturday night, and to ask if she could come home on the following Tuesday instead.

'I'll have to see what your dad says about that,' Christabel told her.

Lewis was as worried about it as Christabel was and decided to speak to Kay himself.

'It seems she's been invited to all these parties with Marlene and tomorrow Alex is taking her and Marlene to the studios where he's making a new film. And the day after that Lilian has promised—'

'Hold on, Lewis. Are you trying to tell me that she has so much to do in London that you have agreed to her staying on longer?' Christabel asked.

'Yes, I suppose I am,' he sighed. 'They've got so much planned for the next few days and there are so many other exciting things going on that she doesn't want to miss out on any of them. If she comes home any sooner it will spoil everything for Marlene as well as for her.'

Christabel was crestfallen. She knew Kay had talked Lewis round and was disappointed in her brother.

'You promised to come home, and do some studying,' Christabel reminded Kay when she phoned her again later in the day. 'Also, you need some clean clothes because you didn't take very many with you.'

'Aunt Chrissy, don't fuss. Aunt Lilian has

259

bought me a couple of new outfits. They're so much more fashionable than any of mine.'

'She's done what?'

'Don't sound so cross. We went shopping, and she bought Marlene some new dresses and said I could have the same.' She giggled. 'Aunt Lilian said it was to celebrate the start of 1930.'

Christabel felt flummoxed. She didn't know what to do for the best. The thought of Kay socialising with Marlene worried her. Although Marlene was a few years younger than Kay, she was very sophisticated and she didn't want Kay growing up too quickly when she still had so much studying to do.

A further point was that she didn't like the idea of Kay being spoilt by Lilian's generosity. Although Kay had never been kept short, she'd always been expected to do some chores in return for her pocket money. As she'd grown older, while they'd always bought her school clothes, when it came to anything special she wanted, she was encouraged to save up to help pay for them herself.

Alex had always been a big earner, and a big spender. He liked parties and entertaining on a grand scale. If Kay developed a taste for their lifestyle it would make it more difficult for her to settle down to a quiet life again like she would have to do. More important still, there had already been far too many interruptions in her routine and, over the next few months, she would have to concentrate on her school work really hard if she was going to pass her exams.

'Please say I can stay here,' Kay pleaded. 'Aunt Lilian won't mind. She said at breakfast time that I was no trouble at all and that Marlene loves having me here.'

'Kay, that's enough. Put your aunt on the line, and leave me to talk to her.'

'Don't you worry about Kay,' Lilian gushed. 'She and Marlene get on famously. Marlene adores her and Kay's enjoying herself.'

'Yes, I'm sure she is! Remind her, though, that she will have to buckle down to some serious studying if she's going to pass her exams.'

Lilian laughed good naturedly. 'You really are quite a slave driver, Chrissy.'

'Not at all. I'm simply thinking about Kay's future. Lewis isn't able to pull strings whenever she needs a favour.'

'Really, Chrissy, you make it sound as if Alex is some sort of wheeler-dealer!'

'Well, isn't he? Come on, admit it. Going behind people's backs and arranging deals makes him feel he's cleverer than the rest of the human race.'

'He's not in your good books these days, is he?' Lilian commented with a smug laugh.

'No, not really, and judging by the mood he was in over Christmas I don't think I'm in his, either.'

'I'd love to stay talking, Chrissy, if only I had the time,' Lilian assured her. She gave an affected sigh. 'When Alex is planning anything he needs as much looking after as a child. I have to make sure his clothes are laid out for him, his meal waiting, at whatever time he is ready to eat it, and, usually, I have to listen to him pour out all his problems before he can unwind from the stresses he's encountered during the day.'

'How terribly worrying that must be for you!'

'Not being married, you wouldn't understand,' Lilian observed. 'Knowing that Marlene has Kay to keep her company and doesn't need me to be with her all the time is quite a relief.'

Lilian was as devious as Alex these days, Christabel thought cynically as, with a gushing farewell, Lilian put down the receiver at her end without waiting for her to say goodbye.

She really must have a serious talk to Lewis about Kay spending so much time with them, she thought worriedly as she went back into the kitchen.

Tragedy struck before Christabel could have her discussion with Lewis. Two days later, while Kay was still in London, Lewis was knocked down on his way to work.

He was rushed to the Liverpool Royal Infirmary and Christabel, as his next of kin, was informed that he was seriously injured and she should come right away.

The weather was appalling. Thick fog shrouded the Mersey in grey, damp mist. It meant that the ferry boat was slow in crossing so the journey took much longer than Christabel had anticipated. The ear-shattering noise of foghorns and hooters from other boats on the river made her head throb and heightened her feeling of apprehension.

When she arrived at the hospital and the ward sister took her into a side room and offered her a cup of tea, Christabel feared the worst.

'I'm so sorry, Miss Montgomery, the doctors did everything they could, but despite all their efforts Mr Montgomery died,' the sister told her. 'Would you like to have a word with one of the doctors?'

Christabel nodded. She knew it was pointless but she found it so hard to believe that he had walked out of the house so fit and well that morning and now was gone for ever. The thought of having to break the sad news to Kay filled her with anguish.

As she waited for the doctor she even began to wonder if perhaps they'd made a mistake and that it wasn't Lewis who'd been knocked down after all. She wished she'd thought to telephone the office to make sure he wasn't at his desk.

Her first words when the doctor came into the room were 'Can I see him?' 'Yes, of course you can see your husband if you wish to do so, Mrs Montgomery. We did all we could; I'm so sorry that it wasn't any good.'

'He's my brother, not my husband,' she corrected him.

There was a moment's silence before the doctor spoke then he exclaimed in an astonished voice, 'Christabel? Christabel Montgomery! Good heavens, we were at Hilbury together. I was a very junior doctor in those days and you were a trainee nurse. You've probably forgotten me by now.'

For a moment Christabel stared blankly at the tall, wide-shouldered man in front of her. He was in his early fifties with thick fair hair, a lean, good-looking face, and deep, intelligent brown eyes. He was wearing a flawlessly cut charcoal-grey suit, a crisp white shirt, and a tie with dark-blue, grey and white stripes.

'Mark Murray? Yes, of course I remember you.'

Chapter Twenty-Three

After she'd viewed the body and identified that it was that of her brother, Christabel felt daunted by the enormity of the task in front of her. As Mark Murray pulled the dark green sheet back over the inert figure she looked at him blankly. She couldn't think what to do for the best. She knew she had to break the news to Kay but she wasn't sure how to do it.

'What am I expected to do next?' she asked in a slightly bewildered voice.

'Are there any other relatives that you have to inform?' Mark asked.

She looked at him and nodded. 'Lewis's daughter, Kay. She's almost fifteen and at the moment she's staying in London with my sister Lilian.'

She stopped abruptly. 'Why ever am I telling you all this? I'm sure you don't need to know,' she added with a deprecating shrug.

'Perhaps you would like me to phone and tell them?' he suggested.

'No,' she shook her head firmly, 'thank you, it's something I must do myself. And I don't think it would be a good idea to tell Kay over the phone because it will be a terrible shock for her and it's only about four years since she lost her mother.'

'I see; and you have taken her mother's place, is that right?' he asked.

'Yes, I've been living with Lewis and looking after Kay ever since Violet committed suicide.'

'Suicide!' There was surprise in his voice. 'That must have been very hard for a young girl to cope with.' He looked thoughtful before continuing. 'I think you are quite right, you should wait until she comes home and then tell her. She will need you and, for that matter, I imagine you will need her.'

Christabel nodded. Making an effort she pulled herself together and held out her hand. 'Thanks for listening and for your advice. I mustn't keep you any longer.'

'Are you sure you are going to be able to manage on your own, Christabel? Here,' he pulled a card out of his pocket and handed it to her, 'this is my home telephone number. If I'm not there I will be here at the hospital. Feel free to ring me at any time if you think I can help or if you want to talk. Promise!'

'It's very kind of you, Dr . . . I mean Mark. I hope you don't do this much for all your patients, or your wife must get very fed up,' she said with a wan smile.

'My wife died about four years ago,' he said quietly.

'Oh, I am so sorry; your poor children. When

you were at Hilbury you told me that you had two boys, if I remember correctly.'

'That's right and now they are grown-up men. One is a dentist and the younger one is still at university and hopes one day to be a doctor.'

Christabel travelled home in a daze. Despite the fact that it was a bitterly cold January day, as soon as she boarded the *Royal Daffodil* she went up to the top deck and walked around. The mist that had shrouded the Mersey earlier on had cleared and she hoped that the strong winter breeze would dispel the fog in her mind and help her to get to grips with what she ought to do for the best.

She wanted to be the one to break the news to Kay but, on reflection, she thought she owed it to Lilian to tell her what had happened first.

Lilian was almost hysterical when she heard the news and agreed immediately that it was Christabel's place to tell Kay.

'I've decided that the best thing to do is to have Lewis cremated at Landican, so if you let me know when you can be in Liverpool, we can arrange a date for the funeral service,' Christabel told her. 'Afterwards, I'll arrange for his ashes to be put into the family grave which is what mother would want.'

Lilian said she was too upset to think of anything like that but she agreed that Christabel must do whatever she thought was best.

'I'll ask Alex to bring Kay home tomorrow,' she promised.

'Won't she think it strange that you're cutting short her stay?' Christabel said worriedly.

'I'll tell her that he has to come to Liverpool on business and that she can come again soon. Perhaps she could come back with us after the funeral; that might help to take her mind off matters.'

'Perhaps. It depends, we'll have to wait and see.'

Christabel found it was very upsetting telling Kay what had happened.

'We're both going to miss him so much,' she murmured as she hugged her close and tried to console her.

'I've lost both my mum and my dad now, so I am an orphan with no one to love me,' Kay sobbed.

'No, no that's not true, Kay; you'll always have me to love you,' Christabel assured her.

Christabel found she missed Lewis dreadfully. Without him to talk to and share things with there was a void in her life, but it didn't seem to be the same with Kay. Kay seemed to retreat into a shell, refusing to mention her father's name or talk about him in any way.

Ever since Lewis's funeral Christabel had been regretting that she'd agreed with Lilian that letting Kay spend some time in London

268

with them and being with Marlene would be a distraction for her. She'd thought Lilian had meant for a few days immediately following the funeral, not every weekend. It had started a routine Christabel didn't approve of and which she found difficult to stop.

It was as if the exciting social scene that Lilian and Alex enjoyed had given Kay a taste of the high life, and consequently she not only found it difficult to settle down again when she was at home during the week but she also didn't even seem to want to try.

The weekends became a constant battle; Christabel thought she ought to stay home at and study, but Kay wanted to go to London to spend time with Marlene.

'We can't afford it these days, Kay, surely you can understand that,' Christabel would repeat time and time again. 'I have to budget very carefully to manage on the money your father left.'

'It doesn't cost me anything to stay at Aunt Lilian's,' Kay would argue, 'and if Uncle Alex is too busy to come and collect me in his car then he always sends me the money for the train fare.'

'I am aware of that and I don't like him doing it!'

'Why ever not?' Kay's eyebrows shot up questioningly. 'He's loaded! Marlene says it's his idea; no one asks him to do so.'

'Apart from that side of things, going off to London so often is interfering with your studies.

You should be spending every minute you can revising.'

'Aunt Chrissy, I keep telling you that swotting went out with the ark. You either know it, or you don't.'

'In your case it will definitely be "not knowing" it and I'm not prepared to stand by and see that happen!' Christabel told her sharply.

'I tell you what,' Kay said in a wheedling voice, knowing she was about to lose the argument, 'if I stay home and study every weekend from now until half-term, then can I go up and stay with Marlene for the whole week?'

'That will depend on how your Aunt Lilian feels about having you there for that long.'

It established a new pattern; one which Christabel still didn't like. Kay did stay at home most weekends, and she studied in between long phone calls with Marlene. At Easter she spent a full week with Marlene, and then persuaded Marlene to come back to Wallasey with her for a further three days, by which time the new term was about to start.

In the weeks leading up to Kay's exams, however, Christabel put her foot down. No trips to London, no telephone calls, and no visits from Marlene.

Kay gave in with a good grace and Christabel thought her problems were temporarily over. She concentrated on making sure that Kay had adequate sleep, a well-balanced diet, and spent every moment she possibly could studying.

Exams over, Christabel allowed Kay to relax. Marlene now had a part in her father's new film so she hadn't as much spare time as before, but Kay still spent a great many weekends in London.

When Kay's exam results came through at the end of August, they were better than Christabel had anticipated.

'This confirms my opinion, Kay, that if you work hard you're quite capable of getting to university,' Christabel told her.

'That means staying on for another two years at grammar school!' Kay groaned.

'Well? You will still only be seventeen.'

'And then you'll want me to spend a further three years studying at university to try and get a degree? By that time Marlene will have starred in at least four films!'

'Possibly, but remember it will probably be the only job she can get without a proper education or any qualifications,' Christabel pointed out rather tartly.

'Uncle Alex said he is going to do a commercial next, and that I can have a part in it.'

'No!' The fury in Christabel's voice startled Kay. 'Any nonsense of that sort and you won't be going up to London to see Marlene ever again.'

'He only meant during the school holidays. He thought I'd like a chance to earn some pocket money. And I jolly well would!' Kay added rebelliously.

Christabel wondered if she should explain her reasons to Kay; tell her how Alex had tried to lure her into the glamorous world of films. Instead, she said, 'If you've any energy to spare, then how about helping to redecorate your bedroom?'

Kay pulled a face. 'What's the point? I only go in there to sleep. It's all right as it is.'

'I thought you might like to get rid of some of the clutter, like the dolls and books that have been sitting on the shelves for years. Why not clear them out and smarten your room up?'

'Yes, I would like to do that,' Kay agreed, 'but I'd also like to go and stay with Marlene and since I did so well in my exams I thought that would be a nice reward.'

The argument went on for several days and eventually Christabel capitulated and agreed that Kay could spend a fortnight in London with Marlene before she returned to school for the start of the autumn term.

From then on, although she worked hard during term time, Kay spent more and more of her holiday breaks with Marlene in London. When she returned home she always looked worn out from all the excitement and late nights.

Christabel would try questioning her about what they did, and where they went, but she was not very forthcoming. Apart from paying for Kay to go out to theatres and dances, she suspected that Lilian and Alex were also buying her clothes which she was keeping at their place in London. Kay didn't deny this, but she glossed over the details and admitted that she often borrowed things belonging to Marlene. There was such a difference in their ages that Christabel knew this couldn't possibly be true.

'Look, Aunt Chrissy, I'm keeping to my part of the bargain. I don't go up there at weekends, I hardly ever talk to Marlene on the phone, and I'm working hard at school.'

Christabel had to admit this was true. Even so, she felt she was losing her and this was confirmed the following summer when Lilian came to stay for a few days and said they would be returning to America quite soon and would like to take Kay back there to live with them.

'Oh, no!' Christabel tried hard to keep the despair out of her voice, even though the suggestion horrified her. If Kay was persuaded to go she knew there was nothing she could do about it, and she would be absolutely heart-broken.

'We would see she completed her education when we got back to America and when she graduates Alex will make sure that she finds a really worthwhile job.'

'Lilian, I've given up the last seven years of my life in order to look after Kay. Why should I hand her over to you now, and be left on my own?'

'She won't stay with you for ever, you know!'

'I'm aware of that. I wouldn't want her to,

but I'd like to finish what I started. We will know her exam results in August, and she will be off to university in September. After she graduates I know she will probably want to leave home and have her own life. When that time comes we can decide what to do, but until then her place is here with me. It's what Lewis would have wanted and it's what I want,' she added forcibly.

'I always think it's tempting fate to make such set plans,' Lilian told her.

Christabel shrugged as she poured boiling water into the teapot. 'I like an orderly life! Anyway, I would have thought you had enough problems of your own to worry about.'

'Really? What's that supposed to mean?'

The two sisters stared at each other belligerently. Both were now in their thirties yet the animosity between them was as forceful as it had been when they were children.

Lilian had put on a great deal of weight, and since she had always been much shorter than Christabel she was now very plump. Her fair hair framed her round face like a frothy halo. She still chose pastel-pinks, and powder-blues, and was never without her big rings, lavish necklaces, and earrings.

Christabel was far more restrained. Her dark hair was neatly styled, and she favoured tailored clothes that suited her tall, slim figure.

'I understand Marlene has a boyfriend?' Christabel commented as she passed her sister a cup of tea. 'Surely she's rather young for that sort of thing; she's only just fourteen.'

Lilian looked startled. 'Who told you about her boyfriend?'

'Oh, Kay let it slip.'

Lilian gave a forced laugh as she stirred her tea. 'Only a passing phase. As I told you, we will be going back to America quite soon, so it's hardly likely that Marlene would become seriously involved with anyone over here.'

'Well, whether she's serious about him or not, it's not a good example for Kay, but like mother like daughter, I suppose. You were always fickle when it came to boyfriends,' Christabel added dryly. 'Anyway, I want Kay to stay away from her and from London for the next few weeks.'

'And then?'

'After her exams,' Christabel said reluctantly as she sipped her own tea, 'she can come to you for a short holiday, if you like, before she starts at university.'

Kay resented being told she couldn't see Marlene until after her exams, and there was an uncomfortable atmosphere between her and Christabel for the next few weeks. The moment her exams were finished in July she packed a suitcase and went to London. She was still there when her examination results came through in late August.

Christabel phoned to tell her they had arrived.

'You haven't opened them, have you, Aunt Chrissy?'

'No, but I intend to do so if you aren't here by tomorrow morning!' Christabel told her. 'If you had come home yesterday, like I asked you to do, you could have gone in to school and known the results a day earlier.'

'Must I come back today? Can't the letter wait until the weekend?'

'No, Kay, it certainly can't. I'm amazed you don't want to know the results. Are you sure you wouldn't like me to open the letter and read them to you over the phone?'

There was a long pause then, with obvious reluctance, Kay said, 'All right then, Aunt Chrissy, perhaps you'd better do that, but only if it means I can stay here with Marlene for a few more days.'

The silence after Christabel had opened the letter lasted such a long time that Kay asked, 'Are you still there?'

'I'm still here,' Christabel told her in an icy tone. 'I simply cannot believe what I'm reading, which is why I've gone through it again.'

'Why? What do you mean?'

'What do I mean?' Christabel's voice was dangerously quiet and controlled. 'What I mean, is that you've failed in absolutely every subject, Kay!'

'There must be some mistake.' Kay's voice held a mixture of fear and defiance.

'You haven't got a pass in anything. Not a single subject! You'd better get back here right away. You've got a lot of explaining to do, Kay, and we've got to have a very serious talk about your future.'

As she waited for Kay's return, Christabel was filled with an overpowering sense of unease. When it came to late afternoon, and Kay still hadn't arrived home, she phoned Lilian.

'Kay left here immediately after your phone call,' Lilian told her. 'Perhaps she stopped off somewhere to do some shopping.'

'Shopping?' Christabel snapped. 'I very much doubt it!'

'Well, don't shout at me about it,' Lilian said coldly. 'I've no idea where Kay is. I've got plenty of problems of my own. Marlene has just told us that she doesn't want to return to America with us because this boyfriend of hers, Bill Wood, wants them to get engaged. As you can imagine I'm out of my mind with worry because she's far too young and—'

'Will you ask Marlene if she knows where Kay is?' Christabel interrupted.

'Marlene's not here, she's gone to meet Bill,' Lilian said irritably.

'So, Kay might well be with her. If she has told Marlene how dire her report is, then Marlene will know Kay's in trouble, and she may be trying to shield her.'

'Shield her from what?' Lilian asked bemused.

'From me, of course! I want her to come straight home so that we can discuss it and talk about her future. Not one single pass! I still can't believe it. I blame you for encouraging

277

Kay to come to London so often. All this gadding about with Marlene has ruined everything for Kay. Heaven alone knows what's going to happen to her now!'

'Well, don't blame Marlene! If you hadn't pushed Kay so hard she would probably have done better when it came to her exams.'

'What absolute rot,' Christabel exclaimed furiously. 'Now, tell me where Marlene's gone with this so-called boyfriend of hers, and I'll phone and see if Kay's with them.'

'I've already told you, Chrissy, that Marlene has no idea where Kay is. After you phoned this morning, Alex told Kay that he would drive her to the station as soon as he'd finished at the film studio, but she said she couldn't wait until then. She said she'd take a taxi to the station.'

'So why hasn't she turned up here? Where is she?'

'Chrissy, I've already told you, I don't know,' Lilian repeated wearily. 'As soon as you get off the line I'll make some calls and find out if any of our friends have seen her, or if they know anything that might be of help.'

'I think perhaps I should go to the police.'

'What on earth do you want to do that for?' Lilian exclaimed.

'Kay's missing, isn't she? The sooner we set the wheels in motion to find her the better. Anything could have happened to her. What was the time of the train she was intending to catch?'

'I haven't any idea. I simply know that she said she was going to call a cab.'

'There you are, then,' Christabel said triumphantly. 'She's probably still in London. Now are you going to tell me where I can contact Marlene?'

'I've already told you that I have no idea where Marlene is,' Lilian snapped. 'I'll ask her to phone you the moment she comes in.'

Marlene phoned Christabel as soon as she got home, but she was not able to help. She promised to contact everyone she knew to see if they had seen or heard anything from Kay.

Another two days passed and Kay was still missing. Christabel was beside herself with worry. It was at times like this, she reflected, that she missed Lewis so much. If he had been there to share the worry with her it possibly wouldn't have seemed nearly so bad.

Next morning, Kay phoned. She wouldn't say where she was, only that she wouldn't be coming back home.

'But you must, Kay. What are you living on? Where are you sleeping?'

'Don't worry about me, Aunt Chrissy, I'm fine. I'm working as a receptionist in a hotel, and I live in. I'm OK, and I won't be coming home – not for a while, anyway. I'm sorry about my results, but don't worry about it. I never wanted to go to university.'

Christabel tried her hardest to persuade Kay to come home so that they could discuss the situation and decide what to do for the best, but Kay remained adamant. She had made her choice, she said, and she was staying where she was.

Christabel phoned Lilian right away to let her know that Kay had made contact and made Lilian promise that if Kay contacted them and they could find out exactly where she was, they would let her know right away.

Chapter Twenty-Four

In the ensuing weeks Christabel felt quite sure that if Mark hadn't phoned to ask how she was and if she and Kay were coping all right without Lewis, she would have gone out of her mind from not having anyone to share her worries with.

'Kay went back to London with Lilian right after the funeral,' she told him. 'She was so quiet and withdrawn that I'm very concerned about her. She doesn't seem to want to talk to me about her father, so I'm hoping that being with Marlene might help her to come to terms with what has happened.'

'It sounds to me as though you need someone to talk to about it, so if you are on your own, what about coming out for a meal with me?' Mark asked.

It had been the start of regular meetings. They'd gone to quiet little restaurants where Mark seemed to be well known. The food and wine were good and the service discreet, so they were able to talk in comfort.

The intervening years since they'd both been at Hilbury gradually vanished; they felt comfortable in each other's company as their friendship blossomed.

Christabel now found herself automatically turning to Mark for advice when Kay insisted on staying on in London and none of them knew exactly where she was or how she was coping.

'She may only have just left school but you've brought her up to be confident and well adjusted so I'm sure she'll be all right,' he pointed out.

'She's also suffered a great loss, the second one in a comparatively short time. Marlene is very impetuous and rebellious, and although as I say it might help her, I'm also worried that Kay may follow in her footsteps.'

'From what you've told me, Marlene may be rather precocious and think of herself as a child star, but Kay is certainly not following in her footsteps or she would have persuaded her uncle to give her a part in one of his films. Instead of that, Kay's not only found herself a job but she's also been very pragmatic and made sure that it is one that also provides her with somewhere to live.'

'When you put it like that, it all sounds very sensible and responsible,' Christabel agreed. 'What we don't know is what sort of hotel it is and whether or not she's safe living there.'

It was several months before there was any more news, and then it was Kay phoning Marlene to find out when she would be returning to America.

Marlene told her that she intended to marry Bill as soon as she was old enough to do so and would probably be staying on in London. 'You will come to my wedding, Kay?' Marlene begged.

Kay laughed a little self-consciously. 'It's a long way off! Would you really want me to be there?'

'Of course I would. Anyway, I want to see you before then, and tell you all about it and introduce you to Bill. So when are we going to meet?'

'If I come to your home, your mother might tell Aunt Chrissy in advance, and I don't want to have to face her yet.'

'OK, we'll make it somewhere else; just the two of us, and I won't tell anyone that we are planning to meet up,' Marlene agreed.

The meeting restored the close friendship between them. It was like old times as they chatted and caught up on each other's news.

Kay confided in Marlene about her new friend, Stuart Blakemore, who often stayed at the hotel where she worked. When she said that he was single and that he always took her out whenever he was in London, Marlene teasingly suggested they should have a double wedding.

Before they parted, they arranged to see each other again soon. 'Why don't you come to the house and bring your boyfriend, and you can both meet Bill,' Marlene suggested.

Kay looked dubious. 'Is Aunt Chrissy going to be there? If so, I'm not sure I want to come.'

'I was thinking of inviting her; after all she's family. You're family, too, Kay,' Marlene insisted, 'so you must come.'

'I don't know; I really am scared stiff of meeting Aunt Chrissy. If Stuart comes with me, I'm sure she'll disapprove of him, and probably try to stop me seeing him,' she added worriedly.

'Rubbish! You're being paranoid. Anyway, how can she stop you seeing him when you're living in London, and she's hundreds of miles away in Wallasey?'

Kay looked uncertain. 'I don't know, but Aunt Chrissy always seems to get her own way,'

'Aunt Chrissy has been desperately concerned about you since you left home,' Marlene reminded her. 'I really think you should get in touch with her to let her know you're all right and to tell her about Stuart and give her the chance to meet him. It might stop her worrying about you so much.'

Christabel felt very relieved when Kay phoned her – until she mentioned Stuart Blakemore. She couldn't believe she had heard aright. It had been bad enough when Kay had told her she'd found herself a job and was staying on in London, but she found this latest piece of news was a great deal more shattering.

'Surely I don't have to wait until Marlene's

284

wedding before I see you?' Christabel pressed. 'It won't be for ages; at least another year or perhaps longer.'

'I think that would be best,' Kay said stubbornly, 'and you'll be able to meet Stuart at the same time.'

'That will be rather a lot to take in all in one day,' Christabel protested.

'Do you mean for you, or for Stuart?'

'For both of us, I should imagine, Kay. Why don't you bring him here for a visit first?'

Kay refused to be enticed even though she was relieved that her aunt appeared to be taking the news much better than she'd expected. Even so, she was not looking forward to a meeting between Aunt Chrissy and Stuart, but if it was at Marlene's wedding, then Aunt Chrissy would have to be civil to him, she reasoned.

Christabel was at the church early, eager to have a chance to talk to Kay before the service started and was disappointed that Kay and Stuart turned up so late that she didn't have an opportunity to do so.

She felt a lump in her throat as she watched Kay make her way down the aisle and slip into one of the front pews. She had always been above average in height, and she looked extremely smart in a turquoise wool suit that fitted her perfectly. She was wearing her straight dark hair drawn back from her face in a French plait topped by a frothy little hat that emphasised her high cheekbones and vivid blue eyes.

She might only be nineteen but she looked a lot older. Very grown-up and sophisticated, Christabel mused, as she studied her carefully. In so many ways it was like turning the clock back to when she was that age, she thought.

Her reminiscing was cut short as the organ music changed to greet the bride's arrival, and Marlene, a vision in frothy white lace, entered the church on her father's arm.

As they walked up the aisle to where Bill Wood was waiting by the chancel steps, Christabel recalled how disastrous her own love life had been. She remembered Dennis Williams, and how she had lost him to Lilian, and then her brief affair with Alex before the same thing happened all over again.

Christabel wished she could have her life over again. If only her first love, Philip Henderson, hadn't been lost at sea and she hadn't been forced to give up their baby, then things could have been so very different.

Christabel smiled to herself. There was still a great deal that no one in the family would ever know about her. She wondered what Lilian's reaction would be if she told her that she, too, had borne a daughter. It was a secret none of them had the slightest idea about since she had confided in no one except Lewis and he had kept her secret.

What had happened was very much in the

past so there was no point in thinking about it now, she told herself. Nevertheless, looking at Kay, standing tall and confident beside the man she assumed was Stuart Blakemore, Christabel hoped that Kay's future wouldn't be a replica of her own, even though they were so alike in looks and temperament.

Marlene, she was sure, would settle down happily, have two or three children, and by middle-age probably be fat and contented in her role of wife and mother.

She wasn't at all sure that life would be such a bed of roses for Kay. She had spirit as well as a streak of independence which Christabel recognised only too well as being a Montgomery trait. It was one of the reasons she was so anxious to meet Stuart Blakemore and to be able to reassure herself that he was the right partner for Kay.

She studied him throughout the service, and she could understand why Kay had fallen for him. He was tall, broad-shouldered, and had a strong profile.

He looked comfortable in his well-cut suit, as though he were used to dressing smartly. His thick brown hair was swept back from his brow, and his general appearance was commanding and self-assured. His manner towards Kay seemed to be very protective. Even though he seemed quite a bit older than her they appeared to be at ease with each other.

Being the maiden aunt in the family had been

her role for so long that she supposed they all thought she didn't understand about being in love and that she had no right to interfere in what Kay did. They were entitled to their opinion, of course, but for Lewis's sake, she was still concerned when it came to Kay's future happiness.

'Telling Aunt Chrissy we would come to Liverpool for the weekend is one thing, actually doing it, is something else!' Kay muttered moodily as she handed her suitcase to Stuart so that he could put it in the boot of his Rover.

'I thought you would jump at the chance of showing me all your childhood haunts,' he teased, turning to kiss her on the cheek before he slammed the boot shut.

'I could have done that without staying the weekend with her,' she told him, turning away.

'You mean you would have preferred simply to drop in for tea, and then be on our way again?' he said as he held the passenger door open for her.

'That is exactly what I mean!' She settled herself in her seat. 'Still, it's too late for that now, if you've already agreed we will be staying with her; I only hope you don't live to regret it,' she added ominously.

'It's not altogether my fault,' Stuart told her as he took his place behind the wheel and switched on the ignition. 'When she phoned me she said she had already spoken to you about it at Marlene's wedding, so I thought it was all agreed, and it was simply a case of confirming a suitable date.'

'That actually goes to prove my point! Get wise to her now while you have the chance. She can be quite smothering.'

'Are you saying that you didn't make any arrangement to visit her?'

'I certainly did not. Nor did she ask me to do so,' Kay laughed. 'She probably knew I wouldn't agree.'

Stuart looked puzzled. 'Why are you so hostile towards her, Kay?'

'Oh, I don't know.' Kay's mood was as grey as the day, as she stared out of the car window. 'I suppose it's because she's always fussed over me so much.'

'She didn't come across like that to me,' Stuart exclaimed in surprise. 'She certainly seemed to be very concerned about your welfare.'

'That's just the point,' Kay sighed. 'You call it concern, but I think of it as interference. Ever since I can remember, Aunt Chrissy has been there in the background, fussing over me like a mother hen with one only chick.'

'You mean she brought you up? You never told me that.'

'Probably because I was trying to forget about it. My mother died when I was about eleven and as Aunt Chrissy was staying with us at the time she stayed on and took care of things. Then, when I was about fourteen, Dad was killed in a road accident so Aunt Christabel was left in sole charge.'

'So how did you end up in London?'

'Marlene and her parents were living there and I used to visit at weekends and stay with them in my school holidays.'

'Go on!'

'There's not a lot more to tell except that I failed my Higher School Certificate exams . . .'

'All because you spent far too much time with Marlene in London instead of at home studying,' Stuart cut in.

'Aunt Chrissy told you, did she?'

'No, as a matter of fact, she didn't. I managed to work that much out for myself,' he laughed.

'And you got it completely right! In fact, I was in London when my exam results came through. Aunt Chrissy told me over the phone that I had failed them all and she sounded so upset that instead of going back and facing a lecture from her I decided the best thing to do would be to find a job and stay in London. You know the rest,' she ended with a wry smile.

'Your aunt must have been very upset; after all, she must have put her own life on hold in order to stay and look after you.'

'I suppose she must have done, I never thought about it like that,' Kay agreed reluctantly. 'My dad was her sister and they got on very well. I know she was terribly upset when he died, and she must have been pretty lonely afterwards. I suppose I should have stayed with her but, at the time, all I could think of was putting it all behind me and getting away so that I could start afresh.'

'Which must have been devastating for your aunt after all she'd done for you.'

'Marlene says she's found herself a boyfriend. Yes, it's true, even at her age,' she laughed when she saw the look of surprise on Stuart's face. 'Apparently they worked together during the war when she was a nurse and she met him again at the hospital when my dad had his accident.'

As silence descended between them Kay pondered on what Stuart had said. It made her think about her Aunt Christabel in quite a new way and she felt that perhaps she had been thoughtless, unkind even, to have deserted her like she'd done when, as Stuart had pointed out, Aunt Chrissy had obviously changed her whole life to look after her.

She stole a sideways glance at Stuart wondering how she would feel if she had to change her lifestyle and never see him again. She knew she would be heartbroken because she loved him so much and was determined to marry him. She'd never thought about it before but now she wondered if perhaps Aunt Chrissy had forfeited the chance of marrying in order to look after her and her father.

When Aunt Lilian had heard that she was seeing Stuart on a regular basis she'd wanted her to tell Aunt Chrissy about him.

'Well, at least bring him here so that we can meet him,' she begged when Kay had refused to take him to see Aunt Chrissy. 'He sounds all right, but there are some very strange people in London, and you are very young and inexperienced.'

Kay had still not done so, preferring to keep him to herself but, in the end, she'd had to give in because Aunt Lilian had insisted that if she wanted to bring him to Marlene's wedding then she and Alex must meet him first.

They'd made quite a party of the occasion so that Stuart wouldn't feel that he was being inspected. Marlene and her prospective husband Bill were there, and Alex had invited people from the film set, and it had turned out to be a very convivial evening.

Afterwards, both Alex and Lilian had said they liked Stuart and kept reminding her that she ought to take him to meet Aunt Chrissy. Aunt Lilian was far too busy with the preparations for Marlene's wedding to follow up her suggestion with any enthusiasm and Kay was happy to let her forget about it.

Kay herself was so involved with work and with Stuart that she'd not checked on whether Aunt Chrissy had accepted an invitation to Marlene's wedding or not and seeing her in the church as they walked in had been a shock. Kay wished she wasn't sitting in a pew behind them. She could feel her eyes on them, studying her and Stuart, and it made her feel uncomfortable all through the service.

Afterwards, at the reception, when Aunt Chrissy sought them both out, Kay had felt cornered, and knew there was no way at all that she could avoid introducing Stuart to her.

She had to admit that her aunt had seemed to be extremely pleased to see her and hadn't reproached her at all for not keeping in touch. However, having to walk away to fetch the glass of white wine that Aunt Christabel had asked for and leave Stuart chatting to her on his own for a few minutes had been almost as great an ordeal as introducing them to each other in the first place.

They seemed to be on the best of terms when she returned, so she assumed nothing untoward had been said, although she thought Stuart looked at her in a rather puzzled way as she rejoined them.

Kay was surprised to find that their weekend in Wallasey was an extremely pleasant one. Aunt Chrissy made them both very welcome. She had put Stuart in the larger of the guest rooms and Kay in her old room, which was at the other end of the long passage.

The weather had brightened up so Kay and Stuart spent Saturday afternoon visiting places she knew in Wallasey and New Brighton. It was the first time he had been there and he was very impressed by the New Brighton Tower and the fact that it was possible to look across the Mersey at the impressive Liverpool frontage and also far away to the West to see the outline of Mount Snowdon and the Welsh mountain range.

In the evening, Mark joined them for dinner and Kay was surprised to discover what good company he was. Afterwards, they'd all talked until quite late and Kay was intrigued to hear that he had two sons who were older than she was and that he had first known her aunt when she was about her own age.

Up until the moment when she went upstairs to collect her suitcase, the weekend had been surprisingly successful. Christabel knew from the look on Kay's face that she'd been greatly relieved because she'd been very tactful when reminiscing about the past and appeared to have accepted without any argument that she now had a life in London.

She wished with all her heart that Kay would come back home but she knew she had to accept that it would never happen now, not since she'd met Stuart. It was so obvious that they were in love and Christabel had to admit that Mark was right and that Stuart was a very solid sort of chap and would make Kay a good husband.

Christabel waited until next morning when Kay was coming downstairs with her suitcase and then asked her to come into the sitting room so that she could have a private word with her, saying they hadn't had a chance for a talk since

Lewis had died and there were a lot of things they needed to talk about.

She realised the moment she shut the door that Kay thought she was in for a lecture and that she was immediately on her guard.

'Oh not now, Aunt Chrissy. Please don't ruin the weekend by lecturing me,' Kay protested.

'I've no intention of doing that, my dear,' Christabel reassured her. 'It's been lovely having you and Stuart here and I hope that you will both come again very soon. It's just that there are several things that we've got to sort out concerning your father's will and where you stand in regards to this house and everything else.

Stuart waited until they were clear of Liverpool, then he pulled over into a layby, switched off the ignition, and turned to face Kay. 'Right, let's hear what it is, then. What was it your Aunt Christabel said to you that has made you clam up and look as if you'd been told the Stock Market had crashed and you'd lost all your money?'

'I'm all right, really,' Kay protested.

'You haven't said a word since we left Wallasey,' Stuart protested. 'It wasn't because you heard me promise her that we'd come back again soon and that next time we would try and stay much longer, was it? I thought you were both getting on so well with each other by the time we left that you would want to do that.'

'You're quite right, I do. I'm very pleased that you told her that. In fact, I think I have been rather mean and made her feel unwanted over the last few years. I'm glad she's got such a good friend as Dr Mark Murray, he seems to be such a nice man.'

Stuart looked puzzled. 'So why such a subdued mood, then?'

'Aunt Christabel was telling me about my dad's will and about the house and I found it rather upsetting. Look, I don't want to talk about it now. I'll tell you all about it some other time.'

Chapter Twenty-Five

With a feeling of dismay Christabel reread the letter from her sister Lilian which had arrived that morning. It certainly put a dampener on her own plans, she thought wryly.

She was sorry to hear that Alex had died but, remembering his lifestyle and the copious amounts he always ate and drank and how overweight he had been for years, Christabel wasn't all that surprised. She felt sad for Lilian because she'd depended on him so much. It had always been Alex who was the figurehead in their family and who made all the decisions.

Christabel reflected she and Alex had not been on very good terms for a long time, because she'd blamed him and Lilian for the rift between herself and Kay after Lewis had died.

She'd had such high hopes for Kay's future and she'd been planning for her to go to university and make something of her life. She was quite sure that would have happened if it hadn't been for Lilian and Alex encouraging her to visit them in London.

Spending so much time there with Marlene meant that Kay had neglected her studies and consequently her examination results had been so dire that Kay had been afraid to come home.

It had meant a long estrangement between her and Kay. If Mark hadn't come into her life when Lewis died and been at her side ever since, she wasn't sure how she would have endured not being in touch with Kay because it had left such a dreadful void.

Christabel sighed, remembering how terribly upset and unwanted she'd felt when Kay told her that she was going to marry Stuart. When she'd confided in Mark about it he'd pointed out that since Kay was already leading an independent life it probably wouldn't make very much difference.

'I know I can't take Kay's place in your heart but I'll always be here for you,' he'd added, taking her in his arms and giving her a reassuring hug.

All that, of course, was in the past and, as Mark was quick to point out whenever she mentioned that she still missed having Kay at home, she now saw her quite regularly.

This was very true and most of the time Christabel knew she was very fortunate that nowadays Kay did keep in touch and included her in her life as much as she possibly could, even though she was still living in London.

Until a couple of years ago, even after they were married, Kay and Stuart had made the journey from London to Wallasey so that they could spend the weekend with her at least once a month. Since Jill was born they'd not managed to come quite as often. She understood that, of course; travelling with a very young child wasn't easy, there was so much that they had to bring with them.

Not for the first time, Christabel reflected on how lucky she was to have met up with Mark again and to have had him in her life for the past six years. He was not only a calming influence but was also dependable, wise and helpful.

She had Mark to thank for suggesting that since she had nursing experience she might find it interesting to come and work at the clinic that was part of the practice where he worked. It had not only stopped her brooding over Kay's absence but had also provided her with a much-needed income.

Their friendship had blossomed into a deep companionship that suited them both and which they both enjoyed. Over dinner the previous night Mark had asked her if she would marry him and she had accepted.

Christabel wondered if she should tell the rest of the family about their future plans when they all came to Liverpool for the service to commemorate Alex's life. She wasn't at all sure that Mark would think it was the right time to do so and wondered if he would even want to be there with them.

He mightn't want to intrude on such a sensitive family affair as the disposal of Alex's ashes. Yet, on the other hand, since they were shortly to be married he might consider himself to be part of the family already, she mused.

Mark was very family orientated and always so considerate and careful to do what he thought was the right thing. She remembered how, when they had realised that they meant so much to each other, he had insisted that she must meet his two sons.

She'd been very nervous about doing so because from what Mark had told her they had both been very close to their mother and had taken her death rather badly. Christabel had been afraid that they might resent her close friendship with their father in case she tried to take their mother's place. They were both so charming and so courteous towards her, however, that she'd felt quite overwhelmed.

Since then she'd grown to know them both extremely well and she now felt a genuine interest in them and was almost as concerned for their welfare as Mark was.

'It always seems to be weddings and funerals that bring about family reunions,' Kay commented as she passed the letter, which had arrived that morning, across the breakfast table to Stuart.

'It's not Aunt Christabel getting married, is it?' He grinned as he took it from her.

'No, I think she's far too set in her ways to do anything as reckless as that.' Kay smiled.

'We really should go and see her this weekend.

She hasn't seen Jill for a couple of months now and you know how much she enjoys spending time with her.'

'I know, but we seem to have been so busy lately. I have written to her most weeks and sent her the latest snapshots we've taken of Jill.'

'That's not quite the same as visiting her, and you know it isn't!' Stuart remonstrated. He looked again at the letter Kay had passed across to him from her cousin Marlene to say that her father had died in America, and that her mother was bringing his ashes back to England:

It's Mum's idea, she wants them to be interred in the family grave in Liverpool. I very much hope you will come because I'm counting on your support.

We will be staying over in Wallasey with Aunt Christabel, of course, so it will be a good opportunity for us all to meet up as a family. You barely know Bill, and I have only met Stuart a few times. You've not seen either of my children any more than I have seen your little poppet.

'Marlene says she's relying on you being there, so when do you want to travel to Merseyside?' Stuart asked, passing the letter back to Kay.

'She'll have her husband and Aunt Lilian so she doesn't really need me there for moral support,' Kay demurred. 'It might all be too much for Aunt Chrissy. I know she has the room to put us up, but I don't think she can afford to cater for so many visitors and you know she's too proud to let us pay for anything.'

Stuart looked at his watch. 'I'm running late, we'll talk about it when I get home tonight, OK?' He stood up, kissed her goodbye and made for the door.

For the rest of the day Kay worried about what to do. She certainly wanted to see Marlene and her family, even Aunt Lilian, but staying with Aunt Chrissy at a time like this could be awkward.

Aunt Lilian was bound to talk about Uncle Alex's will and that would be the opening for Aunt Chrissy to get on to the subject of Lewis's will and there was so much involved that Kay felt this wasn't the right time to deal with it.

Aunt Chrissy had mentioned the will several times before but Kay had always managed to avoid the issue, mainly because she was pretty sure that Aunt Christabel wanted to talk about what was to be done with the house in Rolleston Drive and was waiting for her to say what she wanted to do about it. She knew there would have to be a decision eventually but knowing that it would affect them both, she didn't know what was to be done because selling the house would mean turning Aunt Christabel out of what had been her home for so many years.

Kay knew she ought to talk to Stuart about

it and tell him exactly what was involved and ask his advice, but she kept putting it off mainly because she still had feelings of guilt for having behaved so unfeelingly towards Aunt Christabel immediately after her father had died.

For so many years, she reflected, they'd been almost like mother and daughter but after Lewis had died, Aunt Christabel had started putting the pressure on, determined to make her go to university, and that was when she'd rebelled.

She was quite sure that Aunt Christabel had forgiven her and accepted that was all in the past. They would never be as close as they'd been when she was a child, but they were still very fond of each other and affectionate towards one another.

At the moment, Kay reflected, everything was so harmonious that she didn't want to do anything to upset things – especially the almost-perfect life that she and Stuart were living now that he was working with his father. For many years Stuart's mother had been in poor health due to a heart condition, and when she died a few months after Stuart and Kay married, Stuart's father, who was an estate agent in the picturesque Thames Valley village of Cookham, had suggested that it might be a good idea if Stuart joined him as a business partner.

'You've worked in the housing market ever

since you left college,' he pointed out, 'so you have a fair grounding of business matters and you might enjoy the change.'

'It's an interesting idea but I've no spare money to put into a business, Dad,' Stuart protested.

'I'm not asking you to do that. I'll remain as a sleeping partner, but it will be your business, and you'll be responsible for the day-to-day running of it. I'm not completely useless, so you can draw on my services when you're busy, or if you want to go on holiday, or if you simply want the odd day off.'

It had worked exceptionally well. Kay liked Harvey Blakemore, and he liked her. In so many ways he was an older version of Stuart. He had the same robust build, the same grey eyes and square jaw. The main difference was his paunch and his grey hair.

Kay and Stuart found a house only a few streets away from his father's bungalow and were settled in well before Jill was born. Left to run her own life, look after Stuart, and bring up Jill had boosted Kay's self-confidence. In many ways they'd been the happiest years of her life.

Occasionally she would feel guilty about not seeing her aunt as often as she'd done before Jill had been born, but she knew that Christabel was working at the same practice as Mark and had a very busy life herself these days.

Marlene's letter niggled in the back of her mind for the rest of the day, and by the time

Stuart came home that evening she was feeling on edge and apprehensive. She knew he thought they ought to go and was at a loss to understand her reluctance.

Kay waited until Jill was in bed, and they were sitting down to their meal, before she said anything. When Stuart didn't mention it she forced herself to do so.

'We'll go to Wallasey next Thursday, if that's all right with you,' she said abruptly.

'Good! I'll ask my father to cover for me. Do you want to make it a day trip?'

She looked startled, her blue eyes wide with surprise. 'I hadn't really thought that far ahead,' she admitted.

'Well, we could stay in a hotel at New Brighton for a few days, if you think it would be too crowded at Christabel's place. That would make it more enjoyable for us.'

'I hardly think you should count on it being a holiday,' she said tartly.

'No, but it could be a pleasant break. Our Jill might enjoy meeting her little cousins.'

'Well, yes, I suppose you're right,' Kay agreed thoughtfully. 'Tommy must be about two and Tracy almost four now.

'So they're about the same age as Jill and that means they should all play together quite well while you and Marlene catch up on what's been happening in your lives.'

'And what are you going to do, spend time with Bill?'

'You'll have to wait and see, won't you?' Stuart grinned. 'I know one thing; we won't manage to get a word in once you and Marlene meet up.'

'We mightn't have anything in common after all this time.' Kay grimaced.

Arriving in Liverpool and driving through the Mersey Tunnel knowing that she was going to meet Marlene and her Aunt Lilian was like turning back the clock, Kay thought as they emerged in Wallasey and made their way to Rolleston Drive.

As Stuart brought the car to a stop in the driveway, the front door opened and Aunt Christabel was there to welcome them. Christabel ushered them all inside and as she made drinks and plied them with biscuits, Jill followed her around, chattering happily.

'It really is like being in a time warp,' Kay murmured to Stuart. 'I remember when I was little I behaved exactly the same as Jill is doing now; it's almost as if she's attached to her by an invisible cord!'

'We're meeting Lilian and Marlene and her family at the church in Liverpool,' Aunt Christabel explained as soon as they'd finished their drinks. 'I'll get my coat and then we'll be off. I understand that it's quite a pleasant little ceremony. Not very long, either, so the children won't be bored. Then we'll all come back here and have a meal. I've left everything ready.

The children can play out in the garden after-wards, if it keeps fine, or there's plenty for them to do in the house.'

'She's planned it all down to the last detail,' Kay giggled as they made their way outside. 'I bet she's even arranged for the sun to shine.'

Stuart laughed. 'Like someone else I know who never leaves anything to chance,' he said mildly as he opened the rear door of the car and lifted Jill in.

'I want Aunt Chrissy to sit in the back with me,' Jill insisted as he fastened her into her special safety seat.

'I think Aunt Chrissy would sooner ride in front so that she can tell me which way to go,' Stuart told her.

'No,' Jill told him stubbornly, 'I want her in the back so that I can hold her hand.'

The few days they stayed in Wallasey seemed to pass in a flash and without any unpleasant incidents. The children played well together; they were much of an age. Tracy and Tommy were both rather precocious. Tracy was petite and plump like her mother. She also had curly hair like Marlene's, only it had a slight tinge of auburn in it; Tommy took after Bill and had the same thick brown hair; both of them had greyish-blue eyes like Marlene.

The next day Bill and Stuart took the chil-dren across to Liverpool on the ferry boat leaving the four women to catch up with all their news about family, friends and children.

It was late on Sunday afternoon when Kay and Stuart set off for home with Jill. They'd promised Bill and Marlene that they would visit them in London. Lilian, they were told, would not be returning to America, but would be living with them until she found a place of her own.

'Well, it wasn't so bad, was it?' Stuart commented as they left Liverpool behind.

'Aunty Chrissy said she was missing me and we haven't been to see her for a long time so I asked her to come and stay with us,' Jill piped up from the back of the car.

Kay swivelled round in her seat. 'You did what?'

'I expect it is too far for her to travel all the way to Cookham,' Stuart said quickly, placing a warning hand on Kay's arm.

'No, it's not,' Jill assured them. 'She promised she would come.'

'Yes, your daddy's right, dear, it is a long way. I don't know how she would manage the journey. We'll come back again and see her sometime soon.'

'No, she said she would come and stay with us,' Jill repeated stubbornly, her blue eyes intense. 'She said she would come in her car . . .'

'Drive! Aunt Chrissy hasn't got a car,' Kay told her. 'She can't afford one these days.'

'Yes, she has, and it's a brand-new one,' Jill insisted.

'Mark bought Christabel a new car,' Stuart whispered.

'You're making it up!'

'No, I'm not.'

In the days that followed Jill constantly asked when Aunt Chrissy would be arriving. Intrigued, Kay finally phoned to see if she really had meant what she'd said to Jill.

'I'd love to come for a visit, Kay. I was waiting, though, for you to ask me. I didn't think I could simply turn up on little Jill's say-so,' she chuckled. 'I remember all too clearly how you invited one of your teacher's to come to tea. You never said a word to me and when she turned up I was so surprised that I didn't know what to do. I had nothing special in, and we all ended up eating peanut butter sandwiches, ice cream and tinned fruit.'

Kay didn't recall the incident, but she found herself smiling. On a sudden impulse, she suggested that Christabel should come that weekend and bring Mark Murray with her so that he could share the driving and she could see Christabel's new car.

'Good heavens, however did you know about that?'

'Never tell Jill anything you don't want to hear repeated over and over again,' Kay warned her.

'Dear me, like some other little girl I used to know. She never could keep a secret.'

309

'I wonder if I should phone Marlene, and invite them as well,' Kay said later that evening when she was telling Stuart that her aunt and Mark were both coming for the weekend.

If they were all there as well, she reasoned to herself, Aunt Christabel wouldn't have a chance to bring up the subject of the will or press her for an answer.

When she did phone Marlene, however, her cousin seemed to be rather reluctant. 'I'd love to come and see you, Kay, but some other time, not while Aunt Chrissy is staying with you,' Marlene told her. 'I don't want her taking over my life.'

'What on earth are you talking about? Aunt Chrissy has changed; she's mellowed with age.'

'If you say so.' Marlene laughed. 'But watch out. I noticed the way your Jill was running round after her, exactly the same as my mum always said you used to do when you were small! Jill is such a replica of what you looked like at her age, apparently, that Mum said that seeing them together was like the rerun of an old film!'

Chapter Twenty-Six

Christabel breathed a sigh of relief as she closed the front door behind the last of her visitors and the silence wrapped round her like a comforting cloak. She also felt a twinge of guilt because, although their visit had gone extremely well, she had not told them about her own plans for the future.

She had fully intended to tell them that she was marrying Mark while they were all gathered together because it would have been an ideal time to do so, but somehow there was never the right moment.

Most of the talk had centred around Alex and all the things he had said or done and that had stirred up so many memories and reminded her how very much her life had been interwoven with his in the past.

Perhaps if Mark had been there, standing at her side, holding her hand, or with his arm around her, giving her the back-up she felt she needed when she told them her news, it would have been different. Mark, though, had not been there; he'd had to attend a medical conference in Birmingham.

Now they'd all left she regretted not having

told them but of course it was too late. Actually Kay was the only person whose opinion really mattered. Christabel should have taken her to one side and told her because it was going to affect her and the details were too complicated to put in a letter or explain over the telephone.

'There's an old adage that says absence makes the heart grow fonder, so you should try it,' Marlene sighed. 'You don't have to invite Aunt Chrissy to stay with you quite so often, Kay.'

'I don't, and she doesn't come all that often!'

'You most certainly do! Every time we want to come to visit you she's staying with you for the weekend,' Marlene said crossly.

'So what does it matter if she is here? There's room for you as well, isn't there?'

'Not on your life! I don't want to spend a whole weekend under the same roof as Aunt Chrissy and neither does Bill. I'm surprised Stuart stands for it.'

'He never complains. In fact, he quite likes her. They seem to get on very well.'

'I doubt it! He probably only puts up with having her there for your sake; anyway, what about Jill?'

'Jill loves her. She asked me the other day if we could adopt her as a Granny!'

'I bet Aunt Chrissy put her up to it. She's a cunning old bat! You know how she monopolised you when you were small. I hope you told Jill she wasn't to call her Granny.'

'I did, as a matter of fact, but I don't think it has made a lot of difference. I heard Jill doing so the last time Aunt Christabel was here. She doesn't do it when they know I'm around, so there's not a lot I can do about it.'

'Oh, can't you indeed! I'd do something about it and pretty damn quick. Aunt Chrissy is an out and out fraud. And, what is more to the point, she's trying to take over your life again.'

'Oh, come off it, Marlene, she's not all that bad,' Kay protested mildly.

'She is and you know it; anyway, I didn't telephone to discuss Aunt Chrissy and her foibles,' Marlene said sourly. 'I phoned to ask if you would like to come to London and stay with us next weekend. It's the première of *Rock of Ages*. Bill has been involved with all the promotional work and there will be quite a lavish celebration afterwards which all the stars will attend.'

'Oh dear, it's back to Aunt Chrissy again, I'm afraid,' Kay said contritely.

'What do you mean?'

'She and Mark are coming to visit us next weekend.'

'Then put them off!'

'She'll be terribly hurt if I do that,' Kay said apologetically. 'I suppose we could bring her with us and they could stay with Aunt Lilian and help her look after the children when we go out.'

'Oh, no, she'd probably insist on coming with us and I'm not risking that. I've got Bill's business friends to consider. Can you imagine their reactions?'

'Surely they're all civilised and well mannered, aren't they?' Kay said tartly. 'Anyway, some of them are pretty way out themselves in the way they dress and the things they say.'

'That be as it may, Mark's quite acceptable, but I have no intention of being ridiculed by any of them because of Aunt Chrissy's autocratic behaviour. My God! Bill would never forgive me. Surely you can put her off.'

'You'd better leave it with me then,' Kay murmured. 'I'll see if I can think of some suitable excuse.'

'Why bother with an excuse? Simply tell her that I have invited you for the weekend.'

'And that your invitation doesn't include them?' Kay laughed.

'Yes, do that if you want to. It won't worry me. I hardly ever see her anyway. If you tell her that then she might realise that you have a life of your own and that you can't always be at her beck and call any more than you can include her in everything you do.'

Kay felt that Marlene was being very unfair about Aunt Chrissy and had no intention of being as outspoken as her cousin suggested. Tactfully, she explained to Aunt Chrissy that something had come up, and they would have to postpone her visit until the following weekend.

To her embarrassment, Aunt Chrissy seemed

to be well aware that it was because of the film première and guessed that they'd been invited to attend.

'You really should tell the truth and not make silly excuses, Kay,' she sighed. 'It was the same when you were a child and growing up, you used to concoct the most elaborate stories to try and outwit me. It was such a waste of time because I always found out what the truth was in the end. I would have thought that by now you would have outgrown such petty behaviour. It sets a very bad example for Jill, you know.'

'I was only trying to save your feelings, Aunt Christabel,' Kay told her lamely.

'Absolute rubbish! You should know by now that there's no love lost between me and Marlene. I wouldn't go to one of her flamboyant parties if she asked me. Actors and actresses, I've met them all and I despise most of them.'

'As long as you understand, and you don't mind putting your visit off until the following weekend . . .'

'Of course I don't mind, Kay,' Christabel assured her. 'Go and enjoy yourselves in London but remember, I would like to see you and Stuart soon because there is something of importance I want to tell you both.'

'Can't you tell me about it on the phone?'

'No,' Christabel hesitated. 'I don't really want to do that, dear. Next week will be fine.

By the way,' she added, 'mind you tell Jill that you're the one who has altered the arrangement, not me. I wouldn't want her to think her Granny—' she pulled herself up quickly, 'her Aunt Chrissy had broken her promise about coming to see her.'

The receiver at Christabel's end went down before Kay could make any reply. I must ask Stuart to have a word with her about encouraging Jill to call her Granny, she thought as she replaced her own phone. As Marlene had pointed out, it was all very well to say it was harmless fun but it was probably best to nip it in the bud.

The weekend in London was in such complete contrast to their usual lifestyle. Marlene's two children, Tracy and Tommy, were always pleased to see Jill and once the three of them were together they were inseparable.

'It's almost as though we hadn't got her with us,' Kay commented as they set off for a top London restaurant with Marlene and Bill, leaving the children in Lilian's care on the first evening of their stay.

'All part of the service,' Bill told Kay. 'You get a built-in babysitter when you come to stay with us.'

'Are you sure it's not too much responsibility for Aunt Lilian having to look after all three of them?'

'Not a bit of it,' Marlene told her briskly.

'Mum loves doing it. She says it keeps her young.'

Kay said nothing but she thought Marlene's comment was a long way from the truth. She had been shocked by her aunt's appearance. She seemed to have shrunk to nothing since Uncle Alex had died, and she looked so thin and frail that Kay wondered if there was anything seriously wrong with her. When she finally found an opportunity to mention it to Marlene, her cousin shrugged.

'Simply a matter of getting older,' she said dismissively. 'She is in her forties, you know, so what can you expect?'

'Aunt Chrissy is older than your mother, yet she looks as fit as a fiddle!'

'She's only ever had herself to worry about, that's probably why.'

'Marlene, how can you say such a thing? She brought me up and kept house for Dad until he died,' Kay defended.

'Yes, I know all that, but she's never had to keep a husband happy, or worry about making financial decisions or anything like that. Your father paid all the bills when you were growing up so she had no money worries. When he died she was able to stay on in his house and go on living in comfort on the money he left. Mum says that by rights that should be yours or it should have been shared out between you. Heaven knows, she could do with it now.'

Kay felt taken aback that Marlene knew so much.

'It was probably my dad's way of compensating her for giving up her job and everything so that she could look after us all those years, and for bringing me up,' she countered.

'Is that really what you believe?' Marlene looked sceptical. Her Cupid's bow mouth tightened into a disapproving little knot, and her blue-grey eyes hardened into glassy pebbles.

Kay frowned, puzzled by the bitterness in Marlene's voice. 'I always understood that Uncle Alex was terribly successful. I thought he would have left Aunt Lilian so very well provided for that she wouldn't want for anything.'

Marlene gave a sharp, bitter laugh. 'You're so naïve, Kay,' she said scathingly. 'You believe everyone is full of good thoughts and kindness. The world isn't like that – leastwise, not the real world, the one we have to live in.'

Kay stared at her, bemused, wondering what she had done or said to bring on such an onslaught. Marlene was usually so frothy and bubbly, so laid back, as if she hadn't a care in the world. Now, judging from her outburst, what she presented on the surface was totally different to what she was feeling underneath.

'I don't understand what you are trying to tell me,' she admitted awkwardly. 'Are you saying that Aunt Lilian is in some sort of financial difficulty?'

'Thanks to Bill she isn't. Dad died penniless.

In fact, he died owing money. He was such a great guy.' She sighed. 'He lived life to the full, drank vintage wines and spirits, and ate only at the top restaurants. He had so many friends in high places, but it costs a lot to keep up a lifestyle like that. It took every penny he earned and some. It wasn't until after he died that we found out how little there was left, or how much he owed. If it hadn't been for Bill, I don't know what would have happened to my mother. Their house was mortgaged up to the hilt, and every bank account he had was over-drawn. Creditors swooped on Mum like a flock of magpies.'

'You mean that Bill had to bail Aunt Lilian out?' Kay said in a shocked voice.

'Not only bail her out financially, but we also had to let her come and live with us. I love her, don't get me wrong. It used to be wonderful seeing her from time to time, but having her living with us . . . well, I'll leave that to your imagination!'

Kay shuddered. She could feel the tension, sense the strain.

'What can I say?'

'Not a lot! Watch your own step, though. Don't let Aunt Chrissy impose on you or you might find yourself in a similar situation. Imagine having her move in with you!'

'Why don't you suggest to your mother that she stays with Aunt Christabel for a while?' Kay suggested brightly. 'They are sisters, after all.'

'I had thought of it, but that would put us under an obligation to Aunt Chrissy and then I would have no way of refusing to let her come here for a visit whenever she wanted to. No, it's not so bad, really. Mum has her own room and spends quite a lot of her time up there, especially in the evenings. She's very good with the children, and if ever we want to go out on our own, then we know she will keep an eye on them.'

Marlene's outburst shattered Kay's equanimity. She found herself looking at Marlene and Bill's set-up with completely different eyes.

Bill was like Marlene's father in so many ways, Kay thought reflectively. He was tall but rather paunchy, even though he was only in his early thirties. He had a round face with a small nose and a rather sharp chin. His brown eyes shone like bright beads behind his gold-rimmed glasses and his thin dark brown hair was sleeked back from his high forehead, almost as if he had just stepped out of the shower.

He had a suave, plausible manner, always dressed impressively, and had personalised number plates on his state-of-the-art-Mercedes. She had never been able to pin down precisely what he did for a living, except that it was something to do with promotions and publicity in the film world.

Living up to his flamboyant lifestyle with all the entertaining it entailed had certainly had dire effects on Marlene over the years, Kay noted. Whereas Aunt Lilian was only a shadow of her former self, Marlene was a round ball; her dumpling figure overflowed from her dresses, which were bursting at the seams.

Perhaps that was why the strain was not noticeable on Marlene's face, she reflected. It was full and round and she had no wrinkles or worry lines. She wondered if she indulged in comfort eating.

As they drove home at the end of their weekend jaunt, Kay took an impartial look at Stuart, and felt thankful that she wasn't in Marlene's shoes. Her cousin's outburst had opened her eyes to how lucky she was.

Stuart might prefer the quiet unsophisticated life of a country village to the glitzy glamour of London, but then she did as well. With Stuart you got what you saw. His manner was the same on the golf course as it was in the back garden, or when he was behind his estate agent's desk.

Whenever they entertained, Kay thought with a degree of satisfaction, they thoroughly enjoyed the company of the people they'd invited. They didn't invite them because they had to or because they were trying to create an impression, or curry favour in order to strike a business deal.

As she drifted off to sleep that night, Kay remembered that Aunt Christabel would be visiting them the following weekend and wondered what it was that her aunt wanted to talk to her and Stuart about. She had certainly seemed to be worried about something and had made it sound as though it was important.

She wondered if perhaps Aunt Chrissy was beginning to find that it was becoming rather too much for her living on her own in such a big house. Or perhaps she was finding it lonely there all on her own.

Remembering Marlene's warning she really did hope that she wasn't about to suggest that she should come and live with them. That was one thing she wouldn't be too happy about, especially where Jill was concerned.

Chapter Twenty-Seven

In a contemplative mood, Mark looked round his lounge with its two huge armchairs and matching settee all upholstered in dark red plush, and the highly polished glass-fronted bookcase and radiogram in matching wood as he sipped his glass of whisky and thought about the future.

A tall, wide-shouldered man in his late fifties, he still had thick fair hair, a lean, good-looking face, and deep intelligent brown eyes. He had changed out of his suit into comfortable grey flannels and a dark blue cashmere round-necked sweater.

When dealing with patients he always sounded competent and professional as he explained in a crisp, impersonal way what their ailment was and outlined the treatment he recommended. In his private life, he was much less confident.

Meeting up with Christabel had been like turning the clock back almost twenty years. He had been attracted to her when they'd first met at Hilbury hospital because of the competent way she'd done her job. Dealing with casualties from the Front and administering to their terrible injuries must have been harrowing for such a young girl.

He'd been young himself in those days, he reflected, and newly married with a young family to worry about.

He had been happy in his first marriage and getting married again at his age, he reflected, would be like starting all over again. It had taken him quite a while to be sure that it was what he wanted. His main problem was wondering whether his two children thought it was the right thing for him to do, or would they resent him replacing their mother in his life?

He knew he didn't really have to consider their opinion since they were adults now and both with good career prospects, but they'd been a close-knit, loving family. Their mother's death from cancer while she was still in her mid-forties had come as a shock for all of them. They'd relied heavily on him and he'd done his best to be both mother and father to them until they'd left university.

Since then, although they'd become independent, they still remained close and confided in each other about what was going on in their lives. Leastwise, they'd done so up until now, but so far he hadn't told them that he was about to marry Christabel although they knew that the two of them had been going out together on a regular basis for several years. It was why he was so anxious for them all to meet and it had taken some careful planning to make sure that both of the boys would be at home the same weekend.

He knew they both liked Christabel and that she got on well with them. Nevertheless, their forthcoming meeting might be challenging and he was anxious to have it behind him.

The two boys would be staying with him, of course, and he resolved to tell them over breakfast that he was planning to be married again. This would give them the rest of the day to digest his news before they all met up in the evening for dinner at the Adelphi Hotel. He hoped it would be a celebratory meal that would set the seal of approval on his forthcoming nuptials.

One of the problems he had anticipated was that they wouldn't want him to give up the family home in Formby, the house where they'd both been born and which had been the hub of their family life for so many years. At the same time he could understand that Christabel didn't want to live there and possibly be haunted by memories of his old life there.

Of course he couldn't possibly move to her home on the other side of the Mersey, even if she wanted him to do so. His practice was well established and it would be highly inconvenient to have to travel from Wallasey to Formby each day.

Once Hilbury had closed at the end of the war he had formed a partnership with Cecil Roberts, who'd also been a doctor there. He'd taken a fairly large house and the surgery and waiting room had been attached to the main building at the side of the property, but completely separate.

Over the years he and Cecil Roberts had built up a very solid family practice and he didn't want his new lifestyle to interfere with that any more than was absolutely necessary.

He had already suggested to Christabel that they should start their married life in a completely new house in Formby. So far, though, they hadn't found one that they liked and that could provide reception and consulting rooms completely separate from the main living area.

When they did find one, he realised that it would mean disposing of most of the things he was familiar with; furniture which he'd chosen with his first wife so many years ago, which had become almost part of the fabric of his life but which he couldn't expect Christabel to want to keep.

Over the weekend he intended to ask his boys to take any pieces they wanted as mementoes; anything from furniture to ornaments and pictures. He hoped they would do so because it seemed dreadful to simply dispose of everything that had once meant so much to them all.

He knew Christabel was going to have to do the same but she had only been acting as a housekeeper to her brother so he didn't think that giving up her place in Wallasey would be quite as traumatic as it was for him to give up the home where he'd raised a family.

'Once we've told everyone we are going to get married and have found a house we like, then I'll invite Kay to come for the weekend so that she can take anything she might want,' she'd agreed. 'As well as all the furniture and so on there are a lot of papers and documents, including things like Lewis and Violet's marriage certificate, that will be needed to be sorted. I think it is Kay's responsibility to decide whether they should be destroyed or placed in safe keeping somewhere.'

Christabel had gone on to tell Mark that she wanted Jill, Kay's little daughter, to be brides-maid, but he was not sure how he felt about that.

'Since we're having a civil ceremony, not a grand church wedding, I don't think there is any place for a bridesmaid,' he'd pointed out.

Christabel would not give up on the idea, however. 'Perhaps we should call her a flower girl instead, then,' he'd suggested half in jest.

Christabel had seemed quite pleased with that idea.

'I do so want her to be part of things because I think it will mean a great deal to her,' she'd told him.

He still wasn't sure if he'd done the right thing in agreeing to it, but he hoped for the best. It always seemed strange to him how attached Christabel was to the child. She seemed to take an incredible delight in the fact that Jill occasionally called her Granny.

When he'd asked Christabel if it was right to let her do this she immediately claimed that it was only a game.

This was a very minor problem compared to all the others they had at the moment, he reflected. Another three months and he hoped it would all be over and they would be settled in their new home, enjoying life together.

One step at a time, he told himself. The coming weekend was the first big step and if that went according to plan then he was sure it boded well for the future.

As he waited in the foyer of the Adelphi for the taxi bringing Christabel over from Wallasey, Mark wondered what other shocks he was going to encounter that night.

Maybe he hadn't been giving his two boys as much of his time as he should have been doing. Since he'd met up again with Christabel she'd occupied most of his attention when he wasn't on duty, he thought guiltily.

Still, he reflected, when he'd told them about his forthcoming marriage, they had accepted it quite happily, almost as if they were pleased to hear the news. Perhaps they were beginning to worry about what was going to happen to him as he got older and whether he would feel that they might one day be expected to have him to live with them.

He almost laughed out loud at such a preposterous idea but then, he mused, he supposed
he was old to them. It was a wonder they hadn't
raised the question of his age and the fact that
he was well into his fifties when he'd said he
was getting married.

Still, it was all out in the open now, so hopefully there would be no more shocks of any
kind.

As she studied her reflection in the long mirror
on her wardrobe door, Christabel wasn't at all
sure that she'd chosen the right outfit. The
ankle-length slinky black dress and the white
fur wrap made her look a little too sophisticated
for someone who was about to become step-
mother to two grown men.

They might have preferred someone plump
and motherly, she thought ruefully. Well, they'd
have to accept her as she was, because it was
too late now to change into anything else
because the taxi that was to collect her and take
her to the Adelphi was due in ten minutes.

She wished she didn't feel so nervous. Colin
and Neil would either accept the fact that she
was marrying their father, or they would resent
her, feeling that she might divert their father's
affection away from them.

She was relieved to have Mark alone for a
few minutes when she arrived at the Adelphi.
He helped her out of the taxi and paid the
driver, and she took a deep breath as he took

329

her arm and hugged her before they went into the hotel. His two sons were waiting in the foyer and as they came forward to greet her, as always when they met, she was struck by how like their father they were. Neil, the elder of the two, was taller than Mark, but he had the same colouring and even the same timbre in his voice. Colin was almost as tall as his brother but not as broad shouldered, but she had no doubt that in time that would change.

As they took their seats in the restaurant Christabel relaxed and wondered why she had been so nervous. The conversation was easy and friendly. She was taken by surprise when Neil explained that he was about to get married.

'Your father never mentioned it to me,' she commented.

'That was because he didn't know until today.'

'Well,' she looked questioningly at Mark, who was indeed looking equally surprised, as her fingers closed round the stem of her wine glass, 'perhaps we should be drinking a toast to Neil?'

Mark nodded and raised his glass and Colin did the same.

When Christabel followed it up by asking, 'Where will you be living?' there was a moment's silence before Neil cleared his throat and said a little diffidently. 'I'm not sure yet. Where are you and Dad going to live?'

Again there was a slightly awkward silence

330

which lasted until after the waiter had cleared their plates from the first course and served their main dish.

Mark waited until they were all concentrating on the food in front of them before he said, 'I was going to tell you after our meal that I'm planning on giving up the house, so if there is anything you would like to keep, then perhaps you'd let me know before you leave tomorrow.'

Colin and Neil exchanged perplexed glances.

'How can you move, Dad? The surgery is there as well as your home,' Colin said bluntly. 'Old Cecil won't like it if you move because you've been running the practice from there ever since you've been partners. You're not retiring, are you?'

'No, I'm good for another few years yet, although we are contemplating taking on a younger doctor full time, instead of employing a locum.' Mark smiled. 'At the moment, I'm trying to find a new home for the practice and then I'll buy a smaller house. I thought that in future it would be better for our home and workplace to be separate.'

Neil laid down his knife and fork and took a sip of his wine. 'I've got an even better idea,' he said. 'I'm fully qualified, I'm fed up with hospital routine, so why don't I join you and Cecil Roberts and then I can move into the house and the practice can stay exactly where it is?'

'That sounds a first-class idea,' Colin enthused,

331

'and when I'm qualified as a dentist I can join you, and the patients will have everything under one roof.' He grinned.

Mark refilled his wine glass and took a drink before replying. 'I don't know,' he shook his head doubtfully, 'it certainly sounds like the easy way out for me, but I would have to talk to Cecil about it, of course.'

'He'll say yes,' Neil said confidently. 'Especially when he hears that he will also be getting the service of a qualified nurse at the same time. I know you haven't met Mandy yet, but when you do, I know you'll like her. It would be an excellent arrangement; she could work part time and be a great asset to the practice,' he said thoughtfully.

'She's a corker,' Colin enthused. 'You'll love her and so will the patients. It sounds perfect to me. Can I still keep my room?' he asked, looking across the table at his brother.

'Of course, that's if you can afford to pay the rent I'll be charging you.' Neil grinned.

'What do you think of the idea, Christabel?' Mark asked. 'So far you haven't said a word.'

'I hardly think that I need to do so.' She smiled. 'It's an arrangement that has to be agreed between the three of you. I must say, it sounds like a wonderful opportunity for all concerned, providing, of course, that Dr Roberts doesn't object.'

'I don't see why he should,' Mark admitted. 'He wasn't looking forward to having to move the surgery and apart from all the upheaval of moving all the files and equipment there was the question of explaining to all the patients that it would be at a different venue.'

'It would also save you the trouble of having to interview applicants for the post of new doctor,' Neil pointed out. 'You both know me and my qualifications. The fact that I will be living on the premises and be on hand to take all the emergency and night calls will ease the strain on you both now that you are getting older.'

'Yes, before we know what is happening you will be taking over the reins and pensioning us both off,' Mark laughed.

'Not for a few years yet,' Neil conceded. 'You must admit, though, that it will be easier for both of you when you want some time off.'

'Yes,' Mark agreed, 'I can see it has plenty of good points, but the next question is when is all this going to happen? You haven't yet told us when you are going to get married, Neil?'

'I haven't been able to make any firm plans until I found somewhere for us to live. As a matter of fact, I've been toying with the idea of asking you to help me out with a loan so that I could buy a place. Then when you said this morning that you and Christabel were going to get married . . .' his voice trailed off.

'I see.' Mark laid down his knife and fork and sat back. He certainly liked the idea; Neil moving into the family home was a better

333

solution than he'd dreamed of, but he didn't want to get carried away before he'd had time to think it through.

'Seriously, what *do* you think of Neil's idea, Christabel?' he asked as he wiped his mouth with his napkin and picked up his glass of wine.

'It sounds an excellent idea providing, as Neil says, that your present partner agrees and you can all work together. Oh, and providing the existing practice is large enough to support three full-time doctors as well as a part-time nurse, of course.'

'That's the nub, isn't it?' Mark agreed solemnly. 'You are probably so full of new ideas, Neil, that you may think that our equipment and methods are old-fashioned and you'll immediately want to start changing everything.'

For the rest of the meal they argued amicably about the details, but all of them knew and agreed that it was the perfect solution. Christabel was also aware that both Neil and Colin had accepted the fact that she and Mark were getting married without any surprise at all.

Chapter Twenty-Eight

Christabel felt disappointed when the evening ended. Although Mark insisted on accompanying her in the taxi he'd ordered to take her back home to Wallasey, he said he wouldn't be staying but would be going straight back home.

'There are numerous things I need to talk over with the boys before they go to bed because they're both planning to leave more or less first thing in the morning,' he explained.

'They won't be leaving until after breakfast, surely, so won't you have time to talk to them then?' Christabel asked as she settled herself in the taxi.

'Afraid not, they want to leave very early. You know what it's like,' he said apologetically, 'they both need to have time to prepare for Monday. I'll come back over tomorrow after they've gone home and we'll have a good long talk about everything then. I must say, there have been several surprise developments,' he laughed.

'Things certainly seem to be turning out far better than we had hoped.' Christabel smiled.

During most of the journey back to Rolleston Drive Mark talked non-stop about how delighted he was by what had transpired and he was eager to know what she'd thought about it all.

'I'm so relieved that at last I've told them that we are planning on getting married and I can't wait to get back and hear them enthuse about what they thought of you becoming part of the family. I could tell right away that they were impressed at how elegant you looked,' he said, squeezing her hand.

'Would it make any difference if they didn't want you to marry me?' she asked tentatively.

'No, of course not; that wasn't what I meant,' he blustered. 'Nevertheless, it was important to have their views about us getting married.'

Christabel nodded. What she really wanted to know was exactly when Neil was planning to be married and what Mark had thought about the idea of Neil taking over his house and also becoming a partner in his practice. She realised that Cecil Roberts would have to be consulted before anything could be formally agreed but it was an interesting possibility. She had realised right from the start that Mark was slightly reluctant to sell up his family home, so this seemed to be the ideal solution.

With three of them in the partnership it would certainly help to solve the problem of Mark having to be on call so often. In addition, if Neil's wife was going to be undertaking nursing duties then that would lighten Mark's responsibilities. If she was willing to do the clinic as well, then that would be ideal and she could stop working.

As her thoughts went back to the reorganising she was also going to have to do, Christabel toyed with the idea that when Kay learned that the house in Rolleston Drive that had been her childhood home was to be put on the market, she might decide she wanted to move back there herself, instead of disposing of it.

She supposed so much would depend on how Stuart reacted to the news and whether Kay could persuade him to give up his estate agency in Cookham and move north to Merseyside.

He didn't have to open an estate agency in Wallasey if he didn't like the idea of doing that. There were plenty of small villages like Moreton or Heswall which were within an easy drive. If he wanted to be in a larger, busier place, then even Chester was within motoring distance.

If that happened and they did move into Rolleston Drive she would see so much more of Jill as well as Kay and that would suit her down to the ground. Driving all the way from Merseyside to Cookham was an onerous journey and she couldn't expect Mark to give up what little spare time he had to share the driving with her whenever she wanted to visit them.

She knew Mark liked Kay well enough but he didn't seem to understand how close she felt to Kay and little Jill. In fact, she knew that, like Kay, he didn't altogether approve of her encouraging Jill to call her Granny.

What harm was there in it when it was a game they'd both enjoyed? Jill didn't have a granny and most of her little friends and play-mates did, so she must feel out of it at times.

Probably, Christabel mused, it had been Stuart who had said it must stop but Kay was far too loyal to tell her that.

As the taxi pulled up in Rolleston Drive and Mark accompanied her to the house and opened the front door, then gave her a quick hug and a brief kiss, she laid a detaining hand on his arm. 'Aren't you coming in, just for a few minutes?' she said softly.

He hesitated then pulled away. 'Not tonight, the taxi's waiting with its engine running.' He kissed her again, this time on the cheek. 'See you tomorrow,' he promised as he walked away.

She remained on the doorstep waving as the taxi pulled away and stood there until its tail lights had disappeared from sight.

Although it had been a most enjoyable evening she spent a restless night going over and over everything that had been said and wondering what else the three of them might have discussed after Mark had arrived back home again.

She also spent a great deal of time between drifting in and out of sleep making plans for their forthcoming wedding.

So far they hadn't set a date, but now that Neil had come into the equation, there might be some further delay in order to coordinate their plans. She and Mark still hadn't found the house they wanted but they had looked at several already so it shouldn't take them too long to find one which was suitable.

In her half-awake state she tried to decide which of those they'd already seen might suit them best. It had to be fairly close to the surgery, she realised that, but she wanted it to be far enough away so that their lives were not too entwined with the practice.

This was especially important if Neil and his new wife moved in and were also working there. They didn't want to be living too close to each other. If, in due course, Colin followed through with his intention to move in as well and establish a dental practice there, then she certainly didn't want to be living on their doorstep.

Yet, she reasoned, Mark probably wouldn't want to be too far away because if he was then he might find himself on the fringe of things and even though they would meet up each day in the practice it was possible he might find that they'd already made their decision on whatever was being discussed.

When the telephone rang while she was having breakfast next morning she thought, as she hurried into the hall to answer it, that it might be Mark.

She wished she'd not been so late getting up and that she was not still in her dressing gown.

She'd have plenty of time to dress and get ready, she told herself as she picked up the receiver, because it would take him at least an hour to come across to Wallasey from Formby.

She wondered if he would be coming on his own, or whether he would be bringing the boys for a fleeting visit. After the three of them had talked things over last night it might be interesting to hear what final decisions they'd reached. Then she reminded herself that Mark had said that both of them wanted to make an early start today. Neil had to travel to Newcastle and Colin even further than that.

To her annoyance she was taken aback to discover that it wasn't Mark on the phone but Marlene.

'Aunt Chrissy, thank goodness I've managed to get hold of you at last. I tried to contact you several times last night but you weren't there. You must have stayed out extremely late.'

'Yes, it was fairly late when I arrived home. I went out to dinner at the Adelphi with Dr Murray and his two sons.'

'Really, well, that answers why you weren't at home,' Marlene said dismissively. 'Look, Aunt Christabel,' she went on quickly, 'we have a problem and we hope you will be able to help us solve it. Bill has to go to America on business and he needs me to go with him. We will be away for about a month. Mother doesn't seem well enough to undertake the journey, so can she come and stay with you?'

'For a whole month!' Christabel gasped. 'I can't possibly agree to that,' she said quickly, 'have you forgotten, Marlene, that I'm planning to get married? How can I possibly look after Lilian when I have all that to organise?'

'She isn't helpless, Aunt Christabel,' Marlene said swiftly. 'She can look after herself and she will probably help you with your wedding plans if it comes to that.'

'Then why not let her stay at home, if she doesn't want to travel to America with you?'

'We can't leave her on her own, not when she's only recently buried my father,' Marlene said sharply. 'Surely you wouldn't mind her staying with you. After all, she is your sister,'

'I do know that, Marlene, but you are her daughter, so surely it's your responsibility to take care of her.'

'Look, Aunt Christabel,' Marlene sighed. 'I've turned to you for help because I am out of my mind with worry. If you don't want her for the whole time we are away, then could she come and stay for a week or two? Then if you feel you can't cope with looking after her any longer and that she's well enough to manage on her own, you could suggest she comes back here?'

'Exactly what symptoms has she got that I need to know about?' Christabel asked dryly.

'She's not well, but there is nothing specifically

wrong with her,' Marlene murmured. 'She's just not herself, and she has such set ideas about what she can and can't do. That's why we haven't been able to persuade her to come with us.'

'I would have thought that she'd be really keen on a trip to America and the chance to meet up with all her old friends again. It would probably take her out of herself and help her to forget about Alex,' Christabel argued.

'No, Aunt Chrissy, it would have the opposite effect, because all the places we'll be visiting and the people we'll be meeting would remind her of when she and Dad were living there and it would bring everything back to her and make her miss Dad even more.'

'A month is a very long time for me to have her here,' Christabel pointed out again.

'Does that mean she can come?' Marlene persisted.

'I need time to think about it,' Christabel parried. 'I'll need to talk to Mark and see what he thinks.'

'Heaven's, Aunt Christabel, I never thought I would ever hear you say that you had to ask someone's permission to do anything,' Marlene laughed. 'I've always thought that you were far too independent for anything like that.'

'I'll give it some thought,' Christabel told her crisply. 'I have to go now because there's someone at the door.'

'I'll hold on if you like,' Marlene offered.

'I've already told you, I need time to think it over,' Christabel reminded her. She replaced the receiver before Marlene could reply or pressure her any further.

The idea of Lilian moving in with her for a whole month appalled her. She had evaded her visiting but this was a hundred times worse than having her come for just a few days. All the old animosity there had been between them in the past flooded Christabel's mind. She didn't think she could do it; she didn't want to do it, but how could she refuse without looking completely heartless? What on earth would Mark think if it reached his ears? Her bereaved sister seeking solace in her company only to be turned away; it would look as if she was utterly heartless.

Lilian arrived a week later. Christabel was shocked by the change in her. She looked so frail and her once smooth face was so drawn and wrinkled that she felt quite sorry for her.

Christabel also felt alarmed at the amount of luggage Lilian had brought with her. Marlene had said they would only be away for a month but Lilian had enough luggage for a permanent stay.

As Bill struggled in with the last of the seven huge suitcases and Marlene brought up the rear with two hat boxes, she wondered not only how Lilian was going to get them into the wardrobe in the bedroom she'd put her in but also when she was going to wear it all.

'Don't worry, Aunt Chrissy, I know it looks as though Mum has come to stay for ever but it's just the way she is at the moment. She insisted on bringing absolutely everything she possesses; there's still a big box of shoes to be brought in.'

'I'm not sure there's going to be room for everything in her room,' Christabel protested. 'Couldn't you take some of it back home again with you, Marlene? Surely it won't come to any harm; you'll be locking the house up and putting the burglar alarm on before you set off and there will be plenty of your stuff left there.'

'I know, Aunt Chrissy, but it's no good telling Mum all that. The doctor said she has some kind of phobia about her things being stolen and it's all due to shock because of Dad dying.'

'All this luggage, though, when she's only staying a couple of weeks,' Christabel protested.

'I know, Aunt Chrissy, and we're eternally grateful, but it might end up being six weeks, by the way. It all depends on how speedily Bill's business deals go and if he can get things wrapped up in a month, then of course we will be on our way home again.'

'Six weeks! Oh no, Marlene, that is quite impossible,' Christabel gasped. 'You seem to be forgetting that I have a wedding to plan; my wedding.'

'No, Aunt Chrissy, we haven't forgotten that, and we'll make every effort to come back from

America in plenty of time. If anything goes wrong and we are delayed, then perhaps you can persuade Mum to go and stay with Kay,' she suggested hopefully.

Chapter Twenty-Nine

Lilian took several days to settle in. She didn't like the wallpaper in the guest room and insisted on moving into what had once been Kay's bedroom. The moment all her suitcases had been moved in there she claimed that it was far too cramped.

'I suppose I'll have to use both the rooms,' she sighed, 'because there isn't room in either of the wardrobes for all my things.'

'Perhaps we could change the furniture around and then you could use one of the rooms as a sitting room?' Christabel suggested.

'A sitting room? Why ever do I need a sitting room upstairs when there's already a perfectly good one downstairs?' Lilian asked in a querulous voice.

'I thought it would give you the chance to be on your own when you felt tired or if I had friends in and you didn't really want to sit and talk to them,' Christabel told her.

'What you really mean is that it would be somewhere to send me out of the way when you wanted to entertain your fancy doctor friend,' Lilian retorted tetchily.

*　*　*

Christabel hadn't expected that having Lilian to stay would be easy, but by the end of the first week she was at screaming pitch. She felt so frustrated that she wondered if she could possibly endure a whole month of her sister's company.

The altercation over wardrobe space and the bedrooms was mild compared to all the other things that Lilian considered to be wrong. She didn't like the food Christabel dished up or the times when she served it. The chairs in the dining room were too hard; the ones in the sitting room too soft. The rooms were draughty, but when Christabel rearranged the armchair so that Lilian was directly in front of the fire, she complained that she was too hot.

The only time when she smiled, or was in any way pleasant, was when Mark visited. Apart from the fact that he refused to discuss her ailments, she thought he was a charming man and did her best to hold his attention the whole time he was there.

Christabel struggled to keep her feeling of resentment under control but when Lilian made no attempt to help in any way but sat talking to Mark while she prepared a meal, served it and then cleared away afterwards, Christabel couldn't help feeling rather hard done by.

It was the last straw, however, when Lilian insisted on accompanying them when Mark made arrangements to view the house in

347

Formby that they had decided was the one most suitable.

'You want me to stay home, even though I'd be here all alone?' she questioned in wide-eyed surprise when Christabel told her they would prefer to go on their own. 'Oh, Christabel, what ever are you thinking of? I'm sure Mark wouldn't want that.'

'I'm quite sure he would feel it was for the best since it is a very big decision we have to make and the less distraction we have the better,' Christabel told her stiffly as she donned her hat and coat.

'Supposing I have one of my giddy turns, what ever shall I do?' Lilian asked in a plaintive voice.

'If you stay sitting down in your chair, then you aren't likely to have a giddy turn,' Christabel told her. She felt so cross that she stabbed the hat pin she was holding so viciously into the side of her hat that it dug into her scalp.

'If you don't want me passing remarks about the house, I can always stay out in the car,' Lilian suggested. 'That would be safer than staying here on my own.'

They argued about it for another ten minutes, by which time Lilian was in such an agitated state that Christabel finally gave in and went upstairs to collect her hat and coat for her.

When Mark arrived and she explained the situation he merely shrugged. 'There's no need to sit in the car outside, Lilian,' he told her with a smile. 'Another pair of eyes might be all to the good; who knows, you might spot something that we overlook.'

'What a sensible man you are, Dr Mark Murray,' she told him with a coy smile.

As they walked outside and Mark held open the rear door for her she hesitated. 'Oh dear, I forgot to mention it, but I always have to ride in the front passenger seat otherwise I get car sick.' She gave an apologetic smile in her sister's direction. 'I do hope you don't mind, Christabel,' she said contritely as she stood to one side so that Christabel could be the one to get into the back seat of the car.

Christabel did mind because she didn't believe a word of it. She was sure it was a trumped-up excuse on Lilian's part simply so that she could sit beside Mark. Even so, she decided that it wasn't worth making an issue of it.

Lilian talked to Mark throughout most of their journey in a voice that was so low that, from where she was sitting in the back of the car, Christabel was unable to hear what they said or take any part in the conversation.

Lilian preceded them down the path when they arrived at the house they intended viewing and was rapturous about their choice. Seconds before they reached the front door she appeared to stumble and if Mark hadn't stepped forward quickly to grab her arm, she probably would have fallen.

349

'Oh dear, that has shaken me up,' she gasped clinging on to him tightly. 'I think you'd better allow me to take your arm, Mark, that's if you don't mind.'

'Of course not. Once we get inside we'll find you a seat so that you can get your breath back,' he promised.

'Oh no, don't do that,' she pulled a sad face. 'I very much want to see round the house, Mark, please.'

'We'll see how you feel when we are inside,' he promised as he rang the doorbell.

'I'll be quite all right if you will let me hold your arm,' she assured him.

Their tour of the house seemed to be purely for Lilian's benefit, Christabel thought as she trailed behind them. She grew tired of listening to Lilian's comments, her excited coos of approval or the tut-tutting sounds she made to show her disapproval when there was something she didn't like.

She'd intended making notes of what changes they wanted to make but each time she mentioned any of these to Mark, Lilian would butt in and voice her opinion.

'You mustn't change things simply to please Christabel, you know, Mark,' Lilian told him in a simpering voice. 'I think your taste is far better than hers and so very much more in keeping with the ambience of this house.'

Christabel could see that although Mark protested that this was not the case, he listened politely to her comments and she had an uneasy feeling that the house might end up being much more to Lilian's taste than her own. It seemed to Christabel that Lilian did everything in her power to impose her ideas not only on the changes to be made to the house but also on their wedding arrangements.

If there was any sort of discussion Lilian always sided with Mark and because it was so difficult to get him on his own, Christabel constantly found that she never had the opportunity to put forward her own reasons or explain why she felt it was best to do things her way.

She found she was becoming so resentful about what was happening that she wondered if she was going to be able to tolerate Lilian staying with her very much longer. Knowing that Marlene wasn't due home for another ten days, she even thought about asking Kay to have Lilian for a while so that she could have a break. When she phoned Kay, however, she learned that was quite impossible because Kay had problems of her own.

'Jill has chicken pox, Aunt Christabel,' Kay told her. 'She's so poorly that there is no way I could have Aunt Lilian here.'

'Oh, I am sorry to hear about Jill, the poor little dear,' Christabel sympathised. 'I do hope she is going to be better in time to be my flower girl. The wedding is not all that far off now.'

351

'Oh, she'll be better in plenty of time for that,' Kay assured her. 'I'm sorry about not being able to take Aunt Lilian off your hands, but I'm sure you understand that Jill needs so much attention at the moment that I couldn't cope with Aunt Lilian as well.'

'Of course I understand,' Christabel assured her. 'Well, it is only about another week before Marlene is due home so I must grin and bear it, I suppose,' she sighed.

Two days later she received a cable from Marlene to say Bill hadn't yet completed his business in America and it would be yet another ten days before they would be home.

Lilian gave a smile of satisfaction when Christabel told her about the delay and said there was nothing she could do about it, but Christabel felt quite frustrated.

The next day when her sister complained of not feeling very well, Christabel commented that it was probably because she had overdone things with all her interfering.

'Interfering, whatever do you mean?' Lilian stared at her in hurt astonishment.

'You've done nothing but oppose whatever I want to do ever since you've been here. I never have a minute alone with Mark to discuss things. You're always there putting your point of view forward or agreeing with him when he wants to do something slightly different to what I want,' Christabel pointed out.

'Oh really? I had no idea you felt like that. All I've been trying to do is help you both,' Lilian insisted. 'I realise my taste is so much closer to Mark's than yours appears to be, but even so, there is no need for you to be so high-handed about it.'

'In future, perhaps it would be better if you kept your thoughts and opinions to yourself and stopped interfering,' Christabel told her. 'Mark will be here any minute so, for once, can you go up to your room and leave us to finalise some of our arrangements on our own? Go and have a rest and you will probably feel all right again after that.'

Tears welled into Lilian's eyes and trickled down her lined cheeks. 'Why are you being so very unkind to me, Christabel?' she sobbed.

By the time Mark arrived, Lilian was in full flood, sobbing and crying as if her heart would break.

Mark was immediately concerned and wanted to know what was wrong.

'When I told Christabel that I wasn't feeling very well,' Lilian gulped, 'she implied that I was being a nuisance and that I had outstayed my welcome.'

'Really!' Mark looked at her in astonishment.

'I said nothing of the sort,' Christabel said wearily. 'I said that I wanted to have some time alone with you and that if she wasn't feeling well, then it would be best if she went up to her room and had a rest, that was all.'

Before he could reply Lilian gave a long, shrill moan and crumpled to the floor.

Christabel rushed to her side to help her up but Lilian seemed to be incapable of standing up. As she tried to speak her face became distorted and she started making strange guttural sounds.

Mark moved Christabel to one side; he felt Lilian's pulse and loosened the tight neck of her dress. His face was grave as he looked up at Christabel.

'Phone for an ambulance,' he said crisply. 'Lilian has had a stroke.'

Lilian's stroke was a relatively mild one and four days later they brought her home from the hospital. Although her face was still slightly lopsided she was able to speak and, apart from looking extremely frail, she seemed to have suffered no other ill effects.

Christabel had cabled Marlene in America to let her know what had happened. The reply had been that they were extremely concerned and that they would be coming home as soon as possible but had not given any specific date.

Mark maintained that he was unable to prescribe anything for Lilian because she wasn't one of his patients but he did keep a close eye on her progress. He came over each evening after he'd finished surgery to make sure she

354

was all right. He also advised Christabel about what was the best course of action to take to pacify Lilian whenever she became unduly agitated.

'Lilian is bound to feel frustrated because she is now so weak that she really does find it difficult to walk or even move and do things for herself,' he explained. 'Even speaking is probably a tremendous effort.'

'She does seem to be improving and is a little stronger every day,' Christabel told him.

'Well, that is good. She has been very fortunate in that she isn't left paralysed in any way; in fact, she hasn't lost the use of any of her limbs. She still needs careful nursing, of course, but I know you can cope with that all right.'

'It looks as though I will have to do so,' Christabel agreed, 'but it does interfere with all our wedding plans.'

'I think it would be best if we left those exactly as they stand until Lilian is either a lot better or until she has gone home, darling,' he suggested.

'If I do that it doesn't leave us much time to get everything done,' she warned.

'No, but at the moment you have too much on your mind and you can't do everything. Looking after Lilian is going to be a full-time job for the next week or so. Let's hope that by then Marlene will be back from America and can take her home.'

'There are so many things to do,' Christabel persisted. 'Now that we've decided on the house there is the decorating to organise as well as furniture to choose and buy.'

'Yes, but it will be quicker and less stressful for you if we do that on our own. I'll attend to all the legal formalities in connection with the purchase of the house and I can also arrange for the decorators to do whatever you want done. As for the rest, we'll attend to that together as soon as possible. If the house isn't ready in time, then we will have to camp out at a hotel or something.'

'Even if you manage to take care of most of the things to do with the house, I still have my wedding outfit to buy and I haven't decided what Jill is going to wear,' Christabel sighed.

'If Jill has chicken pox, she's in no state to go shopping at the moment so delaying everything by a week or two is all to the good,' Mark pointed out.

'I suppose you're right. If necessary, Kay can choose something suitable,' Christabel conceded. 'I was looking forward to taking her shopping, though,' she added wistfully.

'There you are, then. Kay will do that and so all you have to do is make sure that Lilian is better in time for the wedding,' Mark consoled her as he took her in his arms for a farewell embrace before he left.

Christabel smiled but said nothing. In some

ways she hoped that Lilian wouldn't be well enough to attend their wedding because she was sure she'd say or do something to spoil everything.

Chapter Thirty

Christabel had never expected Lilian to be a good patient but she was astounded at just how difficult her sister managed to be over the next couple of weeks.

For the first three days she refused even to attempt to get out of bed and expected Christabel to be in constant attendance. Nothing pleased her. She demanded drinks then changed her mind or pulled a face and said there was something wrong with them. She insisted on special foods and then merely picked at whatever Christabel had prepared for her or said it was not what she'd asked for.

She complained that the pillows were lumpy, the under-sheet was creased and uncomfortable to lie on, the bedding was too heavy and then, when Christabel removed the thick woven counterpane, she complained about being cold.

Christabel found that even when she went to bed at night sleep eluded her because she was constantly hearing Lilian's plaintive voice calling for a drink or bemoaning the fact that she wasn't comfortable and couldn't sleep.

There had been no need for Mark to tell her not to try and do anything more about the wedding arrangements while Lilian was in her care, Christabel thought; she was far too tired and stressed out to think clearly enough anyway.

Some nights she felt so utterly exhausted that she wished she was the one who was being looked after. All the many things that still remained to be done and which she ought to be getting on with went round and round in her head in a never-ending loop. When she finally managed to drift off to sleep it was only to be plunged into a world fraught with problems and she would waken with her heart pounding and her head throbbing.

When she told Mark he was most concerned and told her she was probably suffering from stress and advised her to see her own doctor and ask for some medication.

'Wouldn't it be quicker if you prescribed something for me?' she suggested.

'It wouldn't be ethical for me to do that,' he pointed out. 'I can tell you what you can buy from the chemist's, but patent medicines are not usually anywhere near as effective as something that has been prescribed by a doctor.'

'I'll settle for something from the chemist's,' she told him. 'After all, I only need something to calm me down until Marlene arrives back from America and can take Lilian home. I'm hoping that it won't be more than another week now at the most or it is going to stop me from going to Neil's wedding.'

'Well, that's not for almost a fortnight. They'll be away for two weeks afterwards, of course, and then, a fortnight after they get back, it will be our big day.'

The next ten days dragged by and there was still no news from Marlene. Although Lilian's health seemed to improve each day, her demands on Christabel's time remained as great as ever. She refused to attempt anything for herself. She even insisted on Christabel helping her from the bed to the armchair that was beside it.

'I feel far too shaky to move on my own and I feel dizzy at the very thought of attempting to come downstairs,' she said, shuddering.

'You'll have to come downstairs when Marlene arrives to take you home,' Christabel pointed out as she wrapped a dressing gown round her sister's shoulders and put slippers on her feet.

'Yes, but Bill will be with her and perhaps he can carry me down,' Lilian murmured.

'Carry you? I wouldn't think for one moment that would be necessary,' Christabel told her. 'If you attempted to do a little more each day instead of sitting in an armchair all the time then, by the time Marlene comes home, you'd probably be back to normal.'

'You really are very hard on me, Christabel! I'm sure you have no conception of how ill I've been or understand how weak and shaky I feel,' Lilian sighed as she rearranged the blanket Christabel had placed over her knees.

'Then why don't you ask Mark what he thinks? I'm sure he will agree with me that unless you pull yourself together and start making some effort you will never get back to normal.'

'You have only to look at my face to see how unlikely it is that I will ever be normal again,' Lilian moaned. She picked up the hand mirror from the table at her side and peered into it. 'Look at me, I'm a complete freak! My mouth is twisted and one of my eyelids droops. Even one side of my face is different to the other; surely even you can see that.'

'Of course I can, and I'm very sorry about it, but that will probably correct itself, given time. It is unfortunate, but it doesn't mean that you have to stay confined to your bedroom, now does it?'

'No, I could go and join a freak show and let people pay tuppence a time to come and stare at me,' her sister retorted bitterly.

'Now you are being quite silly, Lilian,' Christabel told her as she plumped up the pillows and straightened Lilian's bed so that it would be ready for her to get back into whenever she wanted.

'Oh, I know you are trying to chivvy me up because you want to get rid of me,' Lilian sighed.

'Nonsense! I'm only trying to help you to get back on your feet again before Marlene comes home. Think how distressed she is going to be if she finds you in this state.'

'If I am back to normal then she will never

know how ill I've been, will she?' Lilian responded smugly.

Marlene arrived unannounced early one afternoon and as Christabel had expected she was extremely distressed by the state her mother was in. Christabel tactfully left them together, saying she would make some tea, leaving Lilian to enlighten Marlene about the dreadful ordeal she'd been through.

'Aunt Christabel, I had no idea that Mum was so ill,' Marlene told her. 'How can I ever thank you for all you have done and the wonderful way you've looked after her.'

'I hope you've come to take me home,' Lilian stated as she stirred the cup of tea Christabel had placed on the table at her side. 'I'm sick to death of hearing Christabel saying how having to look after me is stopping her from getting on with her wedding plans.'

'Oh, heavens, of course. Your wedding day is not far off now, is it?' Marlene gasped. 'I'd almost forgotten about that. Is there very much you still have to arrange?'

'Almost everything. I've had to leave Mark to deal with the house we're buying. I've told him what I want doing before we move in, and he has said that the decorators are getting on with it but I haven't had a chance to go and see for myself.'

'Is everything else in hand, Aunt Chrissy?' Marlene frowned as she sipped her tea.

'No, not really. I haven't been able to shop for my wedding outfit yet or decide what little Jill is going to wear as my flower girl.'

'Flower girl! I never heard of such nonsense when you are getting married in a register office,' Lilian commented.

'Jill is looking forward to it,' Christabel said mildly. 'She's had chicken pox so I haven't seen her for quite some time and I expect she's grown. That's why I left it until the last minute to decide what she should wear.'

'It's a wonder you didn't decide to have page-boys as well and then Marlene's two could have joined in,' Lilian commented.

'I don't think they would be very happy about doing something like that,' Marlene chuckled. 'I can't see either of them taking kindly to dressing up in velvet suits.'

Lilian attempted to put her cup and saucer back on the table but managed to place it so near the edge that as she tipped it the spoon fell to the floor with a clatter.

Christabel was so used to this happening that she simply ignored it but Lilian burst into tears. 'I'm so helpless,' she wailed as Marlene bent and picked up the spoon and moved the cup and saucer into a safer position.

'Come on, Mum. It's not all that bad,' Marlene said, trying to comfort her. 'We all drop a spoon now and again.'

'I do it all the time, I can't seem to manage to lift anything or hold anything. I even drop my food down the front of my dress when I am trying to eat and I know it makes Christabel cross. She doesn't say anything but I can tell by the look on her face.'

'I can see that Aunt Christabel has had a lot to put up with,' Marlene commented dryly.

'I'm the one who has had to put up with things,' Lilian protested. 'I hope you have come to take me home. Where are Bill and the children? Has he taken them off somewhere for an hour or so because he doesn't want to be sitting here with a sick old lady?'

'No, Mum, Bill is still in America because he still hasn't completed his business deals over there.'

'Where are the children, then?'

'They're staying with Bill's mother for a few more days and then they'll come back to London with him. I came on ahead so that I could collect you and take you home.'

'I'm not sure that I feel well enough to travel all that way, not if you are doing the driving,' Lilian told her ungratefully.

'I rather thought you might say that, so I've arranged for a taxi,' Marlene told her. She looked at her watch. 'It will be here in a little over an hour so we'd better start getting your things together.'

'A taxi, all the way from Liverpool to London, whatever has got into you?' Lilian asked in horror.

'It was that or the train, and from what I had

364

heard you weren't well enough for the train and now that I've seen you, I'm quite sure you would prefer to be in a taxi.'

'It's a ridiculous expense, though, Marlene. I hope you're not expecting me to pay for it,' Lilian grumbled.

'It will cost even more if we keep the taxi waiting so shall we start getting your things together?'

The next hour was spent collecting up Lilian's clothes and all her belongings and packing them into her numerous suitcases ready for going home.

When they were finally all packed and ready Lilian started protesting that she wasn't sure she was going to be able to stand such a long car journey after all.

'You'll find it much more comfortable than travelling by train,' Marlene reminded her.

'Yes, and I might find it even better if I stayed on here for another few weeks. By then I'd be feeling a great deal stronger and I could come home with you after Mark and Christabel's wedding,' Lilian suggested.

'That's quite a long time away,' Marlene pointed out, 'and Aunt Chrissy has a great deal to do before then. I think Aunt Chrissy said that Mark's son Neil was getting married before them and she will want to attend his wedding; I think she said it was in Scotland.'

'I know that, but I am so much better that from now on she wouldn't need to do anything

365

like as much for me. She could stop fussing over me and get on with preparing whatever she feels is necessary for this wedding of hers. Bill will be coming back from America in time to attend that, won't he?'

'We hope so,' Marlene told her.

'If he doesn't, then how are we going to come back up here again?' Lilian asked.

'By train, I suppose; we'll make all those decisions when the time comes.'

'You could come on the train, but I'm not sure if I could cope with it. All that pushing and shoving at the station. I do hate all the crowds and noise and everything,' Lilian protested, shaking her head from side to side. 'I don't think you realise how this stroke has taken it out of me, Marlene. I really do think it might be best if I stay right here where I am,' she persisted.

Christabel said nothing, even though she was in agreement with Lilian that it was going to be an arduous journey whatever form of travel she used. The thought of Lilian staying on any longer depressed her, so she left it to Marlene to persuade her that it was a good idea to go home with her now.

She felt on edge herself because there was so much she needed to do; so many things she'd had to put off, and she knew quite well she could never do any of them if Lilian was there.

Leaving them to discuss it all between themselves she went through to the kitchen and

366

made a fresh pot of tea, hoping that might help to calm all of them down.

In fact, it had the opposite effect on Lilian because she protested they hadn't time to sit drinking tea and gossiping. Marlene, however, seemed grateful and asked for a refill.

When Lilian and Marlene finally left, just before five o'clock, Christabel went back into her sitting room, collapsed on the sofa, and closed her eyes. For the next twenty minutes she gave herself up to enjoying the peace and utter silence that filled her home.

Half an hour later it was with an over-whelming feeling of relief that she phoned Mark to let him know that Lilian had gone home.

'Marlene and Bill came to collect her, did they?'

'No, Bill and the children are still in America. Marlene came on her own and she'd arranged for a taxi to take Lilian and all her luggage back to London.'

'Whew! Marlene is a very enterprising lady.' He laughed. 'Or one with a conscience,' he added thoughtfully. 'She was probably begin-ning to feel guilty about leaving you to cope with her mother when she knew you had so much to do.'

'Whatever her reasons, it is a tremendous relief,' Christabel agreed. 'I'm looking forward to seeing you this evening and for the two of us having the chance to enjoy a quiet meal on our own for the first time in ages.'

'I take it that is an invitation, so I'll see you as soon as surgery is over,' he promised.

By the time Mark arrived shortly after seven she'd tidied away all traces of Lilian's stay, taken a bath, changed into a dress she knew was one of his favourites and was all ready to be taken out.

'I thought you would want a quiet evening at home and then an early night after what you have endured over the past few weeks.' He smiled, taking her into his arms and kissing her.

'On the contrary,' she told him as she returned his kiss, 'I feel as if a heavy load has been lifted off my shoulders and I want to celebrate with an exciting night out.'

'In that case, since you are bubbling over with energy, get your coat and let's be off.'

Christabel hesitated. 'I suppose I ought to phone and see if Marlene has managed to get Lilian safely back to her place?'

'If they only left at five o'clock, then there's plenty of time to do that later on in the evening,' Mark told her. 'I wouldn't imagine they'd be home much before ten o'clock and if I know anything about Lilian, she will insist on at least one stop on the way so it might even be midnight before they get to London. In the meantime, we can have a nice meal at the Grand in New Brighton and catch up on what still remains to be organised for our wedding,' he suggested.

'We can also make plans on what we are going to do about Neil's, which is sooner than you think. We haven't even booked a hotel and it is certainly too far to come back the same day,' she replied.

Chapter Thirty-One

Christabel couldn't believe how much she achieved during the next few weeks. She could feel the excitement building up inside her as everything began to fall into place.

Up until now she had felt weighed down by all her responsibilities and commitments and the fact that she had had to push all her wedding plans to the back of her mind because there were so many other things going on in her life.

Now she felt that she really could start counting the days, even the hours, until she and Mark were married and could finally begin their life together.

From now on it was all she wanted: a happy, peaceful life with the man she loved and the comfort of knowing that he was always there at her side to support her and share her problems.

Mark had certainly done far more than she had expected. The house purchase had been finalised and the decorating was virtually completed. With his help she organised all the furniture and furbishing that they would need initially.

'Shall we do the rest after we move in?' Mark suggested. 'It might be much better that way because our ideas about what we want may change after we are actually living in the house.'

Even though she'd always tried to be independent she was beginning to realise that there were times when she needed a man to lean on and that she simply couldn't carry all the problems and upsets that life threw at her completely on her own.

She thought back to the months after Philip had died when Lewis had helped her through the greatest problem she'd ever had to face. It was strange to think that she'd known Mark even in those days but that he certainly didn't know anything about what had happened to her at the time or the weeks she'd been forced to spend isolated in the dismal little room in Wilcock Court with only Maggie Nelson as a friend.

There had been so many family traumas since then that she rarely thought about any of it these days. Now, she told herself, she was far too busy planning the future, hers and Mark's, to start thinking about the past.

Christabel thoroughly enjoyed her solo shopping trip in Liverpool to select her wedding outfit. It was the one thing she really had wanted to do on her own. She finally chose a matching dress and jacket in a very pale turquoise blue together with a matching hat which had a neat brim and was decorated with a large white flower at one side.

As she tried it on, she knew she looked elegant. The colour suited her and the outfit was not too fussy. All that remained to be done now was to decide what little Jill was to wear.

When she telephoned Kay and described her own outfit Kay suggested that perhaps a white dress with a pale turquoise sash, some white socks and black patent shoes would complement it perfectly.

'Can you buy those for her in that village where you live?' Christabel asked worriedly.

'I may not be able to buy the right sort of dress in Cookham, but there are several quite large towns nearby. I can probably get what we want in Maidenhead or in Windsor, so don't worry about it,' Kay assured her.

'I wish I was going to have the opportunity of seeing her all dressed up before my big day just to be on the safe side. It would be terrible if the colour of the sash clashed with what I will be wearing.'

'I don't think for one moment that it will but, to be on the safe side, I'll bring along a white sash in the same material as the dress.'

'That sounds like a good idea, or else not have a sash at all.'

'What do you want Jill to wear on her head, a hat or some flowers, or simply a hair band?'

'A hair band that matches her sash would be nice, but otherwise a white one, or flowers; forget-me-nots, perhaps. I'll have to leave the choice up to you, Kay.'

'Forget-me-nots! They'll have to be artificial ones because they won't be in season in September,' Kay pointed out.

'If she has a pale turquoise hair band then she could have white rosebuds attached to it,' Christabel suggested.

'Leave it with me and I'll select whatever I think is going to look best,' Kay promised.

'I'm sure she will look lovely whatever you decide on. Is she still excited about being a flower girl?'

'I think she has more or less forgotten about it because she has been so poorly,' Kay sighed. 'I'm sure, though, that once we start looking for her dress and all the other bits and bobs she'll get excited again.'

'I'm certainly looking forward to her being there,' Christabel said softly. 'You and Stuart as well, of course, Kay. Is there any chance of you coming to stay here for a few days before the wedding, because there are several things I want to discuss with you?'

'I very much doubt it,' Kay told her quickly. 'Stuart's father will have to stand in for Stuart at work when we come up for your wedding and, as you know, his health hasn't been too good lately. Stuart will probably think that if we are away for more than the long weekend we've already planned, it might put too much extra strain on him.'

'Couldn't you and Jill come on your own for a few days?' Christabel persisted.

373

'That would mean taking Jill out of school and her teacher has already expressed disapproval about her missing school for two days for the wedding. It's such a pity you didn't arrange your wedding for before the start of the new school term.'

'Yes, Kay, I do understand. I did intend for it to be in August, as you very well know, but when Mark's son wanted his wedding to be before ours it meant putting it back. Then, with your aunt Lilian being taken ill and having to stay here, it meant delaying everything yet again. You've no idea what a rush it has been to organise everything as it is. Nevertheless,' she went on in a determined voice, 'you must make time to come and see me either before the wedding or as soon as we get back from our little holiday.'

'You mean your honeymoon, Aunt Christabel,' Kay intervened with a little laugh.

'Very well, honeymoon. Now listen to me, Kay, I am being serious. It's to do with this house as well as several other things.'

'Yes, I hadn't forgotten that you are moving to a new house in Formby. What are you planning to do with Rolleston Drive?' Kay asked, her voice laced with curiosity.

'Well, that's something I have to discuss with you, but I am not prepared to do it on the telephone, that is why it is so important that you come and stay for a few days.'

'Well, I'm afraid, Aunt Christabel, that since

your wedding is only ten days' away it will have to be afterwards. Don't forget, I still have to shop for Jill's outfit,' Kay reminded her.

Christabel knew it was pointless arguing. Surely, though, Kay was concerned about what was going to happen to the house that had been her childhood home. Unless, of course, she hadn't realised that under the terms of Lewis's will she was now the owner so she had to be the one to deal with it?

There were probably innumerable questions that Kay would be bound to ask, Christabel thought, and she wondered what her eventual decision about the house would be. She still harboured hopes that Kay might be persuaded to move back to Wallasey. Though by then she and Mark would be living in Formby, it would still mean that Kay and her family would be so much closer and it would be so much easier for her to visit Kay and even to have Jill to stay with her and Mark from time to time.

'Very well, dear, I'll have to be patient, I suppose. Don't forget, though, that there are all your father's papers to be sorted.'

'I don't suppose there are any that are of any importance,' Kay said dismissively. 'Maybe you could sort through them and dispose of any that are not important and bundle up the rest and send them to me or keep them until I see you?'

The next few days, however, seemed to fly by and Christabel had no chance to look at the papers. There were so many last-minute touches because she wanted everything to go like clockwork and that meant making sure that every detail was taken care of.

When Mark phoned her a couple of days before their wedding and she asked him what he was planning to do on his stag night, he confessed that he'd decided that he was far too old for that sort of thing.

'What I'm planning to do is have an evening out with my partner at the practice and my own two sons.'

'Well, at least I can rely on Cecil Roberts to make sure that the boys don't lead you into trouble,' Christabel laughed.

'Since it is unlucky to see you on the eve of our getting married, I think we should have dinner together somewhere special tonight,' he suggested. 'Where would you like to go?'

'Surprise me,' she told him archly.

'Very well, I'll pick you up at seven-thirty, so mind you are ready,' he warned before he rang off.

They dined at the Paradise Restaurant which was one of Christabel's favourites. Mark had preordered when he'd booked, everything from the wine to the dessert.

'All you have to do is relax,' he told Christabel as they took their places at the table. 'I've ordered your favourite dishes, and the wine I know you like. What more could any prospective bride want?'

376

'For her prospective husband to always be so considerate,' Christabel told him. She stretched a hand across the table and took one of his. 'This really is lovely, Mark, and it is just what I need.'

'Why do you say that? You're not feeling nervous about the future, are you?' he asked anxiously.

'Perhaps, just a little; it's a big step we're taking, you know,' Christabel told him thoughtfully.

He squeezed her hand reassuringly. 'You're not regretting it, are you, my dear?'

'Of course not!' She smiled brightly. 'It's simply that I'm worried in case everything doesn't go smoothly.'

'Stop worrying, then, Christabel. You are such a perfectionist. What does it matter if someone fluffs their words or knocks over a glass of wine?'

She nodded in agreement but remained silent as the waiter approached and began to fill their wine glasses.

'To us!' Mark raised his glass and waited for her to do the same, then touched her glass with his before he took a sip. 'To us and our future,' he said firmly.

'May it always be as wonderful as this evening,' Christabel murmured earnestly.

The serious moment passed. The food was excellent and, because the dishes were all her favourites, she enjoyed every minute of their evening together.

'An early night? Is that what the doctor orders?' She smiled.

As they reached her front door she could hear the phone ringing as she preceded him inside. 'Now, I wonder who this can be?' she murmured as she picked up the receiver from the hall table.

'Some last-minute well-wisher, I imagine; they've probably been trying to reach you all evening,' Mark told her.

She smiled as she spoke into the phone, then the expression on her face changed. She drew in a sharp breath and looked at Mark with wide-eyed distress written all over her face.

'Who was it?' he asked anxiously as she replaced the receiver.

'It was Marlene,' she said in a shaky voice. 'Lilian collapsed and died earlier this evening.'

They stared at each other in dismay. A thousand and one questions surged through Christabel's mind. She realised it probably meant that all their wedding plans would have to be changed but at that moment she couldn't think clearly what was involved.

Mark was more practical. 'You've had a shock, you need a brandy,' he said. Taking her arm he guided her towards the sitting room and sat her down in an armchair. 'Sit still while I pour you one.'

'You need one as well,' she said shakily.

Mark said nothing, but concentrated on pouring out their drinks. He handed one of the glasses of brandy to her then sat down in the armchair opposite her.

'Does it have to do that?' he asked quietly.

She stared at him blankly. 'What do you mean?'

'Does it have to change all our plans?'

'Mark! We can't possibly go ahead with our wedding when Lilian has just died,' Christabel said in a horrified voice.

'No, you're probably right,' he murmured as he sipped his drink thoughtfully.

She stared at him bemused. 'I suppose we could, if you really wanted us to do so,' she murmured tentatively.

'What would the rest of your family think if we did?'

Christabel shook her head and took a sip of her brandy. 'Marlene probably wouldn't like it and even Kay might think it heartless,' she said thoughtfully. 'I don't know what Stuart and Bill would think. Jill wouldn't understand – at least, I don't think so. Oh, dear, she's going to be so unhappy if it all goes wrong again. She's so looking forward to getting dressed up in her pretty new dress and being our flower girl.'

'She's too young to understand so that's the least of our problems,' Mark said decisively.

'What about Neil and Colin? What would they think if we went ahead?' Christabel probed.

Mark ran a hand through his hair, 'I honestly don't know. They've never met your sister, so possibly it wouldn't worry them too much, but they might think it was rather unfeeling on our part.'

'Do you think Marlene has let Kay know? If so, I wonder if she will be coming to Liverpool this weekend? It's pointless them travelling all this way if there's not going to be a wedding.'

She put down her glass and stood up. 'Perhaps I'd better go and telephone her.'

'Hold on.' Mark laid a detaining hand on her arm. 'Let's think this thing through first. She won't be leaving until tomorrow so you have time to consider what's the best thing to do.'

'I don't suppose it will be any clearer in my mind whether I phone her now or first thing tomorrow,' Christabel sighed.

'Right, then leave it until the morning,' Mark advised. 'It's almost eleven o'clock and, for all you know, Kay might already be in bed,' he added as if to prove his point.

'Yes, you're right.' Christabel sat back in her chair and picked up her drink and took a sip. 'If Kay already knows about Lilian, then well and good. If not, then tomorrow morning will be time enough. She's bound to be upset so it might be better if it is tomorrow, otherwise she might lie awake half the night worrying about it.'

'What exactly did Marlene say?' Mark asked.

'Not very much, but then she was terribly upset. She simply said that her mother had died earlier this evening.'

'Did she say what had happened?' Mark frowned.

'Only that she'd had a heart attack. Apparently she hasn't been feeling too well ever since she got home. It might have been the long car journey. Then again, she said she wasn't feeling all that well even before they left here and she was complaining that it was going to be a long journey.'

'Yes, well, it would be. She's hardly been out of the house since her stroke. Probably the journey was very stressful for her; that and all the excitement about our coming wedding.'

'I don't think that would have had anything to do with it,' Christabel said dismissively.

'She did say that she would like to stay on here until after the wedding.' He frowned.

'That was only to save her having to travel all the way back here again a few weeks later.'

'Which means that she was probably worrying about the journey. The trouble was,' Mark commended dryly, 'Lilian complained so much about everything that we both had a tendency not to take too much notice of what she was saying.'

'I know.' Christabel sighed. 'It makes me feel so guilty that I don't know what to do for the best.'

'I think we are going to have to postpone our wedding for the time being.'

'You mean until after Lilian's funeral?' Christabel shivered.

'That's right.' Mark nodded.

'How much longer do you think we ought to wait afterwards?' Christabel questioned.

They looked at each other blankly; neither of them seemed capable of deciding.

'It will have to be for at least a month, I suppose,' Mark said thoughtfully. 'It means cancelling the reception and all the hotel bookings for the family as well as our own going-away plans.'

'Possibly we will have to postpone it for longer than that. It very much depends on how Marlene reacts. It's a terrible shock for her. Lilian was her mother, remember.'

Mark stood up and paced the room. 'I've already told Neil he can move in, I'll have to talk to him and see if he will let me stay on there, I suppose. I'll be like a lodger in my own home,' he muttered.

'You don't have to do that, you can always go and live in our new house,' Christabel said quickly.

'I'm not sure I want to do that on my own,' he protested. 'How about you move in with me?'

'Mark!' Christabel didn't know whether to appear startled or amused by his suggestion. 'Now that would give everyone something to be shocked about,' she said wryly.

'What difference do a couple of signatures on a piece of paper make? We're planning to be living together for the rest of our lives, so what does it matter if we jump the gun?'

Christabel shook her head. 'I don't know what to think, Mark. I think that is another decision that is best left until tomorrow, don't you?'

'Whatever you think best.' He picked up his glass and drained it. 'I should probably go . . .'

'Mark, you're not leaving, are you?' Christabel exclaimed in alarm. 'I don't think I want to be on my own; can't you stay here with me?'

He hesitated as she stood up and moved towards him, tears streaming down her face. His arms went round her, holding her close. 'I didn't realise you were quite so upset by the news,' he murmured, stroking her hair as he tried to comfort her.

'No, neither did I,' she sniffed, 'but I suddenly feel so frightened and alone. I think the reality of what has happened has only just sunk in. Lilian was my sister and younger than me, and it is such a shock that she has died.'

'I know, my darling. I do understand.' He held her closer, kissing her gently on the brow.

'So will you stay? Please, Mark. I don't want to be here on my own.' She shivered.

'Of course I'll stay if you want me to, and for as long as you feel you need me to be here.'

'All night?' She hesitated. 'Will you come to bed with me, Mark, and hold me in your arms all night?' she asked in a whisper.

'If that is what you want me to do.' He frowned. 'Does Marlene know that I am here? If so, and she tells the rest of your family, won't that give them something to disapprove of?' He said, raising his eyebrows.

'I don't think I mentioned that you were here,

but does it matter?' Christabel sighed. 'I need you and, as you said earlier, what difference do a couple of signatures on a piece of paper make?'

Chapter Thirty-Two

Christabel was roused from a deep sleep the next morning by loud banging on the front door.

As she struggled to open her eyes she was startled to discover that Mark was in bed beside her. Her sudden movements disturbed him and as he opened his eyes he looked equally surprised then, with a sigh of pleasure, he pulled her towards him and his lips found hers.

Christabel returned his kiss then pulled away as the knocking on the front door was repeated. 'What are we going to do?' she whispered.

'Leave it. Pretend we're not here and they'll go away.'

'No, they won't; your car is outside in the driveway.'

Mark sat up, running a hand through his hair as the knocking was repeated. 'I'll go and see who it is,' he volunteered.

'You'd better slip my dressing gown on, then,' Christabel gasped as he threw back the bedcovers. 'It's hanging up on the door.'

Mark surveyed the pink and white satin garment with raised eyebrows. Then he snatched

385

up the counterpane and wrapped himself in that as he headed for the stairs.

As she heard the front door open and thought that she recognised Kay's voice, Christabel slipped the satin dressing gown on and went out on to the landing.

Stuart and Kay were already in the hallway and Jill was staring up at her in astonishment. 'What on earth is going on, Aunt Christabel?' Kay asked. 'Don't tell me we've arrived too late for the wedding.'

'No, no, you haven't done that,' Christabel assured her. 'Mark stayed the night . . .'

'Yes, we can see that,' Kay said, raising her eyebrows.

Pausing halfway down the stairs Christabel smiled uncomfortably. 'Give me a minute to pop some clothes on and I'll come down and explain.'

'Shall I put the kettle on?' Mark asked, bunching up the counterpane so that he could move more easily.

Christabel hesitated. 'Why don't you all go into the sitting room and make yourselves comfortable while we both go and get dressed,' she suggested. 'We'll only be a minute.'

'Take your time; we'll go into the kitchen and I'll put the kettle on and make a pot of tea,' Kay told them. 'We'll certainly want an explanation about what's going on, though,' she added with a laugh.

Ten minutes later all of them were sitting

386

down round the table enjoying a cup of tea while little Jill had a glass of milk. Kay had made a mountain of toast and scrambled egg for them all.

'I was under the impression that the bridegroom-to-be wasn't supposed to see the prospective bride in that state until their wedding day,' Kay observed with mock severity.

'We're not too sure when there is going to be a wedding,' Christabel sighed. 'Obviously Marlene didn't telephone either of you yesterday telling you the news.'

'News? What news?'

'About Lilian; she died yesterday,' Christabel said very quietly, hoping that Jill couldn't hear. 'It means, of course, that we will have to postpone our wedding.'

'Oh, Aunt Christabel, that's terrible. It's sad about Aunt Lilian, of course,' Kay added quickly, 'but you must feel devastated. Why ever didn't you let us know and then we would have postponed our visit?'

'Marlene didn't let us know until almost midnight. We'd been out for a quiet meal and the phone was ringing when we reached home. I thought she'd probably already told you but, to be honest, I was so overcome by the news that I wasn't thinking too clearly. Mark stayed the night because I was so upset,' she added by way of explanation for his presence.

'So what do we do now?' Kay asked, looking at Stuart.

'Go back home again, I suppose; after we've been in touch with Marlene to see if she needs our help.'

'Can I phone her now?' Kay asked.

'You can try, but she may not be at home. Lilian had a heart attack so she may have been in hospital at the end. Marlene might have had to go back there this morning to sort things out.'

'Have you cancelled all the arrangements to do with the wedding? The register office and so on, Aunt Christabel?'

'No, not yet.' Christabel shook her head. 'It was too late last night for us to do anything and, as you know, we weren't even awake when you arrived this morning.'

'Then probably the best thing we can do is to phone Marlene and find out exactly what is happening. It may be best if you wait until we know when the funeral will be before you start changing all your arrangements,' Stuart stated. 'Would you like me to do it?' he asked, standing up and putting his cup and saucer on the table.

Marlene could tell them nothing; she was far too involved in dealing with things at the hospital concerning her mother. Stuart and Mark took it upon themselves to phone around and cancel all the arrangements that had been made for the wedding and to handle the many complaints because it had been left to the very last minute to do so.

It was late afternoon before everything had been dealt with, far too late for Kay and her family to go back to Cookham.

'You must stay here overnight,' Christabel insisted. 'I'd like you to stay on longer, if you feel like it,' she added quickly.

'No, we'd better get back. We'll probably have to take time off next week for Lilian's funeral,' Stuart pointed out.

Mark insisted on taking them all out for dinner that night, even though Kay protested that it would mean a very late night for Jill as they would have to take her with them.

'I think she would rather enjoy it and she can sleep on the journey home,' Stuart pointed out.

It was a rather sombre evening; talk was mostly about Lilian and tentative suggestions about when the wedding could now take place.

'We seem to have had so many misfortunes when it comes to arranging it that I think a very quiet ceremony is the answer,' Mark commented. 'That's, of course, if Christabel will be happy with that.'

They smiled at each other across the table; after the previous night both of them knew that the wedding was a mere formality as far as they were concerned. The many things that had gone wrong only seemed to prove that the solidarity of their love for each other was stronger than ever.

Christabel wondered how she would have coped with everything if Mark hadn't been there to give her support in every way.

At breakfast the next morning, Christabel brought up the matter of the house with Kay.

'I've mentioned so many times that we need to get together and discuss it,' she reminded her. 'Now that Stuart is here as well, then perhaps it is a good time to do so.'

'Yes, I know, you have mentioned it before, but I had *some* idea that it was partly mine and I didn't want you to feel uncomfortable about living here,' she explained. 'I know you must have given up your own home to stay and look after me. I also remember that I wasn't very cooperative and treated you rather badly,' she added apologetically.

'So you were trying to make it up to me by pretending you didn't know that you were a joint owner of the house, were you?' Christabel smiled. 'Nevertheless, my dear, when Mark and I do eventually get married and move into our own place in Formby then we will have to decide what we want to do with it, Kay.'

Kay looked startled. 'I've always thought of the house as yours, Aunt Christabel,' Kay protested. 'If you are not going to live here, then you should sell it or rent it out. Do you want Stuart to handle all the negotiations for you? I'm sure he has contacts with estate agents in this area and can get you the best possible deal.'

'You don't understand, Kay; I obviously haven't made myself clear. If you had read his Will like I asked you to do time and time again, then you'd understand. The house is yours; your father left it to you. The stipulation in his Will was that I should live here for as long as I needed a home and then it would pass to you.

'There will be certain legal details to be sorted out and that is why you must go through your father's papers and then contact his solicitor.'

'What do you want to do? Do you want to sell it, Kay?' Stuart asked.

'I rather hope that since it is the house you grew up in, Kay, you might like to move back here,' Christabel suggested.

'Move back? How on earth can we do that when Stuart's estate agency business is in Berkshire?' Kay gasped. 'He can hardly be expected to commute,' she added with a laugh.

'I know that, but I thought he might like a change; he could sell his business in Cookham and open a new business somewhere round here. Or, for that matter, open another estate agency in this area and leave his father to run the existing one.'

'That's out of the question, I'm afraid. Dad is not well enough to have the sole responsibility of managing things any longer,' Stuart told her. 'I think he would be heartbroken if I sold up and moved to somewhere else. He has taken such a pride in building up a sound business, and one which is so well known in the Thames Valley area, and in being able to take me into partnership. I'm sure he expects me to go on running it at least for the rest of his lifetime,' Stuart added gravely.

'Oh dear, well, in that case, I suppose it means that this house will have to be sold,' Christabel said sadly. 'That's unless you decide to rent it out for the present so that you can move here at a later date should you change your minds.'

Kay look confused. 'There's no great hurry for us to decide, is there, Aunt Christabel?'

'No, not really. If you want to sell it, then of course you will have to dispose of all the contents.'

'If there is anything you want to take with you, Aunt Christabel, then feel free to do so,' Kay told her, smiling.

'No, I don't think so. Mark is not moving any of his belongings into our new house and I don't think I want to do so either.'

'What are you doing with your place, Mark?' Stuart asked. 'Do you want me to handle the sale of it for you?'

'No, that won't be necessary. My eldest son is moving in and becoming a partner in the practice. Later on, in a year or so, my youngest son is planning to add a dental surgery to the practice.'

'That sounds like an ideal arrangement,' Stuart nodded.

'There are all your father's papers to be sorted

out, Kay,' Christabel reminded her. 'You might like to take those back home with you and then you can do it at your leisure.'

'I suppose. If you think it is necessary,' Kay said. 'After all this time, though, is there anything that has to be kept?'

'That's up to you, dear,' Christabel told her. 'It's a very large package with a wax seal and has your name on the outside. I'm not too sure what is in it. I assume it contains Lewis's birth certificate, marriage certificate, and so on. It may even contain documents relating to the deeds of this house. The package is in his desk, I'll go and get it and you can have a look through it.'

Christabel returned a few minutes later carrying a bulky brown manila envelope. Stuart moved Kay's plate, cup and saucer out of the way so as to clear a space in front of her on the breakfast table.

Kay took the thick brown envelope from Christabel and deciding not to wait, broke the seal, and then tipped the entire contents out on to the table. She handed the deeds of the house, which were clearly labelled and secured by a thick elastic band, over to Stuart.

'I'll leave you to check through those; they'll make more sense to you than they will to me,' Out of the remaining items she picked up a flimsy yellowing slip of paper and unfolded it and smoothed it out.

'This is Dad's birth certificate,' she said, looking up and smiling across at Christabel.

'Lewis Montgomery, 1890. Heaven's, I didn't realise that he was older than you, Aunt Christabel. That means he was only forty when he was killed; and poor Mum must have been even younger when she died.'

She dropped the piece of paper on to the table and picked up another one. 'Here's their marriage certificate and it's dated 1913. They must have married only a short time before the Great War broke out.'

She folded it carefully and put it with his birth certificate, then picked up the remaining piece of paper and gave a little cry of surprise. 'This is my birth certificate – February 1915.' She studied it in silence for a moment, frowning. 'Have you seen this, Aunt Christabel?'

'No dear, of course I haven't. The package was sealed, that's why I didn't open it.'

'I know that, but have you looked at it before and seen the date, when it was issued, I mean?'

'No, of course not.' Christabel frowned. 'Why ever should I?'

Kay stared at her aunt for a long moment before she spoke. 'The reason I'm asking, Aunt Christabel, is because this certificate has your name on it!'

Christabel felt the colour draining from her face as she held out her hand for the slip of paper. 'Let me see; it probably means that you are named after me?' she said in a shaky voice.

'No,' Kay frowned as she stared at the slip

394

of paper again. 'No, Aunt Chrissy, it's not that at all. What do you make of it?' she asked as she handed it to Stuart.

He studied it in silence then, without a word, passed it across the table to Christabel.

Her hand was shaking so much that she could hardly take it from him. The words on it were a blur as she tried to read what was written there.

Memories of that day long ago, when she'd been discharged from the private clinic and had left Lewis to deal with all the relevant paper-work, came flooding back.

She'd insisted that he should be the one to sign everything and she'd never asked him for the certificate; there hadn't seemed any point in doing so. She'd given up all rights to her baby, so there was no reason why she should check the child's birth certificate – she was never going to need it. From now on it belonged to whoever adopted her baby, not to her.

So who had adopted her baby? The sudden realisation that it must have been Lewis star-tled her. She looked across at Kay and it made her feel faint. All these years her little daughter had been within reach and she hadn't known. How could Lewis have been so cruel as not to have told her?

With a feeling akin to guilt she remembered Violet's distress when she'd kept on about Kay not taking after her in any way but looking more like Lewis and the Montgomery family.

Memories of the whispered rumours she'd overheard when her own mother had been talking to her friends about Violet's baby surfaced in her mind; something about it being stillborn. At the time she'd not been interested because she tried to avoid all talk of babies, knowing that she had just given up her own for adoption.

Had Lewis adopted her baby? Had Violet known all along that she was Kay's real mother, or had she suspected that the baby was Lewis's but by some other woman not her?

There were so many questions seething in her mind; so many possible answers. She felt confused. She didn't know what to say as she handed the slip of paper back to Kay.

'Can I have a look at that, Kay?' Mark asked.

'Yes, of course.'

Christabel watched with growing concern as Mark perused the certificate, frowning as he tried to reconcile the date on it. She was sure he was remembering that it was around the same time as when they had both been at Hilbury.

Surely, even though they had known each other fairly well because they'd worked together, he wouldn't remember that she had taken compassionate leave from Hilbury Hospital for several months around that date and, even if he did, why would he connect the two?

396

Mark was a doctor, she reminded herself; he would be able to work out accurately enough to satisfy himself what the dates on the certificate implied and Christabel wondered what he would feel about it when he did.

Chapter Thirty-Three

The tension around the breakfast table was palpable. Christabel could see from their faces that they were all bursting with curiosity, especially Kay. She took a deep breath, but when she tried to speak no sound came so she cleared her throat and, with a slightly trembling hand, reached out for her cup of tea.

It was cold and she shuddered as she swallowed a mouthful. The silence remained unbroken, all eyes fixed expectantly on her, waiting to hear what she had to tell them. She felt uneasy and her mind went blank. She knew it had to be the truth but she wasn't sure how to begin.

She felt that she needed time to sort out her thoughts. Standing up, she held out a hand to little Jill who was amusing herself by making patterns on her plate with some crumbs she'd made out of the remains of her toast. 'Shall we go out into the garden and feed those crumbs to the birds?' she asked.

Excitedly, Jill clambered down from her chair and then reached for the plate.

'Perhaps I'd better carry that,' Christabel suggested.

*   *   *

She sat down on a seat at the bottom of the garden and watched as Jill scattered the bread-crumbs and then waited for the birds to swoop down for them. Each time they did so she clapped her hands excitedly and immediately the birds rose up into the air in fright and the whole procedure began all over again.

By the time they went back into the kitchen again Kay had sorted through the contents of the envelope and everything was spread out on the table.

Christabel noticed that there were a great many photographs of herself and Kay, which Lewis had taken when she'd arrived in Wallasey to help look after them but there wasn't a single picture of Kay as a baby, or any taken of Kay and Violet together.

Christabel wondered what had happened to those. She was sure there must have been some since there was several of Kay taken with Lewis. There were also school photographs and some taken of Kay with her grandparents as well as with Marlene.

Christabel found herself mesmerised by the panorama of the past spread out there. She marvelled at how closely interwoven her life and Kay's had always been even though they'd both been unaware of their close relationship.

Aunt Christabel's relationship with Jill was like history repeating itself, Kay mused as she refilled her coffee cup and watched her aunt sitting on the other side of the table showing Jill a better way of drawing ducks and swans on a pad of white paper. She remembered her own childhood, and the way her aunt had always wanted to teach her new things and also, as she grew older, to exercise control over everything she did.

It was one of the reasons why she had spent so much time in London with Marlene. Aunt Lilian had been so much more tolerant than Aunt Chrissy.

She looked at the conglomeration of pictures arrayed on the table and felt she couldn't discard any of them. Her mind made up, she gathered them together in order to put them back into the manila envelope. As she opened it she peered inside to make sure nothing had been left there and then drew out what looked like a letter of some kind.

Kay frowned as she straightened it out. It was an invoice from a private clinic in London. It was addressed to Mr Lewis Montgomery and it was dated February 1915 and was for a confinement and medical services for his wife Christabel Montgomery.

She studied it with interest; the month and year were correct, but what she couldn't understand was that the mother's name was given as Christabel Montgomery. That didn't make sense!

She looked across the table at Christabel. 'That birth certificate we were looking at a little while ago, Aunt Christabel, *my* birth certificate . . .

400

you still haven't told us why it has your name on it. You must have some idea. Surely it ought to have both my mother's name and my father's name on it?'

'It is all so long ago, Kay, you can't expect me to remember details like that,' Christabel said evasively.

'Perhaps this will help you to remember,' Kay said, holding out the invoice.

As she took it from her, Christabel felt the colour suffusing her face and she felt trapped. She knew all eyes were on her and she could think of no way of concealing the truth any longer. Taking a deep breath she decided to make a clean breast of it all.

'It's obviously the invoice from the clinic where I gave birth to the baby I had in 1915. Lewis, your father, helped me to deal with the situation I found myself in at the time and he also made the necessary arrangements to have my baby adopted. I had no idea what was entailed because I left him to see to all that side of things and to pay the clinic, as well as sign all the legal documents. That was why I knew nothing about the birth certificate.'

'Surely he would hand your baby's birth certificate over to whoever adopted the baby?' Stuart frowned. 'So how is it that it is still here amongst his private papers?'

'I've already told you, I don't know,' Christabel protested. 'I suppose it wasn't collected by the people who adopted her.'

'Or it could mean that your brother adopted your child and substituted it for his own child who had just died,' Stuart said, aghast. 'If that's the case, then it means that Kay must be that child – which means she's your daughter.'

Christabel sighed, a long, drawn-out release of tension. 'Yes, it does, doesn't it, Stuart?' she murmured softly. 'It means that Kay really is my daughter.'

'You used to act as if I was. Does that mean you have suspected all along?' Kay asked in a bewildered voice. 'If it is true and you really are my mother, then who was my father?'

Christabel bit down on her lower lip. She was finding it increasingly difficult to talk about. What did it matter after all this time? she thought despondently. Then, as she saw the bewildered look on Kay's face, she knew she owed it to her to tell her the truth.

'Your father's name, Kay, was Philip Henderson. He was a naval officer; we had been sweethearts for several years and we were planning to be married. My father insisted that we must wait until I was twenty-one before he would allow us to do so. A month after Philip set sail, on what was to be his last trip before our wedding day, his ship sank and all on board drowned. Afterwards, when I discovered I was expecting his baby, I was devastated.'

Kay stretched out her hand and took Christabel's. 'What did you do?' she whispered.

'War had been declared by this time and I managed to convince my family that I ought to do something to help and so I became a trainee nurse at Hilbury Hospital.'

Nervously she glanced across at Mark. So far he hadn't said a word but now he nodded as if corroborating her story.

'By the time I was qualified I realised that I was pregnant. Abortion was out of the question, so I persuaded Lewis to help me and to agree that once I'd had the baby he would arrange for it to be adopted to save both me and our family from disgrace.

'His own wife was pregnant at the same time, so probably because he understood the plight I was in, he agreed to book me into a private clinic as Mrs Montgomery for the birth and then afterwards, unknown to them, arrange for the baby to be adopted.

'Before the baby was born I took several months off from Hilbury and lived in a squalid little room in Wilcock Court off Scotland Road. It was drab and I had only the money Lewis could spare me to live on. Immediately after I'd had my baby, I went back to Hilbury Hospital and carried on as if nothing had happened.'

'And my father never discussed with you any of the details about what happened – not even after my mother died, even though, obviously, he must have known the truth about what happened to your baby?' Kay asked.

'Surely Kay's mother must have known,'

Stuart said in a puzzled voice, looking enquiringly at Christabel.

Christabel shook her head. 'Possibly not! You see, Violet's baby was born within hours of mine, only her baby must have been stillborn. She was desperately ill afterwards and Lewis must have thought that the kindest thing to do was to substitute my baby for hers and save her any heartache over losing her baby.'

'Would it have been possible without telling her?' Stuart persisted. 'Surely he would have had to persuade the doctor to swap the babies over and that would be illegal, wouldn't it, Mark?'

'Lewis probably didn't ask anyone, merely acted on his own initiative, which meant that he was the only person who knew the truth about what had happened,' Christabel said thoughtfully.

'I see. So where does this leave everything now?' Stuart asked worriedly.

'I don't suppose it really makes any difference, does it?' Mark questioned. 'It was highly irregular, but then so were a lot of things in wartime. As I see it now, it's a family matter, and even though Christabel has told us everything she can, we don't know for certain what happened, now do we?'

Kay was in shock but she shook herself and, partly to disguise the torrent of emotions raging inside her, she quipped, 'Well, if I am Aunt Christabel's daughter, then it will make you my stepfather when you two get married,' Kay

404

pointed out. 'You won't be expecting me to call you "Daddy", will you?'

Mark smiled and shook his head but Christabel could see he was still as flabbergasted as Kay by what had gone on. She wished she'd looked through the papers before handing them to Kay so that she could have at least had the opportunity to explain to Mark about everything that had happened in her past instead of it all being disclosed so blatantly.

Stuart seemed to be worried about the legal implications but surely, after all this time, there was nothing to worry about. Lewis hadn't been trying to break the law only to do what he thought was best for all concerned. It had meant that Violet had been appeased over the loss of her baby and at the same time Christabel's child remained in the Montgomery family.

It did answer a great many other questions, of course, Christabel reflected. It accounted for the very strong resemblance between her and Kay. Looking back, she wondered how much Violet had known about what had happened. Had Lewis ever told her that the baby was his sister's child, and was this why she and Violet had never really got on with each other? Or had there been some other reason why Violet had committed suicide? Was Violet so desperately unhappy because she really believed that Kay was Lewis's daughter by another woman?

There were so many questions to which none of them would ever know the answer that

Christabel felt bewildered. She wished the matter had never arisen because it was causing such an unpleasant atmosphere. She had looked forward to Kay and her family staying on for a few days, but now she sensed that all Kay wanted to do was to go home.

When a phone call came from Marlene who wanted to talk to Kay and apologise for not letting her know before she made the journey to Wallasey, Christabel felt a sense of relief.

She gathered from what she could hear of their conversation that Kay intended to go home and then they would return to Liverpool for Lilian's funeral.

Marlene must have said that it was their intention to bring her mother's body back to Liverpool so that she could be buried in the Montgomery grave and she heard Kay saying, 'That's going to be very expensive, so why not have Aunt Lilian cremated where you live and then bring the ashes up to Liverpool for a service of interment?'

'Aunt Christabel, Marlene says she will telephone you as soon as she knows what she has decided to do,' Kay stated as she replaced the receiver. 'It is going to mean another long journey for us, I'm afraid,' she added in a vexed tone.

'And when you decide on a new date for your wedding, we'll have yet another trip to make to Merseyside,' Stuart added.

'We're very sorry about all this, but it is none of our making,' Mark told him.

406

'I understand that,' Stuart agreed. He looked at his watch, 'Look, we must leave. I need to be back at work tomorrow if I am going to take time off again next week.'

'Would you like to leave Jill here with us?' Christabel suggested.

'No!' the refusal came from both Kay and Stuart simultaneously. 'I'll take all these papers that belonged to my dad home with me, Aunt Christabel, and I'll let you know if there are any more surprises after I've gone through them all again,' Kay added tightly as she scooped up the papers and put them all back inside the envelope.

Chapter Thirty-Four

The interment of Lilian's ashes in the Montgomery family grave took place ten days later in Liverpool. All the family, Christabel and Mark, Kay and Stuart and little Jill, Marlene and Bill, were there for the brief committal service.

'Thank goodness that is over,' Kay commented as they went back to Rolleston Drive afterwards where Christabel had arranged a buffet meal for them all.

Christabel sensed that there was still an strained atmosphere between them all and as she made sure that everyone had food and drink she could hear Kay telling Marlene about the discovery of her birth certificate and what it implied.

She heard Marlene's gasp of shocked disbelief and the next time she turned round she saw that Stuart was deep in conversation with Marlene's husband and heard Bill's suppressed guffaw of laughter as they discussed the details.

Christabel knew they were all talking about her and her past and she was glad Mark was there to give her support. Almost before they had finished eating Marlene and Bill were saying their goodbyes.

'We must get back because we've left our two with a neighbour,' Marlene explained.

'We'll catch up with all the rest of the news when we meet up again for the big wedding,' Bill told Stuart, giving him a broad wink.

'Don't leave it too long, Mark,' Bill advised. 'You've had enough disruptions and delays. The next thing we'll know is that you've called it off altogether.'

'There's no fear of that happening but we'll probably leave it for a month or so since we've only just said goodbye to Lilian,' Mark replied, his mouth tightening.

'There's no need to delay things because my mother's died,' Marlene assured him. 'We don't mind how soon it is. Or are you putting it off because of all the revelations in Uncle Lewis's papers about Kay being Aunt Chrissy's daughter? I must say, it has come as a tremendous shock to us all.'

Christabel saw the look of annoyance on Mark's face and hoped he wasn't going to say anything that might upset Marlene; the atmosphere was strained enough as it was.

Marlene's words brought a sharp intake of breath from Kay, and Christabel waited on tenterhooks for Mark's reply.

'Christabel's relationship to Kay has nothing

at all to do with when our wedding takes place,' Mark said stiffly.

'Kay says this house is hers now,' Marlene persisted. 'I suppose by rights it has always been hers.'

'No, Marlene, my dad stated in his will that Aunt Christabel could live here for as long as she needed to,' Kay told her. 'After that the property would become mine. When Aunt Chrissy and Mark move to their lovely new house in Formby after their wedding then the house will be mine.'

'I was hoping Kay might decide to come and live here,' Christabel murmured with a little sigh. 'There's no rush for you to decide, of course,' she said quickly looking across at Kay. 'You can take all the time you need.'

'In actual fact, Aunt Christabel, as soon as your wedding is over we will be putting the house on the market,' Kay stated decisively. 'We'd like to have it all done and dusted, signed and settled, as soon as possible. It will be a chance to draw a line under all that has happened in the past and hopefully help to clear the air.'

'So will you still be having Jill as a flower girl at your wedding, Aunt Chrissy?' Marlene asked.

'Of course she will,' Kay said very firmly, giving Christabel a warm smile. 'It matters more than ever now that I know Aunt Chrissy is really my mother and Jill's grandmother.'

Once more Marlene and Bill said goodbye to everybody and Christabel breathed a sigh of relief when the front door closed behind them.

'We must be on our way as well,' Kay murmured. 'Jill's out in the garden, isn't she?'

'Yes, I fixed a swing up out there for her and she's having a great time playing on that,' Mark said with a broad smile. 'The sun is shining, so why don't you go out there and take Christabel with you while Stuart gives me a hand to make some coffee. The minute it is ready we'll bring it out to you.'

Christabel smiled gratefully at Mark. He knew she was hoping to have a quiet chat with Kay and she appreciated the tactful way he had manoeuvred it.

They watched Jill playing on the swing for a few moments or so and then they went to the bottom of the garden and sat down on the bench under the willow tree. Christabel reached out and took one of Kay's hands and squeezed it.

'It's been quite a difficult time lately with one thing and another,' she sighed.

'Yes, but I'm glad everything is out in the open now,' Kay told her. 'I'm sorry I was so horrid to you after Dad died. I feel so guilty about the way I behaved; you must have felt terribly hurt.'

'No, I wasn't so much hurt as worried because I felt such a dreadful failure.'

Kay looked puzzled. 'Failure? What on earth do you mean? I don't understand.'

'I felt so frustrated because you failed your exams. I wasn't able to make sure you had the sort of academic education that would prepare you for the sort of future Lewis would have wanted you to have,' Christabel explained.

'You didn't know I was your daughter then, so why did it matter all that much?' Kay mused.

'I still felt you were my responsibility; I wanted to do the very best I could for you. In some ways I felt that it was an opportunity to repay Lewis for all he had done for me in the past.'

Kay glanced at her sideways. 'Are you talking about when you had me?'

'Yes, Kay, I am. When I was growing up, to have a baby out of wedlock was considered to be the ultimate disgrace. My parents would have been horrified and probably they would have disowned me if they had ever found out about it.'

'Surely you weren't still feeling guilty about what happened; it was all so long ago.'

'No, not exactly guilty; I suppose in some ways I was hoping that whoever was bringing up my own little girl would be doing a better job than I was and making sure that she was well educated and had a promising career ahead of her.'

They sat for several minutes in silence, each

412

of them contemplating the situation in their own way.

'We've wasted so many years; if only Dad had told us both the truth after my mother died,' Kay sighed.

'Or even before,' Christabel said regretfully. 'I'm sure that if he had told Violet the whole story she would have understood that he was only acting in her best interest; well, in all our best interests, in fact. He prevented her from grieving because she had lost her baby and he certainly saved me as well as our parents from having to hang our heads in shame.'

'Put like that, what he did really does sound sensible and courageous,' Kay agreed.

'Yes, and I think the time has come for us to accept that he meant well and to put it all behind us. The wonderful thing is that we now know the truth and we've found each other at last. You'll never know how much that means to me,' Christabel murmured, wiping away a tear from the corner of her eyes.

'In many ways I think I probably do,' Kay assured her. 'I've got a mother now and Jill really does have a grandmother. Mind you,' she went on quickly, 'Jill may find it easy to call you "Granny", but I'm not sure I am ever going to be able to call you "Mum",' she said.

'I wouldn't expect you to,' Christabel assured her. 'Violet was very much your mother; she brought you up until you were eleven, remember, so I think the best thing we can do is let things remain exactly as they stand.' Christabel maintained.

'You mean you don't want me to make any changes?'

'That's right. We are both quite happy with what you call us at the moment,' Christabel affirmed quickly as she spotted Mark and Stuart walking towards them bringing the coffee Mark had promised and a glass of lemonade for Jill.

They stayed in the garden for about half an hour, enjoying their drinks and mulling over their plans for the forthcoming wedding. Jill made two long daisy chains; one for her mother and one for Christabel.

'This is your very first present from me now that you are my granny,' Jill told Christabel solemnly as she draped it over her head and patted it into place.

'Thank you, that makes it very special indeed and I promise I'll treasure it forever,' Christabel told her.

'How can you do that? The flowers will die in a day or two. Do you mean you'll have a funeral service for them like we had for Aunty Lilian?'

'No, I'll tell you what. When I take my daisy necklace off tonight I'll press it so that it will last for ever and ever.'

'How will you do that? Is it magic?'

'No, it's not magic. What I will do is put the

necklace between two sheets of clean blotting paper and then put them inside the biggest, heaviest book I can find.'

'What will happen to it then?'

'Well, I'll leave it inside for a whole week and when I take it out, the daisies will be pressed as flat as flat can be.'

'What will you do with them then?'

'I'll mount them on to a piece of white card and then put the necklace inside a picture frame and hang it on the wall in my bedroom and keep it for ever and ever.'

'Will I be able to see it in its frame the next time I come here?' Jill asked.

Christabel hesitated. 'It won't be here, in this house, darling, it will be hanging in the bedroom in my new house; the one I will be living in when I marry Mark.'

Jill nodded solemnly. 'Will Mark be my granddad, then?' she asked, her vivid blue eyes fixed on Christabel's face.

'Do you want him to be?'

'Oh yes, if you are my granny, then I want him to be my granddad,' Jill nodded.

'Right, well, he will be, then, and don't forget that when we get married you are going to be our flower girl.'

'I know that, but when is it going to be?' Jill asked, putting her hands on her hips and looking from Kay to Christabel and back again. 'I've got my white dress and my white socks and shoes and the flowers for my hair and I want to wear them.'

'It will be soon, my dear. Very soon now. We still have one or two more arrangements to make but you won't have to wait very much longer,' Christabel promised.

Chapter Thirty-Five

Three weeks later, on a lovely mild day in late September, Christabel and Mark were married. Christabel wore her pale turquoise dress with its matching jacket and pretty face-framing hat. Mark looked very distinguished in a light grey three-piece suit. Jill looked enchanting in her dainty white dress with a garland of rosebuds in her hair.

As she stood beside Mark, Christabel felt calm and happy throughout the short civil service. It wasn't until they took their places at a table in a beautifully appointed private room at the Grand Hotel in New Brighton that she felt slightly apprehensive.

The entire family had now had plenty of time to come to terms with the revelations disclosed by Kay's birth certificate. As they all took their places at the big round table with its gleaming cutlery, sparkling wine glasses and a two-tier wedding cake taking pride of place in the centre of it, Christabel wondered if there would be any adverse comments from Marlene and Bill now that the formalities were over and they were all relaxed.

At the end of the meal, Cecil Roberts, who

was Mark's best man, rose to his feet to say a few words. He regaled them with a history of their friendship, from their first meeting when they'd been young doctors at Hilbury Hospital, to their decision when the war ended to go into partnership and start their own practice, right up to the present day.

As soon as he sat down Mark's eldest son Neil rose to his feet and made a short pithy speech about what a good father Mark had always been. He then asked them all to raise their glasses in a toast to his father and his new bride.

Christabel felt apprehensive the moment Neil sat down and Stuart stood up, and took a long sip of her champagne to steady her nerves.

He started off innocuously enough by making a few complimentary remarks about her and Mark. Then, after a short, rather dramatic pause, he looked across at Kay and waited until she had pushed back her chair and walked round the table to stand at his side.

Christabel's heart thundered. What was going on? She felt Mark reach for her hand beneath the table and squeeze it as Stuart started speaking again.

'Now for a very special announcement,' he said, picking up his glass as though in readiness for a toast. 'As most of you know, Kay's birth certificate was found amongst her father's papers a few weeks ago and Christabel is happy and proud to have this opportunity to be able to officially acknowledge that she is Kay's mother and also Jill's grandmother.'

As they all raised their glasses and chatter broke out all around her, Christabel's head swirled. Then as Kay and Jill came round the table and hugged and kissed her she felt tears brimming in her eyes.

'I now have a complete family,' Mark announced huskily as he hugged all three of them at once.

'This really does mean that you are my Granpy now?' Jill said, looking up at Mark with a beaming smile.

'Yes, I certainly am; that's, of course, if you want me to be,' he told her gravely, looking over the top of her head at Kay who signalled her approval with a smile and a nod.

'What about us?' Marlene demanded. 'Are we part of your family too? I know Aunt Chrissy isn't my mother but I think Tracy and Tommy would like to have you both as Gran and Granpy as well, wouldn't you?' she said, looking at her own two children who nodded enthusiastically.

'That's tremendous news, I'm very glad to hear it; the bigger the family the better.' Mark smiled as he opened his arms for the two children to join them. 'Don't forget you've got two new uncles as well,' he added as he looked across the table at his own two sons, Neil and Colin, who were both smiling indulgently.

It was only afterwards when they returned

to Rolleston Drive and Christabel saw that, while their celebrations had been going on, a 'For Sale' sign had gone up outside the house, that she felt a momentary sadness.

It had been her home, as well as Kay's, for such a long time that it was something of a wrench to realise that this would probably be the last time they would ever all be gathered together there.

She still found it disappointing that her hopes that Kay and Stuart would move into Rolleston Drive had not come to fruition but perhaps it was for the best.

'Our home is in Cookham,' Kay told her when she begged her to think carefully before deciding to sell her family home. 'We have made friends there and Stuart wants to carry on the estate agency that his father started and has worked hard to build up.'

The next time I entertain any of the family, Christabel mused, it will not be here but in my new house. A new life and a new home that was free of any memories of the past. It was going to be a fresh start in every way; both for her and for Mark.

The house they'd bought was slightly smaller and much more modern. Every item of furniture was new; all pieces they'd shopped for and decided on together. Even the carpets and curtains and all the gleaming new fitments in the kitchen and bathroom had that pristine unused appeal.

As soon as they were ready to leave for the two-week holiday they planned to take in Cornwall, Christabel took one last look round. Then, resignedly, she handed over the keys of the house to Stuart to pass on to the estate agents he'd appointed to handle the sale.

As they all came out on to the driveway to wave her and Mark off even though she was leaving Rolleston Drive for the last time Christabel felt no regrets whatsoever.

She felt a sense of peace as well as happiness as she made herself comfortable in the front passenger seat beside Mark. There were no more dark secrets, no hidden scandals. Everything was at last out in the open and her past was accepted not only by Mark but also by the whole family.

A Love Like Ours

Rosie Harris

They shared a secret no one must ever know.

When seventeen-year-old Ruth Davies' father is invalided out of the Great War, the whole family has little choice but to move to the infamous Tiger Bay area of Cardiff. Not only faced with a life of adversity, Ruth and her mother Caitlin also share a secret, one that no one else must ever know.

Ruth and Caitlin's wages are barely enough to put food on the table let alone pay the rent. And an increasingly neglected young Glynis runs wild. When Caitlin contracts tuberculosis and dies they have no option but to move into an even more squalid neighbourhood. But Ruth is still determined to keep their secret, at all costs. That is, until their father dies unexpectedly and an ever more desperate Ruth and Glynis find themselves living hand-to-mouth . . .

arrow books

Love Changes Everything

Rosie Harris

Would she ever have a life of her own?

Fourteen-year-old Trixie Jackson hoped she had a future to look forward to. But when she is sacked from the local factory she is forced to work as a housekeeper for one of her father's friends – a man she instinctively dislikes.

Kept under lock and key, her life soon becomes a living hell. But in her haste to escape she injures herself and ends up in hospital. However, her troubles are only just beginning. When her mother is involved in a tragic accident and dies, Trixie and her younger sister Cilla are left at the mercy of their bullying father. All too quickly he brings his mistress Daisy into the house. And she will stop at nothing to make the girls' lives utter misery.

arrow books

The Quality of Love

Rosie Harris

Would she always be unlucky in love?

The only child of over-protective parents, Sarah Lewis yearns to leave home. Studying hard to please them, she earns a place at Cardiff University. Here she is swept off her feet by handsome Gwyn Roberts, but when she becomes pregnant her parents are devastated and turn her from their door.

All Gwyn and Sarah can afford are two squalid rooms in the infamous slums of Cardiff, and Sarah soon realises she's made a terrible mistake. Gwyn becomes increasingly distant and when the baby dies in infancy, he leaves Sarah with little choice but to fall on her parents' mercy.

But just when Sarah is starting to pull her life back together again, she is drawn to the charms of Stefan Vaughan and finds herself in trouble once more . . .

arrow books